Ask a Dead Man

Ask a Dead Man

Robert S. Levinson

Five Star • Waterville, Maine

First Edition
First Printing: December 2004

Published in 2004 in conjunction with Tekno Books and Ed Gorman.

Set in 11 pt. Plantin by Al Chase.

Printed in the United States on permanent paper.

Library of Congress Cataloging-in-Publication Data

Levinson, Robert S.
    Ask a dead man / by Robert S. Levinson.—1st ed.
      p. cm.
    ISBN 1-59414-255-6 (hc : alk. paper)
    1. Attempted assassination—Fiction. 2. Terrorism—Prevention
—Fiction. 3. Pasadena (Calif.)—Fiction. 4. Northern Ireland
—Fiction. 5. Revenge—Fiction. 6. Widows—Fiction. I. Title.
PS3562.E9218A92 2004
  813'.54—dc22   2004042391

FOR SANDRA
My *Raison d'être*,
Eternally.
LVY
and
FOR LIAM FERRIS
Wherever He Might Be.

PROLOGUE

Always the same dream.

Milly O'Malley's pub is just the way she last saw it that dismal Belfast evening, a fake castle full of false gaiety, the locals inside working overtime to deny the reality of the frequent deaths on the narrow cobblestone streets outside.

The chilling breeze at her back will turn colder than a British soldier's stare and cut clear to the bone later, when they finally shepherd her home, but now it surrenders to the warmth of camaraderie as she pushes past the swinging doors and takes comfort from the tobacco clouds and stale lager air and the thick crowd of locals drinking, bragging over darts and warm beer, having a laughing good time, as if all of life were easy and uncomplicated.

From the ancient jukebox against the rear wall, next to the drawn curtains that hide a short corridor leading to the toilet and the back entrance, U2 is somehow making it sound like happier times.

The kitten cradled in her arms stirs to the music and makes a noise as she acknowledges a finger salute and a smile from eager-faced Danny O'Malley behind the time-scarred bar.

She starts sweeping the room with her eyes, briefly wondering about the solitary drinker at the bar, a stranger, sitting in a way that gives him an overview. He wears a blank expression and a frayed houndstooth jacket and is trying to fit in.

She catches him staring at her.

He averts her gaze by diving his eyes inside his beer mug. After another moment, he sets down the mug on the counter and wipes his prominent lips with the back of his hand.

The regulars at the tables pushed tight in the center have noted her arrival and, as usual, are not being the least shy about exploring her lean, athletic body or passing fractured smiles and side-of-the-mouth whispers shielded by their cupped hands.

She knows how pleasing they find her and wears their inspection with a barely disguised pride while searching about for Frankie.

In another moment, she spots him, leading five other lads in heavy conversation at a somber, back corner table. His face is in three-quarter profile and he is unaware of her arrival, lost in the intensity of his words.

Even in the bad overhead light, Frankie shines as her own beautiful boy.

As she plays with the thought, the Drinker crosses in front of her, heading for Frankie's table. He stops a foot or two away, hands resting in the pockets of his jacket, and quietly waits to be noticed.

One of the lads nudges Frankie, who turns away from the group and stares up at the Drinker. His smile is offhanded. The man responds with his own tense, tight grin as he casually pulls a Luger from his pocket and fires without aiming.

The bullet smacks into Frankie, knocking him backward over his chair and onto the floor.

Except for her screaming, the harsh sound of the shot has killed every other noise in the pub. The kitten springs from her arms, lands on its feet and hurries to Frankie.

The Drinker is striding away, heading for the front door, holding the Luger in a way that says he's ready to use it again.

She is incapable of movement as he brushes by her, but only for an instant.

She wheels around and charges after him.

In a single motion, the Drinker turns and uses the barrel of the Luger to smack her aside.

She stumbles sideways, trips and falls awkwardly onto the sawdust-covered wooden floor. She shakes her head clear and forces her eyes open in time to see him disappear through the swinging doors.

The bartender hurries to her side, gets down on his knees and reaches for her hand, his words assuring both of them that she'll be just fine and not to worry. She looks past her shoulder and sees the kitten licking blood off Frankie's hand. One of the lads picks it up by the scruff of its neck and then doesn't quite know what to do with it.

Another lad heads in her direction, while the three others take hold of Frankie and speed him out past the drawn curtain alongside the jukebox. Sinead O'Connor is singing something she has heard a million times before but, right now, doesn't know by name.

She wants to run after them, after Frankie, but she can't make her body work. Her mouth is open, but she can't put words to her thoughts. There is more to see, but her eyes no longer cooperate.

Always the same dream.

Always, she wakens to the same old sweat and confusion of a new life without Frankie.

Hardly three weeks after the shooting, Frankie's older brother, Liam, comes calling on her, his cap in hand, a crack in his voice, tears staining his cheeks, like he really cares about their loss or her suffering.

Finally, unable to contain herself, she explodes. "Stow it, Liam. I'm not up for your kind of truth."

"Which is what, Bright Eyes?"

Liam knows how much she hates hearing him use one of Frankie's pet names for her. Why he does it. Ever Mr. Hyde to Frankie's Dr. Jekyll. Others see it too, but tolerate Liam because of who his brother was and the McClory family's abiding commitment to the Cause.

The Troubles are over now, maybe; maybe, for good; even Sinn Fein's Gerry Adams preaching the gospel of peace and the brotherly love to come with a cease-fire nobody truly expected this side of Heaven. But not yet this animal, Liam, or any of the boys who once fell in line behind Frankie, the "Thirty Two."

They are outcast toughs who practice violence in the name of a free and united Ireland. All of them up from the dirt of Catholic Belfast and most break their backs in the shipyards when they're not breaking heads for the six counties. Mercenaries for hire. Skilled and well-paid killers called "Plowmen." Anyone's life for the right price and, sad to say, Frankie a hero among them since he was a boy; ultimately, their leader.

Yet, if he had not been, she never would have met him and it would have been one more of the great loves that never happen, that most women experience only in the innermost caverns of the soul.

There would have been no Frankie and Bright Eyes.

She freezes at the thought.

No Frankie and "Face?"

"Face," the other pet name Frankie could always make sound like a poet's reward, the one Liam resents most and never uses as a taunt.

"Which is what?" Liam repeats. "My kind of truth?"

The beatings Liam took over the years have frozen the lower part of his tightly drawn face, and he wears a constant smile. A bramble bush mustache offsets what the Brits left of his lips. A drunk surgeon had botched the reconstruction of his nose. Liam is not yet forty and looks a hundred years older.

"You wouldn't know the truth if it reared up and bit you in the ass, so how do you expect—"

"Right. Like I do expect too much from you?"

"Like you expect from all the girls?"

"And what's that supposed to mean, Bright Eyes?" And, a wicked wink, as if she is another of the young women he bought with a pint or two of ale and lots of hokum about his bravery confronting the damned U.V.F., the double-damned U.D.A., the double-damned, bleeding Brits.

She has seen evidence of Liam's handiwork, in the library, at the grocer's, the black and puffed faces, welts even careful dressing can't hide. But the women never speak out about his tortures, too fearful of the consequences that come in bedrooms and back alleys.

"He is what he is," Frankie told her shortly after they married and he brought her home to Belfast. "Not nothing I could say to Liam or nothing I could do will ever change that, hard as I might try."

"How can you stand to be around them, and not only Liam? Any of those bloodsuckers who take themselves for strutting saints."

"The end justifies the means. Wasn't the first to say it, Face. Won't be the last. This killing will go on, both sides, until someone takes the first steps at looking peace square in the face."

"Who? Who'll take the first steps?"

"Ask a dead man."

"What kind of answer is that?"

"Right now, the only answer, unless you have a better solution."

She did, one to keep to herself until it was the right time and she could confess the awful truth that put them together, about Walter Burkes and the Service and—

Instead, she appealed to him, "Tell me, again, Frankie. I need to hear it from your lips again, that you've never murdered anyone."

"Not by my hand, Bright Eyes, but don't I always say to you that giving commands makes me as responsible as him with his finger on the trigger or lugging a ton of Hell to Kingdom Come explosives? I could never deny giving the commands any more than I would retreat from sharing the bloody blame, but that's ground we already been over enough. The admission of guilt has you in a mood to reconsider being Mrs. Frankie McClory, there's trains running as regular as my heart goes out to you. And I would die without you, as surely as you had your own finger on the trigger."

He always said it so confidently, the part about the trains.

He knew what her response would be, maybe even better than she.

She always reacted with a small, spontaneous gasp at the notion of leaving him, and he would sweep her up into his arms and carry her off to their own private world of love-making. Gentle, torrid, never twice the same, always surprising, astounding in the way it released her emotions, made her believe in herself as much as she believed in Frankie.

Liam has grown impatient. His voice snaps her back to his intrusion. "Tell it, Bright Eyes. Tell me what it is I expect from the girls, or do you need more time to think up something? I'm waiting on you, girl-o."

She changes the subject. "Tell me why you've come into my home, Liam, then go, please."

He makes himself comfortable, slumping into the cushioned chair Frankie always took for himself, and says, "We got a job in America and need you in it."

"I never lifted a hand for Frankie, why should I do it for you?"

"Doing it for me is doing it for Francis. Before they come on after him with a pair of wings, he told me himself he'd be putting the job to you. Here's a golden chance to grant your departed Frankie one last need."

"I don't believe you, Liam."

"You say I'm lying?"

"I say Frankie never asked me to be involved in the business."

"He taught you how to use a gun?"

She lies with a nod. "To protect myself."

"How about to protect your loved ones?" He might be smiling at her. With that face, no way to tell.

"Who? You?"

"That day comes, pigs will shit gold bricks. Does the name Osborne set off any chimes in your belfry?" Her breath catches in her chest. "Judge Noah Osborne? His sainted wife, Dorothy, and the children? Peter and David and Raleigh and the wee girl, what do they call her? Cookie, is it?"

"Bastard!"

"Don't tell me Ma and I'll owe you one."

"Speak to me."

"You mean say what I expect from you?" Liam makes a no-need-to-answer gesture. "We got us a job calls for letting a nigger who fancies himself a world leader get acquainted with one of our Plowmen. We need to send on across some tools for the Plowman to do his work. You make the delivery for us to the Osborne home where you once lived and you're out of it."

"Mr. Mustamba is going to Pasadena?"

13

Mother Mary and Joseph!

The name just slips out.

Maybe, Liam has missed it; he's painting a corner of the wall with his gaze.

"Did I say a name?" The bastard heard, all right.

Thinking quickly—

"—You said a color."

"I didn't say he was a black man. I said he was a nigger, which is the truth. When he's a dead nigger, we have us a tidy sum to keep on with the struggle."

"To line your own pockets, you mean." He shrugs. "Why the Osbornes?" She can't manage her voice. It betrays her concern.

Liam feels himself for cigarettes, lights up and blows a jet stream of smoke across the room. Teases her with time. Finally, lets the hum under his breath turn into words. "Your judge heads some greeting committee bowing down to the nigger chief. So we got us a perfect place to store the tools, convenient and safe, up until the Plowman is ready for them."

She wants to ask, *How do I make contact with the Plowman? Is the Plowman someone I know?*

She needs the answers for Barney Sullivan, who'll get them to Burkes, who'll—

This is the wrong time.

"Go to Hell, Liam. I won't do anything to put the Osbornes at risk."

Liam cackles. "They're in it, with or without you around, Bright Eyes. If we choose someone else for the job, who don't got the same worries about them Osbornes as you, think what could happen to your old family . . ."

"A threat, Liam?"

"Call it whatever you will and, meanwhile, you're there in

Pasadena, California, U.S. of A. and seeing to their safety . . . Look, you want to sleep on it a few days and come on by with your answer?"

"Once and only once?"

"You mean, will we invite you to help us again? Girl-o, do a good job and we'll let you work with us any time you want."

"This one time and never again."

"You drive a hard bargain for a free trip home."

"I may decide to stay in America."

His hand sweeps the air in front of him. "I won't be the one begging for your return."

"If the Osbornes are harmed, if they're hurt in any way, I'll come after you, Liam."

"So long as I come, I don't care who's first."

The way he says it frightens her. She clamps down on her back teeth and shows nothing. "Bastard."

He blows on the burning end of his smoke to raise the glow, finds a viewing range and inspects it for Lord knows what. Nails her with his feral gray eyes and makes a chalk mark in the air between them. "I do this for him, Bright Eyes, for Francis, for him what we both loved dear. What he asked for, otherwise, I had me own way—"

He zips a finger across his throat.

Two days later, she meets for the last time with Barney Sullivan, an Irish patriot who lost an arm standing up to the Brits and found a deep hunger for peace instead of revenge.

Unable to get anyone in or out of the I.R.A. to pay attention, especially not the Thirty Two, he was ripe for plucking by the Service, Sullivan explained to her early on. These were Americans, so it wasn't like going over to the enemy, only to people who shared his need to end The Troubles, and end soldiers coming out of the night shadows in infrared goggles

15

like stalkers from another planet, pointing self-loading rifles with image-magnifying sights at every wind noise and whisper that might be an armed patriot, often killing women and children in the name of self-defense.

They met frequently at Milly O'Malley's after she had settled in as Frankie's wife. Whenever there was news to exchange, she found an excuse to be with Frankie, or Sullivan found her and gave her a signal while she was out marketing.

Sullivan was a Milly's regular, dragging himself in every night around nine, looking and smelling like leftover stew and playing the sot, so anybody watching would figure theirs for friendly chat at the bar, while Frankie plotted with his mates at a rear corner table overhung with smoke.

Her final meeting with Sullivan is different.

She is returning from the grocery, within sight of the Peace Line separating her neighborhood from the one next door, hands laden with shopping bags, when the cop stops her, calls her by name and says she has to come with him to the station.

People watch and make noises and, fearful about stirring up the soldiers backing the cop's action with aimed machine guns, only throw out angry words. The cop broods and insults her, does not try to help her with the groceries on a half-mile march under a blazing sun that makes her sweat with more than fear.

She sits on the only chair in one of the cramped, dimly-lit isolation rooms for almost an hour, ruefully guessing how much Catholic blood has been washed from the walls and mopped off the concrete floors.

The door squeaks open. She expects to be joined by thugs in uniforms, government sanctioned gangsters who will hurt her for whatever truths they want out of her, or just for the sport.

Instead, Sullivan darts inside. He closes the door behind

him and gives her a finger salute. "I got your signal and had to organize the safest way to gab," he says, exposing crooked, tobacco-stained teeth black at the gum line. "Something to do with that damn bleeding Liam's visit, I suppose?"

She collapses with relief, struggles to get her breathing to normal and, once she finds her voice, says, "These bloody walls have ears, too."

"Our walls, our ears. Except to top brass, I'm a carouser caught out late-late with too much Bass on his breath." Sullivan raises his arms and does a turn like a model showing off an outfit. He looks like he's been rolling in the gutter before they took him in; smells like the gutter, too. "So, tell me about Liam . . ."

When she has finished relating the story, Sullivan stretches the rose blooms on his cheeks with a smile. "Fits with the puzzle pieces we already got, so I'll get the news to the Guv and you don't worry yourself about a thing."

"Now I'm worried," she says, adding a look to the sardonic edge of her reply. "The Guv is a king-sized asshole."

Sullivan draws back, barely moves his head left and right, runs his fingers through what's left of his thinning gray hair.

He studies her like she's crazy, the stump of his left arm tapping nervously against his body.

"Serious, girl. Don't you make light. Mr. Walter Burkes always knows what he's doing, so you go and do what Liam McClory says, knowing you'll be looked after. You got my word and you'll have the Guv's word on it."

Well, Burkes can fool others in the Service, but he could never convince her he was more than a despot pretending to have all the answers, like the eleventh commandment was *Thou Shalt Believe Burkes*. Tell that to Moses, not her, who knows someone like Burkes wouldn't last out a week giving orders to Frankie's bunch. The Thirty Two would take only so much before dropping him off in some dark alley, a bullet air-conditioning his brain, and go on to celebrate over a pint of Guinness at Milly's.

"I learned the hard way, Barney; taking somebody's word only leaves the gate wide open for somebody else, somebody wrong, to pass through," she says, her voice rising. "I've met other people in the Service who did that, took somebody's word. They're dead now."

Sullivan signals her to lower her voice and looks at her dumbly, obviously resenting the inference about Burkes.

She waits out the urge to shout. "I'll put it to you as straight as I know how, Barney." Her whisper is dagger sharp. "You get word back to Burkes. I want the Osbornes to have round-the-clock protection starting the minute I leave Belfast. You tell him it's the deal-breaker. If Burkes says it's no go, you tell him I'm a no go."

Sullivan, looking like he has swallowed a skunk, says all he can do is relay the message.

Liam comes calling a few hours after she is back home, demanding to know why she's been picked up by the cops.

"Where'd you hear?"

"What difference it make?"

"No difference. Where'd you hear?"

He circles her like a bullfighter, then leans against a wall and finger-snaps a stick match to light his cigarette. "So happens you was seen being picked up. We got calls."

Something in his eyes tells her there is more to it than that. She moves into the cover story Sullivan has worked out with her. "Was one of the callers Barney Sullivan?"

Liam's face gives away nothing. He makes her wait for his answer. "Matter of fact, yes. Says he was out for a stroll when the RUC bastards come to fetch you."

"Then Barney was lying to you."

"Your old drinking mate? Lying to me?"

"Lying. He was on a bench, either coming or going, when they waltzed me past the barbed wire. Looked like he had drunk all the Lough and half the North Channel."

Liam swallows half the cigarette with his next drag, fills the room with smoke. He looks around for his memory and shrugs. "Maybe how it was, Sullivan told me when he called . . ." Takes another drag. "At any rate, still need to hear about you."

The smug bastard isn't going to acknowledge she has caught him in a lie. Well, tit for tat. "The cops wanted me about Frankie. They made me look at a lot of photographs, mug shots, sketches, hoping I would find the one who shot him."

"That's it?"

"That's it."

"Nothing about your impending journey to Pasadena, California, U.S. of A?"

"Nothing."

"Funny, them being interested in Francis now. All they could do to keep from yawning when it happened. Like they ever bleeding care when it's one of our own takes a bullet . . . What do you say to that?"

"Nothing, Liam. I say nothing." She has decided to take the offensive. "You here to put the shadow on me some more? That what this visit is about? If so, ask the questions you really mean, then get the bleeding hell out of my sight."

His eyes narrow with distemper. "Don't you be challenging me or telling me what to say, Bright Eyes. This ain't Francis you're dealing with now, and you're in no position at all to—"

"I don't have to go to America, Liam. You and the Thirty

Two doubt me for any reason, you choose someone else to take your bloody baggage. Remember, it was you approached me. I'm doing it for Frankie, and I'm doing it to be gone for good from here; forever."

"It can't be soon enough for me, girl-o," he says, in a voice to freeze the fires of hell. "First, though, we need you to do some sightseeing after you're settled with your precious Osbornes."

"You're asking for more than we agreed, Liam!"

"I know that, Bright Eyes. But ain't me doing the asking. Is for the cause that's bigger than us two and any nigger you choose to name."

"Why can't your bloody Plowman do it after we make contact and I deliver to him the—"

He interrupts. "Why can't cows fly? Girl-o, I do what I'm asked and you do as you're told. Then, we're finished one another and I don't ever need set these tired eyes of mine on you again."

"Piss on you, Liam!"

"Fun with somebody else, but I'm not meant to be your wall. You may of blinded Francis to what matters, but rest assured you don't even raise a pimple on me."

He grinds his cigarette into her hardwood floor with a boot heel and eases out like the snake he always was.

That night, she has the dream again.

Milly O'Malley's pub is just the way she last saw it that dismal Belfast evening—

No way of knowing about the meeting Liam is having at the same time, with the Plowman he is hiring to—

"Kill her like I killed her old man?"

20

"More to it than that," Liam says, explaining what he has in mind.

"Easier ways doing it here and nobody the wiser."

"Except the Thirty Two needed convincing she's a traitor like I say. So, after this business with people she knows come along, I said send her to the States as a test and have you stick to her tighter'n glue. If she meets up with someone, does anything suspicious on the train ride, like I expect . . ." Liam aims a finger gun at the Plowman and clicks off a thumb shot.

"And if it don't happen?"

Liam repeats the gesture. "Nobody wiser, excepting for you and me."

"Christ, you are the cold bastard, McClory."

"But warm to the cause, Donahue. You do what you do for the money. I always done it for love."

"Love for country or love for killing, McClory?"

"Who wants to know?"

The Plowman gestures indifference, and leads the conversation to the matter of his fee, the bonus he'll expect for killing her—

—While she is asleep, dreaming the same dream.

Always the same dream.

Awakening to the sweat and confusion of a new life without Frankie.

CHAPTER 1

KC knew about renegade priests. She had met enough of them in Belfast, even got drunk with some on occasion and had to discourage a few whose curious hands roamed too freely under the influence, but none had ever come on to her like Father Shanley.

Jim.

She encouraged him.

By the time the train crossed into California and they were carrying on like old friends, she had decided it was more than the Sex Thing he was after.

She knew she had to kill him.

That or be killed herself.

The Service had taught her never to take chances, take no prisoners, either, after it had stripped her of her humanity.

Survive or die.

Never hesitate to pull the trigger.

You can apologize for being wrong, the world is a textbook of mistakes, but there's nothing you can do if you're dead.

She had first noticed him stealing glances at her in the connector bus from the Sandman Inn in Vancouver to the Amtrak station in Seattle, frequently tugging at the ecclesiastical collar digging into his wrestler's neck, but it wasn't until the train was well underway and the billboards whizzing past began advertising the advantages of living in Oregon that she allowed him to pick her up.

She was relaxing in the nearly vacant club car, concentrating on the monotonous hum of the train in motion, nursing the vodka and tonic she had ordered to take the edge off the trip she'd let Liam McClory bully her into making, when she looked up from an old *People* magazine and saw he was getting ready to make his move.

The priest unwound from his seat, pocketed a Bible and straightened his jacket before stepping forward to her, preceded by the heavy scent of a cologne he must have bathed in.

"You mind a wee bit of company?" he asked.

And winked.

He appeared to be ten or twelve years older than she was, in his late thirties, and five or six inches taller at six feet something.

He was broad shouldered, muscular in a way that gave the impression his cheap, piously black suit was ready to burst at the seams, and frequently tugged at the ecclesiastical collar digging into his thick neck. He wore his dark, rugged good looks as casually as the immense, ornately carved wooden cross dangling from his chest.

She let him hover momentarily, made it appear she was weighing his inquiry and his wink; filled her lungs and let the air sneak back out, priming herself. "Not at all," she said at last. Invented a smile. "Please. Company would be wonderful, Father—"

"Shanley," he said, pretending not to have seen KC gesture him toward the cushioned bench seat across the table and maneuvered for comfort on the seat alongside her. "Father Shanley to me church, Jim to me friends. And, who might you be?"

"I might be Kate McClory," she said, working to sustain her smile.

Father Shanley appeared to exult in the news, as if a papal messenger had just delivered him a red hat. He rolled the name around in his throat several times, acquiring a taste for it. Finally, he rewarded KC with an approving nod. "A lovely Irish name. Pleased to make your acquaintance, Kate McClory."

"Thank you, Father."

"Jim." The waiter took his drink order, another double shot of Jameson's, straight, no ice, with a beer back, but they had no Guinness and he settled for domestic, a Bud. He reviewed the scenery and the weather for her until the waiter returned, mixing in several jokes that sounded like part of a slick routine he'd used before, the smooth salesman measuring his client.

His voice was deep, straight out of evening mass after the whiskey had had all day to scorch the throat raw. She recognized the accent, Belfast, but not the neighborhood.

He toasted to her health and inquired, "McClory, you said?" KC nodded. He took a sip and ran his tongue around his oversized lips, then for good measure wiped them with the back of his hand. There was something in the gesture that stirred a memory, but she couldn't get it to budge from its hiding place. "A good, solid salt-of-the-earth name, McClory. You Irish by birthright or by marriage?"

The question prompted her hand to the plain white gold band on her ring finger. She pictured the engraved message from Frankie, *Katie. Forever, my madness most discreet,* and she felt a momentary longing tug at her chest. "Both," KC said. "My parents were also Irish."

"From the old country?"

"My father was. My mother was second-generation American."

His approving smile quickly faded into a quizzical expression. "Was, you say? I take it then they're with our Lord Jesus Christ?"

"Yes."

"Recent?"

"Long enough for most of the hurt to be gone."

"But never the memory."

"Never the memory."

Father Shanley crossed himself and promised, "I'll add them to my prayers tonight, and a few words about the beautiful creature their daughter has become."

KC whispered a thank you and forced a brief grin.

The priest winked again.

"And your husband?" he asked.

"From the old country."

"I mean, traveling with you?" He looked around to survey the other passengers in the club car. There were five. Two men in their fifties locked in a game of gin. A fat woman whose hot pink outfit matched her beehive hairdo. An attractive young couple, early twenties, in matching Nirvana tee shirts, touching each other like newlyweds.

"Only me," KC said.

"He's back home then?"

"Yes."

KC could almost see his mind working, trying to decide on what to say next, and she was guessing he'd move their conversation to the Sex Thing. The way he was giving the Nirvana girl a second look told her it would be a pretty safe bet he was one of those reprobate, horny, degenerate old priests on the make for some illicit, recreational sex to speed along the hours between here and Pasadena.

Except, the priest unconsciously unbuttoned his tight jacket leaning forward to get a better look at the girl and KC spotted the shoulder holster hugging the space under his left arm.

He must have realized the possibility immediately. He pushed back in the seat, pulling the jacket closed, working the buttonhole, giving KC the once-over in a single movement.

She had been faster and was already staring across the aisle and commenting about the Disneyland billboard whizzing past the picture windows.

"I haven't been there in years," she said. "The Haunted Mansion is my favorite. You ever been, Father?"

"Jim," he corrected her, trying to read her face. "Years ago, but I favor a Holy Ghost what don't reside in any haunted castles."

He grabbed himself by the shoulders and laughed uproariously, and she joined in, maybe too anxiously, because he quit suddenly, leaving her sounding foolish and alone while he strip-mined her face for some clue.

Shaking off whatever he was thinking, he took a casual swallow from the Jameson's and picked up where he'd left off.

"I'm from the old country, too. Hollywood, east of Belfast; on the water. You know it there?"

She nodded and flashed a smile of recognition as he drowned her in his.

"First saw you up in Vancouver, on the ride to the King Street station, long before we reached the shadow of the King Dome. I was hoping then you might be one to indulge a wayfaring man of God in a bit of innocent conversation."

KC said, "I'm flattered, Father."

He made a clucking noise and corrected her again.

She stirred her vodka, but took only a sip, for show. She needed to be as sober as possible. She would continue pretending to be charmed, of course, and hope her eyes didn't betray her to this priest who wore a shoulder holster.

She challenged herself anxiously, Is glimpsing a shoulder holster enough reason for killing someone?

Anyone?

Has it ever been?

After all, Frankie had introduced her to a half dozen priests who packed, like Father Mulroney, who stored his .45 brazenly under the sash of his cassock and foolishly bragged about his sentiments. Dead now, the father, his heart not as strong as the paramilitary sons-of-bitches who used a Wilkinson single-edge safety razor to scrape away his skin layer by layer, demanding information the poor, brave soul didn't have.

She thought back, trying to figure how long it had been since she'd killed someone, Barry Shields, the bastard who murdered her parents.

William and Margaret Cassidy.

Billy and Peggy to their friends.

One minute, her folks were alive and vibrant, away on one of their usual combination business-and-pleasure trips, sending love notes and picture postcards home to their only child, who pasted them neatly in a scrapbook decorated with the crayon hearts and designs you could expect from a ten-going-on-eleven-year-old.

Next, a minute that became a millstone around the rest of her life.

KC was staying with the Osbornes, her godparents, fast asleep in the guest room she had come to think of as her own, when her "Uncle Judge" gently awakened her to share the bad news.

His eyes were red and his voice broke telling her her parents were gone. A car accident along a narrow, rain slicked country road west of London, about twenty miles past Oxford. In fact, exactly twenty-three and a half miles, a distance she verified after the Service sent her to London to eventually wander into Frankie and make him fall in love with her, and she had driven to the crash site once she had settled into a cramped convenience flat the Service kept for its agents near Nottinghill Gate.

She thought she was dreaming, at first, her "Uncle Judge" a welcome shadow, but you don't wake up *into* a nightmare. He wrapped her in his arms and hugged her warmly. Protectively. Shared her grief. Kept reassuring her the Osbornes would continue to take care of her the way her Mommy and Daddy would want. Her parents' trust named Noah and Dorothy Osborne her guardians, but she never doubted they would have taken the responsibility for her under any circumstances.

And so they did, until she ran off to take care of herself and to kill the murderer of her parents, Barry Shields . . .

She wondered if she could kill again, but—

Father Shanley's voice made it impossible for her to concentrate.

"You looked bright to me, and now I can tell you are." He inched away to survey her. "I've always had a partiality for bright women. A bright woman knows how to make a man glow." She dismissed the compliment with an exaggerated gesture. "What it was brung you over to Vancouver anyway? A lot more direct routes from Eire to Los Angeles."

She wasn't about to tell him this was the usual route the Thirty Two and I.R.A. branches had used to transport their most wanted out of the country and to safety, as well as for missions like the one Liam had put her on. She supposed he already knew that, anyway. "Friends there. Ticketed myself to Toronto, then took an Air Canada commuter. The train ride is for fun. I've always loved trains."

He accepted her explanation without comment. "How very, very, *very* lovely!" he said abruptly, reaching out to point at the delicate sterling silver crucifix around her neck, a fifth anniversary gift from Frankie that she never removed. "You are one of us then?"

He lowered his hand and, in passing, made it seem to brush her breast accidentally.

She acted like she didn't notice. "Not a very good one . . . Jim."

"Is that a confession?"

"Close as I've come to confessing in years."

"Me, neither," he said, and winked. He leaned in closer, his upper arm connecting with hers, and in an insinuating tone suggested, "Maybe the both of us will have something new to confess before our journey ends, Kate McClory. How does dinner sound to you?"

She nodded approvingly, certain her voice would betray her thoughts.

There's too much at risk to presume this is about the Sex Thing, KC.

Take no chances.

Nothing you can do if you're dead.

Better the priest.

Father Shanley.

Jim.

Whose real name was Preston Donahue.

CHAPTER 2

Over dinner, Donahue saw KC's mind was somewhere else most of the time, but he kept his broad smile elastic, his laughter rowdy and did most of the talking while he half-watched the California landscape sneak past their window in the beauty of an orange thunderbolt sky.

Ten or twelve other tables were occupied by people who had reserved for the first seating, including some he remembered from the club car, and the air was filled with the intoxicating smells of a busy kitchen.

He wondered if she was so quiet because she was trying to figure him out, or had she truly bought into him as a gregarious priest?

No.

He was still certain she had seen the holster. She had become a different person after he'd made that dumb move, no matter how hard she pretended, but he was not so dumb himself.

He had not survived this long without developing a sixth sense about people, and this one had brains, just like her old man, Frankie, had. The shit was the other McClory, Liam, who always acted like he was smarter and better than Preston Donahue. Straight up a pig's bloody ass, he was.

Donahue sipped at his Jameson's and grinned at her pretty while he tried to picture all the zeros in one million dollars. A lot of zeros, and he deserved them all, given his years of service to the highest bidder.

He reminded himself, Tonight, Donahue, you take the money and run.

A wonderful meal and, afterward, jolly her into her compartment. Bone her for the sport of it, then kill her and find the gold certificate for a million dollars, American, Liam said would be in the luggage, in a plain brown manila envelope. The gold certificate went with the tools and the plan for disposing of the nigger Mustamba, Liam said.

Now, it would be going off with Preston Donahue to early retirement.

Maybe, on an island somewhere, where they'd never think to look or ever find him.

"A penny for your thoughts, Father."

He opened his eyes and looked across the table at Kate, his grin already fixed. She smiled back and could have meant it, he thought. She gave a salty toss of the head, then finger-brushed her blonde hair back into two shoulder-length curtains framing her oval face.

"Jim," he reminded her. "I was thinking, You look like a million dollars."

She did, too.

In the time she had excused herself to freshen up and meet him here in the dining car, she had changed into a blue silk hopsack dress that accentuated her eyes, the neckline revealing more than the blouse she had worn earlier: choice mounds of flesh and the press of nipples ripe for sucking. Before she'd sat down, he looked for a panty line and could not find one. She had to be starkers down there, too, naked as a jaybird, and the thought made his tool grow ramrod straight.

"Jim," she repeated, making the name sound like a mating call. She had chosen the poached salmon salad, and picked at it occasionally. Probably how she kept her figure, eating like a bloody sparrow, he decided.

He mentally undid the gold buttons running down the front of her dress, one by one, while he devoured the last of the well done prime rib steak, chewing with gusto. He followed it down with a heavy swallow of the Napa Valley Cabernet the waiter had recommended.

He reached across the table and took her hands in his, ignoring the confused look of the black-jacketed waiter, who had just duck-walked over to ask if they were ready for dessert. After all, didn't he have the right to administer a little comfort?

Kate freed herself, took the padded dessert menu from the waiter and began reciting in a sultry voice that reminded him of Lauren Bacall in the old Bogart movies.

He said, "Dessert I want not on the menu," and tilted his head at the waiter who, possibly because he understood what Donahue had meant, duck-walked away in double time.

"What kind of dessert did you have in mind?"

"The kind where calories don't count."

"You have a way with words . . . Jim."

"Got a tongue good for a whole lot more than words, trust me on that."

"Trust you, or am I nearer to my God than thee, Father Shanley?"

"I think we're speaking the same language," he said. He cocked an eyebrow, drilled her with his eyes while his mouth curled into a knowing smile. "Today is Sunday, a fine day for a Holy Communion," he said, and waited for her response.

Finally, she placed a hand on his forearm and gave it a gentle massage. "I've been a widow long enough to miss more than my man," she whispered enticingly. "Why don't we finish the wine in my compartment . . . Jim?"

Too easy, Donahue thought. Thinks she knows something, that one. Forget about screwing her. Kill her outright. Take the gold certificate.

One, two.

Easier than one-two-three.

CHAPTER 3

By the time they had reached her compartment door, the priest was stealing gentle rubs of her body and finger-tripping her as if she were a roadmap. KC answered his cooing small talk and smiles with smiles of her own, but said nothing to either encourage or discourage him. Her adrenalin was galloping as she played out in her mind the plan she had rehearsed while dressing to meet him for dinner.

Several times she wondered if she'd be able to go through with it, conjuring up the shreds of decency she had managed to hide and store away from the Service after Walter Burkes did his Pygmalion number on her.

Burkes. She despised him as much as she loathed Liam. Bloody bastards, both of them. But they were her keys to freedom, if she managed to get past this job in one piece. So, he had to go, the priest.

Father Shanley.

Jim.

She visualized the gun in his shoulder holster and wondered if he was a Plowman put onto her by the Thirty Two, maybe, because they figured her for a traitor, the way some of them had come to suspect Frankie.

That's what brought the Plowman after him at Milly O'Malley's pub, isn't it? And, KC winced at the memory of the exploding gunshot that brought the congenial din to silence. Her scream. The Plowman smashing down the Luger on her. And—

Where's the logic, KC?

If they suspected you, too, you'd be dead already, dead

34

and buried; worm food; trying to imagine the sky from six feet under, beneath a cheap wooden marker in the McClory family plot next to Frankie's stone.

She felt goose bumps growing on both arms and inside her thighs and used her hand as an eraser, rubbing hard, but they wouldn't go away.

Besides, hadn't Liam pushed more bloody work on her in Pasadena and touted her off strangers?

To turn around and send one after her was a contradiction.

She shut her eyes—

—and felt the priest's hand intruding on her body, snaking over her buttocks and around her waist. Hot breath at her neck and then his teeth nibbling at her flesh.

She knew if Frankie could be here now it would be over for the priest, Plowman or not, just for thinking he could have Kate McClory for dessert.

KC wriggled free of him and surrendered the wine bottle and the pair of glasses she had taken from the table.

She fished the electronically encoded Saflok from her purse, inserted the slender plastic rectangle into the slot in the door, pulled it out.

The door lock clicked open.

She coughed her throat clear and, speaking slowly to hide the anxiety corrupting her throat, told him to clear some space on the Formica surface of the built-in slab desk for the wine bottle and the glasses.

"Get comfortable while I visit the little girl's room and, you know . . ."

Instead, he moved past her and deposited the wine bottle and the glasses on the desk.

She managed to unbutton her dress down to her waist and was intentionally pulling on the fabric so that both her breasts would be exposed enough to beg his attention after he turned back to her.

He closed his eyes to some thought, then stepped over to the open lower berth and unfastened his jacket button as he settled onto it. He ate her with his eyes and played back her use of the expression *the little girl's room* with amusement.

As KC expected, she didn't go unnoticed.

His voice was hoarse with emotion telling her, "You're not really such a little girl, you know?"

"I don't suppose you're so little yourself," she said, making it sound seductive as she glimpsed an edge of his shoulder holster. When he seemed to reach toward it, her nervous laughter exploded out of control, and she commanded, "Get yourself ready for a sermon on the mount, Father Shanley."

That stopped the priest.

"Romeo," he called across to her before she'd slipped behind the safety of the bathroom door.

CHAPTER 4

The bathroom lock clicked and Donahue withdrew his hand from the holster. Damn! Her breasts, those erect pink nipples challenging his dickie-do to attention, they'd cost him the moment. He counted off ten seconds under his breath, then leaped back to the slab desk, intent upon putting the time to use, and carefully examined the contents of the travel case Katie had parked there.

When he didn't find the gold certificate, he swore under his breath, then moved on to the piece of worn leather hand luggage he had spotted on the rainbow-colored carpeting below the desk.

He dropped to one knee and explored the satchel, careful not to make a mess.

Froze when he thought he heard the bathroom door opening behind him.

Looked cautiously past his shoulder.

False alarm.

Before continuing, Donahue listened harder.

Heard the sound of a toilet flushing, then running water.

A shower? If so, she'll be getting good marks in hygiene from the coroner.

He suppressed a smirk.

The gold certificate was not in the larger case either.

He pushed around the top layer of sweaters and closed the lid and was surveying the small room for other luggage when the water abruptly stopped.

Only the sink then, for a fast go at her hands and pudding pie?

Donahue hastily retreated onto the lower berth.

Saw a chunk of cashmere sleeve stuck out from the case under the desk.

If Kate saw it, she would suspect at once what he had been up to. Raise a bloody stink, especially if he smacked her around until she told him where the gold certificate was. Bring the world down on him, knocking and hollering questions through the door. Can't have that, can we, Donahue? Easier just to do it and get on with a leisurely search, joyous as it was playing all over again with the idea of a screw first.

Maybe, afterward, along with the gold certificate, he'd take a souvenir with him, something to remember her by, the way he sometimes did when the girls were as delicious as this one. Once more show the bastards they weren't the only ones knew how to fight a bloody filthy war so unfair it could make even the devil shed tears.

Donahue dug inside his jacket for the Walther PPK and in the same motion reached across for the pillow. He positioned the pillow in front of the gun barrel and, calmly, as the door handle began turning, he took aim.

CHAPTER 5

Men appreciating KC's breasts was old news to her, but the priest's frequent glances had bordered on obsession and she was confident that exposing them would give her the few seconds she needed to dodge out of gun range and put her plan in motion.

Suddenly, the thought of killing somebody made it difficult for her to breathe.

KC began gasping for air; felt the bathroom space closing in on her.

She pressed a hand to the wall to keep from falling; kept it there until her knees felt strong enough to hold her.

She rubbed her crucifix.

Closed her eyes while she retrieved an image of Barry Shields.

Shields also had expressed an urge to have her, and she'd deceived him the way he had deceived her folks. When he was on his knees, naked, begging and desperate for the mercy he had not shown them, she told him who she was and memorized the surprise on his face before squeezing the trigger.

After that, when Barry was history and the Service had turned her into a performing seal—everywhere but in her mind—she always summoned an image of Barry.

Barry was the excuse that let her get into the Sex Thing, let her squeeze the trigger, let her do whatever it was Burkes expected of her.

Until Frankie came along.

He was her rescue and her salvation, her reason for living,

although Burkes hadn't planned it that way.

She summoned Barry Shields now and used the image for target practice, felt a surge of her old confidence returning. Better. Confidence was important. Confidence and need. Without need, confidence was as meaningless as a marshmallow, Frankie often told her. *You have the need, Bright Eyes, then confidence is a steel wall you stand safely behind until the work is finished.*

"I have it, Frankie," she reflected, whispering the words to the ceiling. "I have it, darling. I do."

She finished unbuttoning her dress and hung it on the door hook. Ran her hands over her body and wished it was Frankie's touch. She flushed the toilet and turned on the water in the stall shower, then stepped to the sink counter and her leather-handled, tufted cotton overnighter.

Inside was the .32 she'd wrapped in plastiç and hidden beneath assorted toiletries.

Next, she took the largest towel on the rack and wrapped it around her wrist and several times over the mouth of the .32 the way she'd been taught, completely obscuring the weapon and creating an instant silencer.

Yes, I can do it, she told herself, over and over, until she'd given herself no other choice but to believe, and suddenly she couldn't breathe again. She pressed her back flat and hard against the door while she tried regaining control.

Her adrenalin was pumping and she heard herself gasping for air noisily through her mouth.

She'd have to be calmer than this to make the first shot the only shot.

Calm down, KC. Calm down.

She closed her eyes and saw Frankie, and imagined his voice gently reassuring her. Everything's gonna be fine, Face. Everything's gonna work out just fine.

At once, she could taste the excitement rushing through her system.

She berated herself for how she had let herself feel before, like a child lost in the rubble of truth.

She glanced in the mirror mounted above the sink and determined to accept who was staring back, what was left of the innocent creature who'd grown up believing people lived happily ever after. She saw what she had come to represent to those who knew her back home in Belfast, a grieving widow who was finally so caught up in The Troubles she could take up arms to help the cause that claimed the life of her man; and, if necessary, kill in the name of the cause, although other mourners clucked with a wisdom that said it was a taste for revenge that would eventually take her to the trigger.

The cause, maybe, but not revenge had brought her to this moment of truth with "Father Shanley." She sniggered as the name sneaked out under her breath.

"Father Whoever Whatever."

"Jim."

Plowman?

KC whispered to herself, "You are my need and my confidence, Frankie. I'm doing this for you. No. For us. For you and me."

She turned off the shower, breathed deeply through her nose, let the air out slowly from her mouth before turning the door knob.

Heard the lock click loose.

Took another deep breath. Exhaled slowly through her mouth.

Pushed open the door.

Stepped back into the compartment.

Her arms reached for opposite walls to give the priest an unfettered view of her naked body, the few seconds advantage she wanted this time.

She saw his eyes trail from her solid breasts to the triangle of blonde pubic hair growing wild between her legs.

Saw how the sight mesmerized him.

Long enough for her to swing her arms together, the free hand supporting the one wrapped in the towel.

Steal a quick aim and gently squeeze the trigger.

Cuh-rack!

The shot barely missed the pillow he held in his lap and caught him in the vicinity of his heart. There was a spurt of blood and only a wordless objection out of his mouth; she had worked far too fast for him to be surprised again.

The impact pushed his upper body forward, then backward. He hit his head against the connecting wall of the berth and slumped over onto his side, his legs still on the floor.

KC felt her heart racing.

The sight of death was twisting her insides.

She forced herself forward and fingered his neck for a pulse, to be positively certain there was none. He was still clutching the pillow.

She worked it free and saw the Walther.

She inhaled sharply, aware that her nakedness had purchased her life.

She mumbled a prayer of thanks and pushed out the air.

Felt an immediate, enormous relief as the tension drained from her body.

Became aware of the tears spilling down her cheeks and brushed them aside, acknowledging that any further emotional release would have to wait until the business here was finished.

She unscrewed the gun from the dead man's grip, then hurried back to the bathroom and dropped both weapons and the towel into her tufted cotton satchel.

She zipped the satchel closed, absent-mindedly patted it the way she might pat one of Frankie's pet cats and at once pulled back her hand. The idea she was thanking the .32 for a job well done heated her cheeks with embarrassment.

KC returned to the lower berth and surveyed the carpet for telltale signs. The bleeding seemed to be confined to the body and the bunk area. She smiled at her good fortune. The housekeeping would be less of a chore than she had anticipated.

She began a struggle to get the dead man onto the lower berth. Heavy cargo under normal circumstances, now as dead weight and positioned as awkwardly as he was, there was more to it than just maneuvering his legs up and inside the berth. She had one hand under his left thigh, ready to lift, and the other about to push hard against his left shoulder, when the gentle knocking on the corridor door startled her out of deep concentration.

KC couldn't be certain how long the knocking had been going on, only that she had a new problem, as well as a fresh dagger carving up her guts.

She shoved and got the dead man to roll over.

His right hand stuck out from the bunk and his right leg stayed married to the ground, but it was progress.

Before she could get too pleased with herself, she heard a new noise emanating from the direction of the corridor and recognized it as a Saflok going into the slot in the door.

Hold yourself together, KC.

Don't lose it now.

Somebody has the wrong room and will reach the same conclusion when the door fails to open. Besides, you always turned the interior security lock as well as the slide bolt after you entered the room, so there is absolutely nothing to worry about, except—

The priest had followed her inside, and she had had more important business on her mind than a security lock and a slide bolt, and—

The door handle was depressing.

She became paralyzed.

Forgot how to breathe.

For a moment thought she might pass out.

Ordered herself, *Not now, dear God! Not now!*

KC swung around. She leaned over and grabbed onto the blanket at the foot of the bunk, yanked it up and over the body. She jumped away from the lower berth, nearer the desk, turned around to confront whomever might be about to come through the door.

As the door started to open, she glanced over to the berth and noticed a hand and foot jutting outside the blanket. Her heart wanted to explode. Her legs were ready to quit under her. She willed herself to hold on. She had not gotten this far to—

"Night porter," the night porter announced, before the smile sank off his fat lips and a desperate look sent his eyes into orbit, and KC was about to lie about the body in the bed when she realized the porter had not taken his eyes off her. She remembered she was naked and was relieved. She and not a corpse had evoked the porter's response.

Her mind responded swiftly to the situation.

She hoisted her hands to her hips and held her ground like the Queen of the Nudist Colony, further unbalancing the night porter, who bore a surprising resemblance to the dining car waiter. He was older by about a decade and what hair remained on his head had turned the same sallow white color as the mustache nesting under his flat nose.

"Come to turn down the bed?" he said, finally, in a gravelly voice. He fixed on her eyes and would not let go.

KC put a vertical finger to her lips and with her free hand pointed to the lower berth.

The porter followed the movement, then locked onto her eyes again. "I guess you won't be needing your bed turned down."

"We're fine, thank you. Oh, wait a minute."

KC padded over to the travel case on the desk. She opened it and found her wallet. The smallest bill was a twenty. She turned again and approached the night porter. "A little something for your trouble and your good thoughts," she said, hoping he wouldn't hear the panic lacing every word.

"Not necessary, miss," the porter said, taking the twenty from her. He nodded and smiled appreciatively as he backed into the corridor. KC stepped forward to shut the door. In the same instant, the porter signaled her to stop with an outstretched palm, startling her.

"Allow me, miss," he said.

He took the plastic *Do Not Disturb* sign off the handle on her side of the door and affixed it to the handle on the corridor side.

"Thank you, you're very sweet."

The porter gave her an awkward smile and pulled the door closed.

At once, KC jumped to the door to activate the security lock and slide the safety bolt into place. Then, she stood perfectly still. Eyes shut. Hands at her side. Measuring her breathing. Pushing air out of her system. Trying to bring her shoulders down from the roof of the train. Unwinding the tight ball of yarn her stomach had become. Licking off the thin ridge of fear sweat decorating her upper lip.

After several minutes, she crossed the room and dropped onto the desk.

She planted an elbow, propped her chin in her palm and took a long swallow from the bottle of Cabernet. Another. Got up and headed to the lower berth, trying to remember the last time wine had tasted this good.

It took KC fifteen minutes of manipulation and tugging to get the body onto the bunk.

Pulling hard on the priest's head, his thick black hair lifted off his scalp, exposing a sad garden of gray hairs that added another ten years to his age. Moments later, the palm of her hand swerved out of control across his chest and hit him in the nose, causing the nose to fold onto his left cheek.

Moving in for a closer inspection, she saw the nose was also part of his disguise, made of some kind of putty or polyester.

She stared, hard and then harder, wondering why the face looked familiar, and—

—realized what there was about him all along that had strained her memory.

The gesture. His gesture. Wiping his mouth with the back of his hand.

She'd last observed the gesture in that brief moment at Milly O'Malley's when—

Mother Mary and Joseph!

"Father Shanley" was the same Plowman they'd put onto Frankie.

Her hands began shaking, and then—

A smile of reward skittered across her face and she experienced a different kind of exhilaration, the temporary euphoria of survival.

KC used the next few minutes to calm down, regain her composure, focus on what had to be done.

She told herself she could feel better for the killing now, only half believing.

She felt miserable rotten, and the fire in her belly raged out of control.

She picked up the hairpiece from the floor and tossed it into the lower berth, then worked on a grip that let her push the berth upward and close it.

She missed trapping the catch lock the first time and the berth fell back down with enough force to bounce the body. She fell across it quickly and grabbed onto the mattress, or the priest would have rolled off.

She got the berth up and locked on the third try, celebrated her success with what was left of the wine, chugalugging straight from the bottle.

At once, she knew it was a mistake.

The walls began spinning, and so did her head; her stomach. Her legs began to fail her. She dropped onto her knees and managed to crawl to the bathroom in time to get her mouth over the toilet bowl.

Afterward, nothing left to puke, she rolled over onto one side and, using her arms for pillows, gladly surrendered to the constant, reassuring sound of the train gliding on the tracks. She closed her eyes and pictured the moon traveling along for the ride, and fell asleep knowing that, for whatever was left of the night, she would be too tired to dream.

She was wrong.

It came back the way it always did, the dream she couldn't forget, and more.

Father Shanley.

Jim.

The Drinker.

He brushes her aside and cracks her face with the Luger. He fades into the night as Liam starts barking orders, as if he's in charge now, commanding the other lads at the table to take careful hold of Frankie and rush his brother out the back, before any law comes asking questions. Liam gives her an ugly glance back over his shoulder, as if this is all her fault, before he disappears himself, and—

She woke up crying, feeling lonely and afraid, furiously missing Frankie.

CHAPTER 6

At approximately the same time in Los Angeles, Police Detective Peter Osborne was stretched out on the bed in his partner's apartment, studying the ceiling, trying to crack through the stucco and sail his eyes to the first convenient distant planet, thinking about KC and feeling like a lowlife.

How can you make love to one woman while you're thinking about another? he asked himself for the millionth time. And that's just today, isn't it, Peter? A million times and that's just today. How can you make love to one woman while you're thinking about another? Quite nicely, thank you, very much, you lowlife son-of-a-bitch.

Did he always despise himself this much or was the loathing more pronounced today, in the wake of the news that KC was about to reenter his life after years of being a memory he couldn't lose, for better or for worse, depending upon what else was happening in his life at the moment?

Like Annie Waterman.

Now.

Stretched out beside him.

"Blow job for your dreams," Annie said again, for the second time, maybe the third. He could tell by her tone how annoyed she was. He continued to ignore the offer. "Earth to Peter . . . Earth to Peter . . ."

After a moment, Annie's fingers settled over one of his eyes and she plied the lids wider, as if she were checking for some flicker of life. Pulling them away, she said, "Blink once for yes and twice for no."

He would have preferred not to blink at all, but Annie was persistent when she knew what she wanted, like right now. Her fingers trailed over his nose, his mouth, and began to work their way down his body. They played with his nipples, fingered his belly button, following the track of hair down, down, down.

When he didn't rise to her challenge, she quit, abruptly let go of him.

He made a noise that was involuntary, meant nothing, and tried to draw a curtain across the latest image of KC. Her image was always strongest whenever Annie touched him there?

Also when others touched him there?

Others too numerous to name or was he just being discreet, if only to himself?

Well, which is it, Peter?

Annie.

Dear Annie. One of a kind.

Like KC.

In the long ago, when it seemed like a good and necessary idea to share his problem with a stranger, the shrink told him he was the victim of guilt not love. The shrink said he would heal with time, but neglected to say how much time, or how much money he'd have to spend before he realized he couldn't buy the peace of mind he so desperately wanted.

As desperately as he wanted KC back?

There you go again, Peter, doing it to yourself.

And, again, now, to Annie, who took a noisy drag on her cigarette and pushed smoke into the air, adding to the thick layer of nicotine death by osmosis she enjoyed creating wherever she went, then worked the butt between his lips.

He sucked and swallowed.

"Better," she said, retrieving the butt to take another turn.

"By the way, Detective Osborne, did I mention yet that the damn rubber broke?"

Peter's eyes popped, like in a bad cartoon.

"You are alive. I had faith. I believed. Thank you, Jesus, thank you. Hallelujah! Kong lives." Her hand found his cock again. "Well, almost . . ."

Peter couldn't suppress the grin forming at the corners of his mouth.

Annie was irrepressible, as always.

Her brunette good looks might be considered harsh by some, too offbeat, but he'd found them increasingly appealing, especially the narrow cast of her eyes, green as a bell pepper, and the hairline scar that trailed from the bridge of her nose down alongside her wide mouth, which seemed to hang in perpetual doubt. She was the best partner he had ever had, the only one he had ever sacked.

He was attracted to her from the first day, when the boss called him into his office and then Annie and told them they were now a pair. Effective immediately. No argument, Osborne; a done deal.

Annie let him know at once she wasn't any happier, but would go along with the joke. For weeks afterward, she referred to him as "The Joke."

He took to calling her by the department's nickname for her, "Dyke Tracy." The nickname was understandable.

Annie was lanky and hard bodied, flat-chested and tight hipped, walked like John Wayne and kept in shape by adhering religiously to a three-times-a-week workout regimen at the Academy in Chavez Ravine.

She was two years older than him, thirty-one on her next birthday, and ten years tougher. She also was extremely intelligent, and that did not sit well with the career cops who let their bellies grow and their brains erode while she devoured

51

the textbooks and cruised through the exams and made the grades they could not score by wishful thinking.

It wasn't long before their mutual animal instincts had brought added meaning and significance to the concept of "Internal Affairs." They worked at keeping the truth about "Dyke Tracy" their secret, but sometimes noticed a telling look or a sarcastic remark that meant somebody else knew. In a way, that added to his enjoyment of the game they were playing and, Peter knew, Annie liked it too.

What they had was not just sex, but it was not quite love, either.

Annie chose to believe it was love and she used most opportunities to stake her case with him, but he was still working on what he believed.

Mutual affection, for certain.

Mutual appreciation, mutual need, for sure.

Some of the reason he told her about KC in the first place, shoved it out into the open real fast, before their twist on the Buddy System could get too convoluted, and, hey, Peter, maybe that makes you not as big a lowlife son-of-a-bitch as you'd like to believe?

Wouldn't a real lowlife son-of-a-bitch have kept the truth to himself?

Maybe, once KC was out of his mind for good, he could find Annie's truth or something close to it.

He mentioned that whenever Annie got too serious.

After all, partners don't lie to partners.

Code of the cops and, he supposed, the Code of the cops could work for marriages, too, sometimes.

Except, KC was coming home, and that would change the rules again.

There would be a real person for the two of them to confront: KC, who left hating him and would return—

"Thinking about her again?" Annie wondered. "The broad?"

Annie being Annie, she didn't have to be told to know. He slipped a sigh past her. She was making it one of those moments again with her question.

He told himself it wasn't jealousy she was laying on him. They had never voted a rule that made jealousy permissible.

"I told you. Not a broad."

"Anyone else you ever fucked is a broad in my book."

Jealousy.

He must have been absent the day the vote was taken. He turned on his side facing her and propped his head against his hand. "And if she's a broad, what are you?"

"Still horny," Annie said.

"Aren't you ever satisfied?" Peter said.

"Not when I'm in love."

She took the burning cigarette parked on the edge of the nightstand and ground it into the dead pile on the ashtray.

"You were kidding about the rubber?"

Annie shot back a sly look. "Why? Didn't you wanna go for broke?"

She didn't give him a chance to answer.

She snapped off the lamp, rolled on top of him and laid a long kiss on his mouth, too fast for him to raise an objection, and somehow, however temporarily, she made KC disappear inside the folds of the pleasure she was dispensing.

CHAPTER 7

The morning sun was casting a sparkling light on the ivy-covered, brick and beam station in Pasadena when the Amtrak glided to a squeaking halt. The city was the next-to-last stop before downtown L.A., a clever debarkation point for informed travelers, less than twenty minutes from Union Station and an easy multiple-lane freeway jump to anywhere else on the 210.

Pasadena had already developed a special place in the history of Hollywood fifty or sixty years ago. The movie studios used it to stage arrival or departure photos and stunts involving stars, designated VIPs and special visitors ranging from George Bernard Shaw to Randolph Barshee, a half-blind, bowlegged cowboy in his late seventies, who had the manufacturers of make-believe at Fox convinced he was really Jesse James. Even Zanuck showed up at the station to greet Barshee, in a chauffeured limo longer than his credits.

Peering out the compartment window for any sign of a familiar face, KC thought about Barshee and some of the other names she remembered from stories she'd grown up with, about the famous and the fakes, performing for the press, or just stepping on or off the 20th Century Limited in a place less likely to draw attention to a questionable liaison than the teeming downtown terminal.

She crossed to the full-length mirror inside the closet door and double-checked her outfit. It was as enticing as yesterday's: Double-breasted blue blazer. Nothing underneath. Matching skirt that quit ten inches above her knees and showed off her elevator legs.

Not wearing panties heightened her sense of the role she was now playing.

So did the three-inch spike heels.

KC ran her hands through her hair, fluffing and roughing, until she was satisfied how it framed her face and fell onto her shoulders. Too much lip gloss, sunbursts on her cheeks, a mask of eye shadow and eye liner further obscuring her features and adding to the Halloween Hooker look she was trying for.

She smiled, confident she'd be remembered for the wrong reasons if anyone spotted her leaving the compartment now and later associated her with the body in the bunk, after it was discovered in Los Angeles or San Diego.

She touched her stomach. It no longer hurt the way it did when she was finished upchucking last night. She knew she had scrubbed off the puke stink, but it still smelled in her memory. She found the cologne spray in her purse and administered another dose, then gathered up her two pieces of luggage and, with a last look at the lower berth, opened the door, took a deep breath and stepped into the aisle.

And saw the same night porter who had walked into the compartment last night.

He was carrying a load of newspapers, propping a *Los Angeles Times* against each compartment door as he worked his way in her direction.

She bit down hard on her teeth, willed her stomach to stay settled. Told herself to remain calm. There was no reason for the porter to suspect anything more than the good time she had given some fortunate john.

KC returned his smile of recognition. She set down the luggage to pull her door shut, test the handle and adjust the "Do Not Disturb" sign.

The porter reached her looking as if they shared some

secret and she was too dressed for his taste.

She swallowed hard and asked, "Pasadena?"

The porter nodded, surveyed her curiously.

She answered the question that must be plumbing his mind. "My boyfriend's going on to L.A. You won't disturb him before then, will you?"

"No need, miss, not even if he's heading all the way for San Diego, so long as that sign is hanging there."

"He's very, very tired. You know what I mean?"

"Been working these rails, man and boy, going on forty-seven years, miss."

KC laughed, and so did the porter.

They understood each another.

She tried tipping him, but he shook his head and insisted she had been generous enough the last time. She thought about asking if he meant with the twenty-dollar bill or the peep show, leaning over for her luggage in a way that gave him a clear parting shot at her boobs. Something better for him to remember. The porter made a sharp undecipherable sound not meant to be overheard and helped her get a grip on the bags.

As she sashayed down the aisle, KC could sense his eyes all over her.

Inside the train station, KC searched the overhead directional signs for the one that would take her to a phone bank with enough privacy to lessen the risk of being overheard. Five minutes later she was talking to Burkes' man, Simmons.

She knew what would happen if Burkes learned about the murder any way but from her.

More of his questions, the usual kind and the kind she never wanted to answer, the ones that made her concentrate too hard on keeping the story straight and increased the risk of her making a mistake and ruining everything.

She knew she couldn't afford that, any more than she could afford for Burkes to know the whole truth.

Somehow it seemed fair.

Had Burkes ever shared the whole truth with her?

KC finished the call and found the loo. She made a career of her hair waiting for the stalls to empty and a slope-shouldered mother in her twenties to change her infant's diaper. The mother was at least thirty pounds overweight, not counting the bags under her eyes, but KC envied her the child.

She and Frankie wanted kids, but The Troubles always got in the way, and Frankie would urge her to be patient, wait for the time it would make more sense to bring children into the world.

"Will we ever see that day, Frankie?"

"We're helping to make that day, Face."

"I'll pray you're right."

"Will take more'n prayers, but I'm confident we'll get there our lifetime, and then crank out babies like an automobile assembly line, and name each one for the saints, beginning with Saint Katie."

"Silly bird, there is no Saint Katie."

"There is in my humble life. She's the patron saint of all that matters most to me."

How she hungered for Frankie's touch. She could remember him pressing his body into hers, and her eyes got wet with need and the black mascara borders began racing down her cheeks. She closed her eyes looking for him and felt his confident whisper at her ear: *Everything gonna be fine, Face. Everything gonna work out just fine.*

It took her a minute or two to regain her composure.

She double-checked to be sure she was alone, then puddled a palm with dispenser soap, but before she could begin scouring away her whore's face a woman, early forties, mammoth hips stuffed inside farmer's bib overalls, entered and chose the adjacent sink.

KC eyed the woman nervously.

Maybe it wasn't just a priest they'd put onto her. She moved two sinks away and quickly rinsed her hands while taking a stance that would allow her to react quickly to any sudden attack.

The woman gave her a curious glance and inched her face to the mirror to work at popping a dime-sized zit on her angular chin.

Finished, she sneered at KC, "Fuck you, bitch," and stomped out, her logger boots pounding echoes on the tile floor.

"Welcome to L.A.," KC called after her, light-heartedly.

The exchange of greetings had relieved some of her tension.

KC headed for the end stall farthest from the entrance and pulled from a travel bag the outfit she had selected earlier. She placed it carefully on the toilet tank lid and stepped from her heels. Undressed. Hung the blazer and skirt on the door hook.

Changing, she thought about the Osbornes and tried to imagine how they would look after all this time. How they would sound. Uncle Judge and Aunt Dorothy. Raleigh and David. Cookie. And, Peter. She said his name again: "Peter." Curious how she'd been able to keep him out of her mind most of the time.

Peter. The deceiving bastard who destroyed her life and at the same time made it possible for her to find her life, her

Frankie. Yet, she could admit to herself, she sometimes wondered about him, Peter, more and more once the trip back to Pasadena became a reality etched in stone.

Frankie, if he were still here, would tell her what he had told so many survivors of relationships cut short by The Troubles: *Get on with life.*

Mourn and move on, he'd urge gently, holding hands and sharing the sorrow.

Mourn and move on.

This wasn't the same thing, though, so screw you, Peter.

And, wondered now if she meant it.

Damn him, anyway!

KC jammed the hooker outfit and her heels into the travel bag, zipped it and went back to the sink mirror. She washed off the face of the woman who had slept with a priest, pulled her hair into a ponytail and tied it with a cloth scarf as undistinguished as the black pant suit outfit a size and a half too large hanging from her shoulders; used a junk jewelry pin to hold the Peter Pan collar of her white blouse in place.

She patted her cheeks to give them more color, added a pair of overwrought frames that removed any magic to be found in her cobalt blue eyes, and took a step backward for one last hard look at herself in the mirror. Satisfied she had completed the transformation into a KC McClory who could be on her way to a Pasadena PTA meeting, she hurried into the terminal.

The crowd had thinned out to maybe a dozen people. Homeless types occupied the benches or wandered aimlessly and let wounded expressions do the begging. One of them shuffled over wearing a costume of poverty and fresh cologne under his stubble. KC fished into her purse for her wallet, pulled out a twenty and handed it over to him. He grabbed it greedily, smiled, saluted and shuffled away.

She thought how good it made her feel to have done that before he could beg, even if he might be a phony, one of the play actors she'd read about. After all, the gift was in the giving, wasn't it? And, besides, wasn't she playacting, too?

Looking around, she saw the night porter passing within five yards of her.

He was struggling with a wheelchair, whose occupant was an elderly, blue-haired woman about two hundred pounds heavier than the chair was meant to support, who kept issuing contradictory directions.

Test the look, KC decided impetuously, and moved into the porter's line of vision. He moved on past her with hardly a nod and no sense of recognition. She was exhilarated by her deception.

A hand pressed lightly on her shoulder, startling her.

"Uncle Judge!"

"Been looking for you, young lady," Judge Noah Osborne said.

He was wearing one of the custom-tailored gray pinstripes he favored and always made him seem to her like a member of the diplomatic corps, the President's personal envoy to some-place important, topped as usual by a hand-rolled bow tie with enough oomph to rumor the playful nature he kept hidden behind his public pose of judicial sternness.

The natural downturn to his mouth contributed to the tough impression, but Uncle Judge could never fool anybody who got close enough to him to see the warmth and sparkle in his alert brown eyes.

He said, "Almost getting ready to send the police out hunting. You still the same old pest?" His resonant voice was spun sugar, firm and self-confident, and went with his look. His thick, unmanageable hair had turned white since she last saw him, although by her count he was still a few years short of sixty. Taking a backward step, he decided, "You have not changed one bit," and held out his arms for her.

Noah Osborne towered over her by almost a foot. She lost herself in his embrace and was immediately aware of his thickening middle and a melting softness to the angular frame he used to keep hard as nails through a routine combining Nautilus workouts with laps in the pool.

"I'm six years older than the last time," KC said.

Noah pulled back, feigning amazement. He studied her from a few angles and began shaking his head in disagreement. "Definitely not," he said. "I'm the judge, you remember? And certainly the best judge of that, young lady. Besides, I haven't aged one single solitary day since the last time, so how could you have?"

"You have, you old devil, but like a good wine."

"A good wine, she says." He gripped her by an elbow and began leading her toward the exit doors to the baggage claim area. "Where do you get off knowing from good wines? A double Shirley Temple, *that* is more your speed."

"A good champagne, then? Something along the lines of a nineteen thirty-two Bordeaux?"

"Better. Much better. Like a good champagne. Like a great champagne." His laughter caromed off the tiled walls of the arched corridor, causing heads to turn.

They picked a spot near the carousel and stood on the outer perimeter of the small clusters of people watching while porters unloaded and stacked luggage sailing by on the conveyer. Almost as if he anticipated the question she was not quite ready to ask, he said, "Peter wanted to be here, too, so blame me. I'm the villain of the piece."

KC took a sharp breath. "How's that, Uncle Judge?"

"I have the rascal and his lady friend tracking after another complete set of the James Bonds. First editions. Absolutely beautiful. Bound in Morocco by Sangorski and Sutcliffe. Boy, did Peter read me the old riot act."

She smiled to herself at the discreet way he had tucked in a reference to *Peter's lady friend.* Wanting to prepare her, yet not entirely certain about the sensitivities of a green widow to old relationships; protecting her the way he always did, as if she were his own flesh and blood.

"I can't wait to see him either," she said, unsure if she meant it. "The lady friend you mentioned? Is it serious?"

Noah suppressed a smile by jamming an empty pipe into his mouth. "Definitely more serious than the last one, I suppose. And, the one before that. Or, the one before that." She noticed the porter studying her from a few yards away, and angled away to obscure the view. Her pulse began to race. Maybe she hadn't passed the discovery test after all. "Peter cannot seem to get a handle on a woman, that son of mine. Not on one woman, anyway. Not since—"

She pressed her fingers against his gentle lips. "Oh, Uncle Judge." Noah seemed relieved to be cut off, as if he'd already rejected his own ruling. "I'll bet you don't talk that way to Peter."

He removed her hand. "I most certainly do! Course, never when we're in the same room."

They shared a laugh while KC sneaked a glance as the porter left the woman in the wheelchair and headed straight for them. A swallow caught in her throat.

"Excuse me, miss?"

KC ignored him.

"Excuse me, miss?"

What could he challenge except her wardrobe? She turned and stared him hard in the face.

"Yes?"

Her manner was the final confusion. She would not let go of his gaze until she saw his mind shift.

"Oh, I am sorry. Thought you might be somebody else."

"She most certainly is, my good man," Noah said, capturing her in his arms and adding a reaffirming squeeze. "She is the best thing to hit town since the last Rose Parade."

KC heard the porter's shuffling retreat while beyond Noah she spotted the small leather and linen trunk that matched her carrying cases. "There, Uncle Judge. That one."

Noah tested the trunk for weight and, over her objections, announced he could handle it himself. He tucked his pipe stem first behind the handkerchief in his breast pocket, lifted the trunk by both leather grip handles, like it was pirate treasure, and charged off for the parking lot.

Noah's walk was not so agile by the time they reached his late model Cad. Beads of perspiration were rolling down his forehead and playing a winking game with his eyes. He refused her offers of help and insisted she climb in while he loaded the trunk.

A few moments later, he slid in behind the wheel and finished wiping his face with his handkerchief, studying her with a curious intensity while catching his breath.

The starch was gone from his shoulders and she wasn't fooled by his fake smile of bravado. Oh, how dearly she loved him and wished she didn't have to play act or deceive this sweet, dear, precious man.

"What?" she said finally, unable to interpret his look.

Noah shook his head. "It's just so darned good to see you whole and in one piece, KC. We felt so terrible about that fella of yours, when we heard the news."

"Thank you."

"Horrible, was just horrible, the way we saw it described on the television."

"In Belfast, people die like that all the time, Uncle Judge, especially the ones like Frankie, who are ready to die for what they believe in."

Noah made a long face.

"You disagree, Uncle Judge?"

She wondered if she had sounded too indifferent for his sensibilities.

It hadn't been her intention, only an honest response to honest concern.

Noah appeared to drift into thought navigating out of the Amtrak parking lot onto Raymond Avenue, heading south on the Arroyo Parkway for California Boulevard on a route she had never known him to vary.

He would travel east, then south again on Lake, straight into the Old Money calm of the Ritz Carlton Estates section, where a series of maneuvers would bring him to Fair Winds Circle and *Noah's Arch,* the entrance gate leading to the family residence. There were more cars on the streets than KC remembered for any time of the year except New Year's Day, but still not enough to make a traffic jam.

"Disagree? Not my place. Except I must say you're taking it rather well," Noah said, finally comfortable about dividing his attention, his eyes pinned to the roadway and the rearview mirror nevertheless. Noah was the most cautious driver KC knew, but driving with him was a test of nerves, anyway. "That's good, KC. That is very good. You always did have a strong spine."

"You'd be surprised at how much mourning a person can do in eight weeks. For our own and for others. And, besides, my taking it badly wouldn't bring him back."

"No, I guess not. I guess . . . Well, enough of that. I just wanted you to—"

"I know, Uncle Judge. No matter what's going on in my

life, I know I can count on you being there for me. And Aunt Dorothy."

"Darn right. Peter, too, you know?"

"Yes, I know."

"Cookie."

"I can't wait to see her."

"The whole family."

His last words on the subject as he eased past Noah's Arch and cautiously navigated the Cad up the paved driveway, past the manicured lawns and formal gardens to the front entrance, a hundred or so secluded yards from the street.

The trip had taken less than fifteen minutes.

Noah honkety-honked before pushing open the door to climb out.

KC stepped from the Cad, took a deep breath of the crisp air.

It felt good to be back.

Aunt Dorothy swept through the door and halted on the concrete portico, her smile as bright as the sun and catching shadows that softened the harsh wrinkles of time using her face as a trellis and took a decade off her fifty-something years. A breeze moving down from the north played with the hem of a springtime bright silk dress fashionably cut off two inches above the knees, calling attention to legs thicker than KC remembered, especially at the ankles, but still shapely. By KC's reckoning, Dorothy was about ten pounds heavier now, deservedly matronly, but still the beauty she'd been in her day, as the silver-framed photos on the baby grand in the salon would reveal to anyone looking for confirmation.

KC let out a squeal and raced up the first flight of concrete steps like she was fifteen years old again, took the landing on a pair of wide swings and hurried up the second set of steps into her aunt's waiting arms.

They embraced, and Dorothy whispered, "You're all right, Pudding?" Like the time she climbed for a branch that was too high and came crashing down from the old oak back by the property line, cracked her head on a rock, passed out and woke up uncertain of the world.

"Uh-huh."

Dorothy stroked her head. She pulled back and took KC's cheeks between her hands, studied her face for the time they had missed together. "Swear on a frog?"

"And a polliwog," KC said, and returned Aunt Dorothy's smile.

Arm in arm they entered the mansion.

Noah trailed them into the foyer, sweating again, locked in another struggle with KC's trunk. They were heavier now with the added weight of her two carrying cases, which he had loaded onto the lid and was aiming for the curved stairway straight ahead.

KC eyed him nervously, fearful over what could happen if Noah lost his grip and the luggage crashed open, revealing the murderous cargo she was carrying—

The Plowman's tools.

She kept quiet and held her smile.

There was never a way of changing Noah's mind once it was made up.

Except for the aging process, everything was the same.

The place looked as it did on the first day she crossed the threshold, a magnificence the architect had modeled after *Le Petite Trianon* in Versailles, but to a little girl it was the palace of her dreams and a dozen movies. Huge rooms and high ceilings. Arched, ornately carved entryways of the finest imported woods. Gigantic doors off central corridors or one leading to the next. Here and there a chandelier with true crystal ornamentation to flatter the Osbornes' exquisite furnishings and decor, many of the exquisite pieces rare, restored antiques going back hundreds of years.

The expectation of a monarch or a musketeer about to
round a corner into view. Her favorite musketeers were Gene
Kelly and Stewart Granger, with their swords drawn, ready to
die for the kingdom and their queen. Growing up, she'd
always be D'Artagnan, except when that bratty Peter insisted
on D'Artagnan for himself. Then, depending on her mood,
she'd be either Constance or Milady DeWinter. Constance
was more beautiful, but Milady was more fun.

Many were the dark Belfast nights—

Tired of cardboard keeping cold air from crashing through
the shattered window panes of the kitchen house—

Tired of outdoor plumbing, squatting indignities and the
putrid smells of a pee wall that sometimes seemed to sum up
life—

Tired of being scared shitless by the slightest noises outside on the street—

She had silently longed to be back here.

Love for Frankie kept her there, yet—

She always had the luxury of letting her mind travel back
here on furlough, and she saw everything in exquisite detail.
Especially her beloved bedroom suite.

It was one of six upstairs that opened off a sparsely furnished central corridor dead-ending at the master suite, to
the right of the landing, across from a bedroom the Osbornes
had converted into a sitting room after they moved in. The
next suites across the hall from one another belonged to Raleigh and David. Peter and Cookie had the set closest to Noah
and Dorothy.

The second floor was an afterthought. The mansion was
pretty true to the original *Le Petite Trianon* and didn't have

one when it was built around 1915 for the famous silent screen comic, Eddie Clockworthy, who had been considered a serious rival to Chaplin and Keaton until the April morning when a member of the kitchen staff discovered him inside the double oven.

Sometime during the night, Clockworthy had turned on the gas burners, managed to work his entire body inside, and pulled the door shut.

A handwritten note pinned to his nightshirt with a big safety pin provided police with their only clue.

Eddie Clockworthy had written, "Nobody laughed."

The second owners, General Henry Rialto and his wife, Rennie, had ordered the second floor addition over loud objections from neighbors and the original architect. Noah and Dorothy became the third owners about twenty years ago, when the judge acquired the property at an estate liquidation sale.

And—

Noah dropped the trunk.

He made a horrific noise just before it hit the parquet flooring and the two smaller pieces toppled off. Dorothy shouted his name. KC's eyes exploded and her hands flew to her open mouth, partially disguising the look that fear of discovery can create.

Noah held them off with his arm extended like a crossing guard, bent over with his hands resting on his knees, huffing and puffing and grunting too thick to be understood. Dorothy was anxious to know if he was hurt. He shook his head and mumbled something about tripping over his two left feet.

"Were you always this clumsy, Dopey?"

"Never."

Dorothy turned to KC, nodding agreement. "Never is right. What he was is pig-headed stubborn, to this very day.

Now maybe you'll let us help you?"

"Absolutely not," Noah said, easing himself up. He made a Y with his extended arms and drew several deep breaths, then spit in a hand and slapped his palms dry. "Just stand aside and watch my smoke. The second time is the charm."

KC said, "I always thought it was the third time, Uncle Judge." Teasing him. Relieved that none of the luggage locks appeared to have been disturbed.

"Not if you're lucky the second time, young lady," he said, and set about organizing the cases on top of the trunk.

A moment later, he was on his way again, Dorothy calling after him, "Just try not to trip and fall on your way up the stairs to KC's room, Mr. America."

"Mr. Universe, you mean. That Schwarzenegger fella has nothing on me!"

"My room," KC said, in an appreciative whisper. "Oh, Aunt Dorothy, it's so wonderful that you still think of it that way, after—"

Her aunt waved her off. "Well, who else's room do you think could it ever be? As long as we're here, it will always be your room, dear."

KC's spirits soared with the declaration.

"I'll be a minute unpacking, Aunt Dorothy, and then I'll be down to help you—"

"Absolutely not! You must be bone tired after your flight, and the train after that. You simply have to relax, take a nice bath, maybe, and then a nap. We'll see to it you're up in time for dinner."

"Please. Let me help with something?"

"Won't hear of it."

Noah was heading down the stairs, using his hand as a handkerchief. "Tell you one thing, young lady," he called to her. "I've carried a good deal of luggage in my time, but that little trunk of yours—Whooooh! What are you lugging around in there?"

"Heavy artillery," she said, illustrating with an invisible rifle, the sight at eye level, wanting to be certain Noah heard it as a joke.

He exploded in mock horror, then, "Did you forget where you are now? Pasadena, California, good old U.S. of A. Not Belfast. Little old ladies in sneakers. Not rebels. Nope. No rebels around here."

"Freedom fighters, Uncle Judge."

Noah cocked his head and studied her across the bridge of his generous nose. "Well, there is no place in the world where you could possibly be as safe as you are right here in Pasadena."

"Maybe I'm here to protect you," she shot back, and the three of them shared a good laugh while KC tried imagining what their expressions might be if she told them it was the truth. She *was* here to protect them.

CHAPTER 8

Walter Burkes knew it was not going to be his day even before he heard his name echo down the long corridors of the Atlanta terminal and responded to the page that was about to bring him the kick-in-the-head news about KC McClory.

Burkes was tired. Cranky. Streaking on a sugar high from the four cups of strong coffee and an assortment of irresistible jelly doughnuts he had wolfed down as breakfast before the drive from the Airport Marriott back to Hartsfield International.

He had spent the better part of last night awake, worrying about his pet German shepherd, Fritz, and the concern was now compounded by mounting irritation over the rendezvous that brought him here from Washington on an NTD priority and hadn't come off.

The department's usually reliable informant was a no-show after sixteen hours of monitoring the Piedmont flights in from Myrtle Beach, and so much for scoring a new lead on where the bad guys planned to pull off the assassination of Mr. Mustamba.

Layton was so positive he had the answer when he called, insisting he had to talk to Burkes and only to Burkes and then having second thoughts about how much he could spill on the safe line.

"Damn it all to Hell, Mr. Layton. They don't call it a safe line because anybody who wants can tune in."

"Tell that to Koffler, man."

Koffler, the agent who'd been working with Layton, had been found two weeks ago floating face-down in the marshes near Murrells Bay.

"When Koffler made the date with you, he was not speaking over a safe line, Mr. Layton."

"Don't have to tell me that twice, man." His voice was full of a gumbo stickiness that followed him out of his New Orleans heritage. "I been watching my ass ever since, and you know my ass. You know that takes a lot of doing, man."

"The call would of shown up on our routing logs, is how we know, Mr. Layton. Careless of him, but these things happen." Koffler always had been sloppy, or the Service wouldn't have wasted him down in the Carolinas, Burkes reminded himself, and choked on the laugh caused by his unintentional pun.

Layton waited him out. "Man, all I know is he's down for the count, Koffler, and I don't need no such thing happening to me anymore."

Burkes was in no mood to argue. He arranged the meeting, reassuring Layton he would bring the usual payment with him to Hartsfield International, and clicked off.

And, here he was.

Sixteen tedious hours and no Layton.

Burkes intended to wait one more day, then turn it over to the Fibbies, like it was a chance to share in the glory of stopping the assassination attempt on Mr. Mustamba, with the caveat they go corpse fishing in Myrtle Beach and environs. The Fibbies would try to grab all the credit if they were successful, like always. Shove it. No time now to defense against their inter-mural shenanigans.

Right now, keeping Mr. Mustamba alive during his visit to the States was the only game in town, one the country could ill afford to lose, and the mandate had come to him straight from the Senior Gees holding court in the White House Big Room.

"Paging Mr. Burkes . . . Mr. Walter Burkes to a red courtesy telephone, please . . ."

Burkes almost missed hearing his name. He was deep into disturbing images of Fritz having trouble walking, eyes signaling grief as he put more and more weight on his front legs, because his hips refused to carry their fair share of the load.

"Paging Mr. Burkes . . . Mr. Walter Burkes to a red courtesy telephone, please . . ."

Oh! It had to be Vonnie. He had phoned her before he left the hotel, patiently instructing her on how to track him down at the airport the minute she heard from the vet about the damn x-rays.

He was still hoping the news would be better than it was last year, when dysplasia brought on the surgery that ultimately killed Fritz's brother, Hans, who had been Vonnie's favorite. Well, Fritz was his favorite, and Burkes was determined not to be stampeded into any damn operation, not again.

Burkes wolfed down his second hot dog hustling for a phone bank. He was still swiping at the mustard stain on his chin when the operator made the connection, and he realized he was listening to the gracious Virginia tones of his aide, Simmons, not Vonnie.

Burkes was in no mood for bad news or surprises.

"Simmons, any good reason you didn't use the bee?"

"Tried, sir, but got a malfunction your end."

Burkes' hand slid into the pants pocket where he kept the small black box. The size of a microcassette, it put out a hum strong enough to send his balls into an erotic rumba whenever he was called. He remembered now. The indicator was showing red, and last night he had turned it off to conserve battery power; forgot to turn it back on, probably because his mind was too full of worry over Fritz.

Fritzie.

Damned dog.

Sometimes he wondered why he never got the knack of feeling for people the way he did for that damned dog. Maybe, because dogs were loyal and devoted. Sure, you had to buy their friendship, but it was all yours after that. Train a dog to your way of doing business and there would never be any of the double-dealing that tarnished your typical human relationships. No wonder, when people called him a son-of-a-bitch, he took it as a compliment.

He snapped on the bee without taking it from his pocket. "It looks A-okay as ever, so don't feed me no more of that molasses, okay? You jumped yourself and went for the phone, just say so. We all make errors in judgment one time or another, don't we?"

"Yes, sir." Simmons never argued with him, one of his better traits. He knew where Simmons stood when it came to loyalty, at his right hand and ready to hop on command, like Fritz in the old days.

"Koffler, he made an error in judgment, look what it got him. This about Layton?"

"No, sir. About the young lady, Mrs. McClory?"

Simmons paused, like he was waiting for permission to continue.

"What about her?"

Burkes felt knots forming beneath both shoulder blades. Simmons' hesitant tone gave away what had to be coming, a new problem on top of a damn snitch who did not keep an appointment and probably was floating face-down beneath the seaweed in some damn backwater Grand Strand swamp.

He pushed out a sigh and tucked the corners of his mouth into his cheeks, wondering what kind of trick KC could have pulled on them.

For every Fritz, there was a KC.

She was the other side of the coin.

He had bought her and trained her, but what did he have to show for it six years later? A lot of her double-talk and enough doubt to keep his nerves on the high wire was what.

"What, what, what, God damn it! What?"

"This is not a secure line, Mr. Burkes. Maybe we should disconnect and channel back before—"

"Save it for the movie-of-the-week, Simmons."

"Yes, sir, but you did mention Koffler, and—"

"Simmons, when they give you the goddam feather to wear, you can call the shots."

"Yes, sir." Choosing his words carefully, Simmons said, "Our friends from across the waters—"

"You mean the bad guys."

"Yes, sir."

"What about the bad guys?"

"It appears they put someone aboard the train to keep Mrs. McClory company."

"In Seattle."

"Yes, sir. First the bus in Vancouver, and—"

"You call in the cavalry?"

"The news came too late for that, Mr. Burkes."

Burkes made an indignant noise. "You where I can find you?"

"The usual place."

"Don't you go anywhere." He hung up and punched in a long series of numbers that connected to a satellite planted in outer space exclusively for the Service during one of the final Apollo missions, on direct orders from the Oval Office.

At the tone signal, he relayed his personal I.D. code and the number he was calling, sending the signal on a series of optional paths back to Earth. The system took maybe ten seconds longer than the time needed to make a normal telephone call and it kept sensitive information that routinely passed among agents safe from hackers, bad guys and bugging devices.

Simmons answered on the first ring.

"What exactly does too late mean, Simmons?"

"Means it was all over but the shouting by the time we heard, Mr. Burkes."

Burkes covered the mouthpiece and swallowed the airport.

Finally, "How did they do her?"

"Not exactly, sir. It was Mrs. McClory doing all the shouting."

Burkes' shoulder muscles sagged with relief. It was a mix of wanting the girl safe and knowing what KC meant to the job. The Thirty Two was out to kill one of the most important good guys in the world, and KC might be the key to nailing them in their tracks. If he could trust her to keep her end of the deal: Do whatever she was instructed by Liam McClory and the other miserable skunks, keep her nose clean and find out the who, how and where of the hit. So, what did the news mean? Where and how had she fouled up so royally that they had gone after her?

"What's the rest of it, Simmons?"

"Seems the young lady shot first, sir, and left her assailant behind when she got off the train."

Burkes groaned.

He could see the whole operation going up in a blaze of headlines if the damage control was mismanaged. Christ! First the snitch and now this.

If Layton materialized and told him where they meant to terminate Mr. Mustamba, it would give a different spin to what happened on the train. If not—

Burkes decided to follow his instincts and give Layton a

few more hours before plugging in the Fibbies and grabbing a flight to L.A.

"What else, Simmons?"

"Mrs. McClory is confident she got off the train clean, except for the housekeeping problem."

That was the KC Burkes remembered from the early days. From a screwed-up kid desperate for attention, recognition and love to some kind of *macho* woman after she'd popped that worm, Shields, her folks' murderer; who took unnecessary chances, her ego inflated by the confidence of someone with nothing new to lose, except her life, of course, and her life meant jack shit to her until he directed her to Frankie McClory.

Now, she was back to the old stand, driven, he supposed, by her determination to quit the Service.

Jesus Edgar Hoover!

How he hated dealing with people like that.

They made errors in judgment.

He hated errors in judgment.

More than he hated mistakes.

Inevitably, errors in judgment brought grief.

And, the shiver passing through his body right now, in every direction, went with his wondering if the decision to bring KC into the operation would go down as one of his biggest errors.

Burkes felt his face hit the ground, recognizing it was too late to make a change, no matter which KC McClory was fronting his Pasadena action. He'd have to cross his fingers and believe her feelings for the Osborne family would ground her against doing something stupid and endangering the whole goddam Mustamba operation. He would have to take it one cautious step at a time.

Burkes mumbled into the mouthpiece, "We know the assailant? She give you a name, any ID at all?"

"Negative, sir. Mrs. McClory said she was calling before we heard it someplace else and was nervous about being overheard. She ordered housekeeping and had a few harsh words for you."

Burkes smiled. "Well, she got that part right . . ."

"Yes, sir."

"Listen, continue to stay clear of Mrs. McClory, like nothing happened. Unless there's an absolute need, follow? I don't want to risk doing anything that sends a signal to the bad guys, understand?"

"Yes, sir. Understood. Anything else, sir?"

Simmons didn't have to hear Layton was lost, so Burkes told him about Fritz. Simmons also was a dog person. He'd understand what Burkes was going through.

CHAPTER 9

The call to head for Union Station came while Peter and Annie were a couple miles away at the Mayflower Hotel, a major garbage pail on South Flower, where they'd been helping Narco Intelligence with an undercover hunt for witnesses to a pair of drug-related killings. The loan-out was temporary and not one Peter was enjoying.

A straightforward homicide was more to his taste, but pickup work was a proven shortcut to making friends and getting boosts up the ladder. The fact Annie felt the same was another reason their partnership worked.

He had already made Detective Two, putting him a rank ahead of her, but the only difference was the pay grade. Annie was as good a cop as he was. Her gender was the main factor behind her slower rise, no matter how the department talked publicly about equality. Annie knew that, too, and never let him forget, except sometimes in bed, when the sex was especially hot and horny.

It was unusual to be pulled off this kind of job so abruptly, given the time they had put in laying pipe to snitches who might be too queasy about turning out for NIN regulars.

Lieutenant Rumpion shrugged the question after he signaled them over to the registration desk.

"Seemed unusual to me, too," Rumpion said, without taking his eyes off the tit-tilted prostie in a sad red dress walking dog circles across the lobby, clearly in deep need of a screw to pay for a fix.

Peter made her out a teenager, fourteen or fifteen, and winced as his mind flashed briefly on his kid sister, Cookie.

He had been in the business long enough to know there were no rules that turned people into meat, but there was a rule that said cops who let emotion govern action would be at permanent risk in the split-second difference between life and death.

"I was just getting used to this place," Annie said. "Even found a couple real rats a lot nicer than all the scummy two-footers crawling around. Excluding present company, of course, Lieutenant."

"Well, we'll miss you, too, Detective."

"Lieutenant Rumpion, is that a note of sarcasm I detect?"

"Course not, Detective. It's a whole symphony," he said, still tracking the troubled hooker.

Rumpion, a clam-faced relic of the Boys Club generation, had been uncomfortable around Annie since the two of them showed up. He made clear his distaste early on, and that was all the excuse Annie needed to make him a victim of her relentless putdowns.

Rumpion kept stepping up to the line and she kept busting his chops.

Peter knew to stay out of the way.

Annie didn't need his help, especially not with pushovers like Rumpion, who was getting on his nerves, too, right now, not hiding how he was mentally undressing the hook. If she wasn't somebody's sister, she was somebody's daughter, and deserved better than a dick-driven cop pulling her into a corner for a fast freebie.

"C'mon, Annie," Peter said, clamping a hand on her shoulder. She wriggled free and issued a tight-lipped smile that meant wait a minute, she wasn't through with Rumpion.

She moved her face closer to Rumpion's nose. Peter could tell what she was about to say wouldn't be pretty, but

Rumpion was already talking again, too low for anyone else to overhear.

"Waterman, you know the difference between a bowel movement and a feminist?"

Annie coughed her throat clear. "No, Mr. Bones, what is the difference between a bowel movement and a feminist?"

"It's the kind of crap you take and where, whether in the toilet or the kitchen," the lieutenant said, and turned to see if Peter was enjoying the punchline.

Looking away was Rumpion's mistake.

Annie used the moment to connect her knee to the lieutenant's groin, vicious and hard enough to make his balls clang if they'd been made of metal. Maybe they were, but the clang would have been lost anyway under the sound of his scream, so loud it startled awake all the sleeping addicts and basket case derelicts who were decorating the lobby.

Rumpion tried to grip the desk for support, but his hand slid on some leftover puke and he crashed onto the disintegrating carpet.

"Wow, Lieutenant, I sure walked into that one," Annie said. She snatched Peter's wrist, "You're right, pard, they're waiting for us. We are out of here."

Rumpion was still moaning as they pushed past the glass doors onto the street. Peter took a last look and saw he was being ignored by everyone but the hook, who had crossed over to Rumpion and was kneeling alongside him, helping him stroke his crotch while her free hand went fishing for his wallet.

"I never want to get on your bad side," he said, climbing behind the wheel of his unmarked sky blue Trans Am, which he'd parked in the red a half block down the street with a blue handicapped hanging from the rearview.

"Does that mean we're engaged?"

"It means I never want to get on your bad side."

"You just did," she said, and gave his cheek what she may have meant as a playful tweak, but it hurt too much for Peter to believe the pain was accidental.

Annie never let up. There was an undercurrent of Love Me or Lose Me to a lot of her talk, and Peter was hopeful it wouldn't come to that. He was far from being ready for—

What was the buzz word?

Commitment?

That was it, and he wasn't ready to make a commitment.

It wasn't Annie.

It was him.

Didn't Annie understand, yet?

How many times would he have to say it before—

"I think Rumpion got us bounced," Annie said. Peter was happy to change the subject on the short hop over to Union Station. She said, "I hear he's been saying nasty things about me to his buddies at Parker Center, you know?"

When her catalog of invention got to be too loud and too much, Peter said, "Maybe, it was just that they needed someone with my brains and my brawn."

"Yeah, and what am I along for?" Annie said, and he felt her eyes beating down on his head.

"The ride," he said, and pulled away before her fist could reach his shoulder. She was faster. The car swerved recklessly across the white lane stripe, almost creaming the rear fender of a snail-paced Honda with out-of-date plates.

The Pullman compartment was stuffed with a uniformed cop Peter didn't recognize, young and uncomfortable, maybe handling his first homicide; Ad Murphy from the coroner's office, who'd just opened his magic satchel and was putting on a pair of rubber gloves, a grim set to the wry old coot's mouth and unhappy eyes where the sparklers used to be, suggesting the rumors were right about Murf's split from his wife of forty-two years; an edgy Amtrak supervisor, Ed McCracken, according to the plastic ID badge on his jacket pocket, who was doing a terrific job of nail-picking; a fidgety Amtrak porter, who kept flicking his pink tongue like a frog after flies; and a body cramped inside the lower berth, dead on sight.

He and Annie were the only detectives, and that seemed to answer the question of why. They'd been closest to the scene when the call came through.

Peter invited Annie through the door and squeezed in after her, followed by the station cop who had led them here.

Ad Murphy acknowledged their arrival with a grunt. The Amtrak guy, his black hair turning white by the second, seemed anxious to say something when he saw their badges, but didn't get past some meaningless arm gestures.

Annie glanced the room and said, "Didn't the Marx Brothers do this scene on a boat?"

"Man's a priest," the porter said.

Annie nodded and told the deputy coroner, "Nearer his God than thee, Murf," then to Peter, "We're sure to get the collar on this one, pard . . . *Collar*. Get it?"

Peter wagged a naughty finger.

The deputy coroner said, "Please, Annie, can we please get down to some major death here?"

"Murf, you sure do take your job seriously."

"It's a living," he said.

"Jesus, Peter. Murf does have a sense of humor!"

It was the kind of joking that made the work possible, but Peter sensed it was a chore for Murf, who looked like he was on the Worry Weight Loss program. His face had more fissures than a walnut, his shirt collar seemed about two sizes too large and he was shrinking inside his sharkskin suit.

"Man's a priest," the porter said again. "I think you should show him some respect."

Not joking.

Peter studied him carefully.

He had the look of a man who thought he knew something. "Anything else you think we should know, sir?"

McCracken said, "I really think we should wait until our vice president for public relations arrives and—"

Annie shot him down with a look.

The porter turned from looking at McCracken to Annie, then back to him, and said, "About the girl, I think. I think you should know about the girl."

Peter checked his watch, certain the day was going to run longer than he thought.

The only girl who interested him right now was KC, but he couldn't tell the porter that. None of his business, anyway. First, picking up the books for Father, and now this. With any luck, I'll be out of here and have the preliminary report on the computer in time to make it home for dinner, he thought. Ironic that I'm at Union Station on what could be the train KC arrived on.

He drew another mental picture of her, adding a few lines and a few pounds, but otherwise did not let time intrude on her beauty.

He glanced at Annie and saw by her frown she was reading his face correctly.

Peter had given Annie a hundred different reasons why she couldn't invite herself for dinner tonight, and she'd given him the same reason why she would be there anyway, a hundred different times.

She'd said, "I want to see the enemy."

"She's not your enemy, Annie."

"And they made *you* the Tec Two?"

"Bottom line. I'd rather you weren't there."

"What are you going to do, lay her hello on the dining room table?"

A moment of anger raced by, and Peter was glad he had caught himself before he said something to Annie he would immediately regret, like telling her to mind her own business.

This was her business, maybe not as much as his, but her business, nevertheless, until they both settled on what their relationship was about.

She called it love. He called it—

What the hell do you call it, Peter?

And, hop-scotched back to KC.

He didn't know what he was going to do when he saw her. He didn't know what he was going to say, or how he was going to act or behave, or why he wanted her in his life again, only that he'd never forgiven himself for—

What about her?

What about KC, Peter?

What do you think is going through KC's mind?

Six years later, does she still hate you or has she found it in her heart to forgive you?

Six years later, will it matter to KC that you haven't forgiven yourself?

Annie's voice drew him back to the compartment.

"Hey, Detective, the porter is asking a question. We want to know about the girl, or what?"

Peter nodded, popped a smile at the porter and passed it along to Annie. "We want to know about the girl," he said.

CHAPTER 10

Luxuriating under a blanket of soap bubbles and bath crystals, feeling the heat relax her muscles and melt the ugly realities of the last twenty-four hours, KC prayed the bath would erode the stench of the man she had killed from her body while she drifted in and out of an easy slumber in the kind of tub she could never run in Belfast.

The old dream came and went, then the image of Barry Shields appeared, like he was some sort of seal of approval on her sins.

He confessed to killing her parents and begged her for mercy. On his knees, naked, surprised to discover the fuck he had bought and paid for would climax with a bullet in the head, believing KC when she said he could buy his life with the truth, Shields related the story she had traveled three thousand miles to London to hear out of his small, off-center mouth.

She had to remind Shields of some of the basic details first.

She was talking seven, almost eight years ago and he had been in the assassination business a long time.

Once he began, his forehead wrinkles filled with sweat, another river above his mouth, one eye blinking out of control, even the smallest details came out in a desperate rush of perfect pitch memory.

How they were American agents he had been paid a fair price to deal with. No explanation why asked for or offered; he never liked knowing more than he had to know. Got them to the rendezvous point with a cock and bull story about having information worth the price he was asking, convincing them with a tidbit he had been given for that purpose. He set the hour. They told him it had to be later. He stood firm, giving them no time to arrange for backup.

"They pull off the road and, quick as a wink, I step up to the vehicle," he said, unable to control a flashing grin that battered his glutinous cheeks. "We do the signals, identify us one another. The gent opens the door and I pop him before his foot's halfway out. Luck would have it, the same bullet catches the woman. Fast and clean. No pain and nothing personal. I locate the cash they brought for the exchange, fully honest that respect, and that's that."

"A lot more than that. They were my parents," she said, and looked at his face before the bullet took it away.

In that fleeting instant KC knew nothing had been resolved. She became sick at once, sick of herself and what she had done, sick of herself and what she had become, sick to her stomach and sick of Burkes and sick of the Service and sick of the whole damned world closing in on her, yet painfully aware that it wasn't over yet, not in her mind, not in her heart, and not in what had to happen next.

Anything else she had to know, she'd already heard from Burkes, how Billy and Peggy should have called in, waited for support, instead of making their fatal error in judgment. About the hastily organized cover-up that turned them into crash victims, in order to protect the operation.

Except—

Who had hired Shields.

Burkes refused to tell her that part.

So, it wasn't over.

Not yet.

"Need to know basis only," Burkes said.

"I need to know," she spit back.

"KC, your clearance level doesn't let me give you access to—"

"The Irish?" Not an entirely random guess. Based on some of the comments Shields had made over dinner, in answer to the kinds of indirect questions from her that let him think he was leading the conversation.

"Listen. Maybe someday. When your emotions aren't running so high. Okay?"

"The Irish. Send me there next, Mr. Burkes. Where I want to be."

"Let me think about it."

"Assign me there or I quit."

"I don't know if—"

"I do. Or I'm on the next plane home."

And, within weeks, Burkes had her ready to charm Frankie McClory.

It wasn't her idea to go to Belfast.

It was Burkes' idea all along, only she didn't piece that out for a long time, until Frankie came to mean more to her than her passion for revenge.

By then, little remained of the old Katherine Mary Cassidy, whose life was a world of joyous anticipation before she was stripped of her dreams and self-respect. By Burkes and the Service. But also because of the boy she had adored as a brother, protector and prince, the D'Artagnan of her dreams, Peter Osborne, who came to be her lover.

Peter knew what he had done to her, but not what he had caused.

The bastard.

She and Frankie had talked about him. She hadn't wanted any secrets between them, especially not about someone she'd thought she loved, before Frankie taught her what love really meant and how it could be.

★ ★ ★ ★ ★

Frankie had become philosophical.

"Bury the past," he said, "or it will always be there to haunt you."

"What if I went back and found I still loved him? As much as Peter hurt me and I wanted to die, what if I still loved him? What would you have me do then?"

"Think of me," Frankie said. "Think of me and, if that doesn't rid you of the demon, well, maybe, there's a case can be made for you and him together again."

"Wouldn't you be jealous?"

"Not if I were dead, Bright Eyes. Alive, I'd kill any man what sniffed about too hard or too long in your direction, or in any way brought about any kind of hurt you don't deserve."

"Oh, Frankie, I like you better alive."

"The thought of any man ever touching you again would be enough to kill me."

KC sunk deeper into the tub, barely more than her face, breasts and toes lingering on the surface, yelled the word into the humid air, and began to cry. "Peter, you bastard! Bastard, bastard, bastard!"

It took fifteen minutes to regain control of her emotions and, swearing she would not lose it again, KC eased out and toweled off, pampered herself with bath powder, wrapped a towel turban-fashion around her damp hair before padding barefoot through the bathroom door.

The room was a *boudoir* more than a bedroom, gold leaf anywhere she looked. The floor-to-ceiling velvet drapes were drawn, revealing a modest balcony the other side of a row of French windows. Her personality was on the walls. Posters of her favorite movie and rock stars taped over flocked, floral-patterned wallpaper. A cork bulletin board buried behind the mementos and souvenirs of cherished times. Stubs from a Barry Manilow benefit concert at the Civic Aud. An auto-graph from Elton John, when she waited at the Rose Bowl backstage gate for an hour. Her dance card from Prom Night, filled with the names of boys who beat out all the others for the right to say they held her in their arms. The scribbled notes from her best friends, full of the code words and catch phrases that no longer had any significance.

Aunt Dorothy had kept things the way they were the day she took off, perhaps sensing she would return, or was it wishful thinking that she would change her mind about mar-rying Peter and come running back?

She paused in front of the free-standing, full length mirror to inspect herself.

Satisfied, she crossed to the vanity and found a comfort-able position on the blue, tufted bench to study her photos. They captured some of the highlights of her life here: KC as a cheerleader, prom queen, Rose Parade princess.

She competed with herself in the three-way mirror, run-ning thumb and forefinger down her high cheeks to the base of her chin, stretching away the laugh lines that refused to stop haunting the outer corners of her eyes. She could admit to herself to liking the way she looked and she could lament how time would take it all away from her, but she was pre-pared for that, satisfied to know the powers of the mind lasted longer.

She picked up the frame with Peter's photograph. Formal portrait for the yearbook. Shirt and a bow tie borrowed from Uncle Judge. Suppressing his off-the-wall smile. His head at an angle, gazing into the distance, as if he were measuring the future. Could Peter already know the grief and melancholy he would introduce to her life? The inscription: *To KC. Love ya madly. Peter.* Had she simply overlooked his penchant for dishonesty and cruelty and—

KC spotted the reflection of her Vuitton trunk on the bed seat. It brought her back to reality. Quickly, she moved the trunk onto the canopied four-poster, dumped its contents onto the embossed satin bedspread. Returned the trunk to an upright position. Dug in with both hands and retrieved a false bottom, which she placed temporarily on the floor.

She reached in again and this time removed the three small rectangular packages that had been hidden underneath.

The packages were identical, about the size of a child's shoe box, tightly wrapped in brown paper.

She maneuvered each one with two-handed caution and, one by one, once satisfied, returned them to the trunk.

She reinserted the false bottom and restored the other contents.

When he carried them upstairs, Noah had tucked the two carrying cases alongside the seat. She settled the smaller of the pair on her lap and checked to make sure her .32 Police Positive was wrapped inside the Amtrak hand towel that bore an unmistakable bullet hole rimmed in powder burn brown, as well as the PPK Walther she had liberated from the priest.

Never take anything for granted, Frankie always told her. She never did. She felt better for having checked. Only, she didn't feel so ready for whatever would happen next.

She wondered, Now what? Next what? How safe are the Osbornes? In my need to protect them by being here, have I only brought The Troubles into their home and moved them closer to danger?

KC raised the Walther and sighted it at imagined shadows on the other side of the door, felt a pounding at her temples, squeezed her eyes tightly to forestall another outbreak of tears.

★ ★ ★ ★ ★

The family sat down to dinner without Peter, although his usual place had been set at the end of the mahogany table that seated twelve comfortably and could take up to sixteen in an emergency. Nobody said why Peter was late or if he would be there at all, and KC didn't want to ask or otherwise give the impression she was anxious about seeing him.

"Dah-dahhhh!"

KC turned in the direction of the sound.

It was Cookie, sweeping through the kitchen door carrying a steaming hot apple pie, beaming a smile at her while her mother cleared a place for the platter.

"You remembered!" KC said.

"Would you ever forgive me if I forgot," Dorothy said, and Cookie, as she slipped into her seat next to KC, added, "If you ask her, she'll have to get the ice cream, too. Tell her the Rocky Road."

Noah, occupying his usual head of the table seat to Dorothy's left, finished off a careful chewing of another precisely-cut cube of prime rib and washed it down with a measured sip from his crystal wine goblet.

"Rocky Road? And here I thought you were on a diet, Sister," he said, using his pet name for his youngest child. "Cookie is always on a diet, KC. You can see where she has a hundred or so pounds to lose."

KC smiled at the concept. Cookie was a fifteen-year-old stringbean inside her jeans and a faded Smashing Pumpkins tee shirt two sizes too large. Tall enough for her age that KC could picture her shooting up closer to six feet, like her father and her brothers.

What remained of the long brown hair KC remembered as always being in pigtails and pink ribbons had been trimmed into an eccentric barb-wired minefield of mismatched colors squashed and hidden for now under an R.E.M. baseball cap resting above her alert brown eyes, the duckbill brim backwards. The cap added to the tomboy feeling, but there were signs that Cookie's emerging features would settle onto a woman whose beauty one day would rival her mother's.

"Fah-therrrrr!" Cookie narrowed her eyes and pursed her lips, held the pose until she was certain Noah had noticed. "Besides, dinner tonight is special."

"Indeed! Your mother is allowing meat into the house. I owe you for the prime rib, KC. What with my cholesterol, it takes a visit from you to—"

"Did you remember to take your Lopid?" Dorothy asked, as she handed a plate with a generous wedge of apple pie to Cookie. "Pass this to KC, please, Cookie."

"Yes. Like clockwork, KC, on the docket every day for a half hour before breakfast and a half hour before dinner. I would hate saying what those little fellas cost every month, but they kill off the bad guys and keep Doc Braithwaite current on his dues at the country club."

"And you healthy," Dorothy said.

"Healthy as a horse," Noah said. "Makes me wonder if I shouldn't consider trading in Doc Braithwaite for a veterinarian." He laughed uproariously at his own joke, to the point of choking, washing away the problem with a new swallow of wine.

"Thank you, Cookie." KC pretended to study her dish of apple pie for a few more seconds, then looked over to Dorothy. "You know, Aunt Dorothy, I've been thinking how a scoop of Rocky Road would sure go great with this."

Dorothy made a face, but before she could voice any objection, Cookie said, "S'okay, mom, I'll get it for KC." She gave KC a fat hug and a kiss, leaped from her chair, almost knocking it over, and dashed for the kitchen, whooping as the door swung closed behind her.

Cookie's hugs and kisses had been constant since she arrived home from school, stormed up the staircase and charged noisily into KC's room. She'd pounced onto the bed, hardly apologetic about rescuing her idol from her nap. The moment had brought back to KC an instant memory of Cookie the day they said goodbye. Cookie was nine and unable to control her grief. She chased the car down the driveway, screaming and crying, and the sight made KC bawl all the way to LAX.

Dorothy and Noah traded smiles. KC added her own, just before they all reacted to the sound coming in the open French windows, a car outside on the drive.

"Sounds like You Know Who," Dorothy said, and began to fluff her hair with her hands and fingers. "Peter can smell an apple pie from anywhere within a fifty-mile radius."

KC felt a rush of anticipation. She felt a tug in her chest and hoped nobody had heard the undecipherable sound she'd made. She was surprised at the strength of her involuntary reaction to Peter's arrival.

"A darn shame that Raleigh and David are away at college," Noah said. "They would have loved to have been here, also, to welcome you home, KC."

KC swept away the thought of Peter and reached across the table to take Noah's hands. "Home. It has such a lovely sound to it, Uncle Judge. I can't tell you how much—"

"Why would you have to?" Dorothy interrupted. "We've always loved you as if you were one of our own." Tears welled in her eyes. The judge's, too. KC brushed at hers and mouthed a silent *Thank you*. Dorothy made a face that meant no further discussion was necessary.

Cookie charged back into the dining room carrying a quart container of Rocky Road and an old-fashioned metal scooper. "Dah-dahhhh!" She dropped onto her seat and set about making a major production of the scooping process.

Peter picked that moment to join them.

He came striding in from the hallway, nursing four thick classically-bound volumes in his arms. Stopped short, turned to glance toward her usual place at the table. Briefly. As if he'd been investigating a shadow. And made a beeline for Noah. As if KC weren't there at all.

"Your James Bonds are all secured and await your pleasure in the library," Peter said.

At the Amtrak station, Noah had told her how Peter had read him the "riot act," because he had to pick up the Bonds instead of being there to greet her. No sign here of any "riot act," so why had Noah said that? She began to feel irritation and disappointment.

Peter said, "And here, as a special bonus from your humble and obedient lackey . . ."

He bowed before placing the books in a stack by Noah.

Noah leaned to one side, his ear almost hitting what remained of his prime rib, to better examine the titles imprinted in gold leaf on the book spines, and began to glow. "Well, I'll be gosh darned. Blackstone's *Commentaries on the Laws of England*."

Dorothy shared Noah's delight.

Cookie finished digging another scoop of Rocky Road for her pie and decided, "Daddy is going to owe you big for that one, Flesh." She leaned in closer to KC to explain, "Like in flesh and blood, you know? My bro?"

Peter's attention was still focused on his father. "The first Dublin edition, printed in 1776 to 1780, and acquired today by yours truly in honor of—"

Now, he pirouetted so that he faced her for the first time.

Pointed at her.

Stared into her and sucked her dry.

KC understood the look Peter was sending her ran deeper than an old friendship resumed, wondered what kind of message he saw her sending back. She was not certain herself, but pushed back the chair and rose anyway as he hurried around the table heading for her.

The kiss was controlled, as if Peter understood something she did not, but the embrace was tight and warm and she felt her heat rising and a body chemistry missing from her life since Frankie was shot.

"Well, well, well. You didn't tell me you were kissing cousins, Peter."

KC didn't know the voice coming from the direction of the doorway.

The woman was leaning against the ornately carved jamb, her arms crossed to give more height to a pair of invisible breasts inside her inexpensive black linen blazer, one foot crossed in front of the other.

Her baggy slacks and Reeboks also were black, and so was her mood. KC heard it in her words, saw it on her face, felt it in the air and knew immediately who she had to be in Peter's life: the "lady friend" Noah had mentioned.

KC smiled at her weakly, and the woman mocked it back, as if wanting to make certain KC understood they would never be best friends. Of course, KC did. She had been there herself over Peter.

CHAPTER 11

The broad looked to Annie just like the picture Peter carried in his wallet and once, in the early stages of their relationship, after they had hit the sack and both recognized they were into something greater than a one-shot violation of Department policy, he had insisted on showing her. Before an objection could clear her throat, Peter was pushing the picture on her, apologizing and at the same time trying to make her understand who this KC McClory was who had complicated his life and—if Annie wasn't careful—her own.

It was KC's Rose Princess photo, in color, modest surface cracks, corners worn from handling, and Annie only looked to please him and get it out of her hand, without really examining the All-American face, but a glance was enough to seize the photogenic blonde with honest blue eyes, perfect Crest smile and a radiant complexion that made her resent her own imperfections, like the small brown mole below her ear, on the left side of her neck, the random zits pits underneath her cheeks and the scar on her nose and mouth that had been the source of taunts since second grade and a playground accident.

Kids have a way of being unnecessarily cruel to each another, and it left Annie uncomfortable with the idea of making friends. She learned how to buy them, with cookies from her bag lunch, with gifts and favors and, when she was old enough, with the kind of fun and games designed for clumsy boys with changing voices and awkward hands, who didn't care how smart she was, only that she knew where to put her hands and her mouth and, if they remembered to smile, how to spread her legs.

How to—

Enough of that!

Entering the Academy and becoming a cop instead of an elementary school teacher put her in a uniform and gave her a sense of self-esteem and belonging. It also gave her a different kind of power over men that, ultimately, she grew bored with. When the "dyke" label came along, she was glad. She was used to being taunted behind her back, and it was easier to put up with that crappola from her fellow officers than taking hits from civilians feeding her a line in the hope of catching some nooky.

Not Peter, though. It was different with Peter.

He seemed to understand her from the moment they met and were married to the same unmarked vehicle by Chief Spence, and she caught a vibe from the way he couldn't look at her for more than a few seconds at a time without clearing his throat, making some visible sign of discomfort.

Annie had the same problem with him. It felt great, the first time in years she had felt like pursuing more than a recreational fuck, but even after they'd sweated through an emotional first night, locked in fire-breathing combat or clinging to each other like petals to a rose, defying their senses, demanding more, challenging the world to rip them apart—

Where had it led?

She loved him.

He was kind, giving, supportive, the kind of best friend who would take a bullet meant for you, but—

Unable to love back.

Peter was a victim of his own confusion and a malady she'd only heard about, ghost love. His shrink had a fancier name for it, but that's what it came down to: ghost love.

And who was that spooking her at the dinner table?

The ghost herself.

KC. Goddam KC.

Alive and kicking.

Looking prettier than the picture Peter carried in his wallet. Making her feel plain and ugly and reminding her of pretty girls who'd never invited her to their parties and boys with bed sheets stained from self-abuse.

The intervening years had added a maturity to her beauty that might go downhill after she turned thirty, but right now KC McClory was Olympic class, a gold medal ghost, and Annie hated her for how she had come between Peter and herself.

She knew she wasn't being fair.

Except for the past, KC had made no contribution to the present. But, she wasn't about to blame Peter.

Peter had enough blame in his life.

And, not enough love.

If she could hold on, ignore the pain of seeing her man chase his ghost, control her mouth against stupid outbursts like the "kissing cousins" remark, maybe Peter would be able to reconcile the past and accept once and for all there was no future with KC, and get on with his life.

Their life.

"Well, Detective, don't just stand there," Judge Osborne called out to her and, indicating, "Come take a seat. Mrs. Osborne has prepared an especially sumptuous meal to welcome our daughter home."

Peter said, quickly, "I think Annie has another engagement, Father." Looked at her not quite begging.

Annie shifted her eyes back to KC, who laced her fingers on the table and sent her a face that said she knew Annie was about to tell Peter he was mistaken.

CHAPTER 12

KC worked at keeping her self-control as Annie pushed and pushed her throughout dinner, trying to provoke her with a barrage of tactless remarks. Peter's detective partner tucked her questions inside questions, like the wooden dolls from Russia, and lurking eyes and a hollow smile went with every one of them. She insisted on calling her "Mrs. McClory," pronouncing it like KC's proper place was in the grave alongside Frankie.

KC scored several times without being as rude or insensitive, but it was evident there was no way of convincing Annie Waterman she had absolutely no desire to steal Peter from his lady friend. She squeezed Cookie's hand to caution her, whenever she saw Cookie's eyes narrowing to a testy squint.

Peter also frowned every time Annie attacked her. Other times, she caught him staring at her. He avoided her eyes, pretending to squander his expressions on everyone else. Noah and Dorothy tried to carry on good-naturedly, as if it weren't happening, Noah leading the conversation along an innocuous path at every opportunity.

"Peter, you said something about being delayed by some murder at the Union Station?" the judge said, to plug an awkward silence after another one of Annie's more provocative barbs.

Peter answered quickly. "Out of the blue, Father. Annie and I were on a vice detail downtown, and next thing we were boarding the same train that brought KC here from Seattle."

KC felt her nerves starting to act up again. "The same train? How do you know?"

"Because he's a Tec Two, Mrs. McClory," Annie chimed in. "Also, it was the only choo-choo train in the yard fresh down from the great Northwest and a stop in Pasadena."

Peter showed an annoyed look across the table at Annie, sitting to KC's left, then adjusted into another apologetic smile aimed at KC.

"C'mon, Flesh, give with the real dirt," Cookie demanded. "Not every day you bring home a Murder One."

Dorothy shook her head. She gestured helplessly and elevated her eyes up inside her lids, as if to tell the world there was another teenager running amok. Peter paused for a mouthful of coffee and asked for a second helping of pie.

He said, "We boarded the train and, next thing I know, I'm eyeballing a dead priest, only he's not really a priest at all."

KC helped herself to the cream and almost missed her coffee cup. Annie must have noticed. She coughed out a sarcastic noise and did a trick with the unlit cigarette she'd been playing with that flipped the cigarette into her mouth.

Cookie whistled sharply between her teeth. "What is he then? I mean, besides a corpse?"

"Cookie!"

"Muh-therrr! That is what they are called. Dead they are called corpses . . . Lots of blood, Peter?"

"The usual amount." He made an approving noise at his joke. "An old guy, about your age, Your Judgeship."

"Thanks a lot."

"Only the victim had tried to skim off some years, fake hairpiece and all, to pass himself off as younger. That doesn't make any more sense than why he was in a sleeping compartment he wasn't registered in with some beaut of a woman."

"Makes sense to me," Annie said, under her breath, but

not so low that KC couldn't hear.

"When we find the woman, we'll probably have the rest of the puzzle," Peter said.

Cookie made a hollow pipe of one hand, inserted the index finger of her other hand, and began sanding the finger. Dorothy shook her head and rolled her eyes.

KC masked the sudden alarm clanging in her head, set off by the concept of being discovered, and said, "A *beaut,* you said? Somebody saw her?"

"A porter," Peter said. "Said she was some looker."

KC willed her face to freeze.

Peter said, "The woman was long gone by the time the body was discovered."

"The corpse," Cookie said.

Peter ignored his sister. "She got off the train here in Pasadena."

"Maybe it's time for you to be questioning KC," Cookie said, giving her a playful jab in the arm. "KC also got off here in Pasadena."

Annie said, "The porter said a *beautiful* woman."

KC closed her eyes to the insult, almost happy for the diversion. Cookie leaned over to her and, doing her best Humphrey Bogart, side-mouthed, "You see a priest on board your train—*Beautiful?*"

What a joy, this child, KC thought. She reached for Cookie's hand to give it a gentle, appreciative squeeze.

"Not that I recall," she said, and distancing herself further, "I spent last night trying to get some sleep without breaking my back, in the coach car."

"I know the feeling," Annie said. "Only so much you can do in an upright position."

KC looked across her shoulder at her.

Enough was now, finally, enough.

She said, "I'm really getting bored with your putdowns, Miss Waterman."

"What would you suggest instead, Mrs. McClory?"

Peter's voice climbed above Annie's, commanding harshly, "Let it go, Annie."

Annie said uncomfortably, "I beg your pardon?"

"I said to let it go. Enough is enough." He shifted to KC. "I'm apologizing for Annie, KC. My partner has had a long, tough day and—"

"Don't make excuses for me! If I thought I had anything to apologize for, I would have—"

"Just kept going the way you've been going. Can you remember? When was the last time you apologized for anything?"

"Tomorrow. When I apologize to the gypsy fortune teller I gave a tough time when she said I'd wind up with an asshole for a partner."

A sound of dismay escaped Dorothy's mouth.

"You don't care who you insult, do you?" Peter said.

"No, only why," Annie used the table to push back in her seat and rise. "Mr. and Mrs. Osborne, thank you for your hospitality, but it's getting to be about that time," she said, trying to sound casual. "Civilians are coming in to talk to us the first thing in the morning, and—"

"We certainly understand, Annie, but you will come again, when you can spend more time?" The judge turned to Aunt Dorothy for confirmation.

Dorothy's head bobbed up and down as she searched for something to do with her hands. "It has been a long day," she said, and seemed pleased for having found any words at all.

"I appreciate the rain check, Your Honor," Annie said, wiping off her hands with the napkin like her pores were leaking water. "Walk me to the car, Peter?"

Peter's chest was heaving underneath his jacket. He avoided Annie's eyes, shook his head imperceptibly. "No, that's okay."

"Please. I think we should talk about—"

"I said I'll see you tomorrow, okay?"

Annie seemed to suck in the air in surprise and straightened herself to a dignified attention before she dropped the napkin on what remained of her apple pie and ice cream, repeated her thanks to Dorothy and Noah and fled the room.

For a minute, the dining room was as still as an unborn thought. Then, Cookie gave KC another elbow in the arm and wondered, "Anyone for more Rocky Road?"

Dinner ended about fifteen minutes later.

Noah retreated to his study, to prepare for court tomorrow, and Dorothy insisted Cookie do her homework after she helped load the dishwasher.

Leaving KC and Peter alone.

Exchanging noncommittal looks over their coffees, then finding other places to briefly park their eyes, neither quite able to start a conversation.

I have a million things I could tell him now, KC thought. Names I could call him. This isn't the time, though, given the way he came to my defense. I owe him tonight. Or, is it a fear of confronting the past now that you have the opportunity, KC?

She started to excuse herself.

He shook his head. "Some fresh air to go with your coffee?"

"Pretty strung out from the trip and don't think—"

Peter flashed the famous Osborne touchdown smile. "Fresh air mixed with all that caffeine will have you on your second wind before you know it."

"Maybe tomorrow, when—"

His expression turned serious. "I'd also like to clear the air between us, KC." She looked at him like she had no idea what he was talking about, saw he was not going to let her get off that easily. "Won't work, Milady. You know what I mean."

"Then you know what I'm thinking."

"I suppose I do. Shouldn't we find out together?"

The expression in Peter's eyes carried the kind of challenge that might help her to untangle her emotions about him, she rationalized. And Frankie was whispering into her ear, *Bury the past, or it will always be there to haunt you.* Peter rose and bowed from the waist, one arm wrapped across his midsection, the other sweeping grandly between them, D'Artagnan style.

She thought, All you have to do is listen. You're under no obligation to tell him anything until you're good and ready, tonight or whenever. Besides, you might learn something about the priest. Father Shanley. Jim.

The possibility she'd left incriminating evidence behind froze her neck and made it difficult to swallow.

And Frankie continued whispering in her ear.

They moved outside to the balustraded veranda, under a moon showing off in the clear night sky, and, at first, Peter seemed satisfied to leave it at innocent, amusing memories. The awkward silent stretches between stories shortened as they grew more comfortable together.

She joined in willingly, sharing one story after another, filling in details on some, being reminded by him on others, laughing at the antics of childhood in the years when they were still young enough to overlook the penalties that come with growing up.

Once or twice, he would fumble his thoughts, stare into his cup as if it were a crystal ball sending back pictures.

She swallowed the carnival smells of the garden and the new-mown lawn glistening with moonlight and girded herself for whatever words he would pick to open the subject that had brought them to this moment.

Unexpectedly, as if he had thought better of the idea before now, Peter apologized for the dinner scene that drove Annie away.

"She brought it on herself, but maybe you didn't have to be that hard on her," KC said, and thanked him anyway.

"I did. I probably came across like a first class jerk, but Annie had no business insulting you."

"You're the one she called an asshole," KC said, wondering if she had sounded too much like she agreed with Annie's judgment. Peter mumbled something back. "Besides, I really wasn't so innocent myself, was I?"

His head shook agreement in all directions. "Gave as good as you got. Better."

"Thank you, kind sir."

"Don't mention it, Milady . . . I don't remember you ever standing your ground like that—"

"Instead of little KC, as usual, being bowled over by somebody's words?" Peter sighted her curiously over a nose bashed off-kilter, the first time the night he was royally creamed by two grossly elephantine tackles in a non-leaguer against Dorsey High, pulled out in the last nine seconds by a fifty-two-yard fake and run play he'd improvised on the spot. "Final score South Pas, seven-six."

"What?"

"Nothing," she said. She hadn't meant him to hear that part. She wondered if Annie was impressed by the fact Peter had been a jock. She tried to imagine them in bed together and wondered why it was starting to make a difference.

"Are you sleeping with Annie?" The question lurched

from her mouth like someone else was doing the speaking.

It surprised him, too. He arched backward, his cup jiggling enough to splash coffee. It splattered innocently onto the concrete. "Am I sleeping with Annie?"

"Is there an echo out here I don't remember?" she said quickly, as if the question had no significance, and said something about Cookie.

"Don't change the subject. Let me tell you—"

"Don't. Please. Forget it. None of my business."

"It might be."

They shared an intense look that only made her more uncomfortable with his tone. "It won't be, Peter."

"How do you know? Didn't I say I wanted to clear the air and . . . ?"

"No. This isn't the time." Head swinging left and right. "I'm exhausted, Peter. It's been a long day, the trip down and all. Maybe when—"

"You're making excuses."

She couldn't bring herself to admit he was right, so she answered with a shrug that could mean anything.

"I've never stopped thinking about you, KC, or—"

"Enough, Peter! Okay? This was a bad idea. I am sorry I asked. I didn't mean to. It proves how really tired I am. I need my pillow time, okay?"

She took a step away, and he reached out and took hold of her arm to prevent her from moving any further. His hand was as exciting as his kiss had been. Her worst fears were landing on her head and hammering her into the ground.

He said, "Tell me something first."

"What?"

"Does it matter to you?"

"Does what matter?"

He moved in tighter, and she turned her face away and

looked at the sky, and felt his breath blowing warm on her cheek.

"Does it matter about Annie and me?"

"To Annie and you, maybe. Not to me."

"Why don't I believe you?"

"Believe me."

"Then why did you ask the question?"

She turned to face him. His eyes burned with the reflected intensity of the moon. "Annie hated me before she met me tonight. She wore it like a shoulder patch. It was like she smelled your scent on my body, the way I smelled it on hers."

"You still haven't answered me. Why did you ask? Why does it matter to you if I'm sleeping with Annie?"

"I don't remember telling you that it does." She was not going to wilt under Peter's interrogation. That KC no longer existed for anyone, especially not for Peter Osborne. "I was just checking out the changes," she said, pushing away from him. "I've been gone from here a long time."

"Yeah. Sure." A million emotions traveled across his face. "A lot's changed around here since you went running off to be a rebel with Frankie McClory."

"I ran off to be Frankie McClory's wife." She gave one temple a series of hard taps with an index finger, a signal urging him to remember. "I still am."

"I'll be sure to tell Annie, she asks."

Was that meant to answer her question? She forced a weak smile that would fool no one and turned to look at the moon.

Peter said, "You never told me why you married him." A modest pleading had entered his voice.

"Because he didn't remind me of you."

Peter made a little grunting sound that, after a moment's reflection, turned into a lingering note of acceptance. "So, here you are. Back in my life."

"Knowing you won't remind me of Frankie."

"The way Annie doesn't remind me of you?"

She bit down hard on her lip and wondered if she had drawn blood. Peter had. "Score one for the All-CIF Player of the Year."

"Should I answer your question about her?"

"Don't bother. I shouldn't have—"

"Around the plant she's known as *Dyke* Tracy."

"I don't think so."

"It's true."

"You also have something in a nice bridge you'd like to sell me?"

He raised his hands in surrender. "I see lots of women, KC."

"Noah told me that."

"He would," Peter said philosophically, and shook his head. "None to compare with you," he said. Spoken softly, like a feather floating on the truth.

KC drifted away from the railing and settled onto the porch swing that blocked one set of French windows. It creaked under her weight while she tried to find a comfortable position. She observed Peter straining to examine her motives and was pleased for the obscurity brought by dark shadows angling across her face as the moon passed behind a deck of clouds.

"You told me once you would wait for me forever."

"It was the truth when I said it."

"And we both knew when it became a lie. Did your nose grow, too?"

"That business with Brenda. It never should have happened. She was drunk, and she decided it was what she wanted. I—shit!—I was drunker. I had to run off and marry her, KC. You think His Judgeship would have allowed it any other way? After that—"

"Please stop, Peter. Stop it there."

In that instant, she knew any more explanation would only upset her. She didn't want any new problems brought on by Peter's old excuses. She hadn't come back for this. She got up from the swing and announced, "I'm going to bed. We'll do this some other time."

"Will we?"

"Yes."

"Swear on a frog?"

"You're not Aunt Dorothy, Peter. The magic only works with her."

Peter put his cup on the concrete surface of the balcony, stepped up and clamped both her arms. His grip hurt this time. She wondered if there'd be bruises in the morning, the way Frankie left her with bruises. Peter studied her anxiously, for history she had no intention of showing him.

He said, "We used to have our own magic."

"We had a lot of things."

"I'd like to see if we can have them again."

"I wouldn't."

"Swear on a frog."

"I told you—"

"Nothing. Nothing at all. Tell me one thing. Tell me I wasted my time waiting for this moment, and then I'll know something, maybe."

She couldn't bring herself to the words and, not understanding why, said, "Let's not rush back to anything, okay?"

"How about a healthy jog?"

"How abut one step at a time?"

"Is there a chance?"

"I don't think so."

"But at least you're thinking."

"I'm thinking."

He held her eyes for a few moments more. "Okay," he said, and released his hold. His expression relaxed. "Lunch tomorrow? You'll come downtown and see where I catch the bad guys."

"Not a good idea."

"The lunch will be better."

"I have things to do."

"You're not back long enough to have things to do."

What now, KC? Tell Peter there are some locations the Thirty Two expects you to check out as part of the deal? "I'll sleep on it."

"And then you'll wake up tomorrow, feeling bright and re-freshed. You'll leap from the bed and you'll say, 'Good morning, world. This is the day I'm having lunch with my old friend, Peter.' " He pitched his smile at her. His smile was always her undoing.

Finally, she turned her palms skyward and gave him a why-not shrug. His smile grew. She responded with one of her own. Real this time.

"Swear on a frog?"

"And a polliwog," she answered back, instantly concerned about the stirrings he was causing inside her. She knew she'd have to resist them. She was not here to reinvent the past.

Heading upstairs, she drew a mental picture of Frankie and used it to remind herself what she had to do next, what truly mattered about her life. Not him. Not Peter. Nowhere in her life was there a place for Peter Osborne. Nowhere.

Hard as she resisted, the stirrings wouldn't quit.

CHAPTER 13

At the same time, Liam McClory was tapping his fingers impatiently on the registration counter of the rundown motel near Venice Beach, while the desk clerk finished checking for messages. The clerk circled his hand inside the empty key box, then shuffled through a small pile of pink slips clipped to a peg board next to the telephone.

"No, sir," he said finally, "none just now, Mr. Ford."

He smiled at Liam across the counter, exposing a crooked mouth full of broken teeth the color of piss water.

Mr. *Ford*, yes, indeed, Liam thought. Not a real name that comes back to haunt you, later.

The clerk had one of those high-pitched voices and a way of carrying himself that would have meant lots of nosebleeds back home, where there was low tolerance for that sort of behavior, especially when it came with an attitude. Here, too, if you didn't know better than to do anything that might draw attention to yourself.

Liam said, "I been expecting ever since I got here. Any come, you'll be sure and let me know?"

The clerk closed his eyes, as if tired of the very sight of him. "Any messages we get, there's a copy put in your box and the little light on your phone will blink, sir. Few ever get past us. Part of the service at the Happy Wanderer."

A smile as real as a coward's kiss. Bloody bastard. Like this was Liam McClory's first time at a motel with clean sheets every morning and more than one towel on the rack. Smug poof, this one. He had half a mind to carve him a new asshole, only the poof would probably say thank you for taking the time and trouble.

Instead, Liam said, "Thanks, mate."

And the clerk smiled, averting his eyes again, like Liam's dismantled face told the bad ending to a fairy tale. *Fairy tale,* good one, that.

Liam tipped his cap and headed back for his room, murder on his mind to go with the murder on his mind.

A poof clerk or a smart-talking nigger, no difference.

He wondered, have you always known how habit-forming the killing can become, Liam McClory?

Probably.

Anyway, since the two soldiers a long, long time ago, the fuzz-faced Brits hardly older them him, when he was fifteen and into throwing rocks and making all the nasty sounds he knew, like all the other lads who rarely if ever strayed out past the sixteen blocks some called home and others said was as much a jail as they ever send you to, for deeds far worse than the rocks or the words aimed at people what had absolutely no right being there in the first place.

Da late coming home and supper growing cold on the table, every new minute adding another worry wrinkle to the corners of the wee Ma's sweet mouth, knowing the Da never strays to pub or club after putting in his day at Harland-Wolfe.

Finn is the best, that way, she's fond of saying to anyone up or down Lower Mervue, who'll still stay around to listen on that subject anymore, given their own men who don't show such passion for home or family near as regular.

Finally, she says, "Liam, you go on out and have a look," knowing a fifteen-minute walk is only a fifteen-minute walk, and nobody is safe from the Brits lately. They've become prone to sudden violence they disguise as interrogation since some of their number been hurt or worse in sneak attacks by friends of the Da, who, like him, have grown tired of abiding the politically polite people on both sides who've been turning a war into a waltz.

Francis goes after his cap, too, ready to run in Liam's shadow, like usual. At nine years of age he's six years younger, but Francis already has a head on him that makes him sound twenty going on forty. Anyone escapes following in the Da's footprints, more likely Francis than his brother, who'll finally scrape out of school with no aptitude for numbers and reading only a little better.

"Only going up the street a bit, Francis, so you stay put."

"He's me Da, too, Liam, you know?"

What not to know? Francis being the youngest and the favorite, something you don't need to be told to figure out. You just listen and watch and know they'll never love you less, even when you want more.

The street isn't so busy now, only a few familiar faces going for their doorways in the last of the half-lit moments before darkness takes over, and they start up the block. Two blocks away, they hear a noise in the housing corridor.

Direct in the shadows, but hard to be certain, is a Brit challenging someone built strong and broad like the Da, dressed for a shift in the foundry. The mouth of the Brit's SLR is poking at the belly of the man, who has arms raised above his head. The Brits know not to patrol alone and, sure enough, his partner's at the other end of the corridor, sniffing and searching.

"The Da," Francis whispers desperately in Liam's ear. Liam puts his hand over his brother's mouth while his mind struggles with what to do next. Francis takes a step away from him, then charges into the corridor, calling after his Da.

"You hold it right there," the Brit says, losing interest in the man long enough for him to make a club of his fists and hammer it down hard on the bridge of the Brit's nose. A crack echoes off the walls. The Brit is stunned and drops his rifle, then follows the SLR to the ground.

The man bends after the weapon, but the other Brit has heard the commotion and come running, a step behind a monstrous stomach, his rifle aimed and nervous enough to squeeze the trigger for any reason at all.

"Do and you are dead," he calls, voice fluttering. "There, that's a good fellow. Now, hands back up where we can't have accident or get into mischief." Without taking his eyes off the foundry worker, he inquires of the soldier stretched on the ground like a babe asleep, "Leftenant, you okay?"

The leftenant says something that sounds like gibberish. He shifts around, looking for a way back onto his feet. Can't quite make it past his knees and sets his head on the ground, like an Arab in prayer, with both his hands aimed at his boots.

Liam in this time has hurried forward and stands alongside his little brother, an arm strapped around Francis. He's close enough to know for sure it is the Da being held to the wall.

"Da!"

"They're me boys," he tells the Brit. "Go on home, boys. I'll be along in a minute."

The Brit's face is telling another story. He says to Liam, "You, the big one, down the corridor, then up about three blocks are a Rover and a Pig. Go find them and say where we're at, but first they're to emergency radio for an ambulance."

"What about the Da?"

"We'll take a statement and send him on his way."

His face still reveals the lie. Liam has visions of his Da being arrested and never coming home. Would not be the first time somebody's father took that kind of journey with the bloody damn soldiers.

"Fuck you," Liam says.

"*You do it, boy, and take Francis, then you go on straight home and tell your Ma I'll be along shortly.*" Take Francis. Always looking out for Francis. "*It's all right for them both to run your errand, sergeant?*"

The Brit thinks about it for a second. "*Yes, but leave now, hurry. Leftenant, you hear? I'm sending off these boys after help for you. Hang on, hear?*"

The leftenant moans. Even in the bad light, Liam can see blood trickling from his nose and, maybe, even one of his eyes, like bone has been broken clear to the brain.

"*Go on now, Liam. Francis, you, too. I didn't mean to hit the soldier boy so hard, and we must do what we can to help out. The sergeant here says to go down the corridor and up three blocks. No time to spare. After, you get yourselves on home and tell your Ma to keep me meal warming in the oven.*"

Only that's not what the Da means.

It's only to throw off the sergeant.

The Da's hands are high enough to be invisible to the soldier and his fingers are sending a different message in the sign language of the shipyard workers, invented as a means of communicating back and forth above the din in the long ago, in the time of the Da's Da and before, when they were building ships like the Titanic and the Queen Mary.

Next to the Da's foot nearest them is his lunch pail, and he tells Liam how to use it as an excuse to make a play for the SLR, only Francis moves first while Liam is thinking it through.

"*I'll go on and take the pail with me back to Ma,*" Francis says, and gives the Brit an angelic cast of his blue eyes. The Brit makes a face, tells him to hurry up again, and reassures the leftenant one more time.

Francis leans down for the pail and, in rising, swings it straight up, just like the Da wants.

The pail hits the rifle barrel and deflects the sergeant's nervous shot, which comes within a whiz of the Da's head before crashing into the wall. Jesus! The sound is loud enough to bring the whole of the British army down around them. How long will the patrol need to steer the Pig back three blocks and find them? Not so long at all.

The sergeant trips backward on his heels and is out to make aim again, but Francis dives forward, wraps his arms around the sergeant's thigh and wrestles him off balance. The Da does a bob and weave, and connects with the side of the sergeant's cheek, hard enough for Liam to hear the bone yield under the Da's knuckles.

Fast as a wink, the Da goes after the leftenant and comes up with his Browning. The sergeant is free of Francis and gets off a shot first. It tears through the Da's chest, throwing him backward. The Da slides down the wall, already too dead to know about the pain his two sons will share for the rest of their lives.

The sergeant seems surprised and unsure what to do next, but there's no hesitation on Francis' part. He grabs for the handgun their Da dropped and fires point blank at the sergeant, whose stomach explodes in death.

Francis gives Liam a look that mixes fear with satisfaction, and Liam wonders to himself if, in that moment, Francis understands he has avenged a death as well as caused one. His younger brother, this nine-year-old, is the first of them to carry the killer's curse.

Liam hears the eerie sounds of a Pig, the screech of the lower gears, closing in on the other end of the corridor. Fucking armored van will be on top of them in a breath, but this is no time to just up and leave and let anyone ever say he was cowardly or not so brave as his little brother.

"Give me that," he demands, in the same breath taking the

Browning away from Francis.

Liam adjusts it against the sergeant's temple and pulls the trigger, then steps over to the leftenant and jams it into the base of the soldier's skull before he pulls the trigger again. Both times, the strong recoil sends shock waves through Liam's arm.

"Now, fast, we got to get us to home before the rest of them fucking soldiers find us here, Francis," he says, jamming the handgun into a trouser pocket; pausing only long enough to steel himself and pull a sterling silver watch from the Da's pocket.

And, after that, after he whispers the story to Finn McClory's compatriots, Liam becomes one of them, welcomed to the ranks like a bloody fucking hero.

The killing is easy from the first.

All he ever has to do is think of that night the two Brits fell, and why, and how proud the Da must be knowing he has been avenged and his place in the struggle for freedom has been filled by family.

CHAPTER 14

KC overslept the alarm. Her night was full of stop-and-go sleep and dreams that rambled between Peter and Frankie and ended on an image of the dead Plowman that snapped her awake. She wondered as she prepared to go downstairs if she should cancel out on lunch with Peter. He didn't matter in her life and never would again.

Dorothy and Cookie greeted her on the veranda off the informal breakfast alcove, with its exhilarating view of the formal lawns and walking gardens. A yellow-striped umbrella pole jutting from the center of the round glass table protected them from the sun.

Despite the early hour, KC could already feel the sun rays having fun with her skin. She pushed her wraparound sunglasses up into her hair to prevent any chance of tan lines and went for a fast shot of orange juice.

Cookie put aside her Anne Rice paperback and Dorothy her newspaper. "Uncle Judge and Peter waited for you as long as they could," Dorothy said. "Peter mentioned the two of you are having lunch today?"

"He invited me to see where he works."

"If you were planning on calling a taxi, you're more than welcome to use the town car, you know."

"Thanks, Aunt Dorothy."

"He's positively drooling over you," Cookie said. Her mother made a face and slapped the table with her open palm. "No sauce, KC. You'd think Peter has gone rabies."

Dorothy said, "They say it gets worse after they turn sixteen." She prepared a plate for KC, scrambled eggs, hash browns, cubed Jell-O salad, while KC poured herself a cup of coffee.

KC made out the two bold headlines across page one of Dorothy's *Pasadena Post*.

One declared:

FIND PASADENA CONNECTION
IN AMTRAK MURDER OF PRIEST.

The other said:

MUSTAMBA VISIT
CONFIRMED BY STATE DEPT.

Next to it was the photo of a dignified black man she recognized as the revered leader in his nation's struggle against white supremacists who'd sworn to seize back control of the government from him.

"Bacon, dear?"

"I don't think—"

"Extra crisp, the way you always like."

"Why not?" She reached for the newspaper. "May I?"

Dorothy said, "That murder business. All there in Tuesday's headlines. Nobody is safe anywhere this day and age. Not even on a train."

"KC, they mention Peter," Cookie said, broadcasting the news with unbridled glee. "How about that wash? I got a famous brother. The big stoop."

KC nibbled at a piece of bacon. "Didn't Peter say the priest wasn't a priest? That's not what it says in here." She recited aloud: "According to authorities, Father Shanley had been traveling on vacation from his parish in Toronto . . ." She looked up, confused.

Cookie said, "Yeah, great, huh? Peter told us to forget what he said." KC looked at her curiously. Why had the truth become a secret? "What he told us last night? He said we're not supposed to say anything. To anyone. He said to let you know when you came down for breakfast."

"Did he say why?"

"No, but I tried. You try when you go to lunch. He has to tell you."

"And why, pray tell, does he have to tell me?"

" 'Cause he's hot to guess what in your Guess Whos."

"Cookie!"

"Muh-therrr! I'm not blind, you know?"

KC showered and dressed for lunch, glad now she had said "yes" to Peter's invitation. It would give her opportunity to lead him into conversation that might expose what really was going on.

She shivered under the warm water thinking that Liam might have put the Plowman on the train to finish her. When the news reached him, would his hobbled face turn colors, the rage draw little pockets of spittle to the corners of his mouth, like she'd witnessed other times when he was crazy for not having his way?

Would he leap into some new scheme for taking her out? No. It just didn't make sense the Thirty Two would send her to Pasadena if the plan was to kill her before her job was done.

She recalled how Liam had looked at her, oh, so slyly, when he came to grill her about Barney Sullivan and give her the news she'd have to survey the Rose Bowl and City Hall, the Wrigley Mansion, in addition to making contact and delivery with the Plowman. He was so pleased to watch her anger rise and crackle like flames in the fireplace.

Maybe, KC considered, her part of the job was over before

121

she boarded the train, only she didn't know it. What if "Father Shanley" was the Plowman, and she only figured on the first leg, down from Belfast? The goods received, her fate sealed, he kills her and takes over.

KC dismissed the notion. Checking out the city was best handled by someone who knew the city, and that was her, not the "priest," same as they needed her to gain entry to the Osbornes.

She thought about the risk to her adopted family until the Plowman was caught and the job finished.

Damn Liam! Damn the Thirty Two!

She would verify Burkes had security running full-tilt, twenty-four hours a day on her next check-in, raise holy hell if it wasn't. Where was it, anyway? She had not noticed one sign of security since getting here. How did Burkes do it nowadays, using the same invisible wires David Copperfield the magician used to soar like an eagle above his theater audiences?

Dressing, a thought caught in her throat and made her pause:

The luggage.

She sat on the edge of the bed, palms resting on her thighs as her fingers tapped out a mindless tune.

The luggage.

"Father Shanley" had gone through her luggage, at least part of it. She made the discovery after he was dead. A part of a sleeve of her best sweater was caught outside the frame of one of the two large cases she had put under the desk, as if someone had opened and closed it in a hurry. She was too neat to have done that, even by accident. Besides, she would have noticed. When she opened her carrying case later, she could almost smell the prowling touch of alien hands.

So, what was the "priest" after? If he knew what she was

carrying, he wouldn't have to look for it. He could simply kill her and take the luggage. Okay, now suppose there was something specific he needed.

One of the weapons?

A chunk of the plastic explosives?

It still made more sense to leave with everything and, after he was safe somewhere, take what he wanted and dump the rest.

She thought harder and came at the problem from a new direction. Suppose, she was carrying something she didn't know about? The tightly-wrapped explosives were hidden under a false bottom in the Vuitton trunk. What if there were more false bottoms or hidden compartments that Liam failed to mention when he and two of his mates delivered the cases to her home and he took her through them one at a time to impress her with what was being entrusted to her care?

She'd taken inventory before leaving the Vancouver hotel to board the connector bus to the Amtrak station in Seattle. Again last night. But she'd never thought to examine the luggage for anything besides what she knew she was carrying.

Was her imagination working overtime or had Liam been overly solicitous, like he was going out of his way to explain everything to her in fine detail, only so she would not think to ask the wrong questions or think about checking out the luggage later, by herself?

KC quit dressing.

She'd made up her mind to go through the cases.

Before she could start, a musical alert startled her and sent her eyes sailing in the direction of the hall door.

Cookie had her hand at her mouth and was using it as a trumpet. She arced it aside and announced, Bogart style, "Gotta get my goodies to school, beautiful. You still up to the ride?"

"Of course, I am, or I wouldn't have offered," KC said, adjusting a smile. Cookie looked at her strangely and KC suspected her expression had given away the fact she was wrestling with problems. Rather than wait to be asked, she explained, "You startled me, Cook. I didn't hear you open the door."

"I even knuckle-knocked. Been standing there for almost five years," she said, sliding into the room.

"I guess I was thinking about something."

"Like you were inventing sex."

"Nothing that heavy."

"Nothing heavier."

"How would you know?" KC asked in a teasing tone. She moved from the bed and took the blue blazer hanging on the silent butler, tugged at the fit in front of the full-length mirror as Cookie approached her and said to her reflection, "The usual way."

"What's the usual way?"

"Guy on top," she said, the laughter rising from her throat like bubbles popping.

"Cookie!"

"Now you sound like my mom," she said, and pushed in for a hug, which KC surrendered gladly.

"Certainly not."

KC lowered her gaze for a better look at Cookie, who was shorter by about half a foot, and now stretching her face into a bizarre mask. Cookie dropped her voice the way teenagers do whenever they discus serious subjects, like not enough cheese on the pizza, and apologized.

"For what, Monkey?" KC said, using a private name they had chosen years ago, when Cookie was barely seven years old and, one day, burst into tears complaining to her how everyone in the family had pet names for everyone except her.

"What do you think 'Cookie' is?" KC had asked at the time, gently, stroking the child's hair and warming her forehead with her lips.

"A nickname," Cookie answered with all the logic her age allowed. KC gave her her choice of three pet names, and Cookie chose "Monkey" over "Dog" and "Cat," because there already were too many pet dogs and cats in the neighborhood, and they laughed over their own special, private joke for a long, long time.

Cookie showed she liked hearing the old name, then shifted into a sadder look.

"Monkey is apologizing for talking about sex," she said.

"After all, you are fifteen," KC said, trying to make her feel better.

Cookie rejected the answer with a wave. "I mean, you being a widow and all. I don't suppose you've had much lube in the tube since your—" She caught herself, pulled free and showed her dismay.

KC pulled her back and kissed her forehead. "It's okay, Monkey, really. Say anything you want to me. I can handle it."

They both strengthened the hug.

"You sure?"

"Certain."

"Positive?"

"Positive we'll never get you to school unless you give me another ten minutes to finish dressing."

"Coolness!" Cookie decided. She ripped free and sprang across the room. "I love you, KC," she declared, twisting out of sight. "I love you in a majorly way!"

KC had often driven the family's town car, an old Ford station wagon with simulated wooden door panels, and it felt like an old friend taking Cookie to school. Every cranky sound was a reminder of the good times she had left behind when she said goodbye to the Osbornes.

Cookie had decided to talk about Peter, and the boundless chatter could have been KC carrying on with Aunt Dorothy years ago. "All Peter could talk about was KC, KC, KC," Cookie said. "KC this and KC that."

"Your brother is wonderful." No reason to burden her with the truth.

"You're not so dreary yourself, you know."

"Thank you very much, and same to you." She took her hand from the wheel long enough to mess with Cookie's hair spikes.

"Wanna hear something fab?"

"Really fab or semi-so-so fab?"

"You know who Mr. Mustamba is?"

"Some news about the world does travel as far as Belfast, Miss Osborne."

"His picture in the paper today?"

"Very distinguished. Very elegant."

"Well, he's not only coming to visit, but he's coming on over to our house for a *tres chic* and *muy exclusivo* reception." KC braked for a Mercedes in a hurry that had charged into a left turn in front of her. She chose not to notice the middle finger that Cookie shot up in response. "It's supposed to be a bigger secret even than the corpse on the train not being a priest. Coolness, huh?"

KC tried not to show more than a normal interest. "Did Peter tell you that?"

"No, Daddy. He's head of the welcoming committee, running the whole show and all. Ceremony at City Hall. And a party at the old Wrigley Mansion—" She made bug eyes and momentarily clamped both hands over her mouth. "Shitsky! Formerly a *secret*. All of it."

"Didn't hear a word."

Cookie was genuinely upset with herself. "I blew it, huh? Well, I'm sure Daddy won't mind you knowing."

"I won't say anything unless he does."

They reached the campus that had been South Suburban High School when KC was a student, but sometime during the past six years it had been renamed in honor of Richard Milhaus Nixon.

"If you bump me there by the gate, super fine."

KC maneuvered the town car into the curb lane, behind other cars dropping off other students. There were pockets of kids on foot, laughing and carrying on among themselves as if their world, tomorrow, would be the one she had looked for and never found. She envied them their dreams.

Cookie must have sensed something, because she said, "Daddy let me tell Andy about Mr. Mustamba, KC, so why would he mind you knowing?"

She nodded agreement and said, "Andy? Something you been holding out on me, Miss Osborne?"

"Somebody I know."

"More."

"Andy Oldenburg. A nerd, but rad."

"Rad. Is that anything like *groovy?*"

"Groovy?"

"Come on. More about this rad Andy."

"We're going to a Trekkers convention next week."

"More."

Cookie weighed her answer. "He kisses with his tongue." A broad smile, abruptly engulfed by a look of panic. "Oh, Jayzoosky! You won't tell Daddy, will you?"

"Cross my heart," and she did.

"Seal with a kiss?"

"Seal with a kiss."

KC stopped the car. They leaned into one another to share a fleeting kiss on the lips.

Somebody was knuckling the front passenger window. This had to be Andy. *Nerd* Andy. *Rad* Andy. In her time, *Geek* Andy, like the boys who never trusted her when she tried to make friends and conversation, scared off by her looks and the lettermen who'd strut in her shadow and treat her like another trophy.

He was short and pudgy and his features hadn't all come together yet, but there was evidence he would grow into a good-looking young man in high school, when his face finally fit his nose, the braces came off and he began wearing contacts or, at least, more appropriate eyeglass frames. Unlike Cookie, he had a reasonable haircut Richard Milhaus Nixon would have understood.

Andy stepped back, so Cookie could open the door and jump from the car after delivering one final peck on KC's cheek. He was wearing a button-down shirt and dress slacks, penny loafers and a thunderstruck look that said everything that had to be said about teenage infatuation.

He engulfed Cookie and leaned in for a kiss, his tongue two inches ahead of his starched lips. The tip caught Cookie on her ear as she swung around her head to deliver KC a *See what I mean?* look.

KC watched them leave, then waited for a break in the line of traffic before pulling away from the curb and heading for the first of the surveys the Thirty Two expected from her. She worked out the best route in her mind. First, the Wrigley Mansion, followed by the Rose Bowl and City Hall. Then, a quick contact with Burkes, and on to her lunch with Peter. She thought, Oh, what tangled webs we weave . . .

KC trailed up Orange Grove until she reached the old

Wrigley Mansion and parked on the street. The front lawn sign had been touched up recently, and the words "Rose Bowl Association" seemed as bright as her mood had become. She waited out the traffic and headed for the visitors' entrance along the side of the building.

She appeared to be the only visitor.

That would change nearer the New Year, when Rose Bowl fever hit the city like the last earthquake and all the local muckety-mucks descended on the stately old landmark to select the Rose Queen and her court, finish planning the parade and events surrounding the nation's oldest bowl game and schedule the parties, celebrations, and social hobnobbing with the same precision that goes into organizing military maneuvers.

And, crap jobs like the ones that had brought her this far. God willing, they would be the last crap jobs she ever had to think about.

After this job ended, they would be lucky to find her.

The Thirty Two or Burkes.

Anyone who came looking.

Savoring the happier times of earlier days, she tracked the Association's row of ceiling-high display cases until she located the one with her year engraved on one of the discreet gold-plated tags. The eleven-by-fourteen-inch color photograph, artfully framed, dominated the shelf at eye level: the Rose Queen and Her Court.

"Katherine Mary Cassidy."

The voice calling her name was brittle, cracked at the edges by age, and had a familiar ring as it charged up the broad corridor.

The woman heading cautiously in her direction, supported by a cane and determination, was in her late seventies. Age had drained her of size and overlaid her tightly drawn skin with liver spots, but it could not deprive her of her carriage or her beauty. Her thinning silver-colored hair was cut extremely tight and tapered into a ducktail. It had a cast that was almost as rosy as her eyes, still youthful in appearance and riveting.

"Miss Everhardt."

The elderly woman stopped alongside her and formed a cautious smile, pleased to be remembered. It seemed to add an inch to her height.

"How sweet it is of you to remember, dear. I thought you looked familiar. And, pretty as ever. How have you been?"

"Thank you. Fine. You were the Rose Queen in—"

"Don't say it." She raised a hand between them.

"And, you were head of the chaperone committee the year I—"

"And still. It's better than sitting in some home for the dying, watching leaves turn brown and falling from the trees. Looking at yourself, were you? I do that, too, sometimes. Down by my case." She leaned in and studied the photo. "Yes. Still think you should have worn the crown, KC. Year in and year out, I never do fathom how some judges vote."

"Thank you, Miss Everhardt. I felt honored just being allowed to serve as one of the princesses."

"They all say that, dear. Year in, year out, I hear it. I don't believe them any more than I believe you. Forgive an old lady for speaking out so frankly, but I hope it's not the kind of playacting you do when you're alone."

"For a while, I did, Miss Everhardt. First I cried and then I pretended."

She made a sound she meant to be an appreciative laugh. "I did, too. And, you know what else? You're the first one who ever come back here and was brave enough to say it."

"I found more important things to cry about."

"Then consider yourself lucky. I never did. Isn't that something, Katherine Mary Cassidy? I never did." Tears began to cloud her eyes.

KC looked away, not wishing to embarrass the old woman.

She made an excuse for leaving and felt the sting of her own tears rising by the time she rushed through the entrance, almost tripping as she took the elegant, freshly varnished porch steps two at a time.

A few minutes later, another overpowering memory came into view, the Rose Bowl.

KC parked the station wagon near the service gates, in one of the patchwork rows of maintenance vehicles and passenger cars, mostly Hondas and Toyotas, and probed until she found a gate that was unchained.

She rolled the gate back enough to sidle in, and a few minutes later was surveying the empty stadium from the mouth of a tunnel at the thirty-yard line.

Once again, she allowed herself to be transported back in time.

When she closed her eyes, she could picture the seats jam-packed with cheering fans; taste their noisy approval as she and the other girls danced fancy steps, sent enticing signals with their pompons, and flashed pink undies beneath outfits that traded sexiness for warmth. She could smell hot dogs and peanuts, and the booze odor that always hung in the air. She heard the band, and when she opened her eyes again she was ready to believe she would see Peter crossing the goal line for another touchdown, doing his little victory dance as he put his name down another time in the Pasadena City College Book of Champions.

Was there ever another time as good as these times were?

she wondered, heading down the concrete steps with more care than she'd shown leaving the Wrigley Mansion, looking for the easiest way onto the field.

Her ride around the track as a Rose princess came close, although bogged down by a truth Noah could not prove to her satisfaction, that civic politics weighed heavily in her failure to be chosen queen.

KC felt her throat closing in the grip of emotion and her eyes grow moist. The need to come here for the first time since that New Year's Day had opened another wound she thought was healed forever.

When is it kids stop being children, she wondered. When are they finally grown up?

Miss Everhardt didn't have the answer to that one, so, why should she?

She smelled evidence of recent rain. There were some mud patches on the running track, but the playing field was covered in a lush, long tropical grass that needed a trim.

She took off the double-breasted blazer, exposing her notable chest inside an almost transparent vanilla turtleneck.

Worked off her blue leather Keds.

Enjoyed the cool sensation underneath her feet striding over to a spot at the fifty-yard line.

She searched for a deep scar on a bleacher post, four initials inside interlocked hearts carved by long-ago lovers, and used it to find the precise point where the City College drill team performed, then counted off backwards to her old mark. She folded the jacket neatly and set it down with the Keds and her tote bag on a dry square of grass.

Impulsively, she stepped out of her stone-washed denims and put them there, too, before she high-kicked into one of her old routines. The victory cheer spilled from her lips like yesterday as she gave herself to the wild music of a phantom band, and thought the applause also was part of her imagination until her eyes reached the highest row of bench seats, left of the press box, where painters had stopped working to watch her.

Her face turned crimson but, instead of quitting, she finished the number and responded with a graceful bow when the painters added hoots and whistles to their appreciation. She washed off the sweat and put herself back together in a ladies' room by the service tunnel. Dabbed on fresh blusher. Reworked her eyeliner. Added some cologne mist from the squeeze bottle she carried in her bag.

Checked her wristwatch for the time.

Acknowledged it was time to grow up, be a spy again and contribute to the plot to assassinate Mr. Mustamba.

The old Pasadena City Hall building dominated a town square complex with towering, faded dignity but it didn't hold any special history for KC, only the opportunity to become an advance man for some Lee Harvey Oswald. She parked in a muni lot a block away and walking over spent a few dollars with some of the homeless, who had discovered the area north of the mall was full of places to hide their carts and steal a few hours' sleep.

Over the next two hours, KC trucked the stairwells and floors without incident, committing certain of the doors and directional signs to memory before she got to a problem.

On the top floor of the central building was a fire door painted a rust color.

A printed sign inside the mounted metal frame advised: ROOF. STAFF ACCESS ONLY.

If she didn't get to the roof and survey all the sight lines, the visit might have to be written off as a waste. Liam had said the roof was where the Thirty Two needed her most accurate reading, hinting broadly that the attempt on Mr. Mustamba's life would happen from up there.

She still doubted it, not only because she knew Liam for the liar he was.

If the plan was to shoot Mr. Mustamba from here, why the explosives?

Unless, of course, they also were planning to blow up City Hall.

KC gripped the door handle and pushed, the way some people dip into the coin slot of a pay phone.

Somebody had forgotten to turn the lock.

She checked both directions before stepping through, pushed the door shut behind her and hurried up the first run of stairs, making echoes with every step.

She reached the landing with her pulse racing ahead of her breathing, grabbed the railing, pivoted around for the next flight and discovered a stern-faced custodian in blue pinstriped coveralls staring back at her through heavy-lidded eyes.

He sat on the landing with his elbows resting on his thighs, his meaty chin wedged between his palms. A joint burning fast, hot and close to his fingers.

KC recognized the smell and knew he was not about to give her grief.

She played it safe anyway, too close now to screw up on spec.

"I think I'm lost," she said, and smiled.

He answered with his version of a grin. "Ain't we all, honey. Ain't we all."

By a half hour later, she had completed her tour of the roof.

Every vantage point was locked up tightly in her mind.

One or two were better than the rest, and one in particular was perfect, if Mr. Mustamba got out of his vehicle directly in front of City Hall.

Shoe prints like the studs of running shoes had marred or scattered the coarse gravel covering, and there were several sets of heel marks embedded in the tar paper underneath, probably made by cowboy boots.

Based on what she saw, KC couldn't be certain how long it had been since other visitors were here, or why. Her first impression was of SWAT cops guarding an earlier VIP. Scratch marks on top of the roof siding suggested where they had rested their rifle barrels.

She intended to include these observations in her report to the Plowman once he identified himself; give the Plowman a problem to occupy his mind in the time it took her to get the word to Burkes and Burkes to charge over and put the Plowman out of business.

Back on the public concourse level, she decided against the pay phones. Too many workers now milling about, giving her curious looks. On the Arroyo Parkway about a half mile north of the 110 entrance, at a self-service gas station peddling a cheap off-brand, she found an old-fashioned coffin booth with a reasonable degree of privacy.

She punched in the series of numbers she knew by heart. After a wait that seemed like an hour but probably was not more than two minutes, she heard a voice she knew as well as her own.

"Peekaboo, I hear you," KC said. She checked her watch and recited the time into the recorder that would have clicked on the moment the connection was made.

"How goes, Mrs. McClory?"

"First, Burkes, tell me about security at the Osbornes'."

"You running the Service now, Mrs. McClory?"

She ignored his sarcasm. "Not a sign of it. Just tell me, is it in place?"

"If you saw the security we both could worry."

"You're saying it's in place?"

"I'm saying that's not the purpose of these calls, Mrs. McClory. The purpose of a checkpoint is to tell me what I want to know."

"Make me a happy camper, Burkes."

"Yes."

"Yes, security is in place, or yes because you want to make me a happy camper?"

"Give me three minutes on the relay line and I'll tell you the color of the pair of shorts the judge put on this morning."

She heard by the shifts in his tone that they were stalemated. She would have to believe him and wait for a better time to go after a no-nonsense answer. Without further preamble, talking over his voice, she told Walter Burkes everything that had occurred since her checkpoint call yesterday from the Amtrak station house.

She spoke quickly and was through in less than ten minutes. Burkes started to ask a question. She hung up as if she hadn't heard him. Whatever he wanted to know, he could get by playing back the tape or trade on the next call for a direct answer about security at the Osbornes'.

She got onto the 110 south and sorted through the questions about "Father Shanley" she planned to snake into her lunch with Peter, with no way of knowing the risk of discovery waiting for her at Parker Center, where an Amtrak porter was describing for a police artist the woman he saw in the compartment where the dead priest was discovered.

CHAPTER 15

Walter Burkes moved the receiver from his ear and gave it a withering glance, wishing it were his hand around KC's throat, and replayed a recurring thought: KC has grown up in the last six years; unfortunately, she'd grown up the way modest pains in the ass turn into bleeding hemorrhoids.

He visualized the two of them going nose to nose, KC forgetting who Burkes was and how he came to direct the Not-So-Secret Service, like she had the right to negotiate her want list into orders any damn time she pleased. He considered rolling up his shirt sleeves and personally administering the spanking she deserved or, maybe, sending for one of those Hong Kong butt whackers who'd permanently imprint a lesson or two on KC's ass.

Order her to write on the blackboard a thousand times, I will obey the boss, or—

Burkes allowed himself a cheap grin.

She was right to ask about the surveillance he had promised her for the Osbornes.

It was just her mouth running out of control that always got them going gung-ho at each other.

Never like that with her folks. Peggy had a temper that could scale the Alps in ten seconds flat, she got irritated enough, but there was always Billy to cap her mouth. They were gems, the Cassidys; their obstreperous daughter, KC, ever a diamond in the rough. A diamond in the butt, more like it.

Burkes replaced the receiver and turned to stare at Simmons across the clean surface of his desk in the borrowed back office of the Federal Building he always used when business brought them to Los Angeles. Simmons' office was next to his and shared an interior door. His office was equally barren, hardly more than a desk and a visitor's chair. A waste basket, and a breakfront on which sat a stack of old *Pet Monthly* and *Sports Weekly* magazines. A top-of-the-line electric paper shredder. A multiple-line phone connected to the world; one line to the White House. Only the priority C&N files, in a wall safe nobody else could find. No identifying signs for a space that never received visitors, just dignified gold block stenciled letters on the corridor doors that read "Private" instead of TRIAD.

That was Burkes' magic kingdom, "TRIAD."

It was named by his late predecessor shortly after President Johnson mandated creation of the agency, in the first months following JFK and Dallas. Thinking he was someone straight out of James Bond, Heitz came up with the name by using the first letters of words that best covered the duty: Terrorism, Riots, Insurrection, Assassination, Devastation.

"Just like the White House to cut the budget even here," Burkes was fond of saying. "We're expected to do five jobs in the name of three."

Of course, there weren't that many people to say it to who would understand what the hell he was saying. "TRIAD" was not a word for the masses. He got more fun out of "Not-So-Secret Service." At least, Not-So-Secret Service covered the bloodshed with a laugh.

Simmons stared back at him. He worked the machine coffee in the plastic cup with a wooden stick, waiting patiently for whatever Burkes chose to tell or ask of him. One of Simmons' best traits: obedience.

Simmons always gave off the impression of sitting at attention, a golden retriever ready to chase after any bone Burkes tossed. Loyalty, another one of his best traits. The same way Fritz was loyal. Ready to turn his bark into a bite defending the master.

"Peekaboo, I hear you? That's how she starts with me, Simmons, like we're into some child's game. Peekaboo, I hear you." He pushed his half-moon glasses up onto his head, Hollywood-style, and appealed for some explanation with a gesture.

Simmons removed his wire-rimmed glasses. Polished the heavy lenses with his pocket handkerchief. Squinted generously. "A joke, perhaps? Mrs. McClory does manage to keep her sense of humor in difficult circumstances. That's the impression I get whenever we connect."

"Peekaboo, I see you? Jack Benny, now he had a sense of humor, you remember? Milton Berle, 'Uncle Miltie,' he had a sense of humor, too. Red Buttons, he—You know what I'm saying, Simmons?"

"The names, sir, of course they're familiar, but I'm afraid they're all a little before my time, other than that . . ." He shrugged apologetically.

Burkes gave him one of the looks he usually saved for wondering what the hell was wrong with the world. Simmons wasn't much older than KC, so, yeah, how much could he know? How much could any of these kids know, who think they know it all?

"Mrs. McClory is not even close to being in that league."

"Of course, not, sir."

Walter Burkes knew it all, of course. He didn't have to remind Simmons of that.

But even that wasn't saying a hill of beans any time push came to shove, like now, with the agency up to its eyeballs in an assassination plot with a deadline, counting on kids like Simmons and KC to make it a pay day for the good guys.

"What we're into is no laughing matter, Simmons."

"I'm sure Mrs. McClory understands, too."

"Well, I'm not so sure. What makes you so sure?"

"Of course, sir. I can see where you might have cause to question—"

"Peekaboo, I hear you!" Someone other than Simmons might have jumped at the way he howled the words, in an ominous rumble from a "Jack and the Beanstalk" animated cartoon that made him duck under his movie seat and hide when he was a six-year-old kid.

The memory never left him, and Burkes often likened his work to young Jack, only his golden fleece was ferreting out extremists, terrorists and all the other crazies, helping them dig their own graves.

This time, too, with Mr. Mustamba.

A lot resting on KC.

Too much, even if he could trust her.

And, he couldn't.

And, he didn't.

Simmons, at least, he trusted past his southern manner and accent. Simmons looked like a comic strip, but he bummed out his knee for keeps protecting Burkes from a bullet meant to turn his stomach into a sieve. A lot of people with more experience would have jumped out of the way, as in, "Whoops," not the least bothered by the act of hiding their guts behind their glory.

Not Simmons, maybe because he was still too fresh off the cob to care, working Burkes' left flank on one of those sad-ass jobs the Service is obliged to handle in the name of First Amendment Rights.

Burkes munched on the last of the potato chips that came with the Subway he had picked up for breakfast. He smiled at Simmons and considered what KC might have done in his place that afternoon. Would she have shifted into a "Save Burkes" mode, the way Simmons did, or duck under the rug with the dust?

She had the training and the moves, but also this fanatical sense he was out to do her harm. Christ! It might come to that. Always the chance it might come to that with any of his people, but he was not out to do any of them harm. He had a job to do, was all. Not the nicest of jobs, but he never supposed coal miners were too happy with their lot, either, and it could be one hell of a whole lot worse.

He could have been a paper pusher like his old man, a file clerk in the basement of the Old Senate Building, inhaling the stale air and watching spiders build their cobwebs while he left his fingerprints on mountains of useless documents nobody would ever want to see again.

KC remained a question mark, a cipher, although she'd been pretty straightforward on the phone just now. So, why didn't he trust her? Call it experience, the same reason he was asking questions about Aldrich Ames years before anybody got wise to that greedy SOB.

"How did she say it was going, sir?"

Simmons must have been reading his mind, although they hadn't been together long enough for him to master the trick the way Vonnie had. Besides, wasn't marriage one of the requirements?

Burkes finished what was left of the potato chips, crumpled the bag and sank it for two points. He fished the file drawer of the desk for the emergency supply of snacks he kept handy and, after some rummaging, decided on the raspberry granola crunch bar. It might be enough to hold him until lunch.

"She didn't have a helluva lot to tell us we don't already know," he answered Simmons, hiding his concern. "She seemed a little testy about her old screwing mate, Judge Osborne's son, the cop, being on the case. Aside from that, she said she did the check-outs on the old Wrigley Mansion, Rose Bowl and Pasadena City Hall McClory insisted had to be part of their deal."

"Any conclusions?"

"She has a feeling City Hall would be the choice if it's on the route that takes Mustamba to the Bowl. She said the way she knows McClory's mind to work, he would choose an Oswald finish so he could tell the boys at the pub he'd helped get even for what the bad guys did to John F. Kennedy. There's some logic to it. I'd bet Kennedy is the only guy whose framed picture is on as many Belfast walls as the Pope."

"You're satisfied the try is going to be in Pasadena?"

"Nashville's still my first choice and Atlanta is second or, maybe, tied with Pasadena. I'm not ruling out Detroit, but think about it. Who do you know ever got any joy from Detroit, except for people with names like Ford and Chrysler?"

"Nashville?"

"Country Music capitol of the world, Simmons. All those Irish have a thing for Country music. They could pop off Mr. Mustamba and celebrate at Opryland."

Burkes saw Simmons fighting the laugh, not certain if he was being serious. "Lighten up, my man. You think KC's the only one with a sense of humor?"

Simmons smiled, and chalked one in the air.

"Believe me, I don't begrudge her. If she knew how dangerous this situation is, she might not have been so willing to go along with the game plan."

Simmons nodded agreement. "What's next, sir?"

"More of the same, kid. We wait." He dumped the granola wrapper for two more points. "Look, give me five minutes to

142

call home to Mrs. Burkes and see how Fritz is doing, and then we'll go snare us some lunch. Maybe, a hike to that grease bucket over in Chinatown for one of their meatball double jamboree supremes and those sensational stringbean fries?"

Simmons returned a weak smile, as if he had any real choice. At the door, he paused to inquire, "What about security at the Osbornes', sir?"

Burkes stirred uncomfortably in his seat, drilled Simmons with a hard look.

"What about security at the Osbornes'?"

"I thought I heard you imply to Mrs. McClory that security was in place there."

"So?"

"We never did lay in security at the Osbornes', sir."

"You're telling me something I already know for a reason, Simmons?"

"Security was something we agreed to give her—"

"Okay, okay," Burkes snapped. "I know where this is heading . . . If it makes you happy, take the security we got there and double it."

Simmons didn't smile back this time. "Is it really something we should joke about, sir? I think—"

Burkes threw his index finger at Simmons like it was a dagger. "Hold it!"

Simmons' jaw hung empty. His eyes looked for some safe haven while Burkes pushed himself up from the desk and wrapped his arms protectively across his chest. How he hated being challenged, especially when truth worked against him.

"We never agree to anything, Simmons, and we never think. It's me who agrees to something. Me who thinks. You do as you're told, you got it?, and I don't give a rat's ass what you think!"

"Of course, Mr. Burkes," he replied sheepishly.

"I'm getting too much shit from her to add you to the list, too. I told her not to worry. I meant that." He'd never been quite this hard on Simmons, whose jaw was flexing, trapping the need to answer back, but his disappointed stare was harder to control. "I want you to understand that, Simmons," he said, pulling back on his breath.

"Yes, Mr. Burkes."

"Telling her what I told her was expedient. It was good business. You see anything wrong with that?"

Simmons' head slid back and forth. "I only thought it might be a good idea to do it now, lay in a security team," he said softly, "given what she told us about McClory, and—"

Burkes reached out and turned an invisible lock on Simmons' mouth. "Let it rest, Simmons. Nothing's in the budget for that. Tight enough as it is. What President Reagan didn't take from us, we've been losing under Clinton. Bush was the only one who had a full read on what the Service is all about. Voted for that son-of-a-bitch, too, and me a lifelong Democrat."

He had given more of an explanation than usual, to remind Simmons of his value to him. Simmons looked like he understood.

"No need to share any of this with the lady, is there, Simmons?"

"You tell me, sir," Simmons said, buffing off the sarcasm before it became more obvious.

"No need, Simmons."

"Of course, sir," Simmons said, sounding desperate to say something else, tougher, meaner; something they would both regret. The anticipation hung over them like Chicken Little's nightmare.

Simmons made a two-fingered salute to the temple, wheeled around like a soldier on parade and retreated from the office, pulling the door closed behind him.

Burkes bailed out a sigh of relief. He sank back onto the seat and was reaching for the phone to call Vonnie when the door opened again. Simmons filled the frame, clearly ready to speak his mind this time, and Burkes steeled himself for the worst.

"When I'm the boss, I'll be the same bad ass as you, Mr. Burkes."

The words felt nearly as comforting as his son's hugs had, before a gangbanger's war of words outside the neighborhood mall cineplex escalated and gunfire left Vonnie and him childless and hurting more than he ever told anyone, except Fritz.

"You could do worse, kid."

"I don't think so, Mr. Burkes."

CHAPTER 16

The porter was hunched forward in a chair alongside Annie Waterman's desk at Parker Center, clearly riveted by the image on an oversized sketch pad being displayed by a uniformed police artist, who was wearing a red beret tilted at a rakish angle.

From the corridor, looking through the glass wall ten or fifteen feet away, KC could make out enough of the pencil drawing to know the porter had given a better than excellent description of the floozie he had encountered twice at the compartment where she'd killed the Plowman. Beneath the dark rushes of shading meant to be heavy makeup, especially around the eyes, was the clean-complexioned face of Kate McClory.

The porter had not known her later, in the Amtrak station, but, as she glided into the detective bureau, KC's back muscles knotted with fear that her luck was about to run out.

Peter was at the desk adjoining Annie's. He rose in expectation, swiped the guest chair clean with his hand and shifted anxiously from foot to foot. Annie also had seen her and made a face that announced she didn't feel any better about KC this morning than she had last night at the Osbornes'.

Peter gave her a tight hug and French kissed her cheeks. She settled onto his guest chair judiciously, aware she was being scrutinized by five or six other detectives desk-bound by paperwork, and angled herself away from the porter's sightline.

His back was mostly to her, but it was him, all right. He had traded in his work uniform for a cheap, flamboyant plaid sports jacket, citrus lemon trousers and two-tone shoes that

146

went out of style a hundred years ago.

"Yes, yes, yes, Detective," the porter said, his familiar gravel voice rising like Mantan Moreland from the old Charlie Chan movies on TV.

He began tapping on the pad, swiveling his head between Annie and the sketch artist. "She's the one, for certain. Not a face I'd be forgetting, not now, knowing what I know."

Annie said, "That's very important, Mr. Anderson. We're counting on that."

" 'Pullman,' remember?" He launched an explanation how he came by the name.

Peter made a face and finger-signaled KC, another five.

She smiled, wishing she had not sat down.

Wishing she were anyplace but here.

Started removing her sunglasses.

Changed her mind.

"And my Daddy and his before him, we all of us made a life on the trains. Grampa decided on calling my Daddy 'Pullman' in honor of the passenger class he come by, and my Daddy went and did likewise on me, naming me 'Pullman,' knowing which direction I would likewise be traveling." He let his gaze ride from Annie to Peter to her. "You also get a look at the lady in question?" he signaled the sketch with his thumb.

KC shook her head, fearing her voice might give her away.

Peter explained, "A friend of mine, Mr. Anderson. By coincidence she was a passenger on your train."

"Pullman," the porter said. He leaned over for a better look at KC. "Uh-huh, uh-huh," he said, the same way Ray Charles did in the Pepsi commercials. "You ride the trains much, Miss . . . Miss . . . ?"

"Mrs. McClory," she said, finally. She knew to continue sitting there dumbly would have been, well—dumb. She would have to brazen out the situation. "Not often."

Nervously, she pushed her hands across the sides of her head. They merged at the scarf holding her ponytail. She yanked the material tighter and fiddled with the visitor's badge, moving it from her blazer to the brim of her turtle-neck, distracting him.

Pullman Anderson leaned back to study KC, licking his lips as if to lubricate his memory. "Missus. Well, people what ride 'em find 'em something aeroplanes never should be—down to earth." He welcomed the punchline like an old friend, contaminated the room with laughter. "You weren't Pullman, were you, miss? Missus."

"No. You're Pullman," she answered, maneuvering her body. Crossing and uncrossing her legs. Once more leading his eyes astray.

The porter got her joke. He cackled reaching for the police artist's sketch and compared her with it. "Only that I don't ever forget a face off one of my passengers," the porter bragged.

"I traveled in coach," KC said, husking a smile. "Have the sore back to prove it."

Pullman Anderson made a new happy sound. He looked from her back to the drawing. "Uh-huh. Dig it. Nothing wrong with that way either, the coach, except when your body isn't used to all that sitting." From the drawing back to her, as if his memory were trying to send him a message. The police artist also studied her intensely.

"I'm starving, Peter."

He checked his watch. "Okay with you, Annie? They're holding a table for us at Mah Jahn Guido."

Annie answered with a look that wondered if what she thought would really make any difference to him.

The porter said, "I thought for a minute—but I don't ever

get to coach. Too busy with my own duties and obligations."
He pronounced it *obbelgations*.

The police artist retrieved his drawing from the porter and
began working it over furiously as Peter helped KC to her feet
and led her out the bureau and down the corridor. KC wondered what the artist thought he'd seen that the porter had
missed.

Glancing across her shoulder through the window, she observed the artist showing off the pad to Annie. Annie shot her
face at KC and, after a moment, her suspicious eyes melted
into a smug look.

KC didn't have to see how the sketch had been modified
to know she might have a new kind of problem with Annie
Waterman.

Mah Jahn Guido was an Italian restaurant on the edge of
Chinatown. It occupied the entire floor above an import-
export shop catering to tourists on a side street just off
Broadway. The maitre d' greeted Peter like a member of the
family and guided the two of them to a small table by a picture window with a good view of a bad part of the city. People
were going about their business as if they were blind to the
alkies and druggies and other misfits on street corners and in
doorways.

Their waiter looked like he was around when the Chinese
cooked their first thousand-year-old chicken. He padded
back and forth in a perpetual hunch that distinguished him
from the other ancient waiters in black and gold silk pajamas
and matching skullcaps.

It was early and the staff was barely outnumbered by the
customers. A group of boisterous tourists wearing Hawaiian
shirts, speaking German and taking photos of each other.
Huddling lawyers, judging by the expensive double-breasted

suits and the bell-shaped cases parked alongside their tables.

A matching set of cops and, at a table near the swinging door to the kitchen, two men who looked like longshoremen and gave Peter a high sign and thumbs-up when they spotted him.

Peter acknowledged the pair and told KC they also were detectives, then leaped enthusiastically into a story about the meaty, red-faced one in the watch cap, visibly happy to have something new and inconsequential to talk about. He appeared determined not to cross into touchy areas.

KC had her guard up, too.

It wasn't easy tracking Peter's story, and she hoped she was laughing in the right places. Her mind was set on what had happened at the bureau thirty minutes ago. Gone was any desire to tell him there was no place in her life for Peter Osborne, certainly not before she pulled out of him the answers she needed about identity of the priest-Plowman on the train.

They were poking through their pasta salads when the waiter arrived with their pizza. The garlic odor clinging to the walls like wallpaper doubled in impact and she swiped at her eyes with the paper napkin. "You were both kidding, weren't you?" She turned from the waiter back to Peter. "Tell me it's not really a chow mein pizza. Is it? Give me a break."

Peter said, "Looks like they forgot the sweet and sour pepperoni, Luigi." The waiter surveyed the rolling table and made a gentle show of agreement. He backed off, turned and shuffled off in the direction of the kitchen. "Trust me on this . . . You simply haven't lived until you've tasted Guido's sweet and sour pepperoni."

KC bit into her pizza. Chewed carefully. Rewarded his inquiring look with arched eyebrows. It was chow mein and not bad at all. Peter smiled and buffed his nails with his breath.

The waiter returned shortly. Peter had him dish out the sweet and sour pepperoni. She might have to beg for the bicarb later, but right now it was sheer bliss. And, it felt genuinely good to be in Peter's company. They'd always made a terrific fit. Mother Mary and Joseph! She was doing it to herself again.

An hour later, by the time Luigi brought fortune cookies, almond cakes and a fresh pot of hot water for a tea bag that had no good dunks left in it, Peter's entire demeanor had changed. He'd become increasingly somber, and his small talk was running on empty.

He seemed afraid to keep his attention settled on her and apologized once or twice, after his manner got too petulant even for him.

When the longshoremen stopped by the table, playfully soliciting introductions, he pretended not to understand, and they got even by winking at her while imploring him to send their love to Annie. Neither was very good with innuendo. Peter didn't bite, except into what remained of their mandarin scampi marsala.

She tapped the back of his hand, for attention. His eyes had wandered out the window again. "It is the wise man who understands friendship lifts the heaviest of burdens."

"Huh?"

"The fortune." She waved the slip of paper at him, then tucked it into a pocket. In fact, the two-line message said something about winding roads, but she hated seeing him this way. "You seem to be carrying the Great Wall of Milan on your back."

He shrugged. "Nothing you want to get into."

"Do I have a vote, too?"

Another shrug. He reached for the other fortune cookie, but she was faster. She recited, "The rich man sooner shares

151

his wealth than his problems," and leaned across the table. "That settles it, then. Unless you're ready to write me out a check right now, your problems will have to do." And pocketed the slip of paper, which talked about dreams.

"KC, listen. Did Mother remember to tell you I said too much last night about the priest not being a priest?"

Wonderful! Peter had raised the subject without prompting. "Even before my first swallow of orange juice. Consider it forgotten." He smiled and seemed relieved. "Can you say how come the newspapers are still calling him one?"

A gesture of helplessness. "I got a wake-up call first thing this morning. Direct orders from my boss, Chief Spence. You know how stupid I feel for—"

"Don't be silly. You can also forget I asked." She wondered, Is he hiding anything else his boss may have said? I'll get him back onto the subject later. "What's really on your mind, Peter?"

"That was it."

"I only have to look at you to know better."

"Then you also know it's nothing you want to talk about."

"It is, if not talking about it does this to you."

"Those fortune cookies. You made them up."

She gave him a gesture of confession. Peter closed his eyes to shut her out and she waited while he sorted out his options.

His head rested on one cheek cradled against his fist, the elegant fingers of his other hand swatting at imaginary crumbs on the checkerboard tablecloth.

She always believed Peter had the fingers of a concert pianist or one of the great rock guitarists, like an Eric Clapton or an Eddie Van Halen. Peter had used them to carry City College to the league football championship two seasons running and still looked like he was in good enough shape to whip those forty-seven yards downfield and into the end zone with the winning touchdown, only five seconds left on the clock.

KC had not really studied his face before now, maybe afraid of liking what she saw too much.

Over the years, the boy had escaped into the man. He had the strong features of his father, softened by a sweet mouth that was his mother's special gift. A broad forehead that angled onto his cheeks and a granite jawline. A modest nose that drifted off course after twice being broken, the second time by her. Thick, naturally-curly light brown hair with drifts of red highlighted by the bright sun pouring through the window, trimmed but shaggy just below the collar line and growing wild as a garden of weeds.

How she loved to run her fingers through his hair, grab hold whenever—

She had to stop thinking about Peter that way. She had an obligation not to do anything to encourage him. "Whatever you were trying to sell me before with that dyke business about Annie, I'm not buying, Peter." That got his attention. Now she would try for the other eye. "The way she is around you, not to mention the way she hunted me down last night. You're lucky to have someone who cares for you as much as Annie does." And, she felt her heart racing, flushing with contradiction.

Peter straightened up, leaned back in his chair. Clasped his hands on the table. Raised his chin high enough for her to see the old scar underneath, an ugly, irregular patch of mottled pink, from the time he came home in time to rescue her from a scavenger dog running wild in the neighborhood, who found a hole underneath the fence, crashed through the hedge into the backyard and was about to pounce, forevermore in her memory the size of a tiger, fangs to match. She was eleven and hadn't lived with the Osbornes long enough for him to care enough to risk his life for her, but he did.

An uncomfortable grin. "Is it supposed to matter when it doesn't matter?"

It seemed to her that Peter was screwing up his face and his courage at the same time.

"Bottom line, I don't love her, KC. It's that old business about loving, but not being in love. Annie loves Peter, but Peter—" He quit the thought and turned from her to work out more invisible crumbs. A painful smile. "Annie and I make love, but it's never the same as when you and I . . . It's never been like that for me with anyone else, but—"

"You're carrying a torch that you have no business carrying. Maybe that's what's getting in your way."

She spoke resolutely, anxious to be believed. Hoping to convince herself, as well. Using the paper napkin to dab at the beads of sweat forming on her forehead, from too much garlic. Or, too much emotion?

Peter said, "Did you care that much for Frankie McClory?" Solemnly. One of those questions that never quite fits with the right answer. And, in that instant she knew what had been on his mind all along.

She said, "I cared for Frankie McClory with more heart and soul than I believed one person could ever manage in a lifetime, Peter."

"The same way you once cared for me?"

"I'd rather not answer that question, unless you want me to lie to you."

A wistful grin. "That answers my question."

"Thank you."

"Frankie McClory." He sounded out the name and considered it for a few moments, then talked past her shoulder. "I never heard much about him, or from you for that matter, after you went running off when . . ."

He let the rest of the thought drift away.

"Say it, Peter: When Brenda Bennington tramped into our relationship, made it ugly, turned my world upside down. I met Frankie in London in that summer between semesters at grad school." He seemed to take shape as she spoke. "He was your typical Black Irish. Dark. Handsome. Brooding. Loved his cold beer and hot women . . . I see the wheels turning in your mind. No, I certainly was not the first woman in his life. If I had been, I would have suspected something was wrong with Frankie. I was the last, though. Frankie loved me, Peter, and I loved him."

A melancholy smile. "On the rebound."

"Nobody as important in my life as Frankie. Never."

"On the rebound."

"Stop flattering yourself. That's another habit you obviously haven't broken, Peter."

If he saw her anger rising, he ignored it. "So, he takes you back to the Old Sod and next thing you know Mr. Frankie McClory has you involved with the problem over there."

"Mister? Mother Mary and Joseph! It's my *husband* Frankie, you mean. It was not the *problem* I got involved with, Peter. It was the *solution* I got involved with, even though I don't expect you to understand that. The *solution*. My husband Frankie was always ready to die fighting for what he believed in."

"And you?"

"I believed in him."

Peter trapped her eyes and held them. His own narrowed into slits and bore deeper.

"There's something you're not telling me."

"Maybe there's something you haven't asked."

"What?"

"You're the big detective? You go figure it out," KC said, confident he couldn't find the lie.

Before he could try, Annie joined them, seemingly from out of nowhere.

The look on Annie's face promised more trouble than KC had feared earlier, when she recognized Pullman Anderson.

It began the moment Annie opened her mouth:

"I thought you'd want to know, Detective Osborne. Rafael put a pair of sunglasses on his drawing and it came up looking like your girlfriend here."

Peter looked at Annie incredulously.

She ignored him, waved off the waiter and helped herself to a swallow of Peter's coffee. "Those glasses made all the difference, you know what I mean? If they were meant to hide a face, they revealed a face, instead."

KC rejected the idea as Peter finger-gripped the edge of the table and struggled to rein in his temper. "Is this some joke? This how pissed off you are about last night?"

Annie gave away nothing. "Rafael's running copies, Detective. You'll see for yourself back at the plant."

"What did Anderson have to say?"

"He said it looked like Mrs. McClory. A different hair style, more makeup, but he saw a resemblance." She nodded at KC. "The more Mr. Anderson thought about it, the more he decided it might have been her he saw coming out of the compartment. I let him run off to connect with his train, but he'll be back in a week. He looks forward to visiting with Mrs. McClory again."

KC's pulse was pounding. She found her voice. "Am I a suspect, Detective?"

"Should you be?"

"KC, you don't have to—"

"It's all right, Peter." She challenged Annie with her stare.

156

"Are you saying I killed that priest or that I resemble the person who did?"

"You tell me." Whatever Annie thought was buried too far behind her eyes to read. Her eyes were red and the lower lids turned out to reveal pink rims, like she had had a bad night's sleep, or no sleep at all.

"Damn it, Annie!"

"No, Peter, really . . ." KC gave his hand a friendly pat and rested her hand on his forearm. She felt a stomach knot tighten, but her mind was working. She knew she had to relax or Annie's nasty scrutiny would catch her. She needed to guide Annie without being obvious to one of the stock alibis the Thirty Two had taught her during a week of heavy prepping for the trip. Chances were she wouldn't need to use any of them, they'd said, but they were leaving nothing to chance.

Chance is for idiots, Frankie used to say.

She wanted to applaud his wisdom, smother him in kisses, but, now, disguising her anxiety—

"Didn't Mr. Anderson say he never goes into the coach compartment, Detective Waterman?"

"So?"

"He was as certain of that as I was of not having been in the Pullman section."

"Maybe one of you is mistaken."

"Maybe, Mr. Anderson noticed me in the club car or the dining car."

"I wondered about that. He didn't think so."

"In the station house at Pasadena?"

Annie shook her head. She seemed amused by the questioning. "Not asked and not offered. We can check with Mr. Anderson next time."

"I think you'll find Mr. Anderson was busy with an old woman in a wheelchair."

"What's that supposed to mean?"

"It's why Mr. Anderson looked familiar to me when I saw him. I'm willing to bet he was the porter I saw helping an old woman in a wheelchair. I may even have asked him for directions to the ladies' loo."

"Why didn't Mr. Anderson say something earlier?"

"Why do bitches howl?"

Peter's scowl tilted into a smirk. Annie let the remark pass.

KC cleared a space on the table for her tote bag and made a show of rummaging until she found her ornate pair of eyeglass frames. She adjusted them on her face.

"These are the glasses that helped do wonders for his eyesight. He'd have seen me wearing them."

Annie strained to keep her temper as KC next dug into the bag for her wallet. She pulled out a business card like it was the punchline to a David Copperfield trick and handed it over to Annie.

"Yeah? So?"

"The gentleman sitting next to me in coach. Very kind, very polite; good company and a good listener. We were together the whole trip. Mr. Ford gave me his card and said contact him if he ever could be helpful."

Annie studied the card. She raised her chin, pushed her lower lip so that it covered the upper one. Lifted her eyebrows. Nodded. Smiled. "John Ford."

"Not related to the famous movie director. I asked."

"Sales rep for a shoe company in Vancouver. Shoe business. Next best thing to show business."

"Mr. Ford made the same joke."

"Doesn't everyone? May I keep this?"

Peter slapped the table. "Enough with this crap! Give her back the card, Annie." Heads turned to stare at them.

"Your girlfriend offered it up, Detective."

"Peter, I don't mind." She gestured indifference. She wished he'd stayed out of it. She wanted Annie to have the card. She knew exactly what Annie would learn, and that would end the problem, but she didn't want to appear too anxious. The knot twisted inside her stomach again. "When you're finished, though? Mr. Ford showed me some great shoes in his catalog. Bargain prices. I'd like to—"

"Give KC back the card, Annie." The irritation was flushing Peter's face. A neck vein had grown thick as a rope.

Annie hesitated, then flashed him a troubled look, her lips puckered, eyes reduced to dark-rimmed slashes.

She took a slim notepad from her purse, copied down the information she wanted, then handed over the card.

KC slipped it back into her wallet and volunteered, "If you check the passenger manifest, you'll see Mr. Ford and I sat in adjoining coach seats, Detective."

Annie assailed her with a stare.

"Amtrak doesn't list its coach passengers, Mrs. McClory. Only Pullman."

KC knew that, same as she knew checking out the murder compartment would lead to a woman they'd never find, because she didn't exist.

"I was just trying to be helpful."

"Save your help for Detective Osborne, okay?"

Peter uttered a garbled noise, threw a hand at the wall and signaled for the check. KC smiled inwardly, but recognized from Annie's determined expression that this was far from being the end of it between them. Hell hath no fury . . .

CHAPTER 17

Annie beat Peter back to the bureau, glowering in the wake of his overbearing insults, too pissed to bother about the mocking inquiries from some of the guys, who were anxious to share with her their theories about her partner and the blonde.

Morons.

She wanted to tell them to shove it where the sun never shined, the dorks, who never looked at her the way they'd looked at KC, not even on a day like today, when she had gotten up an hour earlier and made a special effort to dress up and look pretty. Pretty for her, anyway. If they were searching for some reaction, she'd give them her best dyke indifference. It was nobody's business but her own that KC was walking off with her man. Her man. Bastard. Bitch. Bastard and bitch. Bitch and bastard. Go together like a horse and carriage.

The looks that pass between them, those intangible vibes.

Others might have to guess about the signs, but not her.

Annie Waterman had not made it to detective grade on spec. She did not just see things. She observed. She recognized. She analyzed. She understood.

Okay, so maybe she was out of line last night at the Osbornes', but Peter owed her more consideration than the humiliation he dished back defending his lost love. Because she was wrong, did that make him right?

Okay, so maybe she wasn't the most tactful person in the world when she broke into their lunch without so much as a howdy-do or a cheery fuck-you to lay on them the gospel about Rafael Yneguez's sketch.

She shuffled through the papers in her in-basket for the

Pullman passenger list Amtrak had faxed over.

No "McClory."

No "John Ford."

She pushed the list aside and went to the page in her notepad where she had copied the information off the Ford business card in her precise, schoolbook printing. There had been nothing special about the card. Fancy and inexpensive enough for a salesman to pass out by the hundreds. Embossed. Basic information and a dumb slogan, "They Give Your Feet a Treat."

So, what was it about the card that didn't ring true to her?

Annie traced her scar from her nose to the side of her mouth unconsciously, over and over. She invented a tune to go with "They give your feet a treat" and after a minute or two adjusted the beat to the rhythm of her fingers tap dancing on the surface of the desk.

"*Give your feet a treat. Give your feet a treat. Feet, feet. Treat, treat. Give, give, give 'em. Give your feet a treat.*"

She let her mind wander the room, searching for signs that were not there.

Ignoring the sign on the department wall that was, a red diagonal line through a smoldering cigarette.

More than jealousy.

The sign meant more than jealousy.

More than Peter's bitch girlfriend.

Think, Detective, think.

Annie sucked in the smoke and thought some more.

Studied her scribbling in the notepad while plumes of blue smoke drifted out from the corners of her mouth.

"*Feet a beat. Feet a treat. Feet, feet. Treat, treat.*"

Not the card! It wasn't the card.

It was the way KC had volunteered the card.

The way she had reached into her wallet and found it, as

convenient as a 7-Eleven store. Like she wanted her to have the card, to check, to find out—

What?

Impulsively, Annie reached for the phone. She cradled the receiver between her shoulder and chin and double-checked the number she had copied while punching in the codes for an outside long-distance line, quietly singing to herself, *"Give your feet a treat. Give your feet a treat. Treat your feet. Treat your feet. A treat. A treat. So give your feet a treat . . ."*

Heading up the motel walkway, Liam McClory heard the telephone ringing and knew it had to be his because the rooms on either side had cleared out this morning. The pair of middle-aged wall-bumpers were the last to go, getting in one final charge down the tunnel before the noon deadline, the woman slipping a wink at him as she climbed into their Jap trap, as if she were fit for a fast one while her boyfriend loaded the trunk.

He juggled the key one-handed, his other occupied with a lovely bag of breakfast treats from the Uncle Wiggley's Weenie World, and reached the phone in time.

"Mr. Ford? Mr. John Ford?"

"Indeed," he said, and bit into his third Weenie Wonder while Detective Annie Waterman introduced herself.

CHAPTER 18

"Waterman, Mr. Ford," and she spelled it for him, then recited her credentials. "Detective First Grade with the L.A.P.D. . . . the Los Angeles Police Department. I've been assigned to look into a homicide aboard an Amtrak from Vancouver . . . Yes, sir, exactly. The train you were on . . . You may have read a story in the paper or if you've been watching TV . . . That's right . . . Yes, it was horrible, Mr. Ford, but let me tell you why I'm calling you specifically. A routine question, actually. I'm inquiring about a young woman we were told occupied the coach seat next to yours during—Yes, Mrs. McClory . . ."

Peter gave her a withering look as he passed to his desk and slouched into his chair.

He grabbed his coffee mug, swiveled around to face her and didn't even try to disguise his eavesdropping.

Annie laughed into the mouthpiece, more a chugalugging noise she hoped sounded sincere. "Yes, there are. You are absolutely right about that, Mr. Ford. Lots of Irish in the States. Helped make this country what it is . . . Yes, he was. President Kennedy was one to be especially proud of, but about Mrs. McClory . . ."

He snapped at her cue and, after he finished answering a question she had not quite asked, Annie thanked him. "You've been a really big help, sir . . . Yes, I will. If I have more questions, I certainly will. Thanks, and enjoy the rest of your vacation."

Annie replaced the receiver and stared at it for several moments, her back turned to Peter, while she considered what Ford had said. Rolling around to face him, she turned up her nose. "Ever think about suggesting to Guido he tone down the garlic?"

His expression let her know it was not what he wanted to hear.

"Your girlfriend's story checks out. John Ford. Shoe salesman. Here to mix a little vacation pleasure with business, he says. He says Mrs. McClory was never out of his sight for more than a few minutes. Snoozed the night away with her head on his shoulder. Didn't have the heart to disturb one little blonde hair on her precious little head after she finished telling him about her long trip over from the mother country."

"Putting aside your emotions, assuming you can, do you really believe you had a sane reason for checking her story in the first place?"

Annie wheeled back and pushed out a heavy sigh.

If she were a fire-breathing dragon, Peter would be the new crispy critter.

"A sane reason? Not! Unless thoroughness counts, Detective. If she's a suspect, it's not because of anything personal. Try Pullman Anderson for openers."

"And for closers. You finessed that ID based on a lousy drawing."

"Don't let Rafael hear you. He thinks his work belongs in the County Museum." She took a copy of the drawing from the stack on her desk. "Park your brains above the belt line for a minute and admit the sunglasses made magic happen."

He shook his head, disagreeing or disparagingly, and Annie decided it was both, even before he pointed an accusing finger in her face.

"You're the one who's making this personal, not me!" he said.

"Surely, you jest!" Her shrill laughter was enough to break

the glass in one of those old Memorex commercials.

Peter pulled a finger to his lips, but the damage had been done.

The other detectives were staring at them, some trading smirks that revealed she and Peter had more partners sharing in their secret than they realized. Peter lowered his voice to a whisper and began talking between his teeth like a bad ventriloquist.

"Is that all of it, the drawing?" he said. He turned up his palms and banged them over and over with his fingers, signaling her for more.

She didn't remember the last time she'd made him so angry.

She wasn't far behind in the anger department.

She had never felt so intimidated or threatened in their relationship.

Peter was staring at her like he wanted to say something mocking.

He could get nasty sometimes, but not intentionally, she'd convinced herself early in their relationship, when he said a few things as cruel as anything she'd ever heard on the playground, when she'd win back by letting the boys take her where no one could see them and touch her where no one could look.

Shut up and suck. It became a standing order.

She obliged, because afterward they would say nice things, tell her what a great girl she was, and Stringbean Annie believed them, because she wanted to believe them. It was better than anything she heard at home, where her mother never cared enough to see her pain or how she was helping screw up two lives for the price of none, her own as well as Annie's, whose stepfathers treated her like shit, except for the second one, who told her lies she wanted to hear and threatened her into promising she'd never say a word to mama about their chocolate kisses.

He finally disappeared, but first he beat the both of them and boasted about their secrets, how Annie satisfied him where mama had failed. After that, mama couldn't wait for her to pack her things and move out and take the whole blame with her.

Annie called home every so often, but mama never seemed pleased about hearing her voice, so she didn't try to find her after the day she got the recorded message that said the number was disconnected, or after joining the police force, when she landed in Records and it would have been simple to run a make.

In her heart, Annie loved her mother. She would rather live with the scars than hear anything bad had happened to mama, fool that she was, and, maybe, fool that she also was with Peter.

Peter was different even when he was thoughtless, or so she'd come to believe. He never hurt her and he was honest to a fault, talking the truth even when it was nothing she wanted to hear.

She sensed kindred spirits the first time she looked into his eyes, after they were made partners and sat down to the first greasy kitchen cup of coffee, part of the mating ritual of cop partners, although you don't find it indexed in any of the official handbooks.

Peter treated her like a person.

He kept his hands to himself.

He was the best looking guy who'd ever spent this much time with her, even lots of hours off the job, when they tracked the town sharing common interests and pleasures, and some she pretended about, because she wanted to impress him. He liked her in a way that couldn't be faked, and she was damned if she would let it get away just because Peter didn't appear to know how to take their relationship up to the next step, so she took the initiative, got them to a place and a point where bed was inevitable. She deserved to be happy after so much time.

He made her happy, and it pleased her to make Peter happy. Even when he treated her like one of the boys, she knew Peter thought of her as a lady. She couldn't lose that, she wouldn't lose that, even when he made her mad enough to, to—

Annie flashed on how she had played dress-up this morning.

Had Peter even noticed?

If he did, he hadn't mentioned it to her, but that wasn't their way and not much of a dress-up, either. An outfit she'd bought on sale during a lonely Sunday at Beverly Center, browsing the shops before it was time for the movie Peter had seen with his kid sister and said was worth the seven and a half bucks. The sales clerk was suddenly at her side, while she was checking the jacket and pants set through the window, telling her how the outfit would really show off her figure, how the color was really her, how it caught the green in her eyes and all. So, what the hell, she could always return the outfit and, meanwhile, it was nice to have the attention.

Peter's voice eclipsed her thoughts. "Okay. If you have nothing else, my turn."

She tried to look away, but couldn't.

He seemed to take inspiration from the holes in the acoustic tile and gave the squad room a fast make before asking for the drawing.

The other detectives had gone back to work, but he made an effort to keep his voice down, anyway.

Annie had to move closer to hear him, the way she did

whenever they were alone, their passions spent, and Peter was describing how wonderful, how remarkable she was, as a lover and as a friend.

It was never close enough to the truth she wanted to hear from him, but it was the best thing about her life. He was the best thing about her life. Peter was gentle and giving in a world that otherwise seemed the devil's playground to her. She was not about to quit on him without making a real try at removing the hell from her happiness.

How many chances had she had before?

Not that many and all failures, like her mother's failures, only she had been too wise to tie the knot that chokes.

She sensed the lover in him as Peter characterized the business about the drawing as foolishness without making her out to be a fool.

"I submit we can assume Pullman Anderson confused the woman he saw on the train with the woman he saw in the station and that's who he based his description on. KC, by her own admission." He sent her an easy look.

She protectively crossed her arms over her chest. "I thought you said they taught you in law school never to assume."

"Cop school, too, but I'm making an exception in this case. Just for you."

Grudgingly, she answered his smile.

"Let's say that's not all we can assume. Let us assume that KC did visit Anderson's part of the train. He saw her and, later, he confuses her with the woman in the compartment when he's calling out the specs to Rafael. So, KC lied to us and—presto!—she qualifies as a suspect, except—"

He paused for her nod. Annie knew where he was heading, but let him keep the lead, a habit she developed after realizing Peter often needed to be shored up as much as she did.

"Your call confirmed KC made the trip in coach. She slept the night away on the shoulder of a shoe salesman, who had her in his sights most of the time, which common sense suggests had to include the time the M.E. estimates the killing occurred."

"Go on." Whose fault was it she was beginning to feel foolish, his or her own?

"Amtrak's manifest showed the compartment assigned to a Mildred O'Malley, who also boarded in Vancouver. Can't we then assume that Mildred O'Malley might look like the drawing, with or without sunglasses?"

"You finished?"

He shook his head, and she watched his eyes for mockery. That would be crossing the line, and she knew she would blow. He had done that twice before in their relationship. The first time she warned him. The second time she made it so he was unlikely to commit the mistake again. They went two weeks speaking in grunts and shrugs, until she needed to break the silence, not him, desperate to hear his voice and know he was not beyond caring for her anymore.

"One more reminder. The crime scene. It looked to have been wiped down by a pro. It was clean of prints, stray hairs, whatever might give us probable cause to finagle a match-up with KC. Anyone. Ad Murphy ultimately comes back with different news based on a baggy from the lab, well, we'll throw that into the blender and—"

"I know how it works, okay?" He was playing his courtroom lawyer trick on her, admit to the worst and then tear it apart with the logic of coincidence and confusion.

Peter had confessed he was a lawyer, reluctantly, after they became lovers. He had studied law and passed the bar to please Judge Osborne, but he never intended to practice, he said. His heart was set on being a cop, one of the good guys, he said, and characterized lawyers as piranhas with capped teeth and car phones.

Peter opened up, a drift of light through a keyhole, as if he had to pay her back for her own true confessions, secrets that had kept her on a shrink's ledger for ten years but, if the lover boy stuff was to continue, she needed him to know she had become a cop to keep watch over bad cops like the ones who answered her 9-1-1 screaming appeal on her multiple rape.

They had taken her, in turn, before the medics arrived, while she was unconscious and bleeding, close to death and wanting to be closer, laughing and joking back and forth, stuffing blow that hadn't been stepped on up her nose to erase the memory or, that failing, compromise her accusations.

The experience was degrading, dehumanizing, beyond any simple act of revenge, and it turned her away from men.

Peter was the man who brought her back, among the few she let try, and to lose him would be to lose the best part of her new life in the old world.

Who was a KC Cassidy to come back and presume to turn things upside down?

Fuck.

It is personal, Annie, so why pretend otherwise with Peter, especially now?

He was saying, "Maybe Mildred O'Malley is that person or, maybe, she had an accomplice. What we're after is a person or persons with the motive, the means and the opportunity to do the dirty deed. The best you have with KC is the fact she was on the train. Period. At best, a case of circumstantial jealousy?"

"Peter, you said KC's trying to put her old life behind her and begin all over again. Where do you fit in that equation?"

Annie looked away from him, studied her desk, probed her eyebrows with her thumbs. "Also out with the old, or back in with the new?"

"I gave KC the official word on the victim. She understands our ass is glass if she tells anybody the priest wasn't what he seemed."

Ducking.

Not good enough.

"Have you told her about us?"

"My private life is my own business."

"Why not?"

"Because. That's why not." Lying now.

"What did she say when you told her?"

"Damn it, Annie!" His hands grabbing for the sky, his head ajar, like Mussolini. "Okay, I didn't have to tell her. She knew. All KC had to do was hear you treating her like shit and she knew. She knew how you feel by looking at you, not because of what I had to say."

Where's the smartass comeback now, when words fail and emotions are up for grabs? Punt. Buy time. Empty the mound of butts in the ashtray. Go for a fresh smoke. Pack dead. Scour the trash basket for something long enough to catch a flame. Ahhhhh.

She pushed the smoke out of a corner of her mouth, and said, "Good to hear she knows. You'd have to be a real dope to miss the clues."

Peter turned away from her and settled his gaze somewhere in the middle of the room, on some dangling emotion nobody else could see. He reached over for her hand without asking. She let him take it.

"Over lunch, KC spent half the time telling me how lucky I was to have somebody like you in my life. That was before you showed up leading the tiger, of course."

He turned and drilled her with his hazel eyes, and she knew it was the truth.

"Did you believe her? You never believe it when I say it?" He broke the stare first, but said nothing. "We have a problem, don't we?"

Deep-rooted sigh. "It's the same problem we had before KC came home."

"Worse now?"

"I don't want it to be."

"That's not an answer, Peter, it's an evasion. I don't suppose you can show me something in a smaller bridge?"

"Annie, it's the best I can offer right now."

She reflected on it, and said, "Okay, I accept," as if the choice were hers to make.

"If I were you, I wouldn't."

"In for a penny, in for the pot," she said. She worked her mouth into one of those brave smiles she imagined heroes wore in front of a firing squad, and died only a little less than they did.

CHAPTER 19

In Pasadena, Cookie charged through the door and made a beeline for the mail table in the entrance hall, as she had every day for the two weeks since she'd sneaked off her order to Victoria's Secret for two pair of Technicolor scanties briefer than a blink, barely more than crotch comforters; a bra that promised more than she was able to deliver, designed to show off her nips, and, thank goodness, they were developing on schedule.

When she ordered them, she had not thought to ask the 800 operator if the package would identify Victoria's Secret as the source. Not that she was ashamed, but it wasn't the sort of information she wanted to share yet with Mommy, who still made furtive references to birds and bees and the need for a girl-to-girl sit-down one of these days. Not that either of her folks would violate the family code and open mail not addressed to them, but there was always a first time.

Cookie and Andy, who had his own problems at home, with parents who did a sloppy job of hiding their pot and talked in groovy and far out, had decided that the U.S. government exploded a Stupid Bomb during secret experiments conducted in the City of Pasadena. Ever since, the people here had been trapped in the mid-sixties, living their lives behind a wall, like characters in those gnarly sixth-grade educational films.

She was cursing under her breath when the phone rang. She grabbed for it, figuring it was Andy checking in. They had not been together for almost an hour, not since a sloppy suck of a kiss before Andy fled the secrecy of the hedge to catch the school bus. Cookie missed him.

"I got it!" The flocked wallpaper absorbed her shout. "Osborne residence."

"Mrs. Kate McClory, please."

The voice was unfamiliar, and it had a lilting accent she quickly identified as Irish, because it sounded just like Bono did on MTV.

"Who?"

"Mrs. Kate McClory. I understand she's visiting with you?"

"I don't, oh, wait—You mean KC? KC Cassidy?"

"Yes. That would be her."

Cookie told him to hold on a minute and placed the receiver on the table while she moved over to the head of the stairway. She called at the top of her teenage lung power, "Kay-Ceeeeeee! Phone!" No response. Cookie told the caller, "I guess she's not home, or she would have picked up."

"Might I leave a message then?"

"Are you a friend of hers, or something?"

"Both, I suppose. A friend and a something." She felt his smile drifting through the phone and it made her giggle. "Could you tell her Mr. Ford called? Mr. John Ford?"

She scribbled his name on the message pad. "What's your number, Mr. Ford? I'll tell KC to call you back."

"That's all right. I'll call again."

"It's no trouble."

"That's all right, and who might you be?"

"Her sister, sort of."

"Well, sister sort of, just be sure to tell her Mr. John Ford called and he'll be calling back," he said, and clicked off the line.

"Who was that, hon?" Mommy was standing inside the dining room arch.

"Just somebody for—Mrs. McClory." She ripped the page

174

from the message pad and fled upstairs, her voice trailing behind her. "Andy calls, don't tell him anything. Just say hello, and give me a gasp, okay?"

"I'll just say hello and give you a gasp," Mommy repeated. "And pick up after yourself."

When she reached the upper floor, Cookie grabbed the polished mahogany banister knob and swung around to her right, skidding to a stop at KC's bedroom door. She rapped and, getting no response, called, "KC? Calling Mrs. McClory. Mrs. Kate McClory."

Satisfied KC wasn't there, Cookie stooped to slip the message under the door, then changed her mind. The door didn't resist her gentle nudge. She wandered inside, checking out the room on her way to the vanity mirror. She tucked the message slip inside a corner of its filigreed framework and was turning to leave when her curiosity got the best of her. Cookie rebuked herself in the mirror. How would she feel about KC stalking her room? No big deal, not with KC. Mommy rummaging, that was different. KC was friend and confidante, a sister, sort of. She imagined Mr. Ford's voice after she said that before, and giggled quietly to herself.

There wasn't much new to explore.

KC hadn't been home long enough to change more than the smell of the bedroom. The one item of curiosity was her trunk, which Cookie spotted behind the partially open closet door. She scrunched up her face, eyes skewered, lips pushed to the max. Flipped an imaginary coin into the air and watched it fall heads. She'd called tails, but so what?

Despite its size, the trunk was heavier than it looked and awkward to handle. When she turned to move it outside to better light, a corner hit the door jamb hard and ripped the trunk from Cookie's tentative grip.

The trunk bounced on one end, teetered, seemed to hang

on an edge, flopped face down.

Cookie got a double grip on the leather carrying handle and pulled. The snap locks popped and the lid cracked open. Contents spilled everywhere. Odds and ends, mostly, the kinds of travel items people don't bother to unpack. She rolled her eyes and appealed to the ceiling for mercy, got down on her knees and began collecting.

She maneuvered the trunk onto its back and found what appeared to be an interior shelf the same size as the trunk base had been jarred loose and was, in fact, a false bottom. She took out the bottom and discovered three packages, their outer wrapping too plain to think KC intended them as gifts. Each was about the size and weight of a six-pack of Coke.

She replaced the packages and the false bottom, threw the doodads inside the trunk, then reached for the folded bath towel that had landed about a foot away. It was the only towel KC had left in the trunk and had a curious hole and scorch mark, like somebody had placed it too close to a burning candle.

Cookie grabbed onto the nearest corner and, with the first yank, the towel unfolded and two guns clunked out onto the carpeting.

She arched backward and made an undecipherable noise. Thought about what she was seeing while she caught her breath. She lifted the larger gun first and examined it more from fascination than fear. There were always guns around the place because of Peter, who had dragged her and the folks down to the Academy range all those times. Peter said it was necessary for all the family to know, like learning to ride a bike or to roller skate, even if you hated bikes and roller skates.

These guns were the genuine article.

Cookie set them down on the towel and sat cross-legged,

her tongue working one side of her mouth and then the other while trying to figure out what KC was doing with the genuine article.

"Monkey!" KC was calling her from downstairs.

Cookie's jaw dropped in silent panic.

CHAPTER 20

KC had gone calling for Cookie after parking the town car and one-stopping in the kitchen, where Aunt Dorothy was busy preparing dinner, juggling pots and Pyrex at the counter in the middle of the spacious room filled with the delicious aroma of homemade bread baking in the double oven.

She'd quietly slipped up behind her and whispered, "Boo!"

Dorothy's hands jumped reflexively and she almost lost her grip on the curved stainless steel blade, a good seven or eight inches long, she was using to chop lettuce. An instant later she was composed and smiling back at KC.

"You startled me so! Now I know for certain where Cookie learned that bad habit."

KC crossed to the fridge and found a Coke. "I made Peter promise to be on time for dinner," she announced. "He sends hugs and kisses."

"That means his father is going to be late for dinner." Dorothy set the knife down carefully and began running water through a bowl filled with lettuce chunks, using the left basin. The right basin was full of soap water and cookware. "I can't remember the last time they were both on time . . . Did you get your phone message?"

"Message?"

"Cookie took it. You didn't see it when you came in? Usual place."

"No." Curious. She had checked the pad. It was a habit she'd mastered when things like boys and dating meant something.

Dorothy found a place for the bowl, used the knife to clear the cutting board and began working on green and red bell peppers and three shades of onions. "Oh, wait, right. Cookie took it on up to your room. That child is really crazy for you, KC." She parodied her daughter, "Gah-gah crazy. Drool city, dude." Smiled over her shoulder. "Aren't we all." Not a question.

KC answered the smile, and hoped Dorothy couldn't see her concern. "Same, Aunt Dorothy." She crossed back and wrapped her arms around Dorothy from behind, gave her a generous squeeze. "I'll go track down our cookie monster." The nickname had evolved from Sesame Street's Cookie Monster, whose every appearance elicited cries for cookies from tiny Emma, named after a grandmother, and renamed by KC. "Cookie," short for Cookie Monster.

KC called for her at the base of the stairway, "Monkey!" and started up without waiting for an answer, picking up speed and skipping steps as she played with a mental picture of Cookie using the phone message as an excuse to check out her room, what she often did at the same age.

Often without an excuse.

Often with Cookie a willing accomplice.

KC pictured her checking out drawers and cabinets, the closet, the suitcases. The trunk. Innocent fun. She wondered, did she remember to twirl the numbers on the trunk's combination lock? Yes, of course, but—

Already, she was inventing excuses to explain the Walther PPK, the .32 Police Positive Cookie would have found.

The false bottom, too, and—?

She stepped inside the bedroom and said, "Hi."

"Hi," Cookie said, with a grimace she couldn't reinvent as a smile.

Cookie was sitting at the vanity, rigid, her elbows pressing hard against her body, fingers splayed on her thighs, heels of her dirt-stained, flag red high tops locked tight, the soles spread, forming an eccentric pyramid on the plush carpeting. Eyes conceding nothing as they wandered everywhere but back at KC.

She sent a thumb over her shoulder, indicating the mirror. "You had a phone call. Put the message there. Wanted to make sure you didn't miss it."

"Thank you." Everything seemed in order, as she had left it. Maybe, there hadn't been enough time for Cookie to hunt and peck.

Cookie shrugged, failed her smile again and tried to get to the hallway door.

KC took two quick sideways steps to prevent her exit.

"Gotta hurry," Cookie said. "I'm expecting Andy any minute. Andy says that I'm his main squeeze, and—"

"Is that good?"

Cookie tried to edge around her. KC was faster.

"It's stratos-scopic, but don't tell Daddy, okay?"

"Promise. Anything I learn about you, anything you learn about me, we keep to ourselves. Deal?"

Cookie cocked her head and her eyebrows narrowed, forming a single ridge of interpretation. Clearly, she understood what KC meant, or was KC arbitrarily turning her own worst fears into a false reality?

"Yeah. Sure."

"Seal with a kiss?"

"Seal with a kiss," Cookie repeated, like words stamped on an exit visa.

KC stepped aside and closed and locked the door behind Cookie.

She rushed across the room. The closet door was closed. She worked it back and forth, trying to remember how she'd left it. Abandoned the question. Leaned over to grab the trunk handle and pull it into the room. The combination locks were turned. She dialed them open, to check inside, listening to Frankie recite his habitual reminder, *Never take anything for granted. It's dumb. Turns deaf men blind and blind men dead.* She answered Frankie with a nod and stared back at her worst fear confirmed, evidence that Cookie had been snooping.

And, remembered the phone call.

On the message slip Cookie had tucked into the mirror, she'd written: "John Ford. Kate McClory. Call back later."

KC stretched out on the bed and studied the piece of paper, not pleased with the concept of telling "John Ford" about Cookie and the trunk.

Frankie was always cautious for the sake of safety. Liam was a hard case, capable of advocating the worst and following through. At once, he would see and brand Cookie a threat, dangerous to the cause. He would demand an appropriate solution. It would not be the first time. That Cookie was a child would not matter to Liam.

Burkes would think about it and then tell her it changed nothing, not to worry, and maybe talk about assigning an extra detail to guard Cookie, whatever it took to calm her fears, but doing it was another story. Burkes did what was good for Burkes and passed it off as patriotism, no matter who got hurt.

Whatever Cookie might have found had to stay KC's secret, even at the risk of mucking up the real plans.

Cookie had to grow up and live happily ever after, same as KC was determined to live happily ever after.

Liam phoned her again during dinner.

"Judge Osborne here." Noah was expecting a call from his

181

clerk, so the cordless was sitting alongside his salad bowl, like part of the service. "Who? Oh, sure, one moment, please." He offered her the phone. "It's a gent with a charming Irish brogue asking for Mrs. McClory, dear. Mr. Ford?"

KC put her open palm between them and pushed up from her seat. "That's all right, Uncle Judge. I'll take it in the library."

"Must be the same gentleman who called earlier," Dorothy decided.

Peter's eyes strayed over to her, then back to KC. He shifted in his chair, draped one arm over the back and viewed her like her face was sending a message he didn't want to hear.

Noah moved the phone aside. "He said he was *John Ford*," he remarked, chuckling to himself. He turned to Dorothy. "I'm surprised he asked for KC. When John Ford calls, you figure he wants to talk to the Duke."

Dorothy asked him, "Buddy, am I going crazy or didn't John Ford pass away years and years ago?"

"The Duke, too, hon, everywhere except on the TV. Gosh, I love the movies they made, especially the ones about the cavalry." He speared a large chunk of salad lettuce and garbled his words while chewing carefully. "Peter, what was the one with Henry Fonda?"

Peter shrugged. "I think it was *She Wore a Yellow Ribbon*," he said, sounding like his mind was somewhere else.

"Yes, yes," Noah said grandly. "That one. Little Shirley Temple, she was in it, too."

KC stole a look at Peter just before she passed through the door to the library. He appeared disturbed and was staring distractedly into space.

Cookie had been returning from the kitchen with a fresh

platter of Mother's honey biscuits when Daddy answered the phone and identified the caller.

At once, she retreated through the door, set down the tray on the service counter and had the wall phone receiver to her ear, one hand over the mouthpiece, as a voice she recognized said, "The police, they rang me up asking questions about you."

"Liam?" KC said.

"Jack Ford himself, Bright Eyes."

"Liam, where are you? What are—"

"Close enough to remind you how far we've come in our Frankie's blessed name. Too far to fuck things up now, Katie."

"What did the police say?"

"For later. Meet me."

"A problem tonight. I don't have—"

"Problems are for other people, Katie. We're in it for the solution. Tomorrow then."

"Where?"

"And where would you be expecting to find John Ford? I'll see you first," he said, and disconnected.

"Liam, wait, I—"

Cuh-lick.

Cuh-lick.

Cookie hung up the phone and backed away, grabbed the biscuit tray and scurried back to the dining room, trying to work out what the conversation she had just overheard could possibly mean, troubled by the nagging sense KC was in danger. Why else would she carry guns and talk to a strange man using two names?

What she did know: She didn't like Liam. John Ford. She just might have to have a heart-to-heart with KC, or was this something she should share with Peter? Could she do that?

Anything I learn about you, anything you learn about me, we keep to ourselves. That was the agreement she made with KC, or was it?

Daddy said, "What did you do, Cookie? Make the trip by covered wagon?"

The second click she heard told KC someone had eavesdropped on her conversation. She wandered about the library, absentmindedly reading book titles and making contact with the exquisitely-crafted bindings that had multiplied over the years on shelves rising almost to the entire height of three of the four walls, interrupted only by French windows leading outside or to other rooms.

She stepped onto the ladder and gripped the rail, gave herself a scooter push and sailed half the length of the room, like she used to do while pursuing fresh adventure for her ravenous eyes. *Wuthering Heights* and *Jane Eyre*. *Vanity Fair*. Tom and Huck. *The Turn of the Screw*, and how many sleepless nights after reading that one? Everything by Dickens. *It is a far, far better thing I do . . .* All of Shakespeare, and—

Yes, definitely, someone eavesdropping. She thought she had heard a click in when she first drew the phone to her ear, and wrote it off to nerves. But there were two clicks off for certain. No question. Liam's and one that followed a moment later.

Who? And, what had the person heard? She replayed the exchange. Brief. Safe. Called him Liam. Easy to explain if challenged. Think. What else? Nothing else? Who? Uncle Judge? It'd be totally uncharacteristic of him, especially with three other people in the room, Peter, Aunt Dorothy and—

Cookie. She wasn't at the table when the phone rang. She was in the kitchen getting more biscuits, close enough to a phone to—

Cookie, Cookie, Cookie.

KC felt sweat spilling under her arms and between her breasts.

She laughed nervously while crossing to a reading table. She occupied an edge briefly while regaining her composure.

What if the second hang-up was entirely in your imagination, KC?

Nerves. That's all.

Working yourself up over nothing. Nothing at all. Just nerves.

She returned to the dining room and apologized for the interruption.

Noah dismissed it, wondering, "You get the part?" She looked at him squarely, confused. "Did John Ford give you the part or is he giving it to Maureen O'Hara again?" He cackled delightedly.

She responded by breaking into a few steps of one of the jigs Frankie had taught her, the first one they had ever danced together publicly. It helped to relieve her tension. Noah and Dorothy applauded, Peter less enthusiastically. Cookie, not at all.

KC took the long way back to her place, so she could give Noah and then Dorothy a gentle wrap around the shoulders and a kiss. Peter didn't appear to take offense at being passed over, only fixed his eyes on hers like they would yield a treasure of information.

Cookie accepted her reward indifferently, without answering her smile, and now KC was certain Cookie had been on the phone.

She had no idea what Peter thought he knew, unless Cookie had said something to him. What now? She had placed Cookie on the other side of a line she'd never cross.

The decision was written in concrete. Peter, too, if it came to that?

She excused herself before dessert, claiming a headache, and—

That night dreamed the dream:

Frankie smiles and stares up at the Drinker. The Drinker fires and Frankie is knocked backward onto the floor. The kitten in her arms breaks away and races off to comfort Frankie. The Drinker smacks her with the Luger, but before he charges into the gentle night, she captures his face for now and forever, and—

She woke up, startled, hearing the balance of a single whimper that marked her escape from the dream, and wondering where she was. Uncomfortable. Her naked body drenched between two layers of white satin sheets. For a split second she thought she had fallen asleep in the tub. She moved a hand to her face where the barrel of the dream Luger had struck, just below the left ear. Her eyes fixated on the Drinker. The next time she saw him would be aboard the Amtrak to Pasadena.

"Shanley," he says. "Father Shanley. Most people know me as 'Jim.' And who might you be?"

She freed herself from the covers, wheeled around with her feet on the floor and shuddered at questions she had asked before. Why was Jim ready to kill her? Had the Thirty Two found out she worked for the United States government? What else did the Thirty Two know?

The questions kept her agitated and wide awake for hours, until exhaustion won the battle for her troubled mind.

CHAPTER 21

As Walter Burkes finished mixing himself an Alka Seltzer and stepped out from the built-in bar behind the main sitting area of Judge Osborne's living room, he was wondering how KC would react when she discovered he was here. Burkes decided she'd probably think he was checking up. Spying. Right. The Curse of Vlady Borchenko. Never trust one of yours you got pretending to be one of theirs. They just might get to liking it too much, especially if Cupid came calling the way he did for KC and Frankie McClory.

It was only a hunch growing wild about KC, starting to nag a little, but not worth sharing, especially with anybody who might point the finger at him and tell him he was screwing up a Big One, a Big One, Burkes, and hope God help him if Mr. Mustamba got bumped by that Irish bogey man they called the Plowman because of some Burkes screw-up.

The concept had occupied his mind on the drive over, except whenever he found himself thinking about Fritz. The vets had told Vonnie Fritz's x-rays were an appeal for surgery. Sooner the better. Wait and they would find Fritz putting more and more weight on his front legs as the hip dysplasia worsened. The poor little guy would start tucking his elbows into his belly, trying to balance on his front legs alone, and quietly suffer the pain until—

Damn it!

Vonnie said the vet was suggesting an operation where they reshaped the top of the thigh bones, then reshaped the hip joint, then fitted the bone into the socket. It was a long procedure and, of course, there were no guarantees. They knew that already from Hans, who was younger than Fritz when he underwent the same operation. And was never the same. Never caught another Frisbee. And, one morning, somehow managed to crawl out the doggie door and work his way up the backyard slope to the exercise run, where he appeared to have settled down to a peaceful, welcomed escape from his miseries.

Vonnie had asked, "What shall we do, Burkes?"

"Lemme give it some more thought, okay?"

"I have an opinion."

"Save it as the tie-breaker, okay?"

"If I had to decide all over again for Hans, my answer would be the same."

"I'll remember that, Vonnie."

"Why let Fritz suffer needlessly?"

"You're right on that score, Vonnie. That's what we got people for."

Burkes worked the bar gate back into a closed position and silently admired his surroundings. The place reeked of old money invested wisely and passed from generation to generation. Clearly, the recession had not put a cramp in the Osborne family's style of living. He reckoned the living room was a good twenty-five feet wide and about fifty feet long, close to the size of a grand ballroom. Gilded, carved doorways paying homage to a gilt-framed, inlaid mirror almost as tall as the ceiling, rising above a massive Italian marble fireplace. A symphony of crown molding. Herringbone parquetry, a lot hiding under rugs with names he couldn't pronounce that sold for prices he'd never be able to afford on his salary. A majestic French chandelier worth its weight in crystal.

Burkes shambled across the room and rejoined the judge

and his friends. He settled cautiously back into an armchair by the fireplace and did a mental check of the people. Six in addition to the judge and all of them sounding upper-crust, not like the Georgetown set, where power outranked big bucks.

He didn't belong in this crowd. The judge and his committee knew it, too, but they wouldn't let on. He'd discovered on these kinds of assignments that breeding begat good manners, and he would remain the center of attention, accepted and tolerated and maybe even liked before it was over, the way he liked the Osbornes as an upper-crust Ozzie and Harriet.

"Feel better?" the judge wondered.

Burkes finished the last of his Alky and placed the glass on the embroidered napkin served with his coffee and chocolate cream-filled pastry on the slight end table he harbored visions of accidentally overturning.

"Usually works, Judge Osborne. Glad you had the lemon flavor kind. I'm an expert on stomach disorder, and I am here to tell one and all the lemon flavor kind makes the fizz work better. So—where were we?"

The judge said, "Mayor Isaacs here was asking about the security your fellas will be laying in for Mr. Mustamba."

Burkes nodded. The mayor acknowledged his name and began tapping on the arm of the Chesterfield sofa he shared with the judge.

The realtor, Lester Goodale, sat to his left in the Curule bench and Mrs. Weitzman from the Woman's Society to his right in the other.

Burkes still hadn't adequately locked onto the names of the three other civic movers and shakers, who had taken the equivalent of second-row seats.

"I'll be brief rather than specific in that area, Mayor

Isaacs," Burkes said. "Better for all parties concerned, if you understand what I mean?"

He was talking gobbledy-gook, but the mayor nodded, as if he did.

Isaacs was a handsome man, if not as distinguished-looking as Judge Osborne, probably in his late sixties. The left eye had a lazy lid that caused that side of his face to contort every time he tried to compensate for it.

Burkes said, "During his visit here, Mr. Mustamba will be getting no less protection than we give the President himself."

"Is there something we should know, Mr. Burkes? Anything for us to worry about? I run a safe community and I wouldn't want anything happening to jeopardize—"

Lester Goodale said, "Put a clamp on it, Jesse. You're not running for reelection this morning, so relax, for Christ's sake." Everything about Goodale was average, except for his voice, which sounded like it was shot from a cannon. Burkes put him late forties, same as he was, with the same anxious manner he had observed in other insurance men and real estate salesmen.

The mayor gave Goodale a look of exasperation, not the first this morning and, Burkes supposed, part of a running contest between them. Goodale looked away to the group of paintings on the wall near the fireplace and studied them like he'd never seen them before.

The mayor said, "One incident, just one, while Mr. Mustamba is here, and—" He stretched his tapered mouth into a grim line. His left eye fluttered. He left the thought unfinished.

Burkes signaled understanding. It was important he have the city's cooperation, or SOP maneuvers could get dicey. The Lesson of Dallas. "Let me put your mind at ease, Mayor and everyone. Anywhere on the tour, anyone should get inside twenty feet of Mr. Mustamba who does not pass my department's famous Timex test—said person will take a licking or stop ticking. Even if he only farts funny. Check that. Sorry, Mrs. Weitzman."

"Yes," she agreed, but her eyes said she didn't really care. She kept giving him the look that bespoke one too many lonely night. Mrs. Weitzman was trying to do twenty in a late-forties zone. "Are you saying then that it would be possible for one of those nut cases to get close? To get within thirty yards of Mr. Mustamba or, God forbid—"

"President Clinton, if he decides to Air Force One it here to Pasadena for Judge Osborne's party?" Burkes belched, and rushed a hand over his mouth. "Excuse me, please. Big McHeartburn strikes again. Mrs. Weitzman, anything is always possible. The last time we learned that we learned it the hard way, with President Reagan. Probable or likely?"

Burkes shook his head.

Mrs. Weitzman shook hers in sympathy and shock and moved her hand to cover her mouth. She had a great mouth. Buttercup lips. Great eyes and a body out of a Jane Fonda ad. He wondered what she'd be like in the sack and almost re-gretted not being able to find out, but he'd seen enough spy guys twisted out of business on some mattress where they didn't belong.

Just then, Judge Osborne called, "KC!"

He turned toward an open pair of interior French win-dows. The others followed his lead. They all seemed to know who KC was.

KC glanced at Burkes, hesitated.

Burkes watched as a puzzled look spread across her face, as if she weren't sure whether to join them or retreat into the alcove he had passed through on the way here. The alcove, which seemed to act as a passageway to various parts of the house, was dominated by a luminous, hand-painted Oriental screen mounted on the wall, above a wrought-iron-studded chest about six feet tall mounted on a concrete base and lit by a smaller version of the crystal chandelier.

"Come on over, kid," the judge said, the way somebody might welcome a tax refund. "Come and say hello to some old friends." He rose and held out his arms in invitation. "You remember KC Cassidy, Jesse. Bill Cassidy's daughter? And, you, too, Carlos."

They both nodded. Carlos Montoya, the quiet one seated behind Mrs. Weitzman, wriggled a wrist, like he was asking teacher for permission to go to the can. He was the police commissioner, a small man with a pencil mustache and a hanky in his jacket pocket.

"Hey, Princess!" Lester Goodale said. "Give us a look and a listen, so we'll know it's springtime."

"Hello, it's so nice to see you again," KC said, acknowledging the compliment modestly, in a bright, honey-soaked voice that went with looks Burkes escalated from a nine to a ten as she stepped inside and headed over to the judge.

KC rested one hand on his shoulder, shifting her weight from one foot to the other, like she couldn't find a comfortable position. Her outfit was simplicity itself, black slacks and a gray pullover sweater, straw ballet flats that matched the fedora hiding all but a few strands of her blonde hair. The hatband was made from a blue striped necktie. When she removed her shades, Burkes saw how the band picked up the startling blue of KC's eyes. Her skin was pale white, like sunshine was her enemy.

She caught Burkes staring and responded with a gracious smile and a lift of the eyebrows that could mean *Thank you* or question his presence. He doubted anyone else had noticed the calculation beneath her glow of innocent wonderment.

Mrs. Weitzman said, "We were so, so sorry to hear about your husband, KC." Her glistening eyes adding to her sincerity as she turned to explain to Burkes, "Her deceased husband was the well-known Irish terrorist, Frankie McClory." Expressed like she was identifying some famous movie star.

Burkes said, "Yeah." He looked back at KC, who had accepted Mrs. Weitzman's remark resignedly. "I'm Walter Burkes, Mrs. McClory. With the Not-So-Secret Service."

"How do you do," she said, and signaled him not to bother rising.

"Pretty good, thanks."

Judge Osborne said, "Last night at the dinner table, I was explaining to KC about our forthcoming excitement, Mr. Burkes. Would you have any qualms about my adding her to the host committee? My wife could use the help with the arrangements for our little backyard *soirée*."

Burkes pretended to think about it and tossed a gesture. "Sure, why the hell not? It will be necessary to run a security check on you, Mrs. McClory. It comes with the terrain. You don't have to be the widow of an Irish terrorist to qualify, but we are going to need a social security number."

Mrs. Weitzman interjected, "Even mine. Imagine."

KC's look revealed nothing. "Of course. I'll have to find it for you."

"You don't have it committed to memory?"

She missed his joke. "Usually, I have important things on my mind, Mr. Burkes." The comment was out of character. He decided it translated as a response to the sarcasm of his terrorist husband remark.

Mayor Isaacs rose to the rescue. "I never learned mine either, Mr. Burkes."

Burkes raised his arms in surrender. "I'll let you in on a

secret. Eleven times out of ten, the parties in question don't know their Sosh number. It's a gag me and the special agents play. Linsenmeyer!"

Linsenmeyer stepped up from a corner on the side opposite where KC had entered. He'd been leaning guard alongside the last set of pulled-back crimson drapery. He had the ordinary looks and carriage that never stood out, the way Burkes liked all his people to be, but Linsenmeyer could draw the piece he carried under his armpit faster than he could finish a sentence.

Burkes introduced him. "Linsenmeyer, go with Mrs. McClory while she finds her Sosh number. We'll also need a black thumb." He noticed the usual curiosity stares. "Her fingerprint for the collection. Standard practice, Mrs. Weitzman. The good news is—we provide the Handiwipe after, at government expense."

Judge Osborne said, "Taxpayer expense, you mean," and the others laughed.

Burkes chalked up one for the judge, throwing a special wink at Mrs. Weitzman, whose eyes didn't know where to settle as her cheeks and forehead turned pink.

KC pressed out her palms at him and stretched her fingers. "You can have all ten of them if you like, Mr. Burkes. Mr. Mustamba has been a personal hero for years. What he achieved in the cause of freedom, the personal sacrifice, is greatly admired back home."

Burkes nodded and tried again to see if he could penetrate her mask. "*Back home.* If you're no longer a United States citizen, I'm afraid that'd put a crimp in Judge Osborne's—"

"I'll always be a citizen of the United States, Mr. Burkes. I can show you the eagle on my passport as well as my thumbprint if that's also necessary, but Ireland is *home* to me now."

"Where the heart is?" Lester Goodale said, tilting his head for a fresh perspective. He was more serious than Burkes had heard him before now, sounding like a principal beneficiary of the old Reaganomics.

KC conceded nothing. "Ireland is where I left a piece of myself, Mr. Goodale. Maybe the heart."

Burkes headed off further confrontation. "No. A passport isn't necessary, Mrs. McClory, but why don't you let Linsenmeyer have a look, anyway?"

KC leaned over to kiss the judge, who patted her hand solicitously, and followed the agent out of the room.

Burkes called after him, "Linsenmeyer. When you look at her passport, try not to peek at the young lady's age."

Laughs and titters, even a chuckle from Lester Goodale.

Burkes told him, "We're Not-So-Secret, Mr. Goodale, but we are thorough," and noticed that Goodale wore an enameled American flag on his lapel. A Rush Limbaugh patriot, too?

Turning to the judge, Burkes said, "You know, Judge, your Mrs. McClory is quite attractive, but she could use a week at the beach under your famous California sun."

"Can we talk about Judge Osborne's, please?!" Mrs. Weitzman looked unhappy about being upstaged by KC. "I promised to call the tent people by two o'clock."

As if he hadn't heard her, Judge Osborne said, "Mr. Burkes, I suspect the Belfast sun found it safer to stay hidden most days."

"You're something of a philosopher, Judge."

"An observer. I appreciate your letting KC be part of the committee, Mr. Burkes. After she asked, I could see she so had her heart set on it."

"Her helping out, it wasn't your idea?"

"It would have been two seconds later, except KC jumped

at the opportunity. Mr. Mustamba is quite some Superman in her eyes."

"Yeah. Faster than a speeding bullet."

KC getting involved like that was not part of the plan, Burkes thought.

One more indicator he still couldn't be certain whose side the lady really was on?

Later, by the time he was back at the office, Burkes had decided to move ahead with an idea he'd first had after they saddled him with the job of stopping the plot to kill Mr. Mustamba. Burkes put in a call to Parker Center and arranged a meeting that would include Peter Osborne.

CHAPTER 22

By Peter's watch, Annie arrived almost two hours late, maybe a half hour before the call came summoning him to the boss' office. She smelled like she had removed the perfume cards from a thousand magazines and boiled the scents into a single, awful odor. By the looks of it, she had been working on her appearance.

He decided to say something make-nice and, maybe, the compliment would help get them through the day without yesterday's kind of war of the words that was unfair to both of them and to the relationship Annie wanted out of him in the worst way.

Well, she certainly had picked the worst way to go after it.

He laughed at his joke and himself.

Just like Peter Osborne to go for a gag in order to hide his true emotions.

Haven't I told her enough about myself to deserve the space to make my own decision? he reasoned. Can't she understand that KC was not the only one I torched and tossed away like a spent match, only the one who left me before I could tell her the truth about Brenda Bennington and me; left me with a relentless headache that won't go away?

If only KC had stayed to hear and understand what had happened. No, *why* it happened. And, how I didn't have a choice, just Noah Osborne for a father. Damn it, Peter. Who do you think you're kidding, Peter? KC knew more than she had to know. She learned the truth the worst possible way.

At least, I've never misled Annie.

Annie pushed her way inside me and I was glad to have her

there, wishing I knew how to give her more of myself. Annie deserves that the same way Annie deserves better than me.

She'd come into his life when he was trying to turn over a new leaf, only the leaf kept turning into a rock and he was the snake underneath. *You have no cause to loathe yourself as much as you do,* the shrinks said. *Yeah?* he said. *You ever been me? You try being me for a while, then you come look me in the eye and say it.*

Annie looked him in the eye one lonely night, the second or third time they made love, and he found he was inching open his emotions.

"If you were full of any more shit, I'd smell it on your breath," she said.

She cuddled closer and ran her lips across his mouth and her hand around his body, saying it fueled the fires of love, in some ways like the Indians became blood relations by pricking fingers and rubbing them together.

"Make your senses work for you, Peter, not against you," she said, and, after they had made desperate love again, Annie taking the lead, guiding him to peaks he had never imagined and hardly believed possible, she lectured him about himself.

How Peter Osborne was smart and good-looking, kind and decent, the kind of cop cops were supposed to be: a decent man who believed the worst of the law was better than a society without rules.

"I see how you are with your family, Peter; I see you around people. The good, the bad and the ugly. You ace a case and, no matter how stupid or sinful it is, you do more than read some bum suspect his rights. You grant him those rights and stand behind the old nasty business of somebody being innocent until he is proven guilty. If I've learned nothing else from you so far, I've learned that. You've made it possible for me to put aside my own hang-ups, the mind crap that pushed me to join the department, with a need to dick all the dicks who get away with worse than murder, the ones who kill people and at the same time leave their victims alive."

"A regular Perry Mason, that's me, so why didn't I stay a lawyer instead of—?"

"Oh, no, cowboy. Annie here ain't falling for that one. That's a question you take up with your old man."

Talk to the judge? Argue my case, more like it. So the judge could take it under advisement, then rule by his book, and no appealing the decision?

He had come to hate the judge as much as he loved his father.

And loved KC?

Who also was turning her back on his appeals six years later, although she gave him an opening. She gave him a lunch. She seemed more interested than she let on even when they argued, especially when they argued. And every time she mentioned that Mick killer she ran away with and married, her damn dead Frankie, he felt she was testing him, egging him on to compete with a memory stronger than his worst sin against her.

Peter wished an old wish, to be able to go back in time, be reborn the night before Brenda. He'd behave better, not be manipulated by a young kid's avaricious persuasion that wisdom grew with his cock, and, oh!, how Brenda had made it grow.

He had to know where he and KC stood, for better or for worse. He had to spill his guts, stick with the truth, the whole truth, nothing but. Learn if they had a future as well as a past. Then, he could deal fairly with Annie, who deserved far more honesty than he could give her now.

"Didn't expect to be this late," Annie said, winging to her desk.

"You're late?"

Annie gave him the finger, but her expression said she was suing for peace. He took a heavy snort of her perfume, made an approving face and for a fraction of a second she turned giddy as a child pricking balloons. She was wearing a new outfit, having abandoned her Rescue Mission Thrift Shop look for a double-breasted, tailored jacket tapered at the waist over a high-necked blouse, both banana colored. Her pleated slacks were Cordovan brown, same as her Reeboks. The line was good for her, but spoiled by the outline of her hip holster. She had done something to her hair. The standard wind blitz was gone, cut and styled to emphasize the strength of her face. On top of the dreadful perfume, she was wearing bright green nail polish that picked up the unusual quality of her eyes. Nothing wrong with the new look, except he wished she'd recognize she wasn't in a contest with KC.

"Looking good," he said. It wasn't what he wanted to say, only necessary for Annie to hear. She answered with a silly curtsy. He teased her. "Why you walking so funny?"

"What's that supposed to mean?"

"Like somebody pulled the plug on your hips."

"Giving it an extra bump and grind, just for you."

She oomphed into her chair.

"Well, it's effective. You been practicing?"

"I spent all last night practicing."

They spoke at the same time, and it gave a stereo effect to the word "practicing." Their laughter seemed to take the corners off her reserve. His own, too.

"Practicing, huh?" He realized too late it was not a question to ask. Except, he was curious to know what else she might have done last night. Revenge humping? Something worse? Could he blame her?

"Alone. Just me and my battery-operated vibrator. And you, Detective?" When he shook his head, refusing to bite, she said, "Okay, I gave it a lot of thought. You were right. Guilty as charged. I had no cause to come down as hard as I did on her and I apologize."

He unloaded his best smile. "Ancient history."

Annie couldn't leave it there. "I'd like to show you my appreciation. You know, the old-fashioned way?"

"Don't think so."

"Yeah," she said, and shrugged resignedly. "Got a lot of pile driving that needs to be done on the paperwork." She lit a smoke, forgetting she already had one hanging from the lip of her ashtray.

Peter was relieved. Another time and they might have slipped away to an empty interrogation room.

She worked with her back turned to him, and after ten or fifteen minutes swung around and gave him a look that said, "I can't hold this in anymore." He expected her to start a new chapter on KC. She bought some time by lighting another smoke, waving it like Bette Davis and earning the usual mutters from Schlotter and Dyson at the desk nearest theirs.

She leaned across and settled an elbow on one of Peter's file piles. "I went looking for John Ford this morning," she said, watching the traffic passing across the window wall. "The guy your girlfriend said she sat with on the trip down? The business card—"

"And you just thought to mention it?"

"Slipped my mind."

Peter knew he should be annoyed with Annie for pursuing this foolishness after yesterday's conversation, like his argument had made no sense, but KC's phone call from John Ford last night had put a new spin on the case. He had been debating whether to tell Annie immediately or first do some quiet checking on his own.

"Got news for you, too," he said. She examined him for more. "After you finish."

"Beg for it."

"Screw it then."

She laughed and gave the air a hand job. "A local phone number I got calling Ford's company in Toronto tracked to a motel in Venice. The Happy Wanderer."

"Man likes the smell of salt water."

"Leaky toilets more like it. I wanted to run him through his story again, have him look at the drawing. Wrong! A lot of John Does on the register, but not one John Ford. Ever. Not yesterday. Not today. How much you wanna bet on to-morrow?"

"But you called Ford, you spoke with him there."

"I spoke with Ford, supposing he was there." She shook her head. "Phones operate off a central switchboard, one of those ancient uprights, mission-position plugs. You either have a name or a room number to get through and somebody did put me through. Not the human slug I found behind the desk, the kind who'll pick your nose if his is operating on empty."

"Anybody with an Irish accent?"

"Not on this mope's shift, he swore, although he did re-member somebody coming in who spoke what he made as Middle Eastern. Called it Shish-Kebab. Even when I show-boated a twenty I couldn't rattle his memory. I took a name on the night man, figuring we can fall on back later."

"We. How nice."

"Ever in my mind if not in my bed."

"What do you think it means?"

"What do *you* think it means?"

"Your legwork entitles you to the first guess."

"The usual. John Ford has something to hide, or why else would he be hiding?"

"Before you propose an APB—maybe Ford did that miracle of miracles . . . checked out."

"Right now he doesn't check out with me."

"Why aren't I surprised?"

"Because you don't want to be?"

The voice on the desk intercom interrupted them.

"Pete, you there?"

It was Heintzelman, summoning him to the chief's office, in a voice that always managed to sound like fingernails sliding down a blackboard. He talked back to the box. Heintzelman had not mentioned Annie.

"Only you. The boss was specific."

Annie didn't know what to make of it either.

"I'll let you know when I get back," Peter said.

"It'll be your turn, anyway," she said.

Assistant Chief Russell Spence's office was neat and efficient. Besides the usual personal artifacts, family photos, plaques and commendations, the walls were a lake of mounted fish, and Peter was still checking them out when he learned someone else was in the room with them.

Around the plant, it was said the chief had caught more fish than desperadoes in his thirty-one years with the force. Some believed Chief Spence resembled a fish. Peter saw him as more lupine, although he did have lips that always looked like they were whistling.

Spence was Peter's idea of a damn good cop, one who didn't suffer fools who chose against the department in any public controversy, a loyalist even after twice losing out on bids for the chief's job. He had been a combat Marine, in a teenage recruit, out a lieutenant, stripes earned on a battle-field commission, and sustained an abiding respect for chain of command. And loyalty. He expected both in return from his men.

Spence was pacing back and forth behind his desk, which faced the entrance door, his jaw working hard over a wad of gum, his bald head playing bounce with the sunlight striking through the picture window he always kept open, like it was his main lifeline to a constant understanding of the passing scene, traffic and derelicts who camped on the lawns and pissed in the bushes of City Hall, directly across Los Angeles Street. His ingrown eyes moved from his wristwatch to Peter, suggesting the two minutes it took to arrive here was three minutes too long.

"You wanted to see me, boss?"

Spence replied with a disdainful look, never one to deal with the unnecessary. "Say hello to Walter Burkes," he said, indicating the conversation area on the right. Peter turned and saw Burkes sitting in the middle of the green Naugahyde couch like he owned it, arms stretched out along the back, smiling on automatic pilot. "Mr. Burkes is here in town from Washington on that phony priest business. He's TRIAD, part of the Secret Service. Walter Burkes, say hello to Peter Osborne."

Burkes waved like he was shaking his fingers dry, held out his hand. Peter rated the handshake a showboat ten, and took one of three matching armchairs around a metal and glass table.

Two groomed stacks of magazines bookended a deep, help-yourself ceramic bowl full of Mounds, Almond Joy, Butterfinger and Milky Way miniatures, on hand since the boss quit smoking and began putting on the weight, maybe forty pounds in less than six months.

"The Not-So-Secret Service, truth be known. My pleasure, Detective Osborne."

"Peter's fine."

"Peter it is, and still a pleasure. I also had the pleasure of meeting your father, Judge Osborne, earlier today. He's quite a respected gent where I come from."

"Where I come from, too," Peter replied, at once curious.

Burkes rubbed the side of his nose, giving away nothing with his face, and peered over his half-moon glasses like he was inventing his impression of the judge's son. He had one of those faces people describe as "lived in." It seemed to hang from his skull from the high yield of black hair he wore slicked straight back, Brando-fashion. His gabardine suit was in dire need of dry cleaning.

"Where I come from, too," he repeated Peter's words. Burkes clearly liked the sentiment.

The boss called over to him, "Maybe you can start covering ground, Burkes? Don't mean to rush, but I can only be so late picking up the chief for his Wednesday Downtown Rotary." He came around the desk and plopped into an armchair, urging Burkes to try a Butterfinger while snatching an Almond Joy for himself. He attacked the wrapper like a man who had eaten one Rotary lunch too many.

Burkes obliged Spence, but he only examined the candy wrapper, adjusting his glasses to get a better fix on the list of ingredients. "I know what that can be like," he told the chief, and nodded at Peter. His voice was guttural and resonant. "Peter, I've already laid in the usual disclaimer with Chief Spence. What we're talking about is priority stuff. I only just got a special clearance upgrade from Uncle to enlarge the picture for you."

Burkes waited to be sure Peter understood.

The boss said, "No disrespect, Burkes, but we all seen the movie before."

Burkes weighed the comment, pocketed the Butterfinger and went for a Mounds.

"First some background, and I apologize for repeating myself, Chief Spence, but you know already how important it is we understand about this thing." The boss accepted the observation. "Peter, for years there's an Irish faction been operating a shuttle service down into the States from Canada."

"The I.R.A."

Burkes shook his head. "The IRS for all we know. Actually, it's a Sinn Fein splinter group, running on its own. Out of control most of the time. Even now, with the cease fire and all. Like most splinters, this one can be as painful as hell until you pull it out."

Chief Spence's spit-shine was wagging impatiently on the shag carpet. He started on another Almond Joy.

"Generally, the shuttle is used for the ones who get a little too hot for the old sod and are close to being cuffed by the Brits. Maybe, a courier who's been made, or, a bully boy who's been ID'd once too often. Maybe, somebody really dangerous, with one bomb or one massacre too many on their score sheet. Like that.

"The shuttle service scores them a new identity and sets them up in a safe house environment, then looks after them. In many respects like our own Witness Protection Program—but with a twist . . ."

Peter guessed where Burkes was heading. "This is about the priest?"

Burkes staved him off with an open palm, and rubbed the side of his nose again.

The boss checked his watch.

"Hear me out," Burkes said. "Most of the problem retreads are bagged by us and sent back within a matter of months. We have gotten damn good at it. Some of the minor leaguers—we use them to help lead us to the ones the Brits really care about. Bringing us to—"

"The priest," Peter said again.

"Pete, for Christ's sake, stop interrupting," the boss said impatiently.

"Father Daniel Patrick Xavier Shanley. AKA Preston Donahue. One of the worst of the lot, Peter. The kind who kills for a paycheck. A real cold-blooded bastard. However, there was no reason for Preston Donahue to be shuttled. Donahue was hot, but he also was invisible. Been a lot of years since the Brits had a Clue One to finding him."

"No reason for him to be shuttled unless there was something going on that called for his unique talents."

Burkes rewarded Peter with silent applause.

This was new territory for the boss, who wondered, "The broad who offed him—Are you saying she was one of yours?"

"No, Chief Spence. The killer of Preston Donahue was one of theirs."

Peter watched Spence arch back in his chair, equally surprised.

A grin slithered up one side of Burkes' face, exposing irregular, yellowed teeth. "We don't get to kill them. We're the good guys, remember?"

The boss waved him off. "Yeah, and I'm Charles Keating and you just won a free ride on my yacht, the *S.S. Fuck You, Too.*"

"Mr. Burkes, why would they go to all the trouble of shuttling Donahue down here just to kill him?"

"I could be cute and say, because they didn't want to kill him up there," Burkes said, adding the Mounds mini to his pocket and reaching for a Milky Way. He brought the tiny candy bar eyes-high and played with his glasses. "The truth of it is, Peter? We're hoping you'll help us find out the truth from an old friend of yours, Mrs. Frank McClory. Katherine Mary Cassidy."

"KC? You're saying KC is a terrorist?"

"I'm saying she's one of them," Burkes said.

Burkes saw the detective's eyes snap in the fraction of a second before he shot back, "Just because her husband was a terrorist doesn't make KC a terrorist, Mr. Burkes."

"It doesn't make her Joan of Arc, either," Burkes said, satisfied by Peter Osborne's belligerent tone that he was still tied to her emotionally. It was what he needed reconfirmed before pulling the kid into the action.

"You're accusing KC of murder."

"In a manner of speaking."

"What other interpretation is there?"

"I'm not accusing her of anything. I'm telling you point blank. KC McClory shot and killed a dirt-bag named Preston Donahue."

"Evidence?"

"Take my word for it."

"I don't know you well enough to take your word, and if I did, something tells me I probably wouldn't take it anyway."

Yeah, definitely. The kid still had the hots for her, all this time after he dumped on her and made it possible for the service to turn KC into a Grade A spy. No reason for him to know that part, though.

It was going to become Peter's job to see if the Thirty Two had turned KC around again, the way Burkes had sensed for months. Stronger this morning, hearing it was KC's idea to join the welcoming committee, not Judge Osborne's.

Even if he were only half right, it would help to tip off the truth about the bad guys' plan to terminate Mr. Mustamba.

"How about if I add *Scout's Honor?*" Peter didn't laugh. The line usually won him a laugh or at the least a teensy smile. "Okay, so you got me there. I was never a Boy Scout." Burkes dropped his hand from the oath. "If I swear on my mother's grave, any better?" The look. "Okay, there, too. Mom's still alive and kicking, soon to celebrate her seventy-fifth birthday and making it regular with a Brazilian who has the worst set of false chops I have ever seen. Interprets romance languages for the United Nations." Burkes' nose was itching ferociously again.

"For Christ's sake, Burkes. Climb down from your family tree and tell Pete what you got in mind," Spence said, eying his watch. He shot a nervous glance at the old-style phone. Red. No dial. Incoming only. Just then it rang. Spence frowned the color of gas. "*El Jefe.* He hates like hell to be kept waiting, like Rotary's up there with busting O.J. Simpson or the Menendez boys."

"That streak of sarcasm still runs through you, doesn't it, Spence?"

"Like the San Andreas Fault, Burkes."

"No fault of mine, I'm only a tourist," he shot back, raising his hands in surrender.

"Peter's also got a stupid sense of humor, so the two of you should get along just peachy without me."

"Aren't you afraid you'll miss something exciting?"

"Not as long as I know it's you doing the talking. Feel free to use the office long as you like."

"Better idea." He turned back to Peter, who seemed to be wrestling with the last word on KC. "What say to us grabbing some lunch? A place I hit whenever I'm out here. Not so far away."

"Mr. Burkes, what if I said there was an eyeball witness

good enough to prove KC was never in position to kill Donahue on that train?"

"It sure would help spice up lunch," Burkes said, lifting his eyebrows, acting like he didn't know what Peter meant.

Depending on how lunch went, maybe he'd tell Peter about Liam McClory.

CHAPTER 23

About a half hour later, they were eating curbside burritos at Mission Plaza Park, across from the Old Plaza Church, the city's first church, erected when "downtown" was all there was of Los Angeles and, Burkes was saying, the majority of the jackasses still walked on four legs.

Peter's mistrust of Burkes was still growing, for the best and worst of reasons:

Burkes tried too hard to be liked.

Those were the people who had to be watched most carefully, the ones who tried too hard.

Peter had done most of the talking so far. Burkes had done all the jokes. He didn't tell them well, and only once did Peter get the idea there was a person who lived inside the iceberg, when Burkes talked about his pet dog needing surgery.

Peter had a dog once, but only for as long as it took the judge to decide Sherlock's barking upset the household. It never occurred to the judge how sending his collie away upset Peter, but, at least, he didn't play favorites that time. None of the kids ever got to keep a dog, except the time Cookie fell in love with a stray pooch that wandered into the yard. That lasted a couple weeks, until an ad the judge ran in the local newspaper turned up the owners, and that was goodbye to Madonna. Cookie cried for a week afterward, but the judge stayed firm on the no-pets rule. No way to argue him out of it. Never a way to ever argue the judge out of anything.

Somehow, his one remark back at the boss' office, encouraged by Burkes, had turned him into a waterfall of admission. He told Burkes about KC and John Ford and how Ford was tracked to a motel, where he corroborated KC's story, explaining how she'd slept away the murder night on his shoulder. Peter gave the credit to Annie. She'd done the work and, besides, he wanted Burkes to understand more than Peter's word was on the line here.

"John Ford, huh? What's he look like?"

"Like a voice in your ear. We haven't made eyeball contact yet."

"I'd think that's the next step."

"We're on it now."

"But not yet?"

What did Burkes think he knew? Peter shrugged and bit into his burrito.

"Okay, let us say I buy everything you tell me," Burkes said, addressing Peter with one of those looks that's supposed to mean, I have given what you said a lot of respectful consideration. He swiped at an invisible fly on his nose. "Tell me what else you know."

"I beg your pardon?"

"The part you're holding back."

"I think I take offense at that, Mr. Burkes."

"It's the truth, isn't it? Look, Peter, don't hold it against me that I know my business well enough to know when someone is building me a home and at the same time shorting me bricks. I also think I know why. You once had a thing for the young lady, and it's still there?"

Peter took a deep breath. He did not want to lose his temper, especially since what Burkes was saying was true. "More than a guess?"

Burkes made a chalk mark in the air. "From some of the remarks I happened to overhear at your house this morning, meeting with the judge and his committee. Mrs. Weitzman. You know her?"

The second time Burkes had mentioned being with the judge, but no details. Peter decided to hold off asking the question. Let it play out naturally, like whatever else Burkes was holding face down. "I know Mrs. Weitzman, but not as well as Mrs. Weitzman would like."

"And here I thought it was just me and my raffish charms . . . Anyway, she kind of spilled the beans, saying how she wouldn't be surprised to see you and KC putting some new coals in the fire now that KC's back."

"I don't think so. It's ancient history as far as KC is—"

"But you wish it was otherwise."

He thought about lying, but recognized Burkes wouldn't go for it. "If wishes were roses, I'd have OD'd on my allergies a long time ago."

"Know what you mean." Scratched his nose. "Then, you really have no reason to hold out on me, do you?"

What the hell. Not much of a secret, anyway. It had to come out eventually. Burkes had more than gossip on his mind, maybe the whole truth would work for both of them.

Peter described how Annie went hunting at the motel and found no sign of a John Ford. Before Burkes had a chance to digest the information, he backtracked to last night at dinner and KC's call from John Ford.

Burkes sent him curious looks, but showed no surprise. His voice stretched words to compound his disbelief. "This guy is a total stranger conveniently on the train to provide her an alibi and then he turns up on the phone? Give me a break!"

"Give me a break! KC always made friends easily. It's possible she welcomed the company of an Irishman who reminded her of her home these past six years, and she gave Ford her number and invited him to call."

"And it's possible these burritos bite back, only they don't."

"Kindness to strangers . . . Have you ever been there, done that, Mr. Burkes? I have."

"You probably own all the merit badges . . . Peter, you genuinely believe what you're telling me?"

In fact, Peter was trying not to let Burkes see how tough it was believing himself.

Burkes said, "You're a detective, high up on Russ Spence's list, so I know what you did when you got the drift last night it was John Ford calling. You told her what you knew and pumped her about their conversation. What'd KC have to say, exactly, Peter? Tell me."

Peter wanted to kick himself. Instead of defending her, he was dragging KC nearer to the center of the spotlight.

Burkes made a satisfied grunt and, not waiting for him to answer, said, "Suppose you're right. How'd you like an opportunity to prove KC didn't terminate Donahue and that we owe her an apology?"

"She's not capable of it. I know her and—"

"That's why your government needs you."

The man was relentless. "Meaning what, exactly?"

"Exactly what it sounds like."

Burkes signaled the stooped, white-haired vendor for another burrito, and the old man obliged. He was wearing a sombrero and colorful serape meant to attract the small groups of camera-toting turistas. Burkes made a point of aiming his face to the sidewalk, too casual to be accidental.

He took his change and dropped two quarters in the tip cup, motioning for Peter to follow him to one of the park benches. He walked with his shoulders arched and in forward motion, arms swinging, legs jaunty and bouncing. Like all of them, the bench was chained to the ground, empty except for a street woman watching life go by without her.

Peter waited him out, almost afraid of the latest look on

Burkes' face. He was still on his first burrito and chewed in neutral, still trying to sort the truth from his emotions and not doing a very good job of it.

Burkes appeared to understand and for the moment was satisfied devouring his burrito. He wiped his mouth with his hand, squeezed the wax paper into a ball and tossed it into the trash can a couple feet away.

"I need you to get on her good side, Peter. Make friends again. You were as close as they come before, so you have less distance to go than someone else I could find, only that person doesn't exist. If he did, we might not be here enjoying each other's company." Burkes saw he wanted to speak and gestured for him to wait. "Work at it no matter how KC puts you off. Wear her down. Win her over. Then, when you're finally as close to her as a doughnut gets to the hole, you find out some things for us."

"You want me to lie to her." His legs had started to tremble and he felt a slight give at the knees. His lies had ruined it for them the first time and, on top of his promise never to let it happen again—

Burkes said, "I want you to keep telling the truth to yourself and chasing after that truth like it was a pot of gold at the end of the rainbow."

"You're saying I can screw her for my fun and your profit?" Peter felt his face flush and his free hand tightening into a fist. He jammed it into a pocket, for protection from himself and what he could do to Burkes. He pushed out a breath and said, "I don't think so. No."

"Not an appropriate answer, Peter."

"My answer."

Burkes dropped his voice. "Peter, take as a given that there was nothing accidental about her and John Ford coming down together on the same Amtrak as that son-of-a-bitch Donahue. We have to find out what Mrs. McClory knew about Donahue and how she came to know it. Help us find out how KC fits and we find out what those sons-of-bitches are up to. Plain and simple, and a promotion in it for you, a bounce to lieutenant you do the dance our way. My guarantee is also guaranteed by Russ Spence."

"Fuck you, Burkes."

Burkes fetched an Almond Joy miniature from his pocket. He wadded the wrapper, pitched and scowled at missing the can, then made a show of fishing out the nut with his teeth.

"Peter, you got a real way with words, but they're not the ones I want to hear." His expression suggested the fate of the world rested on Peter Osborne's reply.

The street woman's elbow slipped off the arm rest. Her head snapped. She jumped to her feet. She had been asleep with her eyes open. She made a face at them that said she was fussy about the company she kept, fiddled with the hem and collar of her flak jacket and wandered off. Burkes rose and seemed to follow her. Only as far as the popcorn stand. He was back in a minute, chewing on a mouth stuffed with kernels, and tossed some to the pigeons working the scruffy lawn around them.

Peter broke the silence. "So, you're asking me to seduce KC in the name of Uncle. Is that how things like the Serbs and Bosnians get going, Burkes?"

"The Berlin Wall, too. Listen, Peter, let me get closer to home plate with you. Mrs. McClory was sent over here for a reason definitely not in the best interests of your government."

"You mean taking down the priest?" He wasn't going to let Burkes get away with more non-specifics.

Burkes' eyes drifted away to the pigeons feasting on his

popcorn. "Sure, if that's what it takes to win your cooperation." He offered the popcorn box to Peter.

"What about Mildred O'Malley?"

"What about her?"

"It was her sleeping compartment."

Burkes shrugged. "Maybe Mildred O'Malley is off being friendly with John Ford. When it gets to be the right time, ask Mrs. McClory."

"How about more than that, Burkes? How about a shred of evidence?" He aimed kernels at the pigeons. Their number had doubled. "Explain to me how a train porter who eyeballed the killer and had a chance to make KC on a nose-to-nose didn't know her."

Burkes unwrapped a Milky Way. "Pullman Anderson was distracted by the freckles on the killer's tits." He paused for effect, like a standup comic, only Peter saw he wasn't joking. "He told my people that, Peter. Some gents, when they see a naked lady standing in an open doorway of a moving train, do not necessarily *ever* get to the face. Especially with someone as attractive and let me say as *constructed* as Mrs. McClory . . . Does Mrs. McClory have freckles on her tits?"

Peter reacted angrily. He gave Burkes the Italian salute. He pounded his fist inside his elbow and, as his arm rose reflexively, the popcorn shot from the box and landed on the lawn beyond them.

The flustered pigeons flapped and made tracks. Burkes was unflappable.

He waited a reasonable amount of time, using the time to shove a Snickers into his mouth, feigned interest while Peter told him what he thought, then offered him a Mounds and finished the candy bar without considering what Peter promptly suggested he could do with it.

He said, "You know about Mr. Mustamba's visit?" Peter

217

considered the question, shrugged *So what*. "Not just to L.A., but to your folks' place in Pasadena?"

"Annie, my partner, we were assigned to a special protection detail—" Suddenly, it was like reaching the clearing on the far side of the woods. "You knew that already."

Burkes resisted a grin. He held out his palms and rocked his head, his eyes fixed on Peter. "So, this morning I go on over to talk details with your father and his committee on an upset stomach, when in waltzes KC. Next thing I know, Judge Osborne is wondering at me if she can be part of the festivities, help with the party—"

Peter motioned stop. "That's what this is all about. The Mustamba visit." Burkes nodded. Peter felt good for the guess. "What about Mustamba?"

"I can't tell you that, Peter. Maybe KC can."

A cold front seemed to emerge from nowhere. It clawed through the dense, smog-rich air, burrowed into his chest, found his spine and ran in two directions at once. "Jesus! Mustamba."

"Zero in on KC. Make like old times. Play pattycake or whatever. Find out for us. Okay?" Lie to her, he meant. At the same time, risk winning her back and losing her again. "Okay, Peter?"

Burkes insisted he couldn't tell Annie anything, and Peter knew that wouldn't sit well with her when he got back to the office.

Need to know.

That's what keeps the "Secret" in the "Service," Burkes said. When people only know what they absolutely must know about a mission, it's cleaner and safer, and at this time there was absolutely no reason for Annie to know more than she already did.

Peter argued that he and Annie were partners—partners—so it did make sense.

Burkes wouldn't budge on the point.

Need to know.

He was feeling guilty as hell as he settled behind his desk, thinking, Thanks a lot, Burkes. I have to lie to KC and, at the same time, I can't tell the truth to Annie. Where, precisely, does that put me with me? It puts you sucking hind tit is where it usually puts you, Peter. No, damn it, where you put yourself.

Some day you'll have to stand up to the tyranny of life and declare yourself free. Do what you want to do for yourself. Turning into a detective was an act of defiance. Turning into a man, what's that an act of? Not an act, Peter. A giant leap of faith by the who of what you really are. When will you be ready to make that jump? Ever? Especially, without the hoops others put in the way?

Annie was working at her desk monitor. She turned to look at him, leaned back in her chair, crossed her arms expectantly. When she understood she was getting only a hand sign from him, she rocked forward, planted her elbows on the desk and clasped her hands in front of her face.

"Nice lunch?"

"Uh-huh."

"Long, too. Longies twice in a row. Anybody I know?"

"Unh-unh." He scribbled something on the tracking sheet of the top folder on the pile, to look busy. Put the folder in the holding bin between the In and Out bins. Opened the next folder on the pile.

Annie said, "Heintzelman told me he was a government guy."

"Shouldn't have."

"Anything to do with something?"

"Yeah."

"Anything you'd care to volunteer?"

"The boss is on my case, Annie. I don't get through this shit pile, we're both gonna be wallowing in it, okay?"

"Sure." She lit up and checked her coffee mug. He had given it to her last year for Christmas, a naked woman on Santa's lap, Santa in a stocking cap, jingle bells on his erect dork, telling the woman, *Certainly, little girl, but why don't we try it first without your two front teeth?* She wondered. "Coffee?"

Peter checked his mug. Maybe three-quarters full. Cold. Powdered milk coagulated on top. Strong enough to dissolve a spoon. "Thanks."

Annie moved her smoke from the edge of the desk, where it had started to nip at the wood, tucked it in a corner of her mouth and got up, her coffee mug in her left hand. With her free hand, she leaned over and got Peter's mug.

Peter acknowledged her smile, turned back to his files and in the same instant knew he'd blundered.

He couldn't move fast enough to duck the coffee Annie was pouring onto his head.

He rose from his chair like an indignant emperor, the coffee trails covering his face, raining on the shoulders of his jacket, staining his shirt.

He dragged Annie downstairs to the locker room, demanded she wait for him while he cleaned up.

Then, he told her about his conversation with Walter Burkes.

Everything.

All of it.

Apologized for ever agreeing to hold back on her.

Annie listened hard and when he'd finished, said, "Fuck that asshole and his need to know."

"Burkes is too cunning to be an asshole, Annie, trust me on that."

"I trust you on everything, including my face."

"Annie!"

"Okay, okay. You know I hate it somebody tries to shut me out of the loop because of being a woman."

"I don't think there's anything sexist. Burkes is playing it tight. You can't fault him for that."

"I didn't say *fault* him. I said *fuck* him."

"Annie, please."

"So, why'd you change your mind and tell me?"

He shrugged and gave her the kind of smile politicians used to get elected. "When this is over and Walter Burkes is gone, I'll still be stuck with you."

"Makes sense to me. Anything you've left out?"

He nodded. Bought a moment by clearing his throat.

She pretended not to notice how sheepish he felt while telling her about the phone call KC had received last night from John Ford. If she was gloating over how much closer she was to the truth about KC than he, she gave no outward sign. He could have hugged her for that act of kindness.

Annie said, "I see your wheels still turning. What's Plan A?"

"Burkes' best guess, and mine, too—Ford and KC will hook up soon. I'd like us to be ready for it."

"Mr. Inside and Ms. Outside."

"Nice weather for a stakeout."

"And, I suppose you think we should start tonight?"

"No time like the present."

She looked at her watch. "You think we could delay it long enough for you and me to step into a stall?"

He recognized the animal sound slipping into her voice. Annie wasn't kidding. He removed her hand, which had inched onto his crotch, and said, "I'll owe you one."

"But not that one, okay?" she said. "I'd like to see something in a larger model."

Peter moved his fingers onto her lips. She nibbled at them as he said, "I don't want you doing anything dumb. Just play tag. Keep the lengths, stay the distance and don't force anything."

Annie peeled off his fingers, gave him her version of innocence. "You ever know me to do anything stupid?"

"Yes."

"I mean in the line of duty."

"So do I. You want a few recent examples?"

"I want you."

Before he could move, she pressed her body against his, worked it like sandpaper and with her lips locked out any chance of him protesting.

She marched him backward into a stall, reached back and flipped the latch-lock.

"Not a good idea, Annie. Not now."

"If all I have to look forward to later is a Big Mac and stale coffee in the front seat of an unmarked, it's a great idea," she said.

Even before they were done, Peter was telling himself once more it had never been this good with KC. Telling himself why. More than passion was at play here, although he still was not ready to give it a name.

"Damn you," Annie screamed. Again, before her words dribbled off into a series of moans.

CHAPTER 24

KC recognized that whatever Peter thought he knew covered his face like a bad tan. When he started pushing too hard at the dinner table to let him drive her to her "date" with John Ford, she had no time to measure the right or wrong of her decision to contact Liam and let him know to get ready for unwelcome company. She would have to make an excuse to get Liam alone, give him the parts of the story she'd just invented with glib expediency. Trust Liam not to blunder out the truth to Peter.

Not that she had been so smart herself coming down for dinner wearing a red rose from the lavish bouquet she found outside her bedroom door an hour ago. A peace offering from Peter, whose careful printing on the card apologized cutely and begged her for a fresh start at being friends.

At first, Peter's message blinded her to his studied casualness.

So did his compliments at the dinner table. She let him see she was forgiving him and, as she fussed with the barrette that held the rose above her left ear, he made some of his old jokes about her pony tail. The conversation over Aunt Dorothy's baked ham and trimmings seemed the most relaxed and amiable since her arrival, until she asked about borrowing a car for a couple hours.

The judge groaned something about heading off for a special meeting with Mayor Isaacs. Dorothy explained she was due to join her lady friends at the movies and suggested Peter might take KC wherever she was going, like it was sudden inspiration. The darling playing at matchmaker again?

"Sure," Peter said, too fast. "Not out of my way at all."

KC squeezed on one of her cute faces. "I haven't said where I'm going."

"That's why," he said, brightly. "Wherever, it has to beat sitting with a bad book and worse television."

"I'll go along with television, but no such thing as a bad book," the judge said.

"Your Honor, you'd change your mind if you read a few instead of just collecting them." Peter grinned around the table, pausing to look at her too anxiously.

KC pretended to weigh the idea. "Actually, I have a date, so—"

"A date?" Aunt Dorothy sounded disappointed, maybe concerned about the propriety of a widow dating so soon after—

"Really none of our business," the judge said.

KC sent him a smile and said, "More like a meeting, I suppose."

Dorothy looked relieved.

Peter said, "What do they call a date that's more like a meeting? A rendezvous?"

"A rendezvous, then."

"Anybody I don't know?"

The way he prolonged their banter told her Peter wasn't going to let up without more details. Finally, she said, "John Ford." Telling the truth struck her as a safer course than falling into a new bundle of lies. "Remember?"

"How could I forget?" Peter said.

The judge said, "He was the gent who called last night," and searched the table for agreement.

Cookie made one of her yuck faces.

"That's right, Uncle Judge. He called to say he was going home to Vancouver tomorrow and suggested we get together for a beer—"

"Not a beer, a rendezvous," Peter reminded her, his look turning intense. "Pretty forward for a stranger you meet on a train, no?"

She waved him off and explained to Noah, "We sat next to each other on the ride down. Turned out he was from the same neighborhood back in Belfast. Falls Road. Turned out I knew him."

"What a small world," Peter said with too much wonderment. "You didn't mention that over lunch."

"I didn't get the impression that it mattered," she said indifferently, sure the answer wouldn't satisfy Peter, but it would have to do for now.

He weighed the response and shook his head. "To my partner more than me," he said, giving in too easily.

Cookie eyed her suspiciously.

KC said, "I recognized the name, but there are so many Jack Fords . . . Then, I realized it was his face. Not really disfigured, sort of the end of a horrible accident. I didn't recognize him because it was years ago he left. An accident in the shipyard, the foundry. Why he left, to leave the past behind, he said. Start a new life for himself in Canada." Aunt Dorothy clutched a hand to her breast, the way she often did while watching her soaps on TV. "I even know his Mum. Mrs. Ford lived down the row from us. A dear and gentle little soul who loved Frankie and was always very kind to me."

"He didn't recognize you?"

"I asked why he waited for me to say something first, Peter. Jack said he knew it was me, but wasn't sure he wanted me to know it was him. Then he figured, *Wait a minute, this is Katie from the old neighborhood.* He said he'd heard about Frankie and it was only proper he identify himself and express his condolences."

"Damned proper of him," Peter said. "I wish you'd told this to Annie."

"I know, but she'd made me almost too angry to talk. I decided, let her find out for herself." She leveled him with a innocent look. "I meant to explain it to you after she left, but we got talking about other things, and—"

He spread a smile. "No big deal. I'd like to meet him, though. Say hello to John Ford—"

"No, I don't think—"

"Maybe ask a few questions . . . Think about it, KC. I'll be able to tell Annie I met him and got backup on your story first-hand."

Peter riveted her with his eyes, and she answered with a why-not gesture, knowing she had no choice.

She excused herself upstairs for a quick pee and her jacket, took the phone into the bathroom and chanced it that nobody would eavesdrop on her this time.

CHAPTER 25

Heading for the car, Peter wondered if he'd made the right decision, given anything away by imposing himself on KC. After all, Annie was sitting stakeout on the street outside the house, so it wasn't as if they'd not know where KC went if he'd simply handed her the keys to his Trans Am and let her slip off to meet Ford.

He had used that possibility with Burkes as another argument for involving Annie.

Burkes had argued back that a shadow wasn't necessary, because he already had the situation covered.

He wouldn't go into details, though.

This oh-so-secret guy.

So, Annie outside became his own secret.

Peter opened the passenger door and helped KC slide in.

Gunned the motor and eased the car into gear, for better or for worse.

Noticed her knitting her hands apprehensively, like she was already trying to figure how she'd explain him to John Ford.

Annie kept a discreet distance as Peter played the freeways for most of the trip to the beach, catching the Ventura from the Foothill and then onto the San Diego, exiting at Olympic for a straight run west to Santa Monica.

He turned the Am north onto a commercial street about a mile short of Pacific Coast Highway and three blocks later glided a left into a cramped parking lot behind a chain link fence, adjacent to a disheveled brick building painted in early graffiti.

No effort had been made to clean up the façade or to fix the small, flickering neon sign over the entrance that once identified the pub as "The Quiet Man" and now said "The Qui t Ma ." The sign gave Annie the only laugh she had had since picking up Peter's brake lights, before he charged through the front gate with KC in the passenger seat.

Her unmarked loaner, a red Camaro, was an overnighter borrowed from Saunders in Transportation, who didn't believe her story about not having time to get the requisition countersigned, but he owed her on past favors, and waved her off before she could remind him.

The Camaro lacked most of the usual cop trimmings. It was a clunker whose parts were routinely rescued for use in the newer models. The lock box in the trunk had a two-way radio and a small arms cache, a spare set of cuffs, a Buck Rogers stingray and a plastic soda bottle being used by somebody to cache cheap bourbon.

Annie kept a safe distance, never getting closer than ten car lengths, and regularly switched lanes. She almost lost them to a stop light on Olympic, just past Centinela, when Peter breezed through on a yellow and she was locked behind a trailer and a major asshole in a Rolls Royce, who couldn't find his way out of first gear.

She rolled forward past the all-night diner across from The Quiet Man and cut the headlights before pulling a U-turn and sliding into a parking spot curbside, away from the glare of the lamp post by the entrance to the lot, one of a few that had not been shot out or broken by a well-aimed rock. There were plenty.

Most of the cars on the street were late model wrecks wearing a boot or upscale cars gathering dust. Annie wondered how many had been abandoned, stolen or left by owners courting theft, trying to get a leg up on their insurance policies.

She cut the motor.

Exhaled into the calm night air.

Ground out her smoke.

Shoved herself down behind the wheel.

Peter and KC were just stepping onto the sidewalk.

He was wearing an old pair of faded denims and a multi-colored pullover with a pull-up collar and looked underdressed next to her, although both of them looked over-dressed for a place like The Quiet Man. KC had on a short kelly green knit skirt and matching jacket. Large white button earrings and matched plastic slave bracelets on her wrists.

Peter paused and pointed to the rose in her hair. He said something to make her smile. She fiddled with the flower. He laughed, bowed from the waist and ushered her ahead. His laughter traveling up the street was the only sound, except for a rumble Annie identified as the ocean getting comfortable for the night.

She made a note of the time after they entered the pub and reminded herself this was official business and she was not to be jealous. She called herself a liar. Fired up a fresh Camel. Wondered if Peter ever would laugh with her the way he just did for KC.

Annie ran her tongue around her lips, trying to taste the sensation of their making love and how Peter could arouse all her senses, even the ones she thought were stripped from her by the rapists and every other rodent who ever took her soul.

She wondered why she loved him as much, Peter, and the answer came back one more time—

Because he doesn't want you, girl.

Stupid, huh? He doesn't want you, so you want him.

The ones who hurt you the most, they wanted you.

Peter doesn't want you, so he can't hurt you.

Then, why does it hurt so much not having him, and watching him carry on over some relic from his past who dumped on him once and will probably dump on him again, if she gets the chance before the evidence accumulates to confirm it was KC who hauled off and murdered the priest?

Okay, so he was really a lowlife assassin, the priest, what Peter was told by that fuck Burkes and what Peter told her.

What did that make KC McClory?

KC was still a killer, no matter what the priest was, or who, and it didn't end there.

Annie was being killed by her, too.

Every time KC moved close to Peter, Annie died another inch.

Is Peter really worth the suffering, girl? Fuck shit no.

But he doesn't want me. Peter doesn't want me.

And, I need him so.

That's why.

And, she blew smoke and waited in the pale light outside the bar.

CHAPTER 26

Entering The Quiet Man from relative darkness, it took a minute for Peter to adjust to the subdued lighting in a room about the size of his parents' bedroom suite and figure about sixty to eighty people were sardine-packed inside. The conversations were loud and non-stop, competed with a TV set angled on a shelf alongside the bar, an old Seeburg jukebox and frequent roars from rowdy patrons playing darts. The decor was pure Irish, the air full of boozy nuance. A lethal tobacco mist long ago had given the pub's painted walls a coat of dusty brown and yellow thick enough to scribble messages on.

Peter tasted it on his lips and his eyes watered. He was wondering how long before the meandering crud would eat past his clothing and into his skin when KC gave his arm a *stay put* squeeze and needled a path to the bar, searching faces en route.

She put a question to a chicken-necked bartender from Central Casting, who scratched his cheek and shook his bald head.

They had a brief exchange before she motioned for Peter to join her. He crowded in alongside. A warm Guinness was waiting for him in a slender glass bearing lipstick traces from earlier use. KC was drinking Harp, also from a glass.

"What we drink back home," she said, speaking to be heard over the crowd. She toasted him. Their glasses clinked, and he mouthed, "John Ford?" She shook her head and again made herself understood. "We're early." Peter nodded.

The dark, intense man sitting on the stool beside KC stopped mumbling to himself. A half a dozen shot glasses were lined up in front of him, all but one empty, backed by six water glasses, all filled to the brim. His hand shook lifting the live shooter to eye level.

He investigated its caramel color like it was for the first time. Tilted back his head and swallowed so hard he toppled backward from the stool, into the arms of a blue-haired, pug-nosed woman in her sixties, who needed to lose three or four hundred pounds.

The woman sputtered profanities while tightening her grip on the man, and spirited him away.

Peter helped KC ease onto the stool and turned with his back to the bar, so he could pulse the crowd while they waited. KC seemed satisfied to use the bar mirror as a window, rapping out a nervous melody on the varnished surface with the fingers of both hands. He could not recall seeing her this nervous.

She must have noticed him staring.

She reached over and gave him a friendly set of knuckles on the shoulder, a signal from the old days that showed she knew his thoughts.

Tonight, she was half right and he didn't want to guess how she'd take knowing the other half. In his worst moments since giving in to Burkes, Peter dreaded discovering that everything Burkes had confided about KC was true. In his best moments, too.

He double-gulped the Guinness. Decided it must be what stale whale piss tasted like. Set down the glass. His eyes wandered across the room to the billiards area, carved out of a tight space between the entrance and the dance floor. Two tables. Both occupied.

Peter realized he was being examined by one of the players, who picked this moment to signal a time-out to his opponent, then handed over his cue stick to one of the kibitzers holding up the wall and headed over on a path that opened in front of him like a DeMille effect.

"A good evening to you," he called over the din, and extended his hand. "Can't keep track of me friends, but never trouble a-tall spotting the strangers. First time The Quiet Man?"

He was in his mid-thirties and small, hardly more than five one or two in his black patent leather pumps, wearing a suit that could have cost a thousand dollars, but looked cheap on him. There were half moon stains under his arms, from too much pool hustle or whatever cons kept his close-set eyes busy as a tap dance. Red hair, freckles, an overbite gone gray and in desperate need of a dentist. A smile certain as a light switch.

Peter freed his hand and held up one finger, to let him know he had guessed correctly. He glanced at KC, who barely shook her head to indicate this wasn't Ford. The bartender dropped off a Guinness Stout and hurried back to the other end of the long bar.

The small man took it as his due and held up the glass for inspection. "You might consider trying this your next," he said. "Not what it seems. Hold it up to the light, you'll see the ruby thread among the ebony. Cheers." He finished half the glass in a swallow, split a smile between Peter and KC and toweled his mouth with his free hand. "It takes your taste buds by storm, then lingers in the back your mouth like mother's milk." He looked over one shoulder, then the other, as if all the world was about to agree with him.

Turning to KC, he said, "Can tell at a glimpse you're a fair colleen. New to these parts?"

"Meeting someone."

"Lady friend?"

KC shook her head.

The small man acted surprised. He verified the information with a questioning squint at Peter that merged his heavy eyebrows and formed a hedge across a forehead that dominated his face. "The good man, he's late or you're early."

Peter decided the small man was courting them too hard. He didn't like it.

KC said, "John Ford."

Below a dominating forehead, the small man's eyebrows aimed for his widow's peak. "Funny joke, that, fit for The Quiet Man. So, if you're waiting for John Ford, I must be—"

"Barry Fitzgerald," Peter said, impatiently. He had had enough of him. He watched the ruse leave and return from the small man's eyes.

The small man peeled back his lips to show his irregular teeth and bit hard to abate his irritation.

He tugged at his cuffs, using the green agate links for handles.

Made a senseless gesture.

Made cynical noises meant to pass for chuckles.

Asked KC, "Does your friend what's here tell jokes for a living?"

She quickly covered for Peter. "It was a name we were trying to think of before we headed on over here," she said, politely, staring hard at the small man until he nodded agreement. He held the smile, but eyed Peter warily. "He's Peter Osborne. I'm Kate. Kate McClory."

The small man pushed back with a breast stroke to examine her.

Smiled generously.

Bowed courtly.

Doffed an invisible hat.

Announced, "Danaher's the name, and me father before me. Edward, but I go by Snuffy."

Snuffy Danaher moved forward. On what had to be an impulse, used his nicotine-stained index finger to tuck an escaped blonde strand over her ear, beneath the red rose. KC started at Danaher's sudden motion. At once, she acted a smile to offset any wrong impression and, Peter was sure, limit the embarrassment she blamed Danaher for causing.

Danaher wheeled around and signaled to a woman a few feet away. "May! May! Over here one minute." The woman waved back and moved toward them, walking like her body was about to fall apart.

Danaher said confidently, "She might know about your John Ford. May here knows everybody, going back some."

May towered over Danaher by a foot, but no one could ever mistake her for a high fashion model. She was too thin for that, a scramble of bones endangered by every movement. She wore a polka-dot-and-petunia tank dress that went out of style with Donny Osmond, and clay-stained sandals. Her hair was some off-brand of bottled auburn that seemed to remove what it didn't color, leaving her scalp with irregular patches of red-blotched, crusted skin.

"Give hello to Kate McClory, May," Danaher said, as if Peter weren't there, so he introduced himself.

She grunted at KC without looking at her and took his hand hungrily, massaged the middle of his palm with her middle finger. Peter struggled to get free, and she trapped his hand back. Squeezed hard as she could. Gave a look like she'd just been laid.

Peter coughed and cleared his throat. "We were asking about John Ford. Mrs. McClory is here to meet him, but he doesn't appear to be around."

"Ford. Know that name," May said, satisfied with herself. She exposed two even rows of teeth fresh off the cob for Peter, carrying on as if KC didn't matter. "Runty old guy with an eye patch. Come in here when I was a little girl. He made movies and treated me nice." Her voice was deep enough for two of her.

Danaher corrected her. "Not the one. That's the one what made a picture from *The Quiet Man* with our sainted John Wayne. The Duke!" He stared up at Peter. "And the likes of precious Barry Fitzgerald," he said, mocking him.

"I made a few quiet men in my time," May decided, and looked longingly at Peter. Mid-forties, he guessed. Maybe her IQ, too. Hard to be sure because a cosmetic ski mask supposed to hide the years didn't work, except to harden the resignation and defeat on her mouth and in eyes that delivered their own last rites. He smiled at her to be polite.

"The Duke!" Danaher said again, and raised his Guinness. "May our Lord rest his brave soul, him what certainly got past St. Peter and through the Pearlies long before the devil knew he was passed away."

The toast was loud and drew echoes of "The Duke" and an assortment of blessings from people within sound of Danaher's musical delivery.

May moved closer and gave Peter an alcohol rub with her breath, then backed him into the edge of the counter while applying pressure below the belt. Peter drew in his face. May pointed to his empty glass with spaghetti fingers whose digits seemed to be connected like pop beads. "If you aim for a refill, maybe could you manage one for your new friend, handsome?"

"Delighted," he said, using it as an excuse to turn a shoulder to May and steer her off.

He checked with KC, who capped her glass with a hand, signaled the bartender to bring two more. May shouted for her usual, and the refills arrived a minute later on top of a belligerent voice demanding, "What I tell you about drinks from strangers?"

It was the guy who had been shooting pool with Danaher. He had a tourniquet grip on May's arm, and Peter feared the next sound would be bone snapping.

She looked up at him and said, "Not any stranger 'n you, Mr. Dermot O'Dea." Her tone and her straight-mouthed manner daring him to take it farther.

Dermot O'Dea's eyes shifted to Peter, then back to her. "I warned you, May. Say I didn't warn you."

He had a full head on her, and was built like a muscle fortress. The white block lettering on his black tee shirt paid homage to Gold's Gym.

"Dermot, nothing to it," Danaher said. He stepped up to O'Dea and said, "Relax, boy-o. Go back to the game."

O'Dea looked at Danaher like he was deciphering his instruction. Next he looked at Peter, working on a decision, his bearded face a puzzle in violence. May was trying to peel his fingers off her arm. She turned a beet red when he let go.

"Better," Danaher said.

"All he did was offer me a drink," May said.

"What it was you offer him?" O'Dea wanted to know. A gallery of rubberneckers had formed. "Tell me that, Miss May High-and-Mighty Bleeding Lawless."

"Maybe something you've gone soft on?"

The wrong thing for her to say. The question was barely out of her troubled mouth when O'Dea cracked her cheek with the back of a hand.

May's head recoiled and her legs almost folded, but she managed to stay on her feet. Her eyes narrowed and she stuck out her jaw, like she was defying O'Dea to do it again, and massaged her arm where his fingerprints were still a bold white next to skin turning blue.

O'Dea made a fist and weighed it between them.

The crowd receded several feet.

"Enough, Dermot!" Danaher was tugging at his tee shirt. He turned to Peter. "Dermot, here. Mean when he's drinking and mean when he's not drinking."

May dared O'Dea again, then sidestepped to Peter and put an arm around his shoulder. Her eye would be glued shut and useless within the hour.

Peter noticed the blood filling crevices on that side of her mouth, the lips growing grotesque. He glimpsed KC. She was taut as a tightrope, uncertain what to do, and he waved her out of it.

Restoring peace was his own priority, or chance screwing up a line on John Ford.

"I'm really sorry about this," he told O'Dea. "I didn't mean any—"

"When did I tell you a question?"

"Look, Mr. O'Dea. I apologize for any misunderstanding. Let's have a drink on it, okay? My treat."

"Misunderstanding, says him. His treat." O'Dea explored the room, eyelids hanging heavy, a career bully making certain everybody had heard him.

The crowd shifted farther back, almost clearing the dance floor.

The juke box got louder, like somebody had pumped up the volume. "Bohemian Rhapsody." Queen.

Expectant faces cracked through the tobacco curtain, took up residence on Peter's corner of the world.

A curious look of precognition passed between Dermot O'Dea and May before O'Dea guided Danaher aside and closed in. He composed a rectangular frame with his fingers and held it between them, moving it in and out in front of his eyes.

Peter recognized the signs. He felt his muscles tense in anticipation of O'Dea's attack, stretched and exercised his fingers, wondered how much karate was required to halt a buffalo stampede. He returned O'Dea's oven baked stare and turned up the corners of his mouth, sending a message he wasn't afraid, wishing he'd packed tonight, so he could blow the woman-beating son-of-a-bitch a new belly button.

He gave it another try.

Held up his hands in surrender and said, "Look, I didn't come here to start trouble."

"Course you're not here to start trouble," O'Dea said, eyes flickering. "That's what I'm here for." And connected to Peter's face at the jaw line with a roundhouse wallop that exploded from nowhere.

The blow was too fast to dodge.

It momentarily paralyzed Peter.

He shook his head to clear his mind, hypnotized by the sight of O'Dea spitting in both his left hands and both his right hands. He couldn't raise his own in time to defend against the next slammer, an uppercut that landed squarely on his chin and propelled him backwards over the bar counter.

He hit the floor awkwardly, but alert enough to know better than to move, and took his own mandatory eight count. Struggling onto his knees, his hands sliding out of grips on the wet slats of the floorboard, he heard the crowd roar approval of O'Dea.

Peter spotted a waste bin under the sink for empty liquor bottles, crowns broken off to prevent reuse. A fast rummage. He pulled out the jagged stem from a bottle of Canadian Club, about five inches long. Got back on his feet cautiously. O'Dea was propped against the bar, arched back, relaxing on his elbows, playing hero to the crowd, his back to Peter.

"Dermot!" the bartender shouted from the far end of the bar.

Peter was faster than the warning.

Before O'Dea could react, he had O'Dea's throat wrapped in a choke hold and the broken glass pressed at his right temple.

A burst of noise from the customers.

"Fart funny and you lose an eye, mother fucker!" He felt O'Dea's neck muscles flex with tension. "You hear me you cock-sucker? One belch and you're a candidate for fucking Braille lessons, faggot!"

The customers, quiet now. Not a ripple of sound.

Someone shouted, "Man doesn't fight a fair fight!"

Peter sensed some of them were slipping out of the exit as fast as their fears could move them. "Are you listening, Mr. O'Dea?" he asked, easing the choke hold enough to let him answer, ready to rig it hard again if he felt stupidity.

"Hear you, Boss."

"Louder, Mr. O'Dea."

"Hear you, Boss."

"Loud enough for everyone to hear you, Mr. O'Dea."

"Hear you, Boss."

"Traveling with friends?" No answer. "I asked if you're traveling with friends?" He scratched enough to run a narrow thread of red from the corner of O'Dea's eye to the beard line. He'd cut deeper than intended, somewhere midway. A bubble emerged, popped, and slithered down into O'Dea's cheek. Not by the book, but it demonstrated he wasn't reciting fairytales. In life-threatening situations, better the other guy than him.

The customers inhaled a uniform gasp.

O'Dea hissed, "Behave, boy-o. A barber's switch, inside me left boot."

"Good. Mr. Danaher, would you kindly remove the blade from Mr. O'Dea's left boot and put it on the bar where I can

240

see it, away from his immediate reach . . . Mr. Danaher?"
Peter shifted his eyes. The space Danaher had occupied less
than three minutes ago was empty. So was the bar stool being
used by KC.

If they were there, they were out of his sight line.

"Snuffy up and left," somebody called from somewhere to
his left. Peter's sweat had found a route through his eyebrows
and was salting his vision. If adrenalin were oil, he'd be an
Arab sheik.

He spotted May backing off.

Before she disappeared into the blue haze, she
messengered him a look that said her move on him and the
scene with O'Dea might not be as accidental as it first appeared. Part of a scam to keep him from Ford, or was he just
attaching his imagination to his fried nerve endings?

He ordered a black hole in the smoke, "You, there, do
what I said. Remove the blade from Mr. O'Dea's left boot,
place it on the bar where I can see it, outside his reach," figuring someone would volunteer. The woman who stepped
forward with a dancer's grace was in her mid-twenties and
wore a tank top, leather skirt and crazy-glue hair. Large eyes
dominated her chunky face, visibly hypnotized by the adventure of the situation.

After placing O'Dea's switch on the counter, she stayed
put, like she was waiting for another assignment, waving her
hoisted hand behind her head like this was Disneyland and
the ride was loads of fun.

Peter sensed motion. It was the bartender on a creep, a
Louisville Slugger poised to hit a home run off his head.
"Take another step near and I take the asshole's eye, dick
face!" The bartender froze.

Peter asked the woman to get the bat and put it on the
counter next to the switch. He ordered the bartender through

the flip hatch and into the crowd.

The woman waved behind her again, like she was letting someone know Pirates of the Caribbean would never be the same.

He glanced the crowd best he could; couldn't find KC. Was she still in the room?

"What else, Mr. O'Dea?"

"Only the switch, Boss."

O'Dea was relaxed, beginning to treat the choke hold and the broken glass like paintings on the wall, his mind hatching schemes, as obvious as his lie he'd just told.

"Miss—?"

"Mulhall. Ellen Mulhall. My husband and I are on our honeymoon, just the rest of this week, and—"

"I'm happy for you, Mrs. Mulhall. Mr. Mulhall, too. Can I ask you to search Mr. O'Dea's other boot, please?"

The invitation thrilled her.

She came up with a short-barreled .32 Police Positive and held it for her husband to see. "Buns, look what we got from the mother-fucking son-of-a-bitch this time!" Without waiting for instructions, she placed the .32 on the bar by the switch and the baseball bat, and beamed at Peter like they were a team. He thanked her, and her teeth flashed like sunshine.

Buns Mulhall wasn't so sure. "For Sweet Jesus' sake, Ellen, enough already! Stay out of it!"

"Mr. O'Dea, do you have a license for that gun?" O'Dea didn't respond, but Peter already knew the truth. "Mr. O'Dea, I'm a detective with the L.A.P.D. and advising you that the possession of a concealed weapon, licensed or unlicensed, is a felony in this state. Both your gun and your switchblade meet the legal description of a concealed weapon."

Peter read a compliant O'Dea his rights, thinking about the best way to bugle the cavalry before his arms fell off and O'Dea had second thoughts.

He called out a new request to Ellen Mulhall. She dismissed her husband with a sweet frown to do as he'd asked, heading over to the emerald green curtained passage by the west wall, where the bartender said she'd find the manager. She returned a lifetime later with the manager trailing behind and told Peter, apologetically, "He won't let me use the phone."

"What the hell?" the manager said, throwing out his arms to embrace the room.

"Police officer, sir," Peter called, barely sliding a glance in his direction, holding tight rein on Dermot O'Dea, whose body shimmied like a Cuisinart against his own, malice ready to rampage. "I have placed this man under arrest. Please call 9-1-1 now. Explain the situation and request assistance for me." He called out his name and badge number.

The manager was unimpressed. "You got a badge? I'd like to see some identification. The law says I don't—"

"I know what the law says, sir. The phone, or you're going down with him."

"Don't want no trouble, mister. Run a clean place. Give an honest pour." His voice pure as puss.

Peter decided he had to be part of any scam going on. Meanwhile, his arms and his back muscles felt like they were going into spasm. A fire was burning a hole at the base of his spine. Something had to happen quickly, or O'Dea would be loose.

He flashed on sending Mrs. Mulhall for Annie, but let it go. It made more sense to get out of there with O'Dea before the crowd did something more foolish than send O'Dea signals from the sidelines and voice dirty-mouthed complaints.

243

Peter etched a small blood mark by the wrinkled outer crevice of O'Dea's eye and, as the red seed grew, barked instructions. The people started a cautious, side-stepping dance to the counter trap door at the front of the bar, nearest the front entrance. From there it would be a clear walk outside and backup from Annie.

The crowd danced along.

Peter navigated O'Dea around the bar curve.

He realized he would need someone to open the trap.

Mrs. Mulhall understood his call and started over, but her husband clamped onto her wrist, snatched her to him and locked her inside his arms.

Without thinking, Peter turned to say something to her. At once he recognized his mistake and swiveled his head back. His eyes traveled two more stops. He saw the resolute face of May Lawless turning on and off in the dark corner, exotic in the flutter of a revolving neon sign advertising Guinness. He saw the lethal iron pipe she was ready to rain down on him as she charged.

Whomp.

A sweeping blow to the rib cage. His arm arced out and the jagged glass bounced off the mirror behind the bar and dropped harmlessly onto the floor.

Whomp.

His left arm took the smash and angled down onto O'Dea's neck, useless.

Whomp.

His forehead.

Peter made a worthless noise.

The room turned cartwheels. His tissue paper legs refused the weight of his body, but he didn't go down.

O'Dea had him by the throat and was screaming revenge, pressing his threats while resisting hands that embraced him like a spider's love and voices that screamed for him to quit.

Peter shut his eyes and leaped onto the blissful white cloud waiting for him. Sailing off, he heard his own echo of relief.

CHAPTER 27

Snuffy Danaher had grabbed KC by the arm and tugged her away in the instant Peter disappeared behind the bar. His expression was all the explanation she'd needed not to challenge and to leave behind her concern for Peter's safety. Wordlessly, Danaher led her into the crowd and out the front entrance, across the shadowed street into the diner, cautiously stepping around a cab out front with its parking lights on and the motor running. An orange glow worm the size of a dime disappeared north of them as they checked both ways before crossing the street. Except for four noisy people trading bawdy laughs while heading from the parking lot to The Quiet Man, the area was as still as a cemetery.

The All-American Griddle Cakes & Coffee Emporium had the typical railroad train layout. A counter on one side. Small wooden tables and chairs at the opposite wall. Jutting out to the right of the central corridor, three high-backed booths. The decor, mostly faded and torn travel posters tacked to the plastic-coated walls, yellow edges curled by time. By itself on the partial wall to the left of the door, a mural-sized, color photo in an oxidized metal frame worth more than the furnishings: an unrecognizable football player charging, the ball tucked hard, an outstretched palm aiming for the photographer's lens.

More horse flies than customers this hour, and the buzz of their confusion scouring surface crumbs and pie wedges in a doorless display rack sitting alongside the cash register.

On the pedestal stool nearest the cash register, memorizing his coffee cup, a middle-aged man in a brown bomber jacket that was decorated on the back with the stenciled drawing of a 'cycle exhausting the words "Hell on Wheels" in blazing red script; chauffeur's cap with a patent leather brim and Sony Walkman on the next stool.

Halfway down, a woman in hooker's habit, elbows out, face down on the counter, asleep. Her stiletto heels off her swollen feet; black fishnet stockings as torn as her life. A Latina in a crimson bustier and a matching mini, an elaborate cross tattooed the full length of her meaty thigh, discussing TV soaps with the waitress, also middle-aged, but looking older in a stained yellow costume, her canary-colored hair unkempt, her eye glasses as thick as a ham sandwich.

Television sounds seeping through the food service window.

In the bay window, a calico cat, indifferent to the new arrivals.

Danaher directed KC to the first booth and backed out through the door with a wave and a wink, pulling it closed behind him. He wheeled and jaywalked diagonally, heading for The Quiet Man parking lot.

Liam McClory was waiting for her in the booth, on the side facing the front, a bottle of Guinness at his elbow and the remains of a cigarette nestled between his thumb and fingers, in the German style. Of course, KC thought, sliding in across from him. Liam always was a Nazi at heart.

Liam indicated the uncapped Guinness waiting for her.

"Well, Bright Eyes, and you are looking no worse for wear. No worse, for sure, than your cop boyfriend must look about now, with Dermot O'Dea not even reduced to a wheeze."

She picked up the dirty glass beside the bottle and pulled a napkin from the holder, wiped the rim thoroughly before pouring, Liam tracking her like a camera.

"Not *Bright Eyes,* damn it, and not my boyfriend. If I thought they were going to turn a gorilla loose on a cop, for Sweet Jesus' sake, I wouldn't have—"

"First place, why'd you bring him what's not your boyfriend?"

"I needed a car. It became easier than explaining where I was headed. I told them that when I called. If I knew they meant that ape when they said not to worry, I would have—"

"Doing your own thinking now, are you, girl-o? Francis always did like that about you, he did. Me, I always got meself a better place to put a woman's lips than around a bunch of words . . ." Liam's eyebrows did a little dance.

"You're disgusting."

He looked the question, then pretended to realize she meant the cigarette and made an act of smashing it in the saucer he was using as an ashtray.

"Put your mind to rest. Your boyfriend, he won't be hurt too much. Dermot knows to pull his punches, or bring down a brick wall we let him."

"Liam, you make it so easy for me to despise you."

"Ah, Katie, and to think I was not even trying." He might have been smiling at her; no way to tell on that inhuman face. He spoke slowly, thoughtfully, enunciating the words behind his bridgework. "But, real now, Katie, it's no way to talk about family. Or, you putting family behind you with your man gone so long and the cops them being good ones for understanding, I hear?"

Liam's small eyes were gray darts of fatal malice. He was challenging her, and she had to stand up to him. Backing down would be to surrender any advantage at all.

"I still love him, Liam." She answered quickly, took time weighing her declaration.

This would be the worst time to blunder, this close to getting the information Burkes needed.

"I still love Frankie, far more than *you* ever cared, except for how Frankie made you bigger and more important than you'll ever again be, so long as you live."

Liam moved his elbows onto the table surface and made a pyramid of his hands. He briefly closed his eyes to shut her out. "I suppose. But here I am. The U.S. of A. Maybe them other boy-os of the Thirty Two figgered I had a contribution. Same as you, Katie. Same as you." His stare was full of fresh anger.

She emptied the glass, using it as a buffer, and set it aside. Forcing her voice to be steady and certain, she said, "You the Plowman I'm waiting for? You all along?" He didn't respond, so she added a hard edge. "Answer me, Liam."

"Don't you ever be giving me orders, okay? First things first." He lit a fresh cigarette with a jet flame lighter, blew smoke into the aisle. "From what I seen on the telly, our Francis taught you to shoot good."

"Good enough to make someone dead until the day after eternity."

"I saw."

"He brushed up against me once too often."

"Was your titties then? I suppose I killed men for less. I was hoping actually you'd say something like, 'Liam, I broke ranks for revenge. I picked me a proper moment and broke the rules to do to him what he done to my beloved husband.'"

"The thought entered my mind."

"And if your deed fucked up our work here, what? On what was to be no more'n a free trip home for you."

"The ride down, Donahue asked questions. Finally one too many. He got drunk. He came on to me, and I decided to put it to the test."

"Ah! Thinking some more, you were!"

She bit down on her back molars, determined not to let Liam's sarcasm get to her. His eyes drifted away, as if something out front had trapped attention. She moved to the outside of the bench seat and leaned over to take her own look.

He reached across and grabbed hold of her sleeve. His touch put a spasm of disgust in motion in her stomach. He pulled her back gently, without explanation. "Tell me more about your thinking, Katie."

"Are you the Plowman, Liam?"

"Tell me more about your thinking, Katie."

Her breath snapped. She waited out the aftershock. "I invited Donahue back to the compartment. I went to pee. When I came out he was going through the luggage. He pulled a gun. I was ready for him. Faster."

"Did he find what he was looking for?"

"I don't know what he was looking for. Can you tell me? Are you the Plowman I'm waiting for?"

"Your bra, maybe? Checking out your brassiere size?"

"Bastard!" She pushed the empty Guinness bottle at him. "Is there anyone in this shitter who can get me a drink?" Liam pushed his bottle at her. She threw back her head, swallowed hard, pushed back the bottle.

"You sent Donahue over? The Thirty Two?"

Liam shrugged.

"His face came off in my hands, Liam. He was dead and his face came off in my hands and he was the same Plowman who murdered my husband, your brother, in cold blood. A sick thing to do, put him on the train with me and, maybe, to do the same thing?" Any more words would have been a struggle.

Liam's look denied the fact. He was answering her angry eyes, but his vision was elsewhere.

"Francis needed killing," Liam said, lowering his voice to a whisper. She had to strain to listen. "Francis was the traitor in our midst. Lot you don't know, and me. We just carry the spears, girl-o. It's others what come by all the lines in this desperate little play of ours. And the Cause. The Cause. It always got to stay bigger than our own personal grieving."

He waited for a response. She had none. Liam said, "Free trip home or no, fact is you done good if it's like you said it was on the train with Donahue. Him a traitor, too? Then damn his eternal soul. You stop to reflect, you see—always too lucky, him. And, at that sad moment all too ready and anxious to do in the dear boy of ours. Me brother. Like it would prove him what needed none." He thought through what he had said, and asked, "Tell me again. No revenge?"

She shook her head, made a point of holding his look until he broke it off.

"How long you think the Brits owned Donahue?"

"How should I know? Why these questions, Liam?"

A meaningless gesture. "Or the Americans, maybe? Could Donahue have fallen in with the Americans, not the Brits? Both of them, maybe?"

Questions she didn't want to answer. She had to change the subject. "When you rang me up, you said the cops had called asking questions about me?"

"They had the Vancouver connect number. From the business card. They called up, the referral come down to me like it was supposed."

"Nobody told me you'd be here to stand the alibi if I used the card. Why? Why wasn't I told you were here?"

"Nobody told you I was on the train, either, a free trip me own. So what?"

She pushed back against the booth wall on the weight of what he'd said. "I had a damn watchdog? For what? Why?

Not to keep me safe, so it must have been a matter of trust?"

Her questions bounced off Liam's face. "What made that cop ask about you first place, Katie? What made her ring up Vancouver?"

"A porter. He saw me. The cops made a drawing from his description. I was meeting Peter Osborne for lunch and ran into the porter. Before I—"

"That's it?"

"That's it."

"Not for any blabbing you know of by the newest traitor in our midst, the late Mr. Preston Donahue, or for any blabbing you done to the police detective what brung you over tonight, the self same Osborne?"

"Get stuffed!"

"Your Osborne say his mates are still on the grab for Mildred O'Malley? I suppose I'd be comforted to know the hunt for our made-up traveler continues."

"Sarcastic bastard. Why didn't you let me know you were on the train?"

"Look at Donahue."

"You're disgusting."

"And you make some of us nervous, girl-o. That's what brings us together this soft springtime night. I been instructed to tell you. You make some of us very, very nervous."

The calico cat she'd seen in the window leaped onto the table, startling her. Happy for any distraction, she reached over to pet it.

The cat inflated its back and hissed. In a single move, it bounced onto Liam's bench seat, sprang onto the dismal tile floor and bounded out of her sight. Liam ignored the cat's visit and kept chattering away. She snapped back to attention, hanging onto his words, trying to stay a jump ahead of his thoughts. It was critical she listen carefully, answer him cautiously and not make him any more suspicious than he was already.

Nobody came over to see if they needed another beer or, God forbid, something from the menu.

Another fifteen minutes of intense conversation and Liam announced the meeting ended. He told her the taxi parked outside would take her home and volunteered the news Peter was already there.

KC grunted acceptance, convinced anything more would only produce more stink from Liam. Once or twice in the last half hour she'd caught herself thinking about Peter and letting worry intrude on her focus. She'd willed herself to stop. Told herself even a dedicated killer like Liam was too smart to terminate a cop and further threaten the mission.

As they approached, the man in the bomber jacket got up and tossed some coins on the counter.

The hooker was still asleep at the counter.

The Latina had left behind a half-eaten sandwich, cold French fries and three Bud empties.

The waitress could be hiding in the kitchen, where a TV was making loud, wrestling match sounds.

The man in the bomber jacket hurried outside to open the back door of the cab for her, and passing through the entrance she saw that somebody had shifted the cardboard sign on the wire glass window from "Open" to "Closed."

KC pulled her jacket tight and wrapped her arms over her breasts. A cold wind was coming in from the ocean; it felt good on her face.

Liam helped her enter the cab and through the open window said, "Owney here'll see you arrive in one piece. Think through the story I just give you, have it straight as an arrow, the cops ask you anymore."

"The Plowman. When will I hear?"

Liam's starched face gave away nothing. "When it's ready to happen."

He reached in for her shoulder. She inched back in time to avoid contact, and acted like she was adjusting herself in the seat. He withdrew his hand and his eyes fluttered.

He said softly, "I'm sorry if I upset you, Katie."

"No, you're not," KC said, and she rolled up the window after letting Liam see the world did not need another lie.

Liam watched the cab go. After it rounded the corner, he went back into the diner, slid back inside the booth and opened the napkin dispenser. In it was a state-of-the art gunmetal gray bug, about the size of a pillbox, that operated on a chip no bigger than a sand pebble.

"You heard good, knock once for yes, twice for no," he said, pocketing the listening device.

A pause, then—

A single knock from the next booth.

Liam pushed out of the booth and called for someone to bring him a fresh Guinness while he maneuvered into the adjacent booth, facing the street. He massaged his hip hard where it hurt, the pain immortal against pills ever since the bloody bastard Brits worked on him overtime and left him a limp to remember them by.

"Damn cat could of give all away Katie thought to see where it went," Liam said, rolling his eyes at the ceiling and pointed accusingly.

The calico cat was resting on the opposite bench, paws on the table, lapping milk from a dessert dish.

"We got us more to talk about now than cats and their habits," Frankie McClory said, reaching over to stroke the cat.

The cat ignored him.

CHAPTER 28

Frankie said, "I had my back to her, Liam, only a slab of wood separating us, and I swear to you I could hear through the wall, her dear heart beating with mine."

"Damned fucking romantic you are. What you heard was the white heat of her fears of discovery to go with second thoughts you could be having."

The corners of Frankie's mouth dropped. He stared coldly at Liam and fiddled with the tiny earpiece that connected to the bug. He deposited the listening device in a shirt pocket and made a gate of his hand over his mouth, attached by his thumb at the side of his gently sloped nose.

"You heard real good, Francis?"

The gate swung open.

"Too good, sometimes, Liam, and I say this right out on the table. You ever again talk so filthy a way to Katie, you reckon with me. Guaranteed."

Liam shucked off the threat and brought his voice back to a whisper. "Our business with Mustamba was too important even for Preston Donahue to dare unzipping his fly and turning the monster loose." He checked over his shoulder.

"You like being wrong? Preston Donahue *always* was one for the ladies. Katie not kill him, I would of."

"But no traitor, Donahue. I seen deep in the man's soul a long time ago. Katie done him and it proves our case against her."

"I judge not."

"Francis, listen to me once—" He waited while the waitress dropped off four uncapped bottles of Guinness and retreated. The brothers toasted one another to the clank of glass, and matched swallows. The calico cat's dish was dry. Frankie poured in some of his beer. The cat attacked the dish with relish. "Francis, I still figger Katie works for them bastards. I bloody figger it before we set her to thinking you was a dead man and brung her into this scheme for proof. I figger it now, still."

"Katie's done nothing to show you right, Liam. Katie is where she wanted, like we wanted, and Katie went and got the baggage where it's needed. Confess to that or show me where I'm bleeding fucking wrong."

Liam torched a smoke with his lighter and leaned forward, his elbows outstretched and his shoulders hunched into his neck, studying his brother's blue eyes. The eyes hung like two sacks of cement, defying him to remember what it was like before the woman came between them.

"I never voted Kate McClory part of the program," he said.

"No program without her, not this one, anyway."

"She wore a red rose in her hair, ripe as fresh-picked berries, and I wager it come from the copper."

"You see what you see. I remember her scent."

Damn Francis. Rolling the bottle between his palms and grandly smiling back at him, like only he knew it all. Voice smooth as the satin pillows the wee Ma made for the landlords, and never having more to fear than a dentist drilling at his teeth, knowing only skin under his nails, where his big brother took the slow ride to the edge.

Francis could have made the trip after the Da was cut down and they acted the avengers, except what for Liam taking over the household in the same instant, yanking the boy into an alley shadow after a run that got them away from the dangers of the Brits, who would surely be on an all-night hunt for them who done in the leftenant and the other.

Liam shook him dry of tears and demanded, "You go get now and forget everything just happened. You wasn't there, anyone ask. You don't know nothing."

"Killed me Da, Liam. Fuckers killed me Da."

"You hear me, little boy? You don't know it until someone comes to tell, and then you shed tears and make like its news and go on to mourn with your Ma, same as me, or it's both sons she'll also lose to them villains."

He did for a while, and Liam became the hero, only the movement came to use Francis over Liam's objections, where a boy could do a man's work and not encourage the same risk. He was a courier to begin with, messages and an occasional payoff. When Francis got good at the game, a weapon or two buried in a deep pocket or taped on to places the snakes would not think to look on him with such an innocent face.

Explosives become a specialty, Francis treating the deadly balls of clay like they was mere toys. Once even, when a RUC bastard challenged him, he tossed a wad back and forth, hand to hand, high up in the air, and almost missed a catch while they asked more questions than a school quiz.

Francis became legend after that. Remind Francis it was for the Da and he was ready for anything, while he, Liam, got the short end. It meant nothing to them how he stood up to the Brits by himself when they come crashing through the door after the Da's murder, sent the wee Ma and his baby brother behind him and took the worst they had to offer without giving away anything.

Francis watched with eyes grand as saucers and, when the Ma's screaming was loud enough to draw blood, moved forward like he was going to save Liam with the truth. Before he could open his mouth, Liam put a fist to it, making it look accidental, and that shut the boy up and cost him a tooth besides.

The Brits stopped then, adding to Liam's anger. He didn't need no rescuing by a child, who got thrashed by him later and made to understand how important it was to live by rules after learning them. Better that than to die by them, Francis.

Sure, Liam got his share of assignments, some nice pats, but he never felt appreciated the way they were generous to Francis, and that made him step up to jobs more than others, and set him apart in the minds of Brits and the RUC, who come after him every fucking time was a ruckus, or just for the sport.

Francis was no better than their mates after a while. He grew quiet, introspective, less inclined to share secrets the more he got inside the movement. The movement got to be his family and Liam, he got to be, what? as they drifted farther and farther apart. Liam got to be somebody else his brother knew to order about.

Remember her scent, indeed, her what come between them as good as anyone ever.

Like the time his stunt cost two of their own in a failed snatch in London.

He almost paid with his breath that time, but Frankie made a case with the Thirty Two on his own warrant and so he got sent away for sixteen months, to teach him a lesson, they said.

It was really her doing, he knew, a new way to come between brothers, and he told Katie so when he got back. "You shape the wedge between me and Francis," he whispered, "but you better watch out it don't come to a sharp point between your shoulder blades, girl-o". She made like she didn't know what to make of him, like he was a crazy man, and she was right about that. Crazy where she was concerned.

This time, Liam McClory meant to get Katie where she deserved all along. He stared at his brother across the table, knocked for attention, and inquired, "What if—*if*, I say, Francis, mind you, *if*—if it so happens to turn out how Liam McClory was right in his judgment of his only brother's dear darling wife? What then?"

"Not enough those questions of Katie? Now you're starting your bleeding game with me?"

"Not so easy off the hook, Francis. No games at these prices. You answer me and you answer me good."

Liam reached for the cigarette smoldering on the edge of the table, sucked in enough smoke for a two alarm before Francis' eyes reached out and he sliced a horizontal line across his throat.

Liam nodded approval.

"Excuse me. I hope I'm not interrupting at a bad time?"

Her voice startled both of them.

He and Francis shared an expression that asked how long the woman was standing there and what she may have heard.

Francis' cat hissed disapproval and disappeared.

"The waitress told me Mr. Ford was at this table," Annie Waterman said. "Mr. John Ford?"

CHAPTER 29

The bar had been an easy eyeball for Annie. Only one entrance, a step or two inside two blacked-out windows that might have been displaying five-and-dime store stuff twenty years ago. Customers coming and going with erratic frequency until the pattern changed abruptly, arrivals retreating from the place within a minute or two of entering.

She saw KC precede them, but not by much.

Annie caught her heading across the street for the all-night diner, escorted by a little man whose arm was looped through hers. KC stumbled to keep up with him as he took the rutted asphalt in small, gliding steps.

Until then, Annie had been thinking about the cold and the loneliness and Peter.

KC glanced her way and she ducked fast, getting her smoke below the windshield, hoping KC hadn't noticed anything to send her little friend over to investigate. She mashed out the butt and swore again to quit smoking. One of these days.

After a long minute, she slid back up to the sight line. She saw the little man charge determinedly across the street and disappear into the blind recesses of the unlit parking lot. John Ford? His size didn't fit the voice Annie remembered.

She used the dim bulb of the glove compartment to check the time and update the log. Turning to double-check the name of the diner, she saw something strange.

A waitress had just let out a dark-skinned street hook and flipped the door sign to "Closed." It didn't jibe with the painted sign on the windows that said "All-Nite Number 1

Good Eat" in the curious English lately brought to the local language by immigrant Nams and Koreans.

Peter's sky blue Am barreled out of the parking lot, cut a hard left and flew past her. She felt her gut jam into overdrive. Two men up front. Neither one Peter. She couldn't make the giant with the monolithic puss behind the wheel, but the man who had escorted KC into the diner was angled beside him, an elbow jutting out the window.

A green panel truck followed on its tail, too fast for her to make the driver. The side advertised a West Hollywood plumbing company. She trapped the plate long enough to jot down the license number.

She had to choose between keeping the watch or tracking Peter. Hobson's choice, but she sure as shit wasn't Hobson and had never met anybody by that name. Something had gone wrong inside the pub. Peter wasn't about to surrender his keys, and the little man hadn't earned his wardrobe money hot-wiring cars.

Worse, Peter might have gone out tonight unarmed.

Annie had no way of knowing for sure. If anything happened to him, she knew she'd blame herself from here to whatever cliff she dove off. Her own DS was on the seat beside her. She flipped the barrel, gave it a spin; checked the action; parked it in her shoulder holster.

She rubbed her foot against her pant leg to sense some security from the baby .25 in her ankle holster, forced her feet back inside her black Reeboks, the good luck "Reeblacks" she wore for stakeouts, the way some women favor diamonds and emeralds for fancy dress balls, and headed for The Quiet Man.

Inside, no Peter.

Either that or he was playing the Invisible Man.

She flashed her badge and did the standard growl with the

bartender, who toweled and shelved glasses from the hot, soapy water and shook his knobby head. The manager swore he'd been in the back office all night. A half-dressed brunette ditz backed his story from the Hide-A-Bed there. Another random canvass of patrons came up short.

Outside again, holding up a wall and weighing her options, she decided she should have pressed the young moj in the leather skirt and unmade hair, who'd sent vibes like she was ready to say something, before her bug-eyed old man whispered in her ear and yanked her by her dangling earring to the middle of the dance floor.

Annie was moving to try inside again when a blue Chrysler sub-compact with a rental agency sticker on the back bumper jumped the curb turning south onto the street from the parking lot. The moj was at the wheel, looking pale and scared. So did her old man, who threw a hand between his face and the window when he saw her. Annie jotted down the license, just in case, and shivered knowing what her mind meant by *just in case*.

Action across the street.

The totem pole who had been sitting at the counter came outside and held open the passenger door of the cab parked out front all evening, followed by a new entry in the cast of characters, who put KC inside the cab. They chatted briefly, casting elongated shadows in the bold glow of a bell-shaped floodlight burning over the entrance before the cab drove off.

The man went back inside the diner, heading for the rear.

Had to be John Ford.

Had to be.

One of those things they can't teach at the Academy.

Only her period was more certain.

So—

How to play it?

Peter would safety out, call for backup and an orderly close. Peter . . . It came to her. He was in the diner, too. He had trotted there from the bar in the minutes she was hiding below sight level from KC and the little man. Peter had dispatched KC in the taxi and was going one on one with John Ford. It didn't explain the business with his car, but—

Hell, her cover was busted anyway.

She got out and headed for the diner.

No Peter inside, only two candidates for the role of John Ford. Uneasy looks back and forth between them when she told them what the waitress had said: "The waitress told me Mr. Ford was at this table. Mr. John Ford?"

Neither man answered her question, so Annie flashed her badge. "One of you is Mr. Ford, correct?"

Another exchange before the man on her left, his warped face challenging her stare, let a thought escape through his teeth. "That would be me, and would you be the detective I spoke to earlier in the day?"

She forged a smile. "Annie Waterman. Yes."

"This is an old mate, been showing me the sights," he said, indicating the other man, who certified the ID with a nod. He was about the same age as Ford, give or take. Blue eyes. Brooding, but not as angry as Ford's gloomy grays. Kind of good-looking, an earthy handsomeness, but not her type. "Detective Waterman, say hello to—"

"Parker. Robert Leroy Parker," he said, extending a hand. It was warm, even through a ridge of calluses. A working hand. What you would expect from someone in a garage mechanic's jump suit.

"Not Raymond?"

He was momentarily lost, then smiled and smacked his chest over his heart, where the name "Raymond" was stitched. "New job started today and these just on loan until I secure me own." Head cocked. Laughter rippling from his throat like a tenor's sweet hum. Far too much explanation, like he knew the drill. "Robert. Rob or Bobby to all, excepting them what knows me best. They call me Butch."

"And how did you happen to find me, Detective?" Ford's eyes were a challenge.

Annie improvised. "A suggestion I made to Mrs. McClory when she said she'd be seeing you tonight."

"Mrs. McClory did, did she?" Pointing. "Did she also say we was to meet over at The Quiet Man?"

"They sent me here."

Ford seemed to buy it. "More questions about the unfortunate priest, I suppose?" Used a hand to invite her onto the seat next to him.

"Some." Annie squashed out her cigarette in the saucer he was using for his butts. Remained standing.

"Different from the questions Detective Osborne had?" Fingers playing with his mustache, smoothing it back to the edges.

"My partner." Trying not to show emotion, feeling pulse drilling at her temples. "He said he might get here first."

"He come with Mrs. McClory. Saw them back to the car a few ago."

Rob or Bobby or Butch said abruptly, before she could act on the certain knowledge of her danger, "Liam, you looking? She bloody well knows better, Liam."

Ford giggled madly and aimed a .38 at her belly. "Never the perfect fool. Only toying a bit. Keep your hands steady, Detective Annie Waterman. Lean over and put those lovely palms face down on the table. No more sudden movements. At's a good girl now . . ."

Annie knew this was major trouble.

Peter would be giving her holy hell for making the move

inside this dump, instead of requesting backup on a Code Two. She would confess she did it out of concern for his safety, and the news would drive him absolutely insane with anger, her junking procedure for something stupid and personal, but afterward the lovemaking would be intense and fulfilling and he would be too exhausted to explain away his emotions like he was reciting from one of Judge Osborne's first editions.

Meanwhile, where the hell was he?

She listened for any sound that might be Peter sneaking up on these two bastards.

CHAPTER 30

Peter swung the car around the driveway oval and pulled to a stop by the front door of his home. He cut the motor. Killed the headlights. Stared blankly through the windshield for several moments. He washed sharp, tiny breaths through his nose. Willed the agony clog-dancing on his head to go away. Cursed it for not listening.

The spot on his forehead that May Lawless had decorated during her blindside attack was tender to the touch. He winced. Already, it was the size of a robin's egg and would be nesting there for weeks. He was certain about the cracked ribs, and his entire body radiated the pain he'd rejected on the desperate drive from the site in Baldwin Hills where he had been dumped. To have given in to the pain would have been tantamount to passing out and becoming a new freeway statistic.

Whoever they were, they'd left him stretched across the back seat, parked on a dirt shoulder of La Cienega on the downside south of Rodeo, the open hood signaling distress. There was lots of airport traffic, so the chances of being found were pretty good if he didn't pull it out for himself. Whatever it was all about, they didn't want the heat that comes with a dead cop.

Taking it slowly, keeping to a steady fifty-five, he had picked up the Hollywood and looped through downtown onto the Pasadena. The only potentially serious problem occurred at the interchange. A Porsche cut him off on the passenger side and almost sent him skidding into a mural decorating the embankment. He prayed the brakes through the floorboards, barely pulled out of a fishtail and could still taste his balls between his teeth.

He found a heavy metal station, turned the radio up full tilt.

Thinking about KC also helped keep him awake.

By the time he sprang up from behind the bar to impress Dermot O'Dea with his broken glass collection, she was gone.

Where?

Who with?

If KC didn't slip by Annie, she would have the answers when they caught up later. His money was on Annie. Annie was fail safe at just about everything, except pushing their relationship beyond face value. Yes, he loved Annie. Yes, he had made love to her. No, he was not in love with her, never had been. Annie knew it. Not a secret he'd kept from either of them.

Until today, he also thought he knew how he felt about KC, back into his life in a way that emphasized how vulnerable he had been since the day she ran away to goddam Frankie McClory.

Every single woman he took up with after her had meant something to him.

He had not been so emotionally depraved as to use them, at least that's what he told himself. He believed it even now.

They ended the affairs as often as he did, hardly ever for the same reason.

Did he tell them about KC?

Some of them.

Did they understand?

None of them, not for him, only in terms of what it meant for themselves.

The ones he didn't tell?

They were the ones who never lasted as long—the brighter ones?—who looked into his eyes and never saw themselves looking back.

If they looked tonight, what would they see?

Walter Burkes had changed his emotions from wine into water. He was crazy to tell Burkes he would do it, try making KC fall for him again. So, why, Peter? The crutch you need if it doesn't work out? Is there ever any justification for betraying someone you love?

Betrayal.

Like the last time, with Brenda Bennington. Two kids, too drunk to know better, polluting their lives and tilting them off course, irretrievably for Brenda, a suicide before her twenty-fifth birthday.

One night changed two lives. Three, counting KC. He drank, Brenda drank. She took him before he could take her. And he would have, if she hadn't made the first move, telling him how lucky he was to have her instead of KC.

Shared blame, Peter. Shared guilt.

Stupid, stupid, stupid.

Knocked her up, Brenda Bennington. Scared kid, a little girl again by the time she stood on the front porch with her old man, him demanding to speak to the judge, holding his daughter's hand like he wished it were a shotgun. It was to the judge. A gentleman pays the consequences, the judge said. Our faith does not permit abortion, he said, and if it did, he would not.

Stupid, stupid, stupid.

And a beautiful church wedding to show for it.

The bride wore white.

The groom, his heart behind his honor, swearing to love, honor and obey, meaning it, even knowing it had cost him KC, who was taken aside by the judge and given the grim reality, in his terms, without any thought for Peter's need to speak to her first, with a naked truth that might have kept her from running.

Away from Peter, who loved her.

Away, finally, to goddam Frankie McClory.

Maybe, if it had happened that way, he would have had the courage to stand up to the judge, and Brenda to her father. Maybe. But it did not happen that way and, later, he wept for a child born dead. God's punishment, the judge said, making it sound like God had nothing better to do all day than sit on a bench in His Heavenly courtroom and dish out judgment on Peter Osborne.

Brenda never got over it.

Innocent little Mary Grace Osborne.

Sleep with the angels, dear child.

Mary Grace.

Laid to rest in the Bennington family crypt at Forest Lawn, details supervised by dad, as Brenda sank into a depression that haunted her through the divorce, the doctors, and the pills, the sanitariums and the cures that never pulled her back from the other side of despair.

Brenda.

Joining Mary Grace in the crypt before she was twenty-five. Alcohol and pills.

And, the judge saw to it that the official record said Brenda's death was accidental, as it might have been, but Peter knew better. So did her father, who called him to demand he not attend the services, and put a death wish on Peter's head before his wife was able to get the phone away from him and hang up.

Click.

Buzz.

Hello, hello. Operator?

Peter here, disconnected from life. Except for the overweight burdens of memory, and the consequences of betrayal. Is this what bound them together, he and KC, more than his love for her? Betrayal?

Burkes said it was his patriotic duty.

Screw patriotism. Screw—

Christ!

Was any of this making sense? His head had the kind of buzz he got when a foot fell asleep. That's what he needed now. Sleep. A hot bath and sleep. The hot bath only if he could take it into bed with him.

Peter thought he saw KC charging down the veranda stairs while he inched forward one reasoned step at a time, her arms reaching for him, her terrified voice calling his name. Who was that chasing behind her? Annie? Good. Annie would know. Annie'd tell him.

What? What would she tell, Peter? That KC was a murderer, and a terrorist, and—

Peter was on the ground before she and Oldenburg reached him.

Cookie dropped to one knee alongside his head and felt for a pulse, trying not to gag over a face nearly blown out of recognition.

He winced softly, a baby inside a nightmare, when her fingers checked cautiously for broken bones.

A mad whimper as she glided over his ribs.

No visible wounds, but always the possibility of internal bleeding.

"If we get him under the arms we could probably lift him up and get him inside."

"Crank off and phone the doctor," Cookie said, taking charge. "His number is on automatic dial. Mem 04." Andy hesitated, like he had his own opinion. "Just go and do it. Now, damn it! Straight out of the *Campfire Girl Handbook.* I'm glued down."

They had been swapping spit on the swing when Peter's car surprised them, and Andy went limp with fear, like the Bible Police were about to bust him for playing doorbell with her nips. She was a grab away from his dingus. It would have been the first time. Both of them had been building up to it all evening. She told him to remember his place, darted to the railing and used a pillar to hide her scouting mission.

Instantly, she knew something was terribly wrong by the way Peter tried walking, like his thighs were bolted together.

Cookie watched Andy rush the steps in an awkward, bottom-heavy trot, taking them two and three at a time, almost tripping headlong into the door when he came up one short. Her tears spilled over. She was no longer able to hold them back, to keep Andy from deciding she was still a baby.

She stroked Peter's hair and told him everything would be all right, trying to sound like she believed it herself. She hated seeing her brother this way, and hated whoever was responsible.

It had to be KC.

She and Peter drove off together, but KC had come back alone, in a taxi, just when her tongue action with Andy was starting to get outrageously intense.

Otherwise, she would have marched right up to her and asked what was going on.

This KC, not the KC she cherished.

This one, who had come back hiding guns and Lord knows what else; got calls from strangers with two names; trapped her into secrets sealed with a kiss, knowing she'd have to keep them no matter what, because that's the way she had been brought up. Well, not at my brother's expense,

Cookie vowed, promising to do something besides cry as soon as she could.

She heard Daddy's voice calling to her, "Doc Adams's on his way, so don't worry. Peter will be just fine. Doc will see to that." Like he was trying to make himself believe, too.

Daddy was halfway to them, holding a slipper in each hand while wrestling to get his crimson and black robe closed and the sash tied. He winced every time one of his grasshopper steps landed on a pebble, but didn't let that slow him down.

Mommy trailed him by a few yards, traveling with more caution. Better organized. Equally distraught. A brown night cream mask disguising her face. A finger caught in her mouth. Her other hand trapped in her auburn hair, which trailed loosely down her neck and spread across the front of her shoulders. Framed her beautiful face like a magic curtain.

Behind her, on the veranda, a lumpy black shadow stood by the open door. Andy. Signaling her a thumbs up. She ran a sleeve across her eyes and padded them with her palms as he started down the steps.

She made room beside Peter for Daddy and Mommy. Rushed a silent prayer for her brother. Wondered how she ever could have been fooled for even one minute by KC, and sent Peter a message under her breath: *No more, bro, no more. I won't let her hurt you again.*

CHAPTER 31

Peering from behind the drawn draperies, hands locked onto an inner edge like it was a bell rope, KC watched them, as if she were in suspended animation, until they lifted Peter from the ground and carried him to the house, the doctor calling signals like a traffic cop.

She became aware of breathing again, her lungs working, sprung from the state of suspended animation she'd been in since the cab dropped her off, no sense of time or how long she'd stood vigil at the window, needing to see him and know he was all right, finally admitting to herself—

Even before she boarded the flight for Vancouver, Peter Osborne was packed in her thoughts, like a favorite coat that never gets ratty enough to discard. It had nothing to do with her feelings for Frankie. They were intact, unthreatened by the dormant emotions she drew on whenever she thought about her old life. She had told Frankie about Peter at the start of their relationship. It was important to her there be no secrets between them.

In exchange, Frankie told her his own, full of intimate details that made her blush, and sweeping gestures to go with reassurances that the past was meant for history books and their life together was meant for each other.

Frankie made her feel wanted. Needed. Loved. Respected.

She tried giving back more than she received, an overwhelming task sometimes.

KC had thought it was that way with Peter, before she let him inside her on a night with a moon far too fine to waste.

Peter was the first one, a touchdown that never made the yearbook. They had laughed about a Rose Princess deflowered, their private joke right up until Brenda Bennington robbed her of the punchline.

Dear Frankie got down on his knees and helped her find her ego. Showed her the humor in a straw mattress thick as a playing card, the King of Hearts, on rusty coils of broken bedspring, entertaining family members who tittered among themselves on the other side of a ragged door curtain, their amusement as subtle as the crickets sounding off on the dewswept grass out back.

Now her old life with Frankie was in the past, and Peter was back to haunt her present. She'd understood the truth the moment she saw him at dinner, that she would never be over him entirely. The price of first love, Katherine Mary Cassidy one of those who pay dearly on the installment plan.

Maybe if Peter hadn't looked the way he did, or looked at her the way he did, the chandelier igniting his pleading, almost begging eyes whenever he shifted in his seat—

No wonder Annie hated her.

She had come close to hating herself later, on the veranda, after telling Peter, *Let's not rush back to anything*. She had said it only to put him off and discovered it was a turn-on, an old thrill rummaging between her thighs. And, he smiled. And, that was a turn-on, too. And, she said okay to lunch. And, caught her near the truth when she told him stop carrying torches. And, he sent her roses, and she came to dinner wearing one in her hair.

She shouldn't have let him drive her to The Quiet Man, but Peter smiled and she made excuses in her mind and used them in a voice filled with confidence and concern when she called ahead.

The ride to the beach was delightful, even with all her apprehensions. Peter artfully maneuvered the conversation in and out of their common memories and made her eager to forget the worst. Made her believe a new possibility. Made her want to try it once. Crawl behind a bush or between the covers. Lock the garden house door and rake a bed of brown mowed grass and broken leaves. Under their kind of moon, one too good to waste. See if the woman she had become with Frankie responded differently from the schoolgirl she had been. See if she could retire her Book of Judgment on Peter to the farthest dusty corner on the highest shelf in Noah's library. Except, he didn't encourage her. *Let's not rush back to anything.* Peter gave her what she had asked him for, and that made her want him more.

On the ride back here from her meeting with Liam, she knew she didn't dare to say or show any concerns for Peter. The taxi driver, who lit one butt after another and grunted only to acknowledge her directions after exiting the freeway into Pasadena, surely would have reported it to Liam. Or Snuffy Danaher.

Danaher's diamond-studded cuff links, his black pearl pinky ring and his fake Rolex told the truth about his homespun air. She would bet anyone it was only an act hiding a dangerous man. He didn't have to be a Plowman to kill, whether he called it "patriotism" or by its usual name, "murder," especially when he had Dermot O'Dea tracking after him.

She didn't know Danaher from Belfast, but she knew O'Dea by another name and his picture in all the papers the day after he disappeared, next to the photos of six young Brits he surprised with an Uzi.

Hurrying to the front door after the cab eased down the driveway, KC glimpsed Cookie hanging back in a corner of the swing, cute, pudgy Andy closer beside her than a Siamese twin.

She didn't want to guess why. More than likely, they knew what to do there better than she had at the same age. It was absolutely true kids grew up faster today. Too fast. She didn't want to embarrass them or hear the questions Cookie would likely ask.

Cookie was certain to wonder about Peter and there was nothing she could tell her. It was already bad enough she'd become dog-faced and distant, fueling KC's fears she had learned something she shouldn't know. Tomorrow she would remind Cookie their secrets were sealed with a kiss.

KC had rushed through a warm shower, using the scrub brush like sandpaper. She stretched out on the bed in her bra and panties and tossed for a half hour waiting for some sound of Peter returning.

She grew increasingly tense.

Finally, she threw on a robe and took up a post at the window.

She knew they had lied to her the minute she saw Peter.

Peter was so fragile the breeze might toss him over any second.

She felt a sickness strike her in the stomach, hard blows to go with jutting tears, and held her hands over her mouth until the feeling of nausea passed.

She knew how to get even. Get even. Her first thought. Gone before she could remember it had been there.

Later, back in bed—

The dream she couldn't forget.

Preston Donahue brushes her aside and cracks her face with the Luger. Fades into the night as Liam starts barking orders, as if he's the one in charge now, commanding the other lads at the table to take careful hold of Frankie and rush his brother out the back, before any law comes asking questions.

Gives her an ugly glance back over his shoulder, as if this is all her fault, before he disappears himself, and—

Startled awake by the nightmare memory, a remnant of her woeful scream rocketing in her ears, she bolted upright, drenched in sweat, her hands grabbing for the darkness and clues to where she was.

A burst of light. From the hallway. Hands encased one of hers. Gentle, comforting. Aunt Dorothy. "A bad dream, dear. Everything will be fine. Everything will be just fine."

"Swear on a frog?"

"And a polliwog," Aunt Dorothy said. Leaned over to kiss her on the cheek. Smiled to make it so, the way she always drove the demons away.

"Peter?"

"He has a mild concussion, nothing more serious than that, and nothing broken, thank goodness. Remember how we used to say he was made of iron? Doc Adams says he'll be fine in a day or two, provided we can keep him in bed." Stroked her hair. "Peter asked after you, too, Pudding. More worried for you than for himself."

"Remember, Aunt Dorothy, how we used to say, if Peter were any brighter he could be a firefly? Doesn't that prove it?"

Their laughter washed away a lot of the worry and, after Dorothy was gone, KC fell into a contented sleep.

The next morning, when she went downstairs, the house was empty except for the pair of cleaning women who came in every Thursday and alternate Saturdays.

They were Aunt Dorothy's one concession to age—she had always preferred doing things for herself—and only because Uncle Judge insisted after the old housekeeper, Molly, died.

Molly was a stoop-backed African-American who could have posed for Dorothea Lange, with large calloused hands that once picked cotton. Coal black, eloquent eyes. Her husband had been killed in Korea, leaving her with a small military pension and five kids. She came every day with the rising sun and treated dust like her natural enemy.

When stomach cancer took her, Noah quietly wrote out a check and deposited it in the trust fund he'd arranged for, so there would be enough to guarantee all five of Molly's kids got a college education. The kids were sent to live with her distant cousin in Atlanta. Dorothy sent her Molly's weekly check, every so often adding a raise or a cost-of-living increase. KC knew the stories because, one at a time, Uncle Judge and Aunt Dorothy had taken her aside and confided it to her, first making her swear never to tell the other, as if kindness and generosity were a contest between them.

The current cleaning ladies, also African-American, both in their late fifties, carried the weight of the world in boulevard hips. Robust smiles. A competitive, gentle bickering between themselves that quit when they did, once their brown dusting smocks were back in the broom closet and they could slip out the kitchen door with their rope-handled shopping bags.

A note in Aunt Dorothy's letter-perfect script waited for her on the kitchen table, anchored by the keys to the Ford wagon. She would be out for a few hours with Women's Club friends. Peter was on fresh medication and expected to sleep until late afternoon. The town car was hers to use.

Silver-haired Lillo poured KC orange juice and fresh coffee while her breakfast heated in the microwave. Scrambled eggs. Bacon strips. Two slices of ham. An assortment of the fresh rolls, muffins and coffee cakes Lillo and Desireé always picked up at the bake shop. She ate ravenously, her appetite fueled by the nervous energy and worries that woke when she did.

Lillo and Desireé hadn't waited for an invitation before joining KC. They sat on opposite sides of her with their bosoms resting on the table, passionately arguing soap operas and the morning news, their voices floating across the table.

Lillo's voice was full of Beethoven, while Desireé spoke to a rapper's beat, her arms conducting every word.

The conversation moved along to Rodney King, the black man beaten on a Los Angeles street by four white L.A.P.D. officers, captured on an amateur cameraman's videotape that even played over Irish television. The trial, the riot, all of it ended long ago, but Lillo and Desireé feared the worst for the next Rodney King to come along.

"You'll see," Lillo promised. "They'll go and get them-selves some more white folks on that jury entirely, so there'll never be no righteous chance of justice, just enough to say different anybody care about a black man."

"Be riots then, girl." Desireé's head bobbed like one of those birds at a back seat window. "Watts all over again. Looting and burning and children dead in the streets, only nothing come of it like usual."

Lillo's head moved like an oil derrick pump.

This was as long as KC had ever heard them go without disagreement. They could be discussing Belfast, she thought. Justice governed by law and injustice by mobs until one was indistinguishable from the other. Anywhere in the world, the system serves the system and the people are powerless to do anything but take power.

"What our people need right now is somebody out on the streets, walking the walk and talking the talk that keeps it for the better," Lillo decided. "Telling us all to be calm no matter what."

They, the universal code word that keeps bigotry and prejudice alive inside of everyone, and in every language. KC swallowed the last of her muffin and chose a sweet roll.

"Who that be, girl? Malcolm? He still dead. Dr. King? He still dead. Rev. Jackson? That Farrakhan?"

They laughed and traded knowing looks.

Desireé said, "Oprah?" Puffed her cheeks to balloons and opened her brown eyes as wide as they could go.

"Unh-unh, girl," Lillo said, waving her off. "Mr. Bill Cosby. Take that family of his by the hand and march up and down. People'll be so busy getting autographs, they don't got time to do nothing else."

Laughter.

Lillo slapped her thigh and drew a clown's grin across her broad face, like she had just invented the funniest words of her life. Desireé nodded approval.

KC asked, "Mr. Mustamba?"

His name quieted them.

The look between them excluded KC, as if she could never understand.

Lillo locked her hands under her ample chins, shut her eyes to the notion. Desireé propped a cheek on her knuckles, let her gaze drift with her thoughts. Exhaled soulfully.

"Mr. Mustamba is coming here to give a speech, you know?" KC didn't mean to sound patronizing.

"No offense, but it not about what he got to say, Miss KC. It about what people willing to hear."

"Will they listen to Mr. Mustamba?"

"If they don't, ain't no hope," Desireé said.

"Ain't no hope at all," Lillo agreed.

KC used most of the day on herself.

Window shopping at the Pasadena mall, recession echoing

on every floor. A brisk tour of the Norton Simon Museum, to greet old friends on the walls. A mindless movie in Old Town with a dozen other hooky players in an uncomfortable, tunnel-shaped room; no air conditioning and snack bar smells as bad as the film.

When she got home, two phone messages from John Ford were waiting on the entry hall table. Apologizing for missing their appointment last night. Asking her to call back. She balled the messages, tossed them in the waste basket and called Liam a name under her breath.

She went searching for Cookie.

Come and gone, according to Aunt Dorothy, who was in the kitchen spooning fat over a turkey breast in the oven. She and Andy had spent the afternoon locked away in her room, studying to MTV, and would be having dinner at his house. "She knows to be home by curfew," Aunt Dorothy said, reassuring herself. KC couldn't say her concern was over what else Cookie knew.

Doc Adams arrived shortly before dinner to check on Peter, a tam disguising his bald spot, shrunken inside a raspberry sports jacket old as her vaccination scar. His shirt collar two sizes too large, but no other visible signs of seventy-something years. He was ever the gallant eagle, and still making house calls.

Along with Noah and Aunt Dorothy, she followed him upstairs, moved quietly into the room, found a place out of the way.

Doc Adams parked his leather-scarred satchel on the night stand, pocketed his bifocals and sat on the curb of the bed. Peter didn't stir to his poking and probing.

The doctor signaled reassuringly, and made humming noises while changing the dressing. Layers of gauze following the contour of Peter's head, then across the forehead and under the lips: a mummy's kissing cousin.

More gauze around the chest, shoulders and arm. The taut plastic shell guarding his ribs left in place.

Doc Adams slapped a vein to attention, administered a long needle.

Peter's eyes fluttered and he made a little noise.

"The boy's recovery proceeding on schedule," the doctor announced. "The body healing itself."

"Is there anything I can be doing, Doc?"

Doc Adams nodded to Noah's question. "When you sentence killers anymore, be sure and send them to the gas chamber."

He patted Noah on the back, gave Aunt Dorothy a hug and, turning to KC, poked her on the nose the way he used to whenever he came by with the chocolate and strawberry ice cream after removing her tonsils.

After dinner, pleading a headache, she retired to her room. She left the door open wide enough to catch the sound of Cookie returning.

She climbed out of her jumpsuit and tossed it over the back of a chair. Soaked in the tub. Stepped into a soft knit body suit she'd found at Victoria's Secret, the French cut halfway to her waist. Clicked on the TV and stopped at the first sound of canned laughs. Adjusted the lamp shade. Found a comfortable position against the bed pillows. Turned to Chapter One of the thriller she'd chosen from the remainder table at Vroman's.

The sound of the bedroom door closing awakened her.

No idea how long she'd been sleeping.

Peter.

Using the back of a chair for support.

"Was worried about you." The words droning in his

throat because of the bandages.

"You shouldn't be out of bed."

"What hap—?"

"When that O'Dea hit you, the other man, Snuffy, was worried for me. He dragged me out of the place. Shoved me in a taxi. I didn't want to go, Peter, but he didn't give me a choice . . . I was terrified for you."

When had it become so easy to lie? Was there a date on her résumé? She couldn't see him well enough to know if he bought the story. She rolled off the bed, and started for him, afraid about the damage he might be inflicting on himself.

He pointed her to stop. Coughed his throat clear. "John Ford?"

"I never saw him. He called here today and left a message, but no number." Peter's eyes closed. Nothing left to show on his face, except for purple and blue swelling. "Let me help you back to your room."

He pushed his palms at the space between them. Without the chair, his legs gave way under his full weight, and he slumped to the floor in a series of stops and twists that left him on his back.

KC dropped to her knees beside him, not certain what to do. "I'll get the doctor," she said.

"No! Fine in a minute." He coughed his throat clear. "Head hurts like hell."

"I'll get you a pillow."

He grabbed hold of her wrist before she could move. "Supposed to stay flat." She nodded. He released her and she moved to a sitting position on one hip, balancing on her arm. He said, "Like old times? You. Me. Floor." She leaned over and gently kissed Peter between the eyebrows, ran it down along the ridge of his nose. Warm. Probably running a low fever. Her lips came back moist. "Was scared for you."

"I know. Just stay quiet." She put an index finger to his bruised mouth.

His tongue poked out and began to lick her fingertip, ran it down to the ridge of her second knuckle.

She couldn't bring herself to make him stop.

He reached a hand over his body and found her breast. She remembered the touch and responded after a moment. Pushed hard against his palm. Felt a spasm of pleasure jolt her body and immediately was lost to the sensation.

She bit her tongue to keep from making sounds that might alert the family as Peter's breath became more labored, snapping air like he was catching flies.

He struggled to breathe, but didn't stop.

She didn't resist. Couldn't resist. She tore herself off him long enough to pull back the draperies and let the moon enjoy its magic, and he made a crackling, affirmative noise as alleys of light ran over him. She freed him from his silk pajamas, then threw aside her body suit, straddled Peter and lowered herself like an elevator. Felt Peter reaching every floor of her emotional need. Tossed back her head. Bit down hard into the fleshy part of her hand between the thumb and the index finger to keep from screaming.

Peter reached for her shoulders and pulled her toward him. Locked onto her and somehow managed to land on top.

He pulled at the bandages over his mouth and urged gruffly in her ear, "Tell me when to stop."

"No," she said. "No."

Ripped her nails across his shoulder blades.

He exhaled sounds she knew and signaled her not to stop. Sometimes begging through the bandages. Repeating himself the way he did on the broken record she stored with other memories. Calling her by name.

Whatever else was wrong with the world, KC knew this was right.

If only for tonight.

"You killed him, didn't you?"

"What are you saying?"

"The priest? Father Shanley?"

"That's crazy, Peter!"

"Did you?"

"Stop it! No!"

"I don't believe you."

"Mother Mary and Joseph! Just how hard did that bully in the bar hit you?"

"Not as hard as you hit Donahue. That was his name, you know. Preston Donahue. A paid assassin."

Conversation drifts into silence, and Father Shanley sits across from her, a pillow hiding the Walther PPK he will use to kill her.

She is stark naked. The assassin hesitates a fraction of a second. She squeezes the trigger of the .32 and he is the dead one, not her.

"The same paid assassin who murdered my husband."

"What?"

"He murdered Frankie, Peter. Preston Donahue murdered Frankie."

"What else? What else you have to tell me?"

"Nothing. Please. You know too much already."

A pounding.

Pulling KC from the dream.

A different nightmare.

She opened her eyes to Friday morning and saw the bathroom door ajar, a light hiding behind the vertical crack.

Peter rinsing off the night?

She moved a hand to where she felt him still alive inside of her and froze at the memory of Frankie gently confessing, *"You was ever to lay down with him and that not rid you of the demon, a case could be made for you and him, but, I swear, Face, the truth of another man touching you would kill me . . ."*

You I love, Frankie. Only you. Last night was a weakness of the flesh, a wandering memory. A need came to the surface and—

A knocking that wouldn't quit.

"Your goddam ears go deaf?" Cookie's voice, from the other side of the room.

Her legs apart, left elbow angled from her body in a defiant pose.

Her right fist a hammer banging on the bedroom door.

"I said, Your. Goddam. Ears. Go. Deaf?"

KC rolled on her back and slapped the other side of the mattress. Peter must have left sometime after the spasms that threw her into a sleep that could pass for a coma. She gasped through her mouth and let the breath slide out of her nose. Sucked in the lingering smell of their lovemaking. Couldn't repeal the guilty blush sweeping across her face.

"Good morning to you, too," she said, pushing into a sitting position, pretending.

She imagined the chaos if Cookie had walked in on Peter still in bed with her.

"Mommy said I should come wake you. She's waiting breakfast." She wore her petulance with honor.

"Can we talk first, for a few minutes?" Her eyes averted KC. She didn't respond. "It's clear something's bothering you. Let's talk about it, okay? I'm your friend, Monkey. I want to stay your friend."

Cookie had seen something. She tracked forward a few

feet, bent over to pick up—

—Peter's pajama bottoms.

Where KC had tossed them.

Cookie's face turned bright red, borrowed all the horror in the world. She squeezed the bottoms like an accordion and threw them at her. They unraveled in the air and landed short of the bed as she retreated.

"Cookie!"

"That John Ford person—Mrs. McClory. He's here. Mommy invited him to stay for breakfast."

CHAPTER 32

"You had me worried, girl-o," Liam said, putting down his sweet roll as Katie swept past the French windows onto the patio. He brought the back of a hand to his mouth, remembered his manners in time to substitute a corner of the silk napkin tied around his neck like a baby's bib. He sprang to his feet, reached out for her.

"I had *you* worried?" she said, acknowledging her auntie before stepping into his embrace. He could feel her reluctance. "How could I possibly have you worried, Jack?"

She wore no bra and her nipples pressed hard as German marks beneath a snow white tunic worn over a skin-tight pair of denims that were torn at the knees and pushed into a pair of high top suede cowboy boots. Her hair was shower stall wet and hung out to dry, sunglasses perched on top.

"Like I was saying to the good lady, I come this close two nights ago to calling after police, you not showing for our tête-à-tête."

He stole another squeeze before releasing her, settled onto his chair and speared a slice of golden melon.

"You did what, lying devil?" Tried making it sound like a joke.

She took a seat facing her auntie, away from his reach, and poured herself a cup of coffee from the sterling silver pitcher while the old lady explained that her uncle was off to a meeting and the girl, Cookie, had dashed off for school with her geek of a boyfriend.

She didn't offer him a refill, so he took his own.

"Where were you, Jack? You could have helped fight off

some dirty sewer rats who attacked Aunt Dorothy's son."

He answered her mean eyes with a vacant stare. "Heard something about that. Peter by name, the good lady was telling before you come. A police detective."

The old lady nodded confirmation as he pulled out his pocket watch and clicked open the engraved sterling silver face.

"By this very timepiece me sainted Mum give me for a birthday, a legacy from me late Da and it never runs more'n a minute late, I was prompt there The Quiet Man at seven and quit at half past eight, trying desperate not to fear the worst, except for your faulty memory, Katie. What? Nobody told you?" He pushed up tall in his seat. Shared an open-mouthed amazement between them. "Before going, I left word with the bartender, even wrote it down for anyone come asking."

"Jack, our date was for nine o'clock."

"Nine o'clock? Did she say *nine* o'clock? Well, fancy that. Least we know it ain't the ticker what needs some repairing." He made a show of inspecting the Roman numerals on the brown-edged face before he clicked it shut.

Katie leaned in and pretended to sniff him. She nodded and turned to the old lady.

"Jack wears two scents, Aunt Dorothy, Irish whisky and cheap cologne. One for Jack, one for his women, is what they used to say about him in Belfast. You found both at The Quiet Man and made other plans. Come on, confess."

She sang the word "confess" like she wanted to crawl under his skin. There's a time and a place for everything, Katie McClory, he answered her back with his look. His fingers worked a warning she wasn't fast enough to catch.

"Got me, again, Katie." He held out his hands for her to administer the cuffs. "I never could get away with anything when I was 'round this one, good lady. Found one who was at the special age, Katie, needing a good man to prove herself still a good woman. Always the tall redwoods what fall fastest, even without the cologne." The auntie forked some grapefruit wedges, like that was as good it ever got for her, and pretended not to hear what he had said. Katie kicked his shin under the table.

"I found me a nurse with skin as white as her uniform," he said, ignoring her signal to cut it out. "I told her I was what doctor ordered, in need of some serious nursing. A fine nurse, she was. Maureen. Didn't mind filling her prescription any more'n Maureen minded a face like mine."

He pointed at himself.

The auntie smiled politely.

He wondered if she knew he was undressing her.

The old lady was pretty for her age. He didn't often find them so pretty. When he did, he always made a point of leaving them with something to remember him. He wondered what giving her a ride would be like. Sort of like wheeling out a retired champion on Derby Day for one fast trot around the track? She didn't seem to be put off by his face, and that was always a good sign. The ones in need always seemed to see his face as some aphrodisiac or penance for their sins. Liam McClory, wearing on the outside what most people carry only on their inside, compliments the Royal Ulster Constabulary.

He saw by Katie's reaction she had caught on to his drift. He considered who would put up the better fight, the old lady or Katie? Or, the kid, Cookie?

He could tell the kid was no friend from the way she drilled him with her looks, but she looked feisty. He always had a preference for feisty ones, same as he had for a screamer. Never a problem turning the feisty ones into screamers, easier than water into milk. Like he done the cop, Annie Waterman.

She spit in his face and wouldn't so much as give him an answer until he threatened to cut out her tongue when they were finished with her.

How Annie had struggled added immensely to the pleasure, and he regretted when she started owning up to the facts, not that what Annie knew made any difference, except for her suspecting the truth about Katie and the death of Donahue.

"Mind if I join you?"

Katie pushed out a heavy breath, put a hand to her breast as her shit cop boyfriend's eyes bore into hers. Her face was no longer hard as a winter's night in solitary. Her sulky eyes brightened to full-strength blue and her cheeks blushed red. She looked for a place to hide the thoughts passing in front of her eyes, Liam could see that.

Mind? Liam thought. Is what I come for, shit cop. View the kind of work we did on you and how you come through. Find out why me brother's woman don't return phone calls. Test the waters and survey the territory the way Francis needs it, and know better where we stand without having to depend on her over there. Maybe, set new plans and a different death trap for the nigger.

Liam pushed up from the table and extended his hand. The shit cop took it.

"Peter Osborne."

Except for the bandages, the shit cop was about what he expected from Snuffy's description. Slope to the right shoulder, easing the pull on whatever got busted inside his color-splashed robe. A grip on the door handle and all the weight on his left foot. A third degree stare, between shifts to take in Katie, who kept sending him back a look that could mean anything. A tic playing war games beneath his cheek bones. O'Dea had done his work real good.

"John Ford, Detective Osborne, the original rogue with a brogue. Jack to me friends, which is the world at a glance, so I'll call you Peter. If you were the winner, I'd like to know where the funeral parlor, so I can pay final respects to the loser?"

CHAPTER 33

Peter studied John Ford, trying to decipher how much he knew and how much he was putting on, as he told Ford about The Quiet Man. He reached a pause point and encouraged a response with a look.

Ford shaped a huge boulder with his hands and said, "Dermot O'Dea? An animal, that one. Loves his battles as much as his bottles. May Lawless, just protecting her man, my guess. Some women like that."

"Yes." Peter casually drifted his gaze from Mother to KC, who broke it off and made a career of buttering a wedge of toast.

He chewed his croissant slowly. First real food in two days. Washed it down with the rest of his orange juice. Poured a cup of coffee after filling Ford's waiting cup.

Ford said, "Cheers! Don't know what gets into people sometimes, Pete. Whenever I'm faced with the who of it, sure as the devil himself they feel the what of it." He held up his fist and bounced it against the sky.

Mother said, "The answer to violence is never violence."

"Frig no, good lady, but it puts a body in his place, handled right and proper." He aimed his forefingers at his face, like daggers. "This botch tells you better about violence than any words of mine."

"I'm sorry," Mother said.

"You're sorry? Not like someone told me take a number and get in line." Mother's eyes misted and she bit into her lower lip. Instantly, Ford apologized. "All these years and it stays hard for me to go a day without feeling rotten for myself, good lady."

Peter redirected the conversation. "You go to The Quiet Man often, Jack?"

"Often enough to recognize to steer clear-a Dermot O'Dea anytime at all I'm down here from up there." He illustrated *up* with a thumb.

"Canada."

"Vancouver. I settled there some years ago from Belfast. Never regretted the move, except for family considerations. The work gets me down here regular, and then on up again through Washington and Oregon."

"KC said you sell shoes?"

"No business like shoe business." He discharged a laugh. "Natural footwear's me specialization. The genuine leather. No heel: a flat bottom that matches the foot and lets you walk the way God and Mother Nature meant." Ford grabbed hold of his thigh and worked his leg onto the table edge to show off the beaver brown pair he was wearing with his tan wash-and-wear suit and clip-on red and chartreuse bow tie. "You interested, Pete, I just might have your size out the boot . . . at a special price, if you know what I mean?"

Peter shook his head.

"I know, I know," Ford said. "Not regulation in any of our basic styles, or meant for giving chase to criminals." A hearty laugh, a survey inviting them to join in. Mother smiling, the conscientious hostess.

"When my partner got you on the phone, she came away with the impression you and KC first met on the train coming down."

"I already explained that, Peter."

Peter waved KC off.

Ford tried to sound puzzled. "Your partner?"

"Detective Waterman. Annie Waterman. She located your number here through a business card you left with KC.

We've been working that homicide, the priest?"

Head bobbing. "Yes, yes, yes. Pleasant voice, I recall, and attractive. A bit on the feisty side when she dropped by on me. Said she was an admirer of the late John Fitzgerald Kennedy. Your partner, was she?" He paused, made a face to convey he was wrestling with his memory. "Maybe I didn't follow the question or could of answered wrong, must be it . . ." Something made his face flinch. Question himself before deciding, "I know I told her how Bright Eyes here slept the night with my shoulder for a pillow, but can't say as how she ever asked we were old acquaintances."

"And you are, you and Bright Eyes?" Peter repeated the name intentionally. It had jarred KC floating out of Ford's mouth, and now.

"What her husband called her. Frankie McClory? A name I remembered from being there, it being just the right description and one all the locals picked up on real quick. Ain't it so, Bright Eyes?"

KC answered with a dispirited nod.

"So, you left Belfast sometime in the last six years?"

"Why is that?" Ford said.

"KC was there six years, allowing for some time she spent in London. That so, KC?"

She said, "My comings and goings, better than a calendar."

"Me, not so long ago as six years, but I suppose you ring up the company and they could find a date for you. Wasn't so long after I landed I got the job, on a visit to somebody who knew somebody who knew somebody from home."

"Falls Road."

"Well, Katie, seems you been giving your friend here a geography lesson? Yes. Me sainted Mum and the McClorys was all neighbors over by Falls Road. How I come to meet the lass once she married up with Frankie McClory. A poor but decent man. Ma wrote me about his tragic death. I since been wearing black around me heart, Bright Eyes."

Ford took a different kind of look from KC, as something started nagging at Peter.

The story wasn't ringing true. Some contradiction? He'd caught KC and Jack Ford in a contradiction? No, to the contrary. KC had gone from giving Ford's business card to Annie to rattling off a history. Now, he was starting to get the echo from Ford. That was it. Too much echo.

Ford said, "Funny part is, Katie didn't remember me a whit, and I wasn't so sure of her until we got us to chatting the long ride down. Happens and not just the movies. Ain't that so, Bright Eyes?"

KC waived the question. She looked beautiful. Peter had to work at keeping his mind on business. Her blue eyes blazed like neon. Her skin absorbed the sunshine and gave off a translucent glow. "You ever run into a Preston Donahue, Jack? He came from your neck of the woods."

"Can't say as I . . . ? Wait a minute." Finger snap. "Was an Alby Preston with Bally I run into one time a convention in New Orleans?" An edge creeping into Ford's calcified voice. He fished for a pack of cigarettes, thought better of it. Set the pack next to his plate. Peter didn't know the brand.

"I meant Falls Road, Jack, not shoe biz. Preston is the man's first name. Preston Donahue."

Thinking. Taking his time. Calmly channeling into control with the precision of a professional liar. A signal he forget to rehearse with KC, or just acting?

Finally, "Donahue, you say. Donahue? Preston Donahue? No, not over Lisburn Road. Maybe Brook Street? I wouldn't know him from over on Brook Street. What that's about, or shouldn't I ask?"

KC said, "The third degree, Jack. Peter has been out of practice a few days, so you're elected."

Her face starting to close down. The conversation had made her uncomfortable, or was it her memories of last night, when more than once he sensed she regretted having gone so far with him, and he was too hungry to risk the question?

He'd take it up with her tonight, same time, same floor.

If she didn't open the door, he would have his answer anyway.

"Third degree?" Ford slammed his hand on the table for emphasis, shook his head. "Bright Eyes, not even a first degree! Ask him what knows from degrees . . . More questions, Pete? Happy to oblige."

Ford exchanged smiles with Mother, who nervously fingered the gold link chain around her neck.

Peter knew he was onto something. The son-of-a-bitch was challenging him.

He glanced at KC. She had pushed down her sunglasses and was hiding behind them.

He reached for a strip of bacon, extra crisp, the way he liked it, and aimed it down his throat like a sword-swallower. "My turn to apologize, Jack. I didn't mean for it to sound that way."

"None taken, Pete. You got more to ask, you ask."

KC interrupted, "Didn't you say you had somewhere else to go this morning, Jack?"

"Only the motel. Sit on the side of the bed and ring up customers, spread good cheer and a bit of a word about the new styles."

"Well, I don't have all morning," KC said, rising, flashing a sour look.

And, it came to him.

The bother wasn't a contradiction in Ford's story, or the

echo of KC's story about the train trip down. It had to do with Annie. Annie and the motel. She said she had not found him there when she went looking, but he—

Man, between the clobbering he took and the medication, his memory was a disaster area.

"The Happy Wanderer," he said, matter-of-factly.

"Over in Venice. Near the sea."

"My partner said she couldn't find you when she went looking there."

"Oh?" His eyes ricocheting left and right.

"The clerk told her they didn't have a John Ford registered. Lots of John Does, but no John Ford."

KC gripped the back of her chair. "What's the point in all this?"

Ford wagged a hand at her. "A fair question, that, working up to the first degree, Katie."

"You do seem to know about degrees, Jack."

"Badge of honor where I come from, Pete boy. When you talking about, your partner? She got her information at the motel?" Ford moved his coffee cup aside and leaned into the table. One side of his mouth slowly etched a half-hearted grin. "You know the day? What today is?"

"It's—"

"Two days since your run-in with O'Dea at The Quiet Man. Was yesterday I connected with her, your partner. She hasn't said anything to you?"

Mother shook her head. "Peter wasn't in any condition to—anyone. We have some messages waiting on you, dear, but I don't think from Annie. Strange. I would have bet she'd be on the telephone fifty times by now, or camped outside your door. Annie is very fond of him, Jack."

KC's eyes closed to the declaration.

Ford worked his grin. "Bless the man with women as loyal

as dogs. Well, was on yesterday she come to me with more questions and a drawing of a woman she said was the one done in the priest. Making like it could be Katie McClory on the drawing, but I set her straight."

"At the Happy Wanderer?"

"Nowhere but."

"The clerk—"

"Protecting his sideline, maybe? I know for fact him and his cohorts got them a stable of women they run in through there regular." He winked. "Vancouver got onto me about the police wanting to chat some more. I rang up your partner, and there we were."

"At the Happy Wanderer Motel."

"Gave them a terrible piece of my mind. Could of been a valued customer out of the blue, and where would that put me? Down one commission at a time I got bills to choke a horse."

KC cleared her throat.

Ford swallowed what was left of his coffee and read his wristwatch. "So, now, I think you're right, Bright Eyes. I could spend all day in the comfort of these lovely surroundings, but Pete here reminds me I got obligations to look after." He pushed up from his chair. "You got more to discuss, you don't hesitate to call, Pete—at the Happy Wanderer."

They traded tepid smiles.

Mother urging Ford to come again as she joined KC in walking him to the door.

At once, Peter worked his way to the phone and called downtown.

Annie wasn't there.

Nobody in the bureau had heard from her since the night she tooled off to track his shadow. He tried Transportation and learned Annie was overdue in returning her Camaro loaner. He called her home got the recording on first ring, meaning other messages. How many? Piling up for how long? He told her to call him the minute she got his.

He got the Happy Wanderer number through Operator. The clerk sounded like he'd been caught in a nap. Shuffling of register pages. No John Ford on the books. Lying son-of-a-bitch. Who? The clerk or John Ford?

"Plenty of John Does, I hear?"

"And John Smiths," the clerk said. "You a cop? Show me your warrant." And hung up.

Peter cradled the phone. He felt a new layer of sweat building under his bathrobe, concern for Annie adding to his exhaustion.

KC passed him wordlessly, barely a glance, heading for the kitchen. He wanted to shout her to a stop and get answers, but there was Burkes to think about, the deception he'd agreed to undertake, his own lies to KC to deal with.

Yeah, she was part of something, all right, and another thing for certain. If anything had happened to Annie, KC would be on his personal hit list, along with John Ford.

CHAPTER 34

KC had walked Liam outside, to have their last words in private, alongside his late model black Toyota Celica with Nevada plates. If it was like back home, the car was stolen, plates clean, and would defy anyone tracing it before it disappeared for good.

"Guess we showed him, girl-o."

"You damned fool. He's no dummy. Why did you lie about seeing his partner?"

"I saw his partner, like I said."

"Not at the motel. The lie was as clean on your face as—"

"G'head. You can say it."

"The new number you gave me last time. Not the motel. You said you had moved on. Never in one place long enough for the law catch up, you said. How much did you pay the clerks to shut their mouths?"

"I paid 'em a compliment is all. The dump is owned by one of ours. He takes care of them details good as I care about my own."

"Peter will check. He'll check and get to the truth. Then it's my ass he'll be on."

"Not a new position from what I make the looks passing between youse."

"You piece of filth!"

"They call me a bachelor boy where I come from, and what's the name for you, girl-o?" She wanted to strike him, but there wasn't even time to be clever before he said, "I give you the new number, but you didn't ring me on two messages I left for you."

"I forgot." It was a foolish answer, but better than admitting she threw his messages away, furious for Peter's beating. "I meant to, but I didn't have the chance, and then I forgot."

"She forgot," Liam said to himself. "Got to make a note to remember that."

"Was it so important? End of the world important?"

"Don't toy with me, Katie, not when you're certain to come up short. We agreed other night I would call to come here and have a look? We got our story straight to make certain we wouldn't open ourselves to any problems we couldn't handle?"

"You agreed. I had no choice."

"Seems you did. Seems your choice was to forget. Problem turns out to be you and your bloody fucking memory, but here I was anyway."

"Like a bad penny."

"Same difference." He shrugged, made a visor of his hand against the sun to study her, his look as rude as a piss on the wall.

KC said, "Well, it's done. Are you satisfied?"

"Satisfied something's not right."

"Why?"

He shrugged. "You'll know when I know."

"Why did you need to come and look anyway?"

"See how the other half lives. Shame I didn't get upstairs. I planned asking the old lady for a tour, but then thought better of it, the way your shit cop boyfriend was raining down me neck."

KC recognized there was no percentage in arguing the point. "Is there a date with the Plowman?"

He considered the question. "Soon."

"You still don't trust me, do you?"

"Never said so."

"You don't have to."

"Good. That kind of clear thinking appeals to a man of few words."

He climbed behind the wheel, turned the engine. Lowered the window.

Called her back to say, "Trusted Francis and look at where that put us. Trusted Preston Donahue and look at where that put us. Now, you being under the same roof as a sniffing cop, and you got to ask? Anything go wrong with the plan, I come straight-away to haunt you. Lob off you and the rest of them and never once stop laughing, Bright Eyes, never once." His eyes shut down. A dirty giggle behind his carnival mouth.

KC understood Liam was crazier than she had ever imagined, but his instincts were right about her. He was getting too close on guesses. Something had to be done about him before it was too late.

She thought about Frankie and the world separating him from his crazy brother as she returned inside. God, she missed seeing Frankie, being with him, loving him. Last night with Peter hadn't changed that.

She hurried past Peter on the phone, before Peter could think to play third degree with her. She helped Aunt Dorothy with the dishes, borrowed the town car, drove to the mall and chose a pay phone as private as the one she'd used yesterday.

The call to Burkes took two switchovers. KC quit the first when a volleyball of a man in dark glasses and a ten-gallon hat limped to the end of the phone bank and made the first of several credit card calls.

She waited for him to finish and limp away before she hit the number pad again. When the connection came through, after what seemed like hours, she told Burkes, "I think whatever is supposed to happen happens soon."

"You got a name on the Plowman?"

"Just a feeling, a hunch . . . John Ford came to the house this morning. He surprised me. I didn't expect him, and—It was wrong. Felt wrong. Was your security ready, in case he—"

"Save it for now. Any chance you're being followed?"

"Followed? No. I'd almost swear." Checked across her shoulders.

"*Almost* is an invitation to disaster," Burkes said. He told her where to meet him.

Back behind the wheel, KC studied the rear view mirrors for signs of a tail. After a while, all the freeway traffic looked suspicious.

CHAPTER 35

A rain forest had settled in Peter's ears and his body parts felt like they'd been used by the circus as an elephant stool, but he was determined to quit playing invalid. KC and John Ford had done more to heal him than all the chicken soup in the world, but mostly it was the worrying about Annie. Ignoring Mother's objections, he took a cautious soak in the tub, grunted himself dressed and headed downtown by way of her apartment.

She didn't answer the buzz, and a glimpse through the peek slats showed a mailbox stuffed with envelopes. Annie, the Queen of Mail Order.

The manager shook her head like a dust mop, and Peter's worrying grew all the way to Parker Center.

He scanned the radio for music hard enough to cut the racket inside his head, was halted by two names on one of the all-news channels—

Mr. Mustamba.

And, the president of the United States.

A sonorous voice recited:

"Spokesmen would neither confirm nor deny that the President has added a visit here to his calendar, but they reminded reporters he recently expressed a strong hope of having the opportunity to meet and confer with Mr. Mustamba during the revered African leader's series of appearances in Southern California. A spokesman for Mr. Mustamba said only that he would consider it an honor to—"

He lost the rest of it flashing on Burkes.

Not just Mr. Mustamba.

Also, the President of the United States.

Need to know.

Check, Burkes, and not half as much fun as *Need to figure out.*

Peter found a jazz station playing early Satchmo, used the dash as a drum kit while trying to lay down a logical rhythm to his concern for Annie.

Parker Center.

He parked and headed for Transportation.

Saunders began complaining immediately about Annie not advising him she'd be late, and his needing the Camaro for a narc spritz in Watts tonight and over the weekend. Peter spiked Saunders' mouth shut with one sideways glance.

He hit his desk and saw a scribbled note taped to the phone. The boss wanted to see him first thing. He let Linsenmeyer know he was there and got a time.

Looped through a stack of new files.

Old cases that refused to go away.

Paper shuffle on court appearances; one missed yesterday, an ice-eyed Korean gangbanger who offed a Crip, getting even for the drive-by murder of his five-year-old sister in the front yard of a nursery school. Reset for next month.

He glanced occasionally at Annie's empty chair.

Scarfed a handful of aspirin from the bottle in his bottom drawer. Chewed them to death.

Called across to Skolnik, who was on logging duty today. Asked for an ARD on Annie. Skolnik gestured *No idea.* Tapped out Debbie Gwyn's extension in Dispatch. Asked if she had any late reading on Annie. Debbie said nothing for today.

Why weren't they worried like he was worried?

Because they assumed she was on stakeout, stripped of obligation to ride the rules until the gig was over. Even his presence didn't raise questions, because they knew he had been flattened out of service for two days.

Annie, carrying the torch alone.

And, maybe, that's all it was.

But she would have called him, damn it. She would have checked with the house, to see how he was doing and found an hour to visit. There was nothing about the tail to The Quiet Man to keep her underground and invisible.

Peter flipped desk calendar pages forward. He found a note from her on a sheet of memo paper Annie had bought him as a gag, a sketch of Hans Brinker doing what he did best, Peter's name in graffiti on the wall of the dike. She had scrawled a kindergarten heart pierced by an arrow in red pencil. Inside the heart she'd written: "P. O. + A. W." Below the heart, in block letters: "No More Up the Irish!"

Peter's smile drained into a flash of misgiving. He taped the drawing to the side of his out basket, glanced at the clock, saw it was time for his meeting with the boss.

Chief Spence gave him a wave in, motioned him to a pair of hardback chairs angled for conversation and grabbed a handful of candy bars on his way over.

The boss decided, "You got bags under your eyes twice the size of Dolly Parton's bazooms." He settled into a slouch with his legs crossed at the ankles. "What is it, forget how to sleep since the whole Israeli Army came down on you?"

"Off and on last night," Peter responded, smiling inwardly.

Spence's eyes narrowed over his nose, like he was trying to confirm a suspicion.

Peter pushed hard against the high back, used the arm rests to defend against an explosion of memory pain along his fractured ribs.

"Talk to me," Spence ordered, lacing his fingers behind the back of his head. The boss was in full dress blue today, going somewhere public. His head glistened from a fresh shave, where he'd missed with the talc. A spit shine heavy enough to trap reflections.

Peter told him about The Quiet Man and Annie.

Spence tried to appear unconcerned.

When he was sure Peter had finished, he asked a few questions, then pinned Peter to the chair with a gesture and headed for his desk without excusing himself. He mumbled something into the phone, parked it between his shoulder and ear while stuffing a pack of gum in his mouth. Two minutes later, he was grunting into the mouthpiece.

Peter used the time wondering what Annie would say when she learned about the breakfast game he had played with Ford. She'd be able to identify Ford's lies better than him. He traded a picture of Annie for KC, sure of some things about her now, sure as Annie had been from the beginning, but—

The lingering *but.*

"Relax, Pete!" The chief replaced the receiver and rejoined him. Threw a leg over an arm of the chair. "I held on while Linsenmeyer checked. He tells me Annie did call in yesterday in the a.m. She advised she was still hoarding a stake."

"Nothing today, Skolnik said. The same from Debbie Gwyn in Dispatch."

"Our girl's TCB, Pete, a pro . . ."

"Boss, she would have called me."

"Maybe she called Larry King, instead." Spence leered and sucked in the flavor of his joke. "Neither did I. I didn't send you a card or flowers. I protected our pension fund reserves." He stretched forward to pat him on the knee. "She's fine, Pete. Annie's a good cop, and careful."

"I don't know."

"Listen, check in with Burkes, then get thee home for some more sack time. I told Linsenmeyer to assign a team to that bar, The Quiet Man. Clear the jurisdiction thing on reciprocity and have them look up this Snuffy Danaher. Dermot O'Dea. The Lawless dame. See what they come up with . . . Where do we turn for John Ford?"

Peter explained the contradiction of the Happy Wanderer.

"Ford says he's staying there, we'll start there. Maybe the clerk'll be more receptive to a push that goes to shove from a pair of our finest gentlemen from vice. If Ford isn't on the register, we'll threaten to play room roulette."

"That failing?"

"By then we'll have tried the Vancouver number again. If that doesn't work—Maybe by then we'll have Annie back to tell us what we don't know. You go on home, Pete. Let me sit on this egg for you."

Peter agreed, not meaning it. He got back to his desk and punched out the number he had for Walter Burkes. He was overdue for more answers, more truth than Burkes had bothered to share with him, and intent on settling for nothing less. Most of all he needed to tell Burkes he wasn't playing "Fuck Her for the Feds" anymore.

CHAPTER 36

Peter pulled up the Trans Am to the high curb outside the Federal Building, where Burkes was waiting for him. Burkes checked his watch, opened the passenger door and inched inside.

"I like a man who's punctual," Burkes announced. He reached over and gave Peter's forearm a friendly squeeze, taking care to avoid the bandages, and toned down the radio without asking permission. "You said you know where the place is?"

"It's not a secret." He navigated the one-ways onto Alameda and kept going north, across Macy, until the familiar green canopies that identified *Philippe's* came into view. He parked illegally out front, dropped the visor so his police ID showed to any three-wheeler cruising for tire chalk.

"I been busting my gut for a French dip since the middle of the night," Burkes said, stepping aside so he could enter first.

Ten or fifteen degrees cooler inside. The overwhelming smell of an open kitchen. Too dim to check for moving parts on the meat being piled inside the buns by the service crew.

Burkes kissed his fingertips French style and gave a circled thumb and forefinger to the attractive, leg-weary brunette behind the counter. "That's Nancy with the secret smile," he volunteered. "My favorite. Always manages to slip extra slices into my beef dips."

They waited their turn in line. His body was a garden of aches. The pain killers he'd swallowed an hour ago hadn't kicked in yet.

Burkes went on and on about his pet German shepherd, like the rest of the world was on hold. "You got an opinion, Peter? The dysplasia's an ultimate killer, a sad and sorry sight, but we go for surgery we risk shortening Fritz's life, like happened once before to the wife's pooch."

"You do nothing and watch him go slowly and painfully. I don't see where there's a decision."

"Logical, very logical." Chewing the word logical like it was a conclusion he would not have reached without help.

He ordered a cheeseburger, vegetable soup and an iced tea.

Burkes asked for fries with his beef dip, a side of coleslaw, a side of potato salad. The meat Nancy loaded into his sandwich was burned to a five-alarm black. Fat clung to it like a spurned lover.

"That stuff can kill you," Peter said, as Burkes guided him toward a nearly empty communal table by the picture window.

"Life does that Peter. This way, at least, I go out with grease on my lips and a smile on my face."

He took a gargantuan bite and chewed like it was his first meal of the century.

Peter dumped sugar into his iced tea and made the cubes swim with his spoon.

"Grease, a smile and barbecue goop on your suit," Peter said, pointing to a spot just below the enamel D.A.R.E. pin on Burkes' lapel. Looked away to mark the crowd while Burkes finished scouring the stain with a paper napkin. Recognized a few people from the Civic Center buildings, who were lingering over dime coffees and homemade doughnuts.

He returned the wave of a Superior Court judge he knew from one of his earliest court appearances, when his testimony clinched a Murder One for the D.A. and the judge, who was acquainted with his father, put some nice words into the record.

He bit into the burger, studied the action on the street.

Nothing and nobody outside to write home about, unless home was the jungle.

Burkes finished cleaning up. He had left a damp spot the size of a half dollar. "Have I mentioned you look like shit?" he said.

"You the expert on what shit looks like?"

Burkes aimed a chin in his direction and quieted his eyes. Peter knew he was pressing for the moment of serious conversation, whether or not Peter was ready.

"Your case does not call for an expert," Burkes said. "Mrs. McClory play that rough in bed?"

"Off limits, Burkes."

"I know, you don't have to tell me . . . I have one of those prurient personalities. Sorry. Sometimes I think that and my undeniable charm is what originally got me the White House detail."

White House. He said it like he was painting it, the way he was certain Burkes intended, making sure he had jump-started the serious talk with Peter's complete attention.

"The President figures in this, right?"

"Figures in what, Peter?"

"The Belfast shuttle business. The business about Mr. Mustamba."

"Are you reporting? Is this something you got from Mrs. McClory? Or, are you on a fishing trip?"

"KC didn't mention the President or Mr. Mustamba."

"Who did she mention?"

"Nobody."

"John Ford."

Peter arched back, sent a stiff pain shooting down parts of

his body that were new to him. He had expected to say the name first. Made like he had been caught on an *Oops*. "Ford, yeah. Ford came to the house for breakfast this morning."

"That's what you said when you called. What this meeting is about?"

The pain had made him forget most of what he had said to get the lunch. Burkes watched him wince again, showing less sympathy than he had put out for his dog Fritz.

"Yes and no."

"Why don't I get you a fence to sit on? Then your answer can be complete."

"I made love to her last night, Burkes. At no time did I know if I was doing it for me or for you. It's been fucking up my head, so I thought I'd put it to you straight. Face to face. I want out."

"You've hardly been in."

He batted the remark with the back of his hand. "KC may be as guilty as sin, but I can't do it to her anymore."

"You mean like you're doing it to yourself?"

"Very funny. So, why aren't I laughing?"

"Maybe you should be laughing. Remember what Adlai Stevenson said after he lost the election? 'I'm laughing because it hurts too much to cry?' "

"He said, 'I'm too old to cry and it hurts too much to laugh.' "

Burkes shrugged. "I may know you better than you think I do, Peter, maybe better than you know yourself. You're a lot like your old man, I think. Judge Osborne is the kind of gent who knows when to put country before self. Straight out, this is one of those times for you, Peter."

Peter felt his expression start to hurt as much as the rest of him. The son-of-a-bitch had scored big with that one.

What Walter Burkes really meant was, Do what your

father would do, Peter. That's the only answer. That's the one the judge can accept; therefore, you should accept without question. He grabbed a chocolate doughnut from the plate Burkes had pushed to the middle of the table, wolfed it down looking for a sugar rush to keep him from nose-diving onto the table.

Burkes saw what he was going through. Maybe why he eased up. "I understand you almost took O'Dea."

Peter thought about it in slow motion. "Where'd you hear that?" Grudgingly.

"Uh-huh. Anyone tell you they call May Lawless The Bitch of Venice Beach? You could've done the impossible, marched King McKong out of The Quiet Man, if May hadn't delivered you a pipe dream, or so I'm told."

"Don't be coy, Burkes."

"O'Dea, Dermot. AKA Denis Moore. The rap sheet I read says he beat a man to death with his fists back in the Old Sod and a few more came this close." He used a thumb and forefinger to illustrate a half inch of space.

"Saved to kill another day by the shuttle."

"Yeah. Up to me, I would of pushed the stem right down his esophagus and probed for his asshole. Danaher, as well. Eager Eddie. The Snuff Man. That insidious little fuck of a leprechaun's been under our microscope for years."

Peter used his fist for a gavel. "Check me out on this one. At The Quiet Man, you had someone smelling my sweat."

"Give the man a four leaf clover."

"The one who helped me . . . Ellen Mulhall."

"By any name. In her case, Reparata. Rep and Bunny were sent pedal to the metal after you phoned the magic number and told us what you were up to. Orders to watch your back full time. They got nailed by locals complaining about Rep's unpatriotic behavior and had to buy a few rounds of forgiveness. They thought about passing word to your partner when she came looking, but did an E.T. instead."

"Annie went inside?"

"And then she went out. Last Rep and Bunny saw of her." Peter could tell he was losing color faster than Michael Jackson. "Peter, we had an arrangement? Annie Waterman wasn't supposed to be in on this."

"We're a team, Burkes."

"Astaire and Rogers are a team."

"Where is she?"

"Rodgers and Hammerstein."

"Damn it, Burkes!" He judo-slashed a swift path above the table, almost knocking over his water glass.

A middle-aged Chinese man dressed like everybody's favorite waiter, a braided white pigtail jutting out from under a black box beanie, rose with quiet dignity from his seat halfway down the next table. He folded his *Racing Form*, stashed it under his arm, picked up his tray and navigated across the room.

Burkes dropped his voice a pitch. "Where Annie is not, Peter. Annie's not available. My people were out checking while you were sleeping off your headache. Maybe, you should add it to your list of questions to drop on Mrs. McClory."

Peter went for Burkes' coffee and gripped the cup with both hands, nervous on the implication. "You are some piece of work, Burkes. A regular bastard."

"Practice. Practice. Practice," Burkes said. He used a doughnut to build in thinking time. "Peter, the raff we're up against only know how to play down and dirty. It would be cruel of me pretending otherwise to you."

Burkes pulled an eight by ten glossy from a pocket, worked out the creases and held it up for Peter to see. Black and white. Grainy. The man was about to cross a street, unaware of the camera. "Anyone you know?"

Peter eyed him suspiciously. Put down the coffee. Took the photo for a closer study. Nodded agreement. "John Ford. Maybe five or six years younger, before his face went to pieces." He sent a facial telegram across the table: *What's this new trick of yours all about?*

Burkes produced another eight by ten. "Then how do you explain this?"

He was looking at a clear view of the kind of gravestone rare today in America, where small plaques rule the grass like dominoes. Matching tablets large enough for ten commandments, both moss-covered arches topped with a finely chiseled cross. A small bouquet of wildflowers, fresh as someone's memory, placed at a base picked clean of the tangled brown weeds gnawing at other stones visible in the picture.

"Catch the name and the date, Peter. That's the most recent picture we have of John Ford, dead and mourned, lo!, these many years by his sturdy widow, Sioghan, who's in her late seventies. Sioghan still lives next door to the McClorys over Duncairnes Gardens way. Knits for the grandkids and in her spare time packages nitro."

Peter weighed the two photos with his eyes.

"The John Ford who you met is Liam Arthur March McClory, the older brother of Francis Charles August McClory, for whom Katherine Mary McClory still weeps. Liam is full of charm and not as bright as Frankie, but just as dangerous. Liam's been missing since Frankie was killed . . . What do you think of her story now, Peter?"

"What else don't I know?"

"How to sidestep a lead pipe."

Burkes excused himself. Peter tracked him as he loaded up

with two fresh coffees, a dish of pickles and sour tomatoes and a half dozen assorted doughnuts. He lingered in line to say something to Nancy that converted her smile into a salacious smirk.

"Nancy wants my body," he said, settling in again. "Told her I wasn't through using it, yet." Probed for jelly with his finger. Licked it clean.

Peter waited Burkes out, resisting an anger that could make him lose if he wasn't feeling so shitty. Burkes tried to make his eyes look honest and stared right back without faltering.

"The widow McClory's playmates from Belfast are gathering here faster'n maggots for an assassination play on Mr. Mustamba," Burkes said, dryly, like he'd just reported the weather. "Somehow, they picked up early on your father's involvement with the Pasadena leg of the tour. Deciding to use Mrs. McClory to put pieces of the plan in place didn't take any great brainpower."

Peter thought about it, briefly. "Doesn't compute, Burkes. Anywhere you read, they regard Mr. Mustamba as one of their own. Like them, freedom fighters for their people and a cause they believe is just. Equality."

"What are you? Today's guest editorial?"

"Jesus! He visited Ireland last month. If what you say is true, why didn't they pull his cork then?"

"Two reasons, Peter. For one, these penny ante shits didn't want to be so close to the actual deed, knowing they'd automatically be ripe to take the heat. Second and more to the point, the program underwriters want the spilling of the wine over here, to embarrasses our government."

"The program underwriters."

"The same South African yahoos who've been feeding on their own entrails ever since the ruling powers and people like

317

Mandela finally cracked *apartheid* like the Berlin Wall. They ponied up a million pounds sterling for those renegade freelance terrorist fucks to take down Mr. Mustamba before he can close the gate and toss the key on their bastard mentality."

"I don't believe it."

"Did you believe Mountbatten? Remember how he was blown into a jigsaw puzzle in nineteen seventy-nine? Almost the same scenario."

"The Irish loved Mountbatten."

"The Irish, they loved him, but the Indians—the ones who worship cows—they hated him. They saw Mountbatten as a symbol of their own enslavement for all those years under the Brits and under him. They shelled out the same fee, a million pounds sterling, all in the name of getting even. Don't you know yet? Revenge is an equal-opportunity employer."

"I can't—"

Burkes warded him off with a hand. "We're not talking real people here. We are talking here people who even the IRA regards as outlaws. Outlaws who loved the payday more than any Lord Mountbatten. The payday bought 'em more guns, better hiding places. It kept shuttle services operating. It kept those bum fuckers in business."

Burkes patted his pockets until he found what he was looking for, a roll of antacid tablets. Chewed and swallowed two. Two more.

He continued, "We're chasing a killing machine known as the Plowman, Peter. The Plowman, for J. Christ's sake! Comic book stuff, but his victims die for real and stay dead. What we know for sure—Pasadena is the Plowman's target location. It can happen anytime, anywhere on Mr. Mustamba's schedule. The Wrigley Mansion. At City Hall. Maybe when the Rose Bowl gets full up with fifty thousand or more people wanting to see and hear Mr. Mustamba's pearls of wisdom drop."

"Best guess."

"You don't want to know."

"Need to know, Burkes."

Burkes showed Peter he was thinking about it.

"Your folks' house." A dozen emotions passed through Peter's eyes at once. "They got Mountbatten at home. They got the guy who did the Guinness Book of World Records on his front doorstep. They got this thing about homes."

"KC wouldn't—"

"But she knows who would, Peter. The Plowman. Get her to tell you who he is, before it gets to be too late for damage control. If you can't or won't do it for your country, do it for the safety of your family."

Peter was too stunned to respond, but Burkes was smart enough to know he didn't need to hear him say the words to know his decision.

Burkes pointed to the cheeseburger. "You gonna finish that?"

CHAPTER 37

The antiquarian book store on Melrose resembled a Magic Kingdom castle, in the theme park style of architecture that had polluted Los Angeles in the years around World War II. Originally a mortuary, owners afterward had retained the stained glass panels balancing the solid oak door. They depicted St. George slaying the dragon. Appropriate, KC thought, as she was buzzed inside. She signed the leather-bound guest register sitting on the exquisite lecture stand to her immediate left and waited to be noticed.

A few customers were touring glass-enclosed bookshelves. Three clerks stationed at desks positioned indifferently in the dimly-lit main room glanced at her before returning to their chores. Business must be good, she thought, just before she heard a clack of hard-heeled steps on the marble floor.

"Something I might help you with? I'm Jerome." He put a price tag on everything she wore. Not interested, otherwise. Mid twenties. Small hips. Submissive eyes. A voice the color of toothpaste.

"I phoned earlier . . . About an edition of works by Sir Arthur Conan Doyle?"

Pointing, already out of interest. "That would be Gus Furness in Contemporary Fiction. I'm Literature."

"What's the difference?"

A side of his mouth pushing the cheek out of joint. An exhausted sigh. "The quality of mercy." Pointing again, just in case she was a slow learner.

Gus Furness sat at a partners' desk stacked high with books and reference materials, looking more like a retired

biker than a book scholar. Fiftyish. White hair pulled back into a tight ponytail.

Furness rose to the sound of her boots, even before looking to check, his pregnant belly sagging over brown slacks that buckled around hard-soled shoes in desperate need of polishing. Saturday night smile in place. "Mrs. McClory?"

"Yes. Mr. Furness?"

He came around to take both her hands, gripping them like handlebars.

Eyes beaming excitement.

"Your uncle will never stop thanking you for this generous gift you've got in mind." Let go to take the pledge, a hand over his heart. A New York cadence to his voice. "Like I said, this is the Crowborough edition of Doyle, the one from nineteen thirty, hardly ever available."

The only other person in the room was a man in a double-breasted blue seersucker suit, inspecting books on the long wall across from them, craning forward for a better look at the titles, hands clasped behind his back.

Furness called an excuse to him, took KC by the elbow and guided her through a door connecting to a solemn, oak-paneled viewing room, lecturing again.

"The set we offer is Number fifty-two of only seven hundred sixty sets printed. As I'm sure you've got to know, it was signed by the great man himself."

In the center of the room was an antique work bench table and two mismatched chairs. On one wall, an elegantly framed photo of Edgar Allen Poe, his stare challenging time better than a withering, handwritten inscription scrawled across the bottom of the picture.

Furness cleared his throat, for attention, and pointed her to six uniformly bound volumes arranged in an orderly row on the table, illuminated by a ceiling-height row of horizontal

stained glass windows, and enhanced by a single baby spot-light mounted in the ceiling. He indicated a single inlaid walnut shelf of similarly-bound volumes and removed one, handling it like treasure.

"In all, twenty-four volumes. Quarter natural linen over brown paper boards. The paper spine labels. The top edge gilt. You can see the spines are faded and some light shelf wear, but all in all a good, clean, tight set. I believe that three thousand would be a fair and reasonable price." He observed her wince. "Doyle, Mrs. McClory. Sir Arthur Conan Doyle. Sherlock Holmes."

"Yes. He's Judge Osborne's favorite, but—"

"Judge Osborne?"

"My uncle. Do you know him?"

Furness stepped back, grinning. "The judge is one of our best customers and so very, very knowledgeable. If your gift is for Judge Osborne, we'll work out something on the price. Don't worry."

"May I look them over for a few—"

"Of course." He placed the volume he was holding on the table and stepped away. "Take your time, Mrs. McClory. Take all the time you want. Never any deadline comes to great literature. They outlive us all."

She sat down facing the volumes, her back to the door, dropped her handbag on the floor.

Began leafing through the volume Furness had set down, in case he returned.

Wondered how long she'd have to wait.

Ten minutes later, she felt a whisper of breeze when the door opened and shut. She looked behind her. The man in the blue seersucker suit stepped forward, asking, "You hear that?" A mellow Southern voice to match an engaging smile. Familiar voice.

"Hear what?" Her answer stopped him.

"The pop, like—" He stuck an index finger inside a cheek, made a popping sound. "Like that. Like in snap, crackle and—" He did the cheek trick again. "My knee. The left one. It was reconstructed after it got shot off. There's a steel pin makes it hurt like hell just before it rains. Goes—" He did the trick again. "Every time I sit down. Sometimes, when I stand up, too."

He was in his late twenties or early thirties. Cartoon eyes behind thick lenses. Nose too large for his chinless face. Frozen, straw-colored pompadour adding four inches to his anemic, six-foot frame.

"You also come about the Doyles?" Testing him.

"The who?"

"Sir Arthur Conan Doyle." Introducing him to the books with a gesture.

"Oh." Sheepish grin. Hand tracing the contours of his pomp. "No." His other hand reaching into a hip pocket, tugging at his jacket, exposing the outline of a shoulder holster underneath. Flipping open his wallet to display the shield; at arm's length, to catch some of the light from the baby spot. The golden glitter of a federal shield. Just as she thought.

"I'm Simmons, Mrs. McClory. Mr. Burkes sent me to tell you that he apologizes for being unavoidably delayed over lunch. Whatever you have to report, I'll carry on back to him." He moved to the door and locked it, his knee popping to the motion. Returned to the table and sat expectantly, hands clasped against his face.

"Need to ask you something first." KC inhaled the room and said, "Has Burkes been playing straight with me, Simmons?"

He leaned back in his chair and studied her. Took off his

glasses. Polished the lenses with a handkerchief from his pocket while his eyes blinked out a Morse code she couldn't read.

KC knew better than to expect the truth from Simmons. His loyalty was where it belonged, with Burkes, but in some of Burkes' remarks to her lately, in the body language of his conversation, she had felt a difference, like he knew not to trust her. So, why wave a flag? If she was right in her thinking, to throw Burkes off balance.

Anything to keep the other side off balance helps keep you upright and moving ahead, Frankie was used to saying.

And, she was used to Frankie being right.

Simmons said, "Ma'am, as witnessed by my presence, if Walter Burkes is playing straight with anyone, he is playing straight with you."

"Thank you. That's the answer I expected."

"What even made you ask the question?"

She shrugged in a way that told him it was the best answer he would get.

They sat at the table for an hour, unbothered, the rare Doyle untouched, as she recounted Liam's breakfast visit, the grilling Peter gave Liam and, most of all, Liam's threats.

Simmons listened carefully, encouraging her to remember everything Liam had said. At first, he contributed nothing but his silence, the sound of courteous listening KC knew from their phone calls. When her voice grew too loud with the memory of Liam's murderous intentions, he angled forward to place one hand over her lips and a finger to his mouth.

KC apologized. Took a deep breath. Swallowed hard to keep from crying. She had not meant to get this emotional. "It's just that I won't let anything happen to the Osbornes. I can take care of myself, but they—"

His hand silenced her again. "Mrs. McClory, don't you think Mr. Burkes knows that, how you feel?" Gently. His soft southern accent as soothing as warm milk. "He has no intention of letting harm befall any of them; you, either." She challenged him with a look. "Listen, whatever else Mr. Burkes told you or whatever else you may think of him, Mr. Burkes has said that straight to my face more than once. His word is total precious metal. So, please, believe me, even if you doubt him."

She recognized he was massaging her. Responding to her question about Burkes playing straight. "The Osbornes, they mean the world to me."

"We know that."

"They took me in when I was a child, not even half Cookie's age now. They knew my parents, but I was just another kid in the neighborhood. Not related. Nothing special. My parents died after the accident; they told me I was part of their family now, to never think of myself as otherwise. I won't have the Osbornes hurt or this close to the mayhem Liam and the Thirty Two are capable of. I just left too much of that in Belfast—"

"Please, Mrs. McClory. You've done a wonderful job up to now. If Mr. Burkes has said that once to me, he's said it a hundred times. He respects everything that you've done for the agency. I promise, nothing bad will happen to any member of the Osborne family, you have my word." He smiled in all the primary colors. "You, included."

Massage, massage, massage. "Are you also speaking for Burkes?"

"You've been around us long enough to know nobody does." She gave her head an *Ain't that the truth* shake. "But knowing how he feels is what makes me feel comfortable enough giving you my word. You all right with that? Feel better?"

KC shook her head because she had no choice, told him, "I will kill Liam before I let him—"

"Heavens, ma'am. You help us get through this and we'll do it for you. It'll be like your going-away gift from the agency."

"You don't mean it."

"I mean it." He smeared another smile across his face. "You just help us to get to the Plowman and write an ending to this plot against Mr. Mustamba, and I will personally volunteer for the assignment." He patted his shoulder holster.

"I'll remind you."

"Knowing what I know about Liam McClory, none necessary, ma'am . . . You get a feeling the Plowman is around?"

"A feeling, yes."

"Then you be double extra careful, ma'am. The trouble with killers? Once they start, they don't know when or where to stop. You get the name, you get it to us, you get out of the way and keep out of the way. The one, two, three of it. I can't be clearer than that."

"If I'm not fast enough to get out of the way?"

"Don't even think it, ma'am. That kind of thinking will only slow you down."

"Nothing is going to slow me down."

Simmons grinned, nodded like he understood, and after that it was his turn. Nothing he said changed how KC felt, but she left sensing a light at the end of the tunnel.

CHAPTER 38

Another murder on the angry streets of Venice.

The responding officers' notes described how one Elmo Pogue, a toothless, tattered relic of better days, had made his regular mid-afternoon pilgrimage to dumpsters behind Uncle Wiggley's Weenie World on the southeast intersection of St. Pierre and Via Viva.

Elmo (he told the officers) trolled through the dumpsters, selecting only the choicest remains from the more than two hundred varieties of hot dog featured daily at every Uncle Wiggley franchise, including his personal favorite, the Rin Tin Tin.

The best Bowser Wowser leftovers he had seen in a week were out of reach.

He loved Bowser Wowsers almost as much as he loved the Rin Tin Tins.

Saliva thickening inside his mouth, Elmo stacked three blue plastic milk containers and used them and metal grips jutting from the rusted wagon.

He feasted on the Bowser Wowser scrap and other chunky leftovers, padded out the supper with a dozen varieties of bun ends and a tasty selection of chips, started to assemble tomorrow's breakfast using the plastic pouch he carried for that purpose.

Elmo sloshed forward like General MacArthur, calf-deep in refuse, and tripped, landed on his belly.

Swam in a paper-infested sea of mustard, catsup, pickles and assorted relishes.

He grabbed hammer-fashion onto something that was not

on any Uncle Wiggley menu anywhere in the world:

A human hand, severed at the wrist.

A warm stream of urine rolled down his leg as he flung it aside.

The dismembered hand hit the side of the dumpster and bounced onto the heap.

Elmo recoiled at the sight, fell a perfect swan, somehow got himself back up into a sitting position, clutching a wobbling ball of—

A naked, scuzz-smeared breast.

Mesmerized by the dark nipple, his other hand unable to ebb the vomit flow that added globs of color to his salt and pepper beard, he began with a meaningless vowel that built from inside his stomach into a gut-wrenching howl heard all the way to the ocean.

And, that's how the cops found him on a Code Three response to a frantic Uncle Wiggley manager's call about a lunatic loose in the garbage dump.

They were down to stomach-contorting dry heaves by the time backup arrived, followed within minutes by the M.E.'s team, carting the gear needed to sift through the dumpster and put together the pieces of a puzzle that once had been a human being.

Most of the rest of the victim was in a double-sized, green plastic bag, the kind used to line trash cans. Her hand and her breast apparently had fallen out when the loose knot keeping the bag closed had come undone.

Peter got there about an hour later.

He had been halfway home on the Pasadena, singing along with Aretha to forget the worst of what Burkes had revealed, when the RTO summoned him to switch from division frequency to a tac.

He charged across the lanes and spun off at the first exit ramp, circled around and crossed over the bridge to the southbound entrance. Veered onto the Harbor Freeway and shot through Civic Center. Swung onto the Santa Monica. Exited at Lincoln and barreled through two miles of surface streets, revolving red chimney and the traffic whoop helping him shear through early rush hour gridlock.

He screeched to a hot brake stop in the Uncle Wiggley's Weenie World parking lot. Four marked and unmarked vehicles were on the site, within ten feet of the dumpsters. The boss was leaning against his command car, furiously chewing gum, arms locked across his chest, studying a spot on the ground like it answered all of life's questions. He saw it was Peter as the motor cut and the siren wound down. Signaled him to stay put. Headed over.

Spence's presence ended the guessing game in Peter's mind.

He knew who the victim was without having to ask or be told.

No other reason for the boss to be called.

The boss didn't do drop-ins on routine homicides.

Spence ran a security arm through Peter's and led him away from the dumpsters, tenaciously, talking fast to get it all said while he could. "We'll find the rat bastards who did this to Annie, Peter. My solemn word."

Peter stopped listening, except to a voice drifting with the erratic sound waves in the ocean between his ears. Explaining how to rescue himself from the inability to cry. Reminding him how emotions came later, after the shock and the disbelief wore off.

Before the cry for revenge.

He twisted himself free of the boss and ran screaming to the dumpsters.

Briefly collected his breath, studying the graffiti and the gang porn that only makes sense in a free port for the criminally insane.

Attacked a dumpster with a hard right.

Another punch.

One more.

Again.

His knuckles making breakfast cereal noises under his skin.

Feeling nothing but the pain of loss.

CHAPTER 39

Peter navigated through *Noah's Arch*, pulled the Trans Am to a stop in front of the house, unable to return the judge's semaphore wave. The damage he had done to himself at Uncle Wiggley's had put a plaster cast on his right hand that ran from his wrist to the crook of his elbow, supported by a criss-cross sling. Fingers spread in a fixed position. A stainless steel insert keeping the wrist straight, immobilized.

The judge was on the veranda, angled over the railing on his palms, a cold pipe jutting upside down from a corner of his mouth. He rose soldier-stiff. At once, his broad shoulders stooped involuntarily. His chest fell into his stomach.

They met halfway. Father gripped him, the way he always did his children when they needed support and comfort for stubbed toes, lost Little League games and any other disappointment. Those times, he knew how to be a father. Provide love and affection. His Judgeship was a complex man, and Peter had come to understand the fruit hadn't fallen far from the tree.

Father rested a hand on his cheek and kissed the other. "Russ Spence called," he said, a breath above a whisper. "I liked Annie, Peter. Liked her a whole heck of a lot."

"Me, too, Daddy."

They headed up the porch stairs with his hand in Father's hand, the way they had wandered Disneyland and the old amusement park at Beverly and La Cienega, where he rode the bumper carts and lapped the other kids on the fastest pony tickets could buy.

"Mother put a plate aside for you. She wasn't sure if you'd be hungry after—"

"Not really . . . KC around?" Stuttering on her name, a puff of breath before the second try, hiding the intent of the question best he could. If Father saw the acrimony in his eyes, he was not abiding his curiosity with a question.

"She and your mother have been comforting each other. I don't know who took it the hardest for you. Both of them—"

"Yeah."

Passing inside, Peter saw Cookie and Andy seated at the base of the stairway. Andy was hugging himself, studying Peter over his nose; grim; not exactly sure what message he was supposed to be sending. Cookie's tears were washing her cheeks.

He signaled her to stay put. Blew her a kiss.

Cookie returned it. Indicated the sitting room.

Father led the way. Mother was on a sofa, adrift in her thoughts. The draperies were drawn. The diffused light of an end table lamp worked like a time machine and he wanted to run to her, climb onto her lap, sense her making nice, hear her gentle voice promising him the hurt would go away. Nothing complex about Mother. She was the model for Mrs. Anderson, Mrs. Cleaver and that whole television world of make-believe she managed to make real for him.

She turned in their direction and showed immediate alarm at the cast. He crossed to her, leaned cautiously to kiss her on the forehead. She removed the hand she had draped on the back of his neck and tilted her face up to trap his eyes with a mother's smile. It faded at once. Peter knew she had seen what Father missed: his repressed anger desperate for release.

He backed off and left her wondering, summoned Father to join her on the sofa.

Closed the hallway door on them and asked, "KC?"

Cookie frowned, tilted her head to the ceiling, shunted

aside so he could pass between her and Andy.

KC's door was unlocked.

She was sitting at the vanity table and seemed unaware of his presence.

By reflection, he saw her eyes red, cried out, intent on the framed photographs.

A floorboard creaked as he advanced.

She saw him in the mirror, turned, started to say something.

He didn't let her finish the thought.

He whipped his good hand across her cheek, then back across the other one. Her neck snapped with the fury of his slaps. She toppled off backward from the bench, quickly got to her feet and retreated.

He charged shoulder first, dumping her backward onto the bed. Quickly straddled her at the waist, with her arms locked tightly against her body and her legs folded uselessly over the edge.

He fumbled into a left-handed grip getting the Smith & Wesson free of his belt holster.

Jammed the .45 under her right eye.

He felt her body freeze. Tension in her arms and her hips.

"Tell me everything. No more lies, KC." He moved the snub-nosed barrel inside her mouth. "The truth. Starting with Preston Donahue . . ."

Her eyes analyzed his demand. Conceded nothing. Turned cold and clicked off like television. Closing him out of her life.

Her body sagged under his weight and he saw her fright fading.

First, it softened into the confusion he had seen in the mirror, then it resolved into a defiant hardness. He moved the

.45 back under her eye. She said, "Kill me, fuck me or get off me."

Hard.

Emotionless.

Daring him to pull the trigger.

CHAPTER 40

KC knew Peter wouldn't shoot.

She was certain he still loved her too much for that. Whether she liked it or not. Whether she wanted it or not. Just now, she'd wanted to take Peter in her arms, tell him how sorry she was about Annie and kiss away his wounds, but he only wanted the one thing she could not give him: the truth.

She had to get away from here before he made the situation worse.

Ruined everything.

Peter said, "I saw a photograph today, of a tombstone in a cemetery in Belfast." Virulent. Relentless. "The final resting place of the *real* John Ford. Saw another one, too. Liam McClory. The brother of your dead piece of shit husband. You tell me something or you get ready to join Frankie McClory in Hell."

She knew it had to be Burkes. The only way he could have seen the photographs was if Burkes showed them to him. That bastard. What else didn't she know? She should have taken Burkes' absence from the meeting as a sign, a bad omen; come down harder on Simmons.

"Get off me, Peter."

"Liam McClory killed Annie, didn't he?"

"Get off me, Peter."

"Where is he, KC?"

"I don't know."

"I don't believe you."

"What happened to your hand?"

She felt the .45 quaver in Peter's grip. He was showing the rigors of emotion.

Whatever the doctors had pumped him full of had stained his eyes yellow. A thin row of sweat globules had formed along the bridge of his nose and above his lip. Mucous coagulated inside the rims of his nose.

"I swear, KC, I will hurt you if I have to. I don't want to, but . . ."

Let Peter see you're turning over his demand in your mind. Make a face. Cinch your mouth. Drag out your cheeks. Flatten your eyes. Good. Now, appeal to him once more. He sees what you're doing and wants you to recognize it's not going to work. Give in. And, now. Not all at once.

"In my handbag. On the vanity. My address book. I'll show you." Suspicious eyes. "I'll show you, Petey."

She hadn't called him Petey since she was eleven years old. Remind him who she was. Put a lock on his conscience. Put a lock on his trigger finger. She knew he wouldn't, but she also knew about accidents. She'd been taught how to handle situations like these. She wasn't ready to become a statistic, not even for him.

"I didn't know about Annie until Uncle Judge got off the phone. I swear on my parents' graves."

"Annie loved me, KC." Voice husky, tense.

"So did I, Peter."

He broke the connection. "Stay put . . . the way you are, okay?" Uncertainty in his voice. Looked back at her.

"The address book. A cordovan cover, button snap on the side."

He started to slide off her, first one knee, then the other.

In a single sweeping motion, the instant her arms and her hands slipped free, she reached over and clutched the neck of a sculpted bronze lamp on the night table, arced up and crashed the multi-colored glass shade against the right side of his face. The Art Deco lamp hit the floor hard, causing a noise she feared would carry downstairs.

As Peter fell backward, dazed, he lost his grip on the revolver. The .45 dropped onto the mattress.

She scooped it up and sprang off the bed, stepped close to him, but not too close, spread her legs, took a two-handed aim at his crotch. "I'll blow your brains out. Don't think I won't."

He stared up at her, his knees aimed at the ceiling, his face fueled with contempt.

His face contorted. He gasped, painfully pushing the plaster cast back into position. Blood stained his bandage wrap near the cheekbone. He pressed down on the spot, winced and, after inspecting the damage, wiped his fingers dry across his shirt. The stain continued to spread.

KC suppressed a desire to tell him she was sorry. She kept her eyes set to cold. "Frankie worried about someone coming after him through me, so he taught me how to take care of myself. He was a great teacher."

"Bitch!"

"And, he never laid a hand on me, the way you did." She briefly moved a hand to her left cheek. It felt the way she imagined a hairline fracture felt. "When did you become such a coward?"

"When did you become such a cunt?"

"Didn't Walter Burkes tell you that, too?"

His appearance gave him away, told her she had guessed right about Burkes.

"Oh, my God!" Aunt Dorothy called.

Aunt Dorothy was standing just inside the door, Noah to her right. Cookie and Andy edging around them for a look. The lamp crashed.

KC ordered, "Over there, please, Aunt Dorothy. You, too, Uncle Judge. All of you. Please." She indicated the wall by the bathroom. She needed a clear path out.

"What the heck is going on here, KC?"

"Do it, Father!" Peter called. "Do what the lady says." He brought down his left knee and eased the leg onto the floor. The other leg remained elevated. He was flushed, snorted air in short bursts through his nose.

Uncle Judge looked back at her, trying to make sense of the situation, shook his head disbelievingly. He moved to Aunt Dorothy, got a grip on her and guided her deeper into the room, instructing Cookie and Andy to follow. They formed an erratic line along the wall between the dresser and the bathroom.

KC kept the .45 trained on Peter, and cautiously tread around him, embarrassed to be doing this to her family. Her family. Nothing she could deal with now. If it was Liam here with the gun, they'd be dead.

"Sealed with a kiss!" Cookie spit out the words, fists balls of fury shaking at her hips. Wriggled free. Stepped forward from the line. She wiped an imaginary kiss from her lips. Flung it to the floor.

"Cookie!" Aunt Dorothy covered her daughter's mouth, wrestled her back in line. Cookie struggled to get loose, momentarily distracting KC.

Peter kicked for the gun.

KC saw it coming and raised it away in time, her finger reflexively yanking the trigger.

The .45 exploded.

The bullet clunked into the wall.

A few inches to the left, the shot would have hit Aunt Dorothy in the heart.

KC heard herself making noises more terrifying than the

others. Froze. Fell to the floor. Peter had managed to roll onto his side, grab on and yank her feet from under her.

The gun went off again.

The bullet dug into the ceiling.

She jammed her boot against Peter's bad shoulder. He cried out and rolled onto his back. Anybody else, she would have squeezed the trigger and finished him.

Uncle Judge shouted, "That's enough! Enough, God damn it!"

KC had never heard Uncle Judge use a four-letter word.

"My son! Petey!" Aunt Dorothy charged forward. Lost her footing. Stumbled and fell at an angle over Peter. Reached up for the .45. KC leaned away, slapped her wrist with the barrel, scrambled onto her feet.

Aunt Dorothy made a noise, began whimpering.

"How dare you!" Uncle Judge thundered at her, already halfway to Aunt Dorothy.

He faltered. Swung a hand onto his chest, like he was pledging allegiance. His look went sterile. From deep inside his throat, a sharp cry. He crumpled to the floor. Mouth agape. Eyes staring blindly.

"His heart!" Aunt Dorothy screamed.

She had pulled herself off Peter and onto her knees. She crawled on all fours to Uncle Judge.

Cookie was alternately crying, screaming and shouting names at her.

"Shut up!" KC ordered. "Shut up and call 9-1-1!"

"If anything happens to Daddy, I'll kill you!" Cookie swore. She jumped for the desk phone.

Andy studied the gun, ignored it. He hurried to Uncle Judge. Began administering mouth-to-mouth resuscitation.

Peter was turned from her, trying to get to his feet.

KC threw him a melancholy look and fled. Hit the veranda

running and was almost at the town car when she realized he was tracking after her.

The engine wouldn't turn over.

Peter closed the gap.

Ignition.

Power up.

Peter had a two-handed grip on the passenger door handle. He looked at her like he was Superman and that was enough to anchor the car.

She shifted into gear, curved out of the parking space, rolled forward onto the exit drive. He trotted alongside, lost his footing, fell beneath window view.

She felt the drag, heard Peter's feet scraping the ground until the car leaped forward like a freed rabbit.

In the rear view, she saw him stretched on the ground, cheek to concrete, still as men and boys she'd seen fall on the streets of Belfast.

She hit the brakes and, loudly cursing herself, jammed into reverse. Screeched to a stop five yards away. Ran to within five feet of him. Took a shooter's stance.

Could she?

Pull the trigger?

Any more than him?

What they had was not love anymore, but a spark, kept lit by the promise of their childhood years and dreams never meant to be. She knew it. Deep down, he knew it. Now they were learning together.

"Peter?" Nothing. She called his name again. "Are you all right? Peter!"

She started to lower the gun when he stirred.

She brought it up and aimed it at him. "Petey?"

He rolled over onto his back. "All present and accounted for."

She saw Peter was desensitized to any disaster messages his brain was receiving. "Sticks and stones may break my bones, but you will never harm me." Bullshit bravado, but his grin refused to play along with the joke.

"Uncle Judge?"

"Andy's handling it best he can." Words coming hard. Eyes gliding behind lids he could not seem to keep raised. "You remember how to pray?"

"I didn't mean for that to happen. You know that."

Peter said, "I don't know much of anything anymore."

"I love him. Uncle Judge. All the family."

"Maybe, you should love us a little less? Might be safer all the way around."

"Did Walter Burkes tell you I work for him?"

"You have the right to remain silent . . ."

He wasn't going to tell her. "I work for Walter Burkes. I work for the government. Ever since college." Peter was having trouble accepting the news. "They bagged me in college. Waved the American flag in front of my face, and I saluted. Their timing couldn't have been better. You were busy screwing and being screwed by the Rose Queen, leaving plenty of time for me to screw up my own life."

"Frankie."

She had his attention now. "Don't misunderstand. I fell for Frankie hard. It stopped mattering how good Burkes had brain-bombed me about Frankie being one of those outlaw terrorists in Belfast. How they were no damn good for our country. Our way of life. Future generations. You think those Scientologists are something? Those Hara Krishnas? Walter Burkes knows how to make brain cells dance on a dime . . . Walter Burkes promised me they wouldn't hurt Frankie, Peter. I made Walter Burkes promise that."

In the distance, growing louder, an ambulance siren.

"A regular Mata Hari." He ignored the .45, sat up on one haunch, using his good hand for support. "Mata Haris I deal with down on the streets of Los Angeles usually go for enough to buy a couple dime bags. What was your payoff, Mrs. McClory?"

"That's what you think, screw what you think."

"Wouldn't be inconsistent."

She had told him too much already, but she wanted him to hear it. If he was going to judge her, let him hear it. "Soon after, something strange happened." She searched the tarnished white sky for words. "Frankie got tired of the senseless killings. He grew sick of the miseries. Women crying for dead husbands never coming home. Kids clinging to the bricks and stones they would never get a chance to throw. I turned him. I turned Frankie against his own. Frankie turned and began working with me for our side, helping me find ways to cut through the chaos and get his world to someplace besides the local cemetery and a graveside mass."

"And he got killed for it."

"By people who only know how to kill . . . Preston Donahue was the Plowman . . . Once Frankie was gone, doors and windows closed behind him, and I was left standing outside."

"Why didn't you quit then and there? Come home? Get the hell out?"

"I owed Frankie. I had to go inside again and pay them back for Frankie . . . The same way you owe somebody for Annie." Peter understood that. His jaws flexed and cable-sized veins pushed inside his neck. "Frankie's own brother, Liam, let it happen. You asked before if Liam killed your partner. I don't know, except I can spell out dozens more reasons Liam McClory is not fit to breathe on this planet Earth."

"Mr. Mustamba."

She shrugged. "What's one more? When they were hired to send a Plowman here to kill him, Burkes was already ahead of them. He came up with your folks as the hook to get me back inside. Why Uncle Judge and Aunt Dorothy were invited to host a reception for Mr. Mustamba, because their little KC was a doorway inside security. I could make the job lots easier. Pack a bag and carry my mourning to Pasadena."

"Preston Donahue."

"He executed Frankie. He came after me on the train. I got lucky."

"You got revenge. I meant, he was supposed to be the Plowman?"

"I got lucky, I got revenge, but I don't think they wanted it that way. Donahue the Plowman? I don't think so. If he was, they would have played out the strike against Mr. Mustamba before turning Donahue loose on me. Until then, Donahue was along for the ride. I'm safe until—"

"Burkes told me you know the Plowman."

"One of us is lying then. Burkes always has been one to hedge his bets."

"Burkes was counting on me to get the name out of you. Fuck it out of you, it came to that."

"I thought you really cared about me."

"So did Annie."

"Bastard."

"Me, too . . . for about five minutes."

"I loved you once."

"The other night make it twice?"

She fired. The bullet popped a concrete cloud inches from his thigh. That was good enough to send Peter the message he was already dead in her eyes. The spark was alive, but he was dead in her eyes.

The Fire Department ambulance sped past on the other

side of the grass island, its siren wailing loud enough to bury the shot as a backfire, and squealed to a stop in front of the house.

Twilight had sneaked around the corner of eternity and the first stars were sending soft signals.

Cookie's familiar shape appeared outlined in the open doorway. She signaled for the two blue-uniformed paramedics and followed them inside. The driver hung back on the ground, finishing a radio check and killing the last of a smoke.

KC fired an innocent shot.

She called out, waved her arms like she was guiding a jet onto an aircraft carrier until the driver found her in the blinding glare of his wandering spot.

She pointed to Peter. The spot trailed down, caught him.

She jogged to the town car.

Peter called after her.

KC ignored him.

He had just found out he was dead in her eyes and now he knew he was dead in her ears, too.

Only the spark was left, and how much could the spark really mean?

CHAPTER 41

KC took the freeway off at the Sherman Oaks interchange, hid the car in plain sight in the Galleria garage and called Burkes from the ladies' room. Told she would have to wait for a call-back, she faked a conversation, refused to surrender the telephone to a grande dame with flaming pink hair and, afterward, to two teenagers who were inventing excuses their mothers might believe.

The phone rang after ten minutes.

Burkes identified himself the moment she snapped her finger off the disconnect lever and let her rattle through the news about Peter and the Osbornes, ignoring the names she called him.

"Yes, I showed him the pictures," he said in the space she needed to regain control of her voice, which had inched high enough to startle a few arriving women back out the door. "He had to see them sometime."

"They made me out to be a liar," she said, her voice a shrill whisper.

"Mrs. McClory, you are a liar. We are all liars. It comes as part of the territory. There's no rule that says we can only lie to strangers."

"You didn't have to do it that way, bastard."

"You know a better way?"

"What kind of information was he supposed to fuck out of me, Burkes?"

"What are you talking about? What does that mean?"

"What kind of information, Burkes?"

Silence, then, "You tell me."

345

"I told him about Frankie, Burkes. I told him how you got me and how you got me to fuck Frankie, the way you got Peter to fuck me, and about my turning Frankie. I told him about Preston Donahue. I told him how much I hate Liam. I think the only part I didn't get a chance to mention was how much I hate you."

"You didn't—"

"God's honest truth, Burkes. I know you wouldn't recognize it unless it came dressed as a lie, so either believe me or don't."

A heavy sigh. "Calm down, Mrs. McClory."

"Stop giving me orders, Burkes. It's over. I think I'm almost better off taking my chances with Liam than I am with you."

His voice began to crackle in her ear, signal that he was losing patience. "Calm down, please, and don't be so damned emotional. I thought we drained that out of you a long time ago."

"Didn't I make myself clear enough?"

"If it's over, I pull security off the Osbornes."

The announcement was like firecrackers going off in her ears. A cry stuck in her throat.

"You hear me, Mrs. McClory? The security goes."

"You would, wouldn't you, you son-of-a-bitch." She knew he would. She'd heard about worse things Burkes had done in pursuit of his kind of justice.

"The minute I hang up, I make that call. No lie. I order off the watchdogs and then I make another call and order you picked up for treason. I have more than a couple pictures to make that charge stick to you like a lover's hands, don't I, Mrs. McClory?"

"And you would."

"And I would."

"What do you want from me now?"

"I want you to stop talking. Take a deep breath. Remember who you are on the phone with. When you are ready to behave again, I want you to tell me."

She stared at the receiver for what could have been five minutes or fifty. "Okay, Burkes," she said, defeated.

"What do I want from you? Nothing new. The truth, and I don't think I've been getting the truth from you for a long time. You know what I mean, Mrs. McClory?"

KC pressed a hand against the wall for support. There was something in the way he said it that made her afraid. "What?"

"Frankie McClory."

"What about Frankie McClory?" She fondled the sterling silver crucifix Frankie had given her.

"He wasn't knocked off by a Plowman's bullet. It was staged to make us think so, to make us think they got wise to Frankie. Why, Mrs. McClory?"

She closed her eyes to the truth. "I don't know what you're talking about. Where did you get that—"

"You think you were our only source? Not by a long shot, Katie McClory. British Intelligence has been at it a whole lot longer'n us."

Get a grip, Katie. Play dumb. Too close to the pie to screw up now. "You're saying Frankie is alive?"

"I want to hear you say it."

"If you say so."

"Not good enough."

"I saw him murdered."

"You saw his murder staged."

"I buried him."

"Tomorrow. I'll ask BI to dig up the coffin."

"Son of a bitch. Bastard."

"Why, Mrs. McClory?"

347

She told herself it was foolish to pretend any longer.

"To get away from you, son-of-a-bitch. To put an end to the games on both sides. For both of us. Frankie told that gang of murderers he was getting too much heat to be an effective leader. Best thing was stage an assassination, let him go undercover and operate from there. Disappear. Even from me until it was safe for him again, and we could make plans to run away somewhere and escape all the killing and the double-dealings. I would tell you they got wise to Frankie. You would believe it because it happens all the time. An informer, followed by a death. I'd be out, too. No use to them, no use to you. The plan was working until Liam came to me, talking about my obligation to revenge my dead husband. They didn't know I knew what really was going on. I was playing the Irish colleen, stuck in a kitchen and still crying over my man."

Burkes said, "Can anyone hear this?"

She looked around. The bathroom was empty. "Little late for that?" She really didn't care. "As a matter of fact, there's a reporter from the *Times* who's standing next to me taking notes."

"Why didn't you level with us from the start, KC? I would have helped get you out then, without getting you tied to this job." His voice was distant, at the same time firm and caring, as if he meant what he was saying. She knew the act.

"Your nose is growing, Burkes. You would have had me on a plane to Iraq or one of those countries with a name I can't spell, all the while reciting the Pledge of Allegiance in my ear. Just tell me what you want, okay?"

"I said you're out after this one, and I mean it. God's honest truth."

"God's honest truth. Three words I didn't ever think were in your vocabulary."

She thought for a moment he might not let the insult pass. Wrong. "Have you identified the Plowman they're sending after Mr. Mustamba? How the work is going down?"

"No, only what I've already told you. When I find out, you find out and then I am out of here for good. That was our deal and I'm sticking by it, just to prove one of us still has morals. Like the wicked woman says, 'I know I'll regret it in the morning, but it feels so good right now.' "

Silence.

Burkes seemed to have his hand cupped over the mouthpiece and was mumbling.

Then, "We have reason to believe the Plowman is Frankie McClory."

Burkes' pronouncement wasn't what she expected to hear. KC's head felt ready to explode. Her body trembled at the significance of what Burkes had said. She sucked up air and inherited the foul smell of a toilet someone had neglected to flush.

"You hearing what I said, KC? We think Frankie is the Plowman. We think he never turned at all. We think he's down here now, getting ready to do the work on Mr. Mustamba . . . KC? What do you think, KC? Mrs. McClory?"

"I'm supposed to believe you?"

"You're supposed to do as you're told, whether or not you believe me." Tough again. "Now, I want you to listen carefully . . ." When he was through giving her instructions that meant she would have to go back to The Quiet Man, he asked, "Questions?"

She eased into her voice. "Can I have a front row seat at your funeral?"

"Get in line."

"No, wait. One question. Is Simmons there?"

"I'll be talking with him shortly."

"Just tell him Mrs. McClory wanted to thank him again for his concern."

"I don't understand."

"That's okay. Simmons will. One other thing. Did he mention he fucked me, too?"

"What?"

"Did he mention he fucked me? When we met at the book store. He locked the door and screwed the truth out of me, the way Peter was supposed to. Ask him. If Simmons says anything else, he's lying to you."

Silence, then, "It's a good thing I have a sense of humor, Mrs. McClory."

"Yeah, pretty funny, Burkes, all of it."

KC hung up the phone fearing what Burkes said was the truth. If so, Frankie was the liar. For how long? Since when? And what would the truth do to the hungry love she had for him?

Burkes hung up the phone and turned to Simmons, who had been listening in on the extension. Simmons' head was twisting back and forth. A few more turns and it would whip off completely.

"I can assure you, sir. Absolutely not true."

"Shame, Simmons. I would have had to reevaluate you, maybe even write another letter of commendation." Simmons nodded, like he got the joke, but not entirely certain. "You think you can beat her to The Quiet Man?"

He examined his watch. "If I leave now, sir."

"Then what are you waiting for?"

Simmons looked like he had something else to say, but he retreated out the door, instead. Loyal, but a shame he doesn't have KC's balls, Burkes decided. He'd be after my job if he did.

Burkes finished what was left of the fudge brownie on his desk while switching to the direct line out. He called home. Vonnie answered on the third ring.

"Hello, you dazzling creature, you . . . What do you mean, who is this? . . . Aren't I ever allowed to get lonesome for your sexy voice? Okay, then . . . I've heard enough of your voice for now. Will you put Fritz on, please . . ."

CHAPTER 42

KC found The Quiet Man was filling fast. Early Friday night revelers with their payroll checks begging celebration, their work sweat not yet dry, joining the extended lunchtime crowd of congenial, booze-inflated regulars. Irreverent banter sailing with every dart. The clack of billiard balls making contact. A smell in the air as fresh as her last day in Belfast. The bartender pushing his shaved scalp to the back of his furrowed neck.

May Lawless was propped on a stool at the far end of the bar in a three-quarter profile, one shapeless matchstick leg separated from the unkempt floor by the three-inch spike of her open-toed pump. Dressed for a carnival. Entertaining a man sitting hunched over a beer mug to her left; laughing uproariously, her hands as animated as her mouth.

KC tapped May on the shoulder. May turned to see who it was without dropping a word until she recognized KC. She gestured the man to wait a minute, took an easy grip on KC's chin, steered her face in the pale light. Made a clucking sound. Called the bartender loud enough to be heard over the crowd hum and MTV rapping, "McGovern, hurry some ice cubes in a nest over here."

May moved in for a closer inspection. Shook her head. "Girlie, vessels broke under the skin-a them pretty cheeks. Swelling and your left eye's an ugly sight. Lucky nothing looks to be broken, so I know it wasn't the work of nobody I hang 'round."

She tittered outrageously, jabbed an elbow into the man's arm, seeking agreement.

He swiveled, stared past May to her, through lenses thick

as a bread slice. It was Burkes' man Simmons, trying desperately to look like his Diesel rig was parked outside. Simmons mumbled something filled with Southern grace, tugged the brim of his Angels baseball cap so it rested tighter above his blonde eyebrows and returned to his ale.

KC touched her face and wondered why she had not felt pain. Even now the hurt was minimal. It had to be the adrenalin rush. A miracle nobody at the Galleria called a cop on her. Not really. People don't look at problems. They turn away rather than risk being drawn in. She spent a moment thinking about the pandemonium that would break out if she passed the word about the federal shield in Simmons' wallet.

The bartender handed May a towel sack of cubes, and May tamped it carefully against one cheek, then the other, assuring KC she would be pretty again. "More'n I can say for your fella what mistook my Dermot for a fair fight," May said. She cackled and elbow-attacked Simmons' shoulder again. Simmons nodded into his beer, reached for a handful from the popcorn bowl. Changed his mind.

"I need to speak with Snuffy Danaher," KC said. Her shoulder ached from the added weight of the .45 inside her creel bag, as large as a photographer's tote. She shifted the strap to her other shoulder, so that it ran diagonally across her chest, accentuating the natural curve of her breasts. That way also made the bag harder to steal, a trick picked up in Belfast, where street thieves preyed indiscriminately.

"Most people would pay for the privilege of not," May said, cupping a hand to the side of her mouth. She had had a lot of whatever she was drinking. "Unless, of course, all you need is small talk no bigger'n him."

"It's talk like that brings tears to my eyes and cracks my Irish heart," Danaher said.

KC turned, became aware of strong cologne, looked down

into Danaher's bad teeth.

Danaher directed her attention across the room, to a corner cloaked in shadows.

"Couldn't help noticing you come in, Mrs. McClory. That's O'Dea giving you the cheery wave."

"Jack Ford."

"O'Dea, I said. How's your hero?"

"I have to see Jack Ford."

Danaher's eyes shifted. His voice dropped. "Don't know as I can help you. Mr. Jack Ford don't ever set no schedules by me."

"You can't afford not."

Reading her face for clues, Danaher raised furrows in his wide freckled forehead, puckered his lips. He saw what she wanted him to see and slacked down his foxy stare. "That the way, is it?" He adjusted his silk, floral patterned tie and moved to the ivory buttons of his tailored, double-breasted russet sport coat. Told her to wait. Disappeared through the stained, emerald green curtain behind Simmons.

Simmons downed his ale and signaled the bartender for two more, for him and May. "Hold my place, May," he said, casually.

"What's 'at, honey?"

"Time to drain the pump again and make the usual call to the old ball and chain."

Simmons eased off the stool and, after May pushed her ruby cheek forward to take his kiss, aimed for the rest rooms off the front entrance. As he passed by her on shaky legs, May patted him on the rump and stage-whispered her plans to free him from his sperm.

"What's Dermot going to say about that?" KC asked, inventing conversation.

"What he always says—How much?" She tossed back her

head and drowned out the bar noise with laughter.

Danaher reemerged from the passageway, made a discreet circle at KC with his thumb and forefinger.

And, if Burkes had it figured out right, if she got Danaher to take her to Liam, she'd also find the Plowman. What added insult to injury was knowing how right the bastard was when he snapped out instructions over the phone.

CHAPTER 43

Burkes took Simmons' call and said, "Didn't we just talk, Simmons, less than five minutes ago?"

"When I went back, Mrs. McClory was gone. Thought you better know. Told the old whore I had to come call home again because I got busy signals last time."

"Gone where? And don't tell me with the wind."

"No position to inquire, Mr. Burkes. First checked the parking lot. Not a sign of her station wagon. Then, I—Yes, like I said, darlin', just funnin' here a bit longer with the good ol's . . . Home soon as I stew another brew or two . . . Promise. No more'n that . . . Y'all be needing the phone, Mr. O'Dea? I'll be right off in a jiffy . . ."

Burkes hung up instantly, concerned over how much O'Dea may have heard. For all his worrying over KC, now he could add Simmons to the list.

CHAPTER 44

Doling out the directions one at a time, Danaher had KC aim for the HOLLYWOOD sign once she'd turned up onto Beachwood Canyon from Franklin. He sat with his back tucked between the passenger seat and the door, aiming his chain smokes and his tobacco exhaust out the window.

KC climbed the narrow road at a cautious twenty miles an hour. The old-style street lamps were spread wide, burned dim. It was difficult reading the white and blue metal road signs.

"When you get to the next cut through, you'll be making a hard right turn, so keep a sharp eye. It will be coming up right fast . . . There!"

Danaher had begrudged her conversation most of the forty-minute ride, except for directions, hiding concern behind his junk smile. She didn't press. It was Liam who knew the words to her tune.

"Slow now, girl. Watch them fenders sticking out a mile and I'll tell you when. Gets narrower still . . . You're going for a white picket fence and a lot more flowers'n any one man deserves. Whoa, whoa, now. Just over—there!"

KC angled a left turn through the open fence gate, braked halfway up the driveway opposite an irregular stone path leading to a fairy tale cottage, indistinguishable from other homes along this section of the hill except for the garden. Someone had made over the front yard into a rose garden. In full bloom. Lush colors. A sweet perfume that shamed Danaher's scent.

Danaher hurried around the Ford and extended a hand to help her out.

"He's expecting you, so go on in. I'll just be here waiting, enjoying the evening and the view," he said. A nod, quick steps away, leaving her no choice.

KC used the handrail navigating warped slat-board steps that groaned under her weight. A sassy calico cat steamed out of the darkness. It brushed against her leg on the way to disappearing again. The curved stained oak door and the rusted screen door opened noisily, before she could ring.

Liam gestured for her to enter.

He wheeled around and headed inside.

The calico cat dashed past her and raced ahead of Liam, who adjusted the piano stool, made himself comfortable and began practicing gentle chords, like he knew what he was doing. A tyke showing off for teacher.

"If looks could kill, Katie, you would already have me halfway to Hell, ahead of the devil himself."

She couldn't control her anger. "Nothing you can say will convince me Annie Waterman had to die."

"Who? The lady bull? Then I'll say nothing, Katie. Happy to oblige you. All over the telly, you know? Like nothing else real ever happens. Was Dermot's idea to do her. Easier disposing the body; settle ourselves back and wait for the garbage truck to come collecting, O'Dea, Danaher and me. A decent plan, except for the bleeding beggar went looking after scraps and spoilt it for us."

He switched to something up-tempo and bouncy on the piano. Riding her. Gloating. Sticking every word under her nails, she believed, for the imagined thrill of her screams. The idea of reaching for the .45 and blowing him away repeated itself to KC.

"You bloody rotten sociopath," she said.

"Climb off your tree, girl-o." Liam quit the keyboard and rose to face her. For a moment, it was ominously quiet, the stale air hard to ingest. "I done people for less." He crossed in front of her, collapsed onto a tired couch covered in protective plastic, used his arms for a pillow. "Besides, never been my purpose to convince your majesty . . ." He made a laugh to frame her insignificance in his life.

KC ignored his invitation to sit and went instead to the tinted picture window. It was open to the night. She looked up beyond Danaher touring the roses, fixed on the first O in the HOLLYWOOD sign. Wondered about flying through it, past the bleakness of reality. The calico cat nosed around her, got away before she could take him in her arms.

". . . so, remember it's a fucking bloody awful war we're in," Liam said. Arguing in the tone he normally saved for people who thought he was important. Banging his fist on the table. "Fucking. Bloody. Awful. The lady bull, she come spying and rested her eyes on something she ought not see, so . . ." He hummed a funeral dirge.

KC wheeled to confront him.

"What could she have seen, so crucial she had to be—?"

Liam stopped her with a gesture. "Not *what* she seen. A case of *who* she seen. She seen someone who's not to be seen until our deed is ready for doing."

"The Plowman?"

He nodded and wheeled into a sitting position, reached for an opened bottle of Guinness, sucked it dry. She noticed a second opened bottle on the table. Two packs of smokes, a jet lighter and a flip top. A butt still sizzling on the lip of the ashtray. Liam hadn't been alone when she arrived. And, Burkes hadn't been wrong in his guessing?

She said, "I see the Plowman, and then what? Do I get butchered by you? O'Dea? Danaher? That how you run the show?"

"Would that I could, girl-o." His ugly face shook to the

slither of his reply. He wanted her to know he meant it. "We made you a bargain and we'll stand by it. Do your part and you're through. Exactly like agreed."

Another voice joined in:

"That was the agreement, Bright Eyes."

The words had a lilt that had been living in her dreams, as warm and as nourishing as a fresh broth. KC spun toward the half moon wall separating the living room from the dining room. Frankie was leaning against an arch, stroking the imperious calico cat in his arms. The cat was crooning to his touch.

Frankie said, "Now, Face, what say you to skipping on over with a fit greeting for yer old man?"

That enchanted grin . . .

Her heart began tearing through her chest, and her legs said they'd had enough.

Frankie. Dead Frankie. Born again Frankie. Frankie the Plowman? She had to find out. She had to know. Then what?

CHAPTER 45

Burkes went looking for Peter at St. Truffaut's Hospital in Pasadena, a hospital older than the tenacious ivy on its imposing walls, named for the patron saint of the underprivileged by one of California's railroad robber barons, who built it during his dying years, trying to buy a ticket to the Pearly Gates. He had to know how much KC had told him, make sure Peter couldn't throw off the hunt for the Plowman more than it already was, which was more than enough.

Burkes found him in the cramped waiting room outside ICU, one arm draped around his mother, the other hiding one of her hands. His sister and her boyfriend were in their own private oblivion in another two-seater, arms and shoulders rubbing discreetly. She reminded Burkes of his own kid at that age, never quite sure how to behave when he'd accidentally catch her dusting the couch with some guy; always a different guy, except for the acne. The room smelled sterile, medicinal, under an odor of fear that came with visitors. Not of death, so far. That was the good news.

The TV mounted in the wall was turned to the ten o'clock news, sound barely audible as the toothy, visibly pregnant anchor segued her smile from a random shooting in West Hollywood to Mr. Mustamba, the camera tracking him as he moved from a limo through a crowd outside the hotel to a standing ovation in the massive banquet room.

Sudden, violent death could be anywhere.

Not if Burkes had his way.

It would be easier if the bad guys played by the rules.

361

It would be easier if there were rules to the game of assassination.

Get them before they get us.

That was a rule, Burkes supposed.

So far, he was losing this game. He had to remember it wasn't his fault and to keep the mantle of guilt hung in the closet. Isn't that what the shrink always says? Yeah, and the shrink couldn't fire a cap pistol to save her own black ass.

He caught Peter's eye and motioned him outside.

Peter whispered something to his mother, signaled the kids to stay put. They took the stairs up to the staff cafeteria, the only one open this late.

They had it to themselves, except for a doctor alone in a corner, still wearing his blue surgical gown, indifferent to the blood, stirring his coffee with wistful eyes, a grim set to his mouth Burkes recognized. Losing a patient isn't what doctors do best.

He almost excused himself for a minute, to step over and say—what?

Better luck next time?

Burkes took another hit of berry pie and made a "not too bad" face, washed it down with full-strength Pepsi, working the crushed ice around in his mouth. Peter nursed his Sanka, waiting out the silence that followed his detailed account of the day. His version was close to KC's, but there were omissions that told Burkes she'd shaded the story enough to confess without revealing Frankie was still alive. Well, that gave them something to talk about.

"The truth, Burkes, or did she feed me a crock of crap when she had me staring at the mouth of my piece?"

He sensed what was racking the kid besides his father and a love affair that was absent love and not much of an affair. If

Peter Osborne was like any other cop, it was losing his piece to a woman.

"I tell you I peeked in on your dad first, Peter? He was all rigged up, under sedation, but looked to be recovering. First jolt to the ticker, no signs of any permanent damage or a stroke, they told me."

"Yeah."

"They told me Judge Osborne's chances for pulling through are better than eighty percent. They said he's in good condition for a man his age, although they'd like to see him drop ten or fifteen pounds once he's out of here."

"He could be in the worst condition of his life and he'd still pull through." Peter sounded almost disappointed.

"Is that the good news or the bad news?"

"He's my father, what do you think?"

"I think you're damned lucky to have him."

"That's what he says."

"Oh, I get it now. Tough living in his shadow."

"For a lawyer, maybe not. For a cop, impossible, but I love my father, Burkes, or I wouldn't be here."

Burkes knew he'd taken the subject as far as Peter would let it stretch. He signaled a time out and patted himself down for his antacid. Peter ran a hand through his hair, nailed him with his hazel eyes, at their most unrelenting. "I'm still waiting for an answer, Burkes. Was KC telling me the truth?"

Burkes let the question hang in the sanitized air while he chewed a handful of Di-Gel into mush, followed it with a full glass of water and used a fresh paper napkin on his mouth. "Yeah. She's been working for us."

"You signed her up and then sent her off to join Frankie McClory. She was supposed to fuck secrets out of him . . . The same way you wanted me to fuck the story out of her." A mirthless smile was painted on his face.

"Gives new meaning to the notion that the whole world is fucked, huh? You really should go for a piece of this pie. It's sensational."

"You asshole!" Peter swiped the table with his arm. Everything on the yellow-speckled Formica crashed to the tiled floor, noise bouncing into every part of the room. The doctor looked over at them reflexively, not really caring. The Filipino woman behind the cash register stepped away from her stool and retreated through the swinging door to the kitchen, a Danielle Steel novel she'd been reading clamped to her chest.

"When I said go for the pie, it's not what I had in mind, Peter."

Peter angled over awkwardly to snare a fork from the floor, bolted to his feet. The prongs were digging into Burkes' Adam's apple before he could finish his grin. Burkes closed his eyes to the possibilities. It would be no trick at all taking back the advantage. A hammered fist on Peter's bum arm. Wham. The .40 caliber Smith & Wesson under his shoulder. Bam. Bam. Before Peter had time to exhale. If it were Liam McClory being stupid, wham bam, finito, and Burkes could mosey over to the doctor who'd lost the patient and explain how the battles you win make up for the ones you don't.

"After Mrs. McClory got away from you, we found her." The kid held his place, as dangerous as sushi. "Then we lost her again." He pointed to the fork, but Peter kept it there, stabbing harder.

"Meaning what?"

Burkes had seen it before, worse than this, with cops as good as Peter, who stay working on guts long after the bulb burns out in their brains. Peter's eyes were drowning in painkillers.

"Meaning Mrs. McClory may be with Mr. McClory."

The declaration roped Peter like an anchor and dragged him straight to the bottom, his face a jumble of uncataloged emotion. He managed himself back into his chair. Rested his head and arms on the table like he was taking a kindergarten nap.

Softly, in the library voice teachers use for sex education classes, Burkes said, "Frankie McClory isn't dead, but KC may soon be, if we don't find her fast."

He let the news sink in while he put his mind to work on how to keep Peter involved.

The answer came to him in a flash.

He stored it away for the right moment.

Peter was confused again by what Burkes had revealed.

Angry, getting angrier, and confused again.

Frankie McClory, alive.

Why hadn't KC told him that part?

Burkes said she knew, but she didn't tell him. She told him a lot, but not that. She went to bed with him, fucked him for more than old time's sake, but neglected to mention Frankie wasn't dead.

Take it personally, Peter.

She climbed into the sack because she wanted to; not just husbands who cock around in these enlightened times. Or, did KC expect to pillow talk you into giving away handy hints they needed for the hit on Mr. Mustamba, knowing you were part of the beefed-up security team, you and—

"—Annie?"

Burkes said, "My sense, from what KC told me?" Peter hurried him with a gesture. "I don't believe she knew about Annie, not until she heard it from you."

He couldn't tell anything from Burkes' expression. "I think the only reason you're saying that is because you still have plans for the two of us."

Burkes took an oath with his right hand.

"Hey, Bro!" Cookie calling from across the room.

She inched around the sleepy-eyed custodian, who was down on his hands and knees in the aisle, working a soapy bucket and scouring brush. Andy hung back, neck buried in his Kings windbreaker, hands in pockets.

"Bro, the doctor's ordered Mommy home. He says he'll call if there's a change in Daddy's condition."

"I need to be here a while longer, Cook. Take a taxi, okay?" He dug after his wallet.

"Andy has his father's Buick and a permit, okay?"

Peter threw a glance at Andy, who made a stupid face, expecting the wrong answer.

He got it.

"Permit doesn't work without an adult," Peter said.

"My pop lets me do it all the time, sir. I'm really quite good behind the wheel, and safe. Especially when I got her, your sister, with me."

Cookie's head started bobbing. Peter saw the pleading in her eyes. The cop in him said one thing, the brother another.

Burkes said, "I can have one of my guys—"

Peter flashed him to quit. "S'okay, thanks . . . Andy, watch the streets and stick inside the speed limit."

Andy made the A-OK circle and beamed.

Peter exchanged a hug and kiss with Cookie and waited until the kids were gone before he turned back to Burkes, who was working on a new piece of pie, apple this time. "Burkes, KC said she got Frankie to drop the dime on his people."

Burkes jigged to a hiccup. He clasped his chest and held a palm between them until he had swallowed another mouthful and rinsed clean with a shot of Pepsi. Ran an index finger around his teeth, searching for residue and pounded out an open-mouthed, growling burp.

"She helped us get Frankie turned, all right. It made sense until it stopped making sense at all. Too many signs. Too many signals that it was not the case and never had been. KC, all of us, had been taken in by Frankie McClory. McClory had played us for saps. Lot of ways, worse than his brother."

"How did KC answer to that?"

"We never told her. Better safe than sorry."

"Is there anyone you trust?"

"Fritz you know about . . . I've been married going on twenty years, and my wife thinks I'm the national sales manager of a tire company."

"Need to know."

Burkes' smile was genuine this time. "Need to win. Look, Peter, as sure as we stand here, KC knows Frankie isn't dead. Only she doesn't believe he isn't one of the good guys. Before we had Frankie made for certain, we weren't so sure about her anymore. We had reasonable doubts about her still being on our side, thinking Frankie may have managed to get her onto their team for real. A question up in the air to this minute."

"KC talked to me like Frankie was murdered after they made him as a traitor," Peter said, covering old ground. Maybe it would help to get the story straighter than some of Burkes' answers had been the first time. "Killed by a Plowman, by Donahue, and—his brother let it happen."

Peter felt idiotic just saying the words.

"She weeps for a dead husband with a brother who helped get him that way, then has him over for a meal at your place? Makes a lot of logic to me. You, too?"

Gold Medal stupid.

"She said Donahue was aboard the train, that he came after her the same way he came after Frankie . . ."

367

He had to turn away from Burkes' gloating look. He lowered his eyes onto the table and invented finger designs on the surface.

"KC's alive, same as Frankie stayed alive, so, at least, that part rings." Burkes dramatized a sigh of frustration. "We were still trying to read her right when the Mustamba business came up. A cool million to Frankie and his scum for shuttling a Plowman down here to dispose of him. Mr. Mustamba! You understand, it was absolutely vital we play it right from the inside, from the git-go. No second chances. Too much at stake to go by our guts or trust some stray hunch."

Peter looked up and grabbed Burkes by the eyes. "So you added Pasadena to the itinerary once you knew Mr. Mustamba was coming to Southern California. That locked in KC."

"She tell you that?"

"Elementary, my dear Burkes."

Burkes made a finger pyramid and a ludicrous look. "Hell, my man. We added Southern California."

"My father and mother, the party at our home . . ."

"To make KC the shortcut between two points. All in all, that connection was too irresistible for them not to use. If we thought Pasadena's famous little old lady in tennis sneakers had value, we'd of added her."

"And, me? I was—"

"An afterthought. You may find that impossible to buy, but it's the God's honest absolute truth. You were nothing on our mind, then—" Burkes made one of those *world opening up* hand gestures. "I remembered love conquers all. Maybe Peter Osborne could *dig* out of Kate McClory what we couldn't. Maybe, Peter Osborne can stir things, rattle their cages, by having those turds wonder about her playing toesies with a cop . . . Good news, bad news?"

"The bad news first."

"If she's still playing with the good guys and we're right about her holding a reunion with Frankie McClory, one slip and KC could wind up the way Annie did. Assuming KC isn't dead already." Burkes sneaked a small white pill and washed it down with water. "The good news? There is no good news."

Peter forgot to breathe. His mind began spinning.

"Wait, one item, depending on where your head is at, Peter . . . That last conversation I had with her before she disappeared? KC told me she loves you. It made me feel like a shit for what I've been putting you through."

CHAPTER 46

Pillow talk.

"How long since?"

"Do you want it in months or weeks and days?"

"I just want it, Frankie."

"Again?"

"We've already done *Again*. I thought we could try *Once more*."

KC rolled off him onto her back.

Frankie reached over and began massaging her.

She shuddered and made a noise and wanted to tell him not to stop.

Frankie knew that without any help from her.

He dissected her body with his lips, licked her wounded cheeks, stopping abruptly to say, "This Peter Osborne, he did that to you." Anger shook behind his whisper. "I'm going to kill that bastard first chance." He tongued the swelling and the purple welts.

She should not have told him what had happened at the Osbornes'.

She had to be more careful with her answers.

Frankie was playing with her and with her emotions at the same time. He was using the weapon he knew always worked with her. Who else was it that never loved wisely, only too well?

"Once more, Frankie."

"Any man what lays a hand on my woman gets no quarter."

"Once more, Frankie." More urgent than before.

"Bloody paramilitary. All bloody alike."

Begging. "Once more, Frankie!"

"What else did he lay on you, Face? Bloody Liam thinks the worst, swears you two—"

"Nothing, nothing, nothing. No. I wouldn't. You know. You know that." Speed-speaking. Exploding into a desperate command, "Once more, Frankie!"

He obliged, finally, and her sighs grew louder, noisier, finally rambled out of control. Her voice became incapable of words.

She didn't need them.

For now.

When her mind was her own again, she shouted to herself, I'm doing this for you, Burkes, but most of all for me! If she was to learn the truth, Frankie had to believe nothing had changed between them.

She wasn't certain what she believed.

For now, ignorance was bliss.

Being with Frankie had brought back the memory of happier times six years ago, when there was innocence to their love. First, Frankie showed his American sweetheart London, then all the towns that smacked of a history she'd known only from textbooks.

They spent one night in Stratford-Upon-Avon, a girlhood dream ever since Uncle Judge pulled one of his leather-bound volumes from a high shelf and told her, "If you're going to read what matters, here's the fella to show the way."

She and Frankie made the ninety-mile journey to Warwickshire in a train that left from Paddington Station, sharing the ordinary economy compartment with a middle-aged couple from Missoula, Montana, who exhibited photos of their five children, but claimed not to miss them; an austere man with bad teeth, traveling alone, certainly British, who'd climbed inside a Times when the train started from the station and thereafter seemed to live within its pages, at no time trading more than a gloomy look with either Frankie or KC; and a girl who looked in her mid-teens, also traveling alone, who slept through most of the two and one-half hour trip and sometimes startled them with sobbing that fell without warning.

They hugged one another, tight and warm, and traded secrets.

KC decided they were on the Orient Express, sharing the clack of the tracks with a pair of spies, a secret agent and an Irish revolutionary.

"Would that last be me now?" Frankie wondered.

"Would it?" she wondered back.

"Mine to know and yours to find out, Bright Eyes."

"Yes, only one of the mysteries I want to solve."

"What are some of the others, then?"

"Where we're heading?"

"To Mr. Shakespeare's beginnings, and not another like him until Mr. James Joyce himself come along."

"You know James Joyce?"

"No, but I read him some."

She pulled away from Frankie. "I'm sorry. That was stupid of me, sounding like the big know-it-all."

"A usual mistake, Katie. I sprung from the earth, but it don't mean I haven't used books to steer me head through the clouds and into the far horizons."

When they arrived, they found that nothing looked permanent in Stratford-Upon-Avon.

The village had been modernized to suit the tourist hordes searching after anything Shakespeare. They pretended not to notice, even let their imaginations turn an overpriced, ordinary hotel room into the thatched home of Anne Hathaway on Shottery.

She was Anne and Frankie was Will, and when she nudged

him indiscreetly there was a smile as well, and he told her, "Love is a madness most discreet."

"You know Shakespeare!"

"A whole lot more than I know Mr. James Joyce, but only because there's a whole lot more of him to know."

KC rolled closer to Frankie. She touched her lips to his and kept them there, telling him, "Love is not love which alters when it alteration finds, or bends with the remover to remove."

"I like that," Frankie laughed, "and I like you and I want you for my own."

"Don't you have me already?"

"Yes. Yes. Yes."

And they made more love, like she knew love was always meant to be made, and—

She already was having trouble remembering Peter.

No, not Peter.

What's-his-name, who had taken away her dreams and sent her out to the real world.

Now—

If Frankie McClory was the Plowman—

Her dreams would be shattered once more, and she would have to deal with Frankie in the real world, using the harsh lessons she'd learned from Burkes after he made her more than a Rose Princess.

Burkes, who had trained her to use all the weapons of war, including her body.

Donahue had learned that about her body, the hard way. Not the first one.

Frankie next?

Truth, the destroyer of dreams and love?

She reached over to find his hand and laid it upon her

breast. Slowly, she guided it down her body and heard his breath intensify, his body twitch alive.

"Please be wrong, Burkes," she thought a prayer. "Be wrong, you bastard."

CHAPTER 47

Liam stood near the bedroom door, open just enough to let him watch his brother's hairy back arching backwards, like he was riding a bucking bronco in one of those cowboy movies that, growing up, were his favorites on the telly. To this day. The most important business always could wait the extra few minutes if it was going to get in the way of the end of another one of Frankie's bloody awful cowboy movies.

He checked his watch.

Time to leave.

The McClory brothers. Coming and going, as usual. Same as it was the night when the bloody cops rearranged his face for good. Francis, too busy with his cowboys and his woman to make the date. *I'll owe you,* he swore, so Liam did it for him and was done by a waiting bleeding brigade of Brits and paramilitary bloodhounds, not caring which McClory walked into the setup. The older brother become the wiser brother as well after that.

I'll owe you.

Some debts remain outstanding, don't they, Francis?

After the Da, Liam had gone into the foundry and kept up the odd jobs same time, to make ends meet and so Francis could keep up his schooling between missions for the cause. He'd hoped Francis would get smart enough to get them away from Springfield Estates, only Francis liked it there the smarter he got and the more important he become.

He grew up to push his big brother Liam down, like Liam didn't know any more than using his fists for brains and a

Smith & Wesson to conclude a dispute. And, doesn't that show how smart Francis become? He got that part right.

I owe you, too, Francis.

Owe you big.

I got a eye out on something suitable all the time, especially after you come back from doing good in London Town, with a sweetheart, who fit right in too comfortable from the start, also too smart to have the time of day for Liam McClory, though pretending she did, and shoved another wedge between a brother what cared and one what knew to say *I'll owe you* and get what he wanted.

Liam inched the door shut again, as if either of them would hear something less than a cannon roar, and quietly moved from the hallway into the living room and over to the sofa table. He finished the last of the Guinness before he got his jacket from the closet and headed outside to the pale darkness considering who he had come to despise more, Francis or the girl.

Danaher was asleep behind the wheel of the Ford wagon, adding a strapping good snore to the night sounds, his head tossed back on the seat and his mouth open wide enough to berth a delicious arrangement of garden-fresh, long-stemmed roses between his wickedly decayed teeth.

Liam stooped, sifted the dirt until he found a suitable pebble.

Held it four or five inches above Danaher's mouth.

Let go.

Danaher flashed awake to the sound of his own choking, his face blue in the moonlight, pounding at his chest until he coughed out the peewee-sized stone. Called Liam names and let him know what he thought of the prank.

Liam quit laughing. "Almost time for us to move, Snuffy. Go find Dermot and we'll do us some business."

"Couldn't we of just worked it out for the girl to bring the stuff to us?"

"No. We could not just work it out for the girl to bring the stuff to us," Liam mimicked. Where'd Danaher get off calling orders? "We goes and we gets and we got nobody else to trust but ourselves."

"He's a judge, is he? The man of the house?"

"I think of him as a cadaver. Time allows, I just might look in on him and make a case for what I think."

"And not?"

"Plenty of pickings, mate, plenty of pickings," he said, and dressed his mind with images of the sappy Mum with a body tasty as potato pudding and, especially, the odd daughter, acting feisty around him, almost like he was something beneath her.

This night, just where she might wind up.

The both, maybe.

CHAPTER 48

Pillow talk.

Cuddling under the quilt. The calico cat at the foot of the bed, telling them whenever they disturbed his nap, often purring in competition with her. However long the cat thought he owned Frankie, he knew better now. You can call a cat *Pussy,* but it's never the same thing.

KC stared at the ceiling, stroking Frankie's chest hair, and confessed, "Having to pretend you were dead, Honey. Having to grieve and mourn, knowing how close you were and how we couldn't be together. You know how hard it was?"

"Know how hard it is now."

"Terrorist!" She found what she was looking for.

He tugged at her crucifix. "Oooch! Me, too, Face. A terrorist. But so important to show Liam and the lads you were forever for the cause, just as you forever been for Frankie McClory."

KC visualized the snake and skull's head tattoo on his thigh while encouraging Frankie not to stop what he was doing. The teasing would continue until neither was able to resist the jungle of their love.

"Soon, Face. We catch 'em all, together. We satisfy that God-bereft Walter Burkes, and then it's truly you and me happily ever after." His breathing grew labored and he had to work on producing understandable words.

"Liam doesn't trust me, like always. He's made it a nightmare for me ever since you—"

"Got cut down in me prime." Frankie laughed a rich

378

man's laugh. Told her not to stop. "The old feelings of inadequacy. Everyone is at guilt, but him. You heard my stories. Been like that since we was lads and had to look after one another. Liam come up helpless after the Da was killed, you know? Stood around and watched it go on, the Brits doing the old man in, until I got close enough to put it to them in a language they understand. The old me, Face. Killing because it was the answer and taking it for the solution to everything, encouraged by the Da's cronies and others what saw shooting and bombs as the end to it, not another sad, desperate beginning. You got me straight on that, Face."

"Like I'm getting you straight now," she teased.

She wanted him to keep talking. Drop more information than he meant, the way he did in the old days, coming in from one too many at the pub or because it was news he wanted to share with her, but had to disburse in a way that honored the confidences he was sworn to keep.

"Keeping me straight," he corrected her. "Liam has always been a queer one, unhappy in the shadows but not quick-witted enough for even the second rank, yet there in the leadership by grace of a brother always looking out for him, the way it's supposed to be between brothers, ever afraid of the dire consequences Liam drags after himself like his bad foot."

"He'd kill me if he could. Every time he sees me, he wishes me dead with his eyes. He's never forgiven me for coming into the family, Frankie, like I committed a mortal sin."

"Liam, he knows from mortal sins all right, but not how to stand up to me anymore. He knows my last word on the subject. He won't go against it. Liam would like nothing better than to prove you're on the other side, but he won't go against his brother's last word. He'd soon as be proven right and kill you dead, Face, but he's not brave enough or dumb enough yet to go against his brother's last word."

"You might not think that if you watched him when I read him off for killing—"

"Bastard Osborne's partner. Tell you, Face, I have me own bullet with that one's name on it. Osborne. Touching you the way he did."

"No, you won't, Honey, not when we're so close to winning." She brushed her lips along his chin. "We satisfy Burkes and then we get the hell away. Your slate wiped clean. A new start someplace where nobody knows us. Finally, the children we always talked about, brought into a world where we don't have to worry about boot steps in the night and doors broken down."

"Yeah, right. S'pose . . ."

"Can I ask a question?"

"If that's how you want to waste your mouth."

"Did you know what Liam planned for Annie Waterman, that detective? Were you—?"

Frankie stifled her with his fingers, pressed his lips against her cheek.

"As God is my witness, Face. He sent her packing to that better place before I knew, or it never would of been. I come around too late to even meet her. That life over for me, absolutely, and wish I could take me brother along to where we're going, crazy bugger that he is, but been too late for Liam for years. Liam only knows one way. There's too much debt on the ledger for him to get away clean, like us. Wasn't that the final word handed down by Burkes?"

"Yes."

"Liam ever figured the real truth about us, it would be like the detective all over again. Dead as ducks in the water. You in a minute and me, too, a minute later, on a temper ten times worse than me or anyone else the family. Why we got to be so careful playing this final hand."

KC sensed distraction turning into determination and chanced asking, "Liam told me you're the Plowman who's here for Mr. Mustamba?"

"Come on!"

"He said."

Frankie hit the wall with a hoot. "What would be worse would be your believing it. Say anything to come between us, Bright Eyes. I'm here because nobody in a reasoning state of mind would let Liam come on over to supervise the licking of a postal stamp."

"To wait for the Plowman."

"To wait for the Plowman."

"He's not here yet?"

"If he is, he hasn't held out his arms to me. You know how it works, Face. Left hand and right hand work apart and never come together until the last minute."

"Is the Plowman even coming here?"

"Or someplace else, you mean?"

"Yes."

Frankie inched his body free, rolled over on his side so that his face was close enough for her to take a cloud of his heavy breathing. "I know, you'll know. We know, bastard Burkes will know, and then it ends all but our new beginning." He moved onto his back. "Enough questions. Time for an answer."

KC lowered herself onto him.

And heard something besides his ecstatic groan.

Outside.

It sounded like the town car starting up.

She pulled away abruptly, straining to hear.

The calico cat sprang from the bed, protesting loudly.

Frankie opened his eyes, looked at her and seemed to read

her thoughts. "Canyon echoes. Been hearing them since settled in . . ."

"Honey, it sounded like my car."

"Not with Danaher posted guard. Okay, I know the look. You'll feel better I go and check for bogeymen." He rolled into a sitting position and said, "Don't lose our place." Laughed to win Heaven on a pass and inched off in the dull light of the bed lamp.

She watched as Frankie turned the knob and pushed open the door, blew her a kiss before passing through. She sent one back and, when the door closed behind him, counted to a slow ten. She hurried to the lounging chair, where she had tossed her jeans and tunic in a way that buried her creel bag on the seat.

Felt inside the bag for the comfort of Peter's .45. Crossed to the window. Peeked out a ripped corner of the organdy pull shade.

The town car was gone.

Where?

What for?

When Frankie came back two minutes later, she was sitting up in bed, holding the quilt for protection. He smoothed a spot on the edge and sat beside her, began stroking her hair. His face supportive of her concerns.

"Everything just fine. Like I told you. Liam, he's practicing his anger out there on the settee, counting all them leprechauns wheedling past our garden gate."

His smile was seductive and equipped with its own happy ending.

"Danaher, too?"

He made a game of wiping away the quotation marks by her mouth and stretching the laugh lines alongside her eyes. "No. Danaher where you left him. Parked on the bonnet of your fine old wagon and dueling the fresh air with one smoke lighting up the next."

Frankie was lying to her.

She heard Burkes' voice telling her, *We are all liars. It comes as part of the territory. There's no rule that says we can only lie to strangers.*

She forced her eyes to settle down. Made her own smile as real as possible.

Recognized Burkes may have been telling her the truth when he said Frankie was still one of them, his crossing over an act.

Since when?

Always?

If Frankie saw her doubts, he was keeping it to himself under the evolving grin of a lover about to claim another prize. He pulled aside the quilt and said, "You're safe as you can be, Mrs. McClory. From one and all, excepting me."

She gave him her body willingly while her mind refused to quit the questions. Why the lies? Why the lies, Frankie? Because Burkes has been telling me the truth about you? Why the—

Oh, wait, don't! Not yet, until I—

No, please. No.

Yes! Yes! Yes!

Again.

Once more.

CHAPTER 49

When they got to the Osborne house, Liam, Danaher and O'Dea were dressed in khaki pants and black turtlenecks they'd bought at a surplus store on Hollywood Boulevard a week ago. The ski masks and black rubber-soled shoes were from a bargain shop three doors down. Everything was easily disposable.

Liam had Danaher park the station wagon on the almost empty street, about twenty yards down from the entrance to the driveway entrance, chancing that a security patrol might recognize the car and find it curious it was outside the gates, but still less threatening than a car strange to the neighborhood.

He found the breach in the bushes he had scouted during his breakfast visit, high and wide enough for the three of them to belly crawl through, and signaled with his pen light. One long. Two short.

They joined him within moments, O'Dea resting three baseball bats against his shoulder, their narrow handles invisible inside his grip. This was not a visit that needed harsher weapons, Francis reckoned while the job was being planned. Bats would do fine. In case.

"In case, what?" Liam had demanded. "In case Katie is the traitor I suspect and there's a welcoming committee waiting for us with their own bats?"

Francis had strapped him with his stare. "Get in, get the stuff, and get out. Don't make a mess. Leave me to worry about Katie."

Liam remembered the argument growing like a mushroom cloud until they were at each other's throat and it took the whole bloody pub to pull them apart. They kissed hard on the lips, made up and got drunk like always, even that a contest.

Well, the time is at hand and remains to be seen, Francis, remains to be seen, so worry away about her.

One after the other, Liam, Danaher and O'Dea used the railing to work onto the veranda. Liam looked for a French window that would give them the smartest access.

A bat and the coil of cheap bonding tape in his pocket would do a neat job of breaking a glass panel, if he didn't detect an alarm. Not necessary. A library window had been left open to the overnight breeze, as well as one off the dining room and another one after that.

Liam stopped outside the dining room and signaled. Danaher and O'Dea moved forward on a line close to the wall, five feet apart, nearly invisible in the shadows cast by overhangs and awnings.

Danaher bumped a shoulder against an earth-toned ceramic pedestal supporting an immense hammered copper pot in front of one of the colonnade columns. He made a startled noise. Caught the pedestal with one hand and the copper pot with the other. Caught his breath. Moved forward anxiously.

O'Dea made the accident a joke. He did a little jig around the pedestal, step-dancing backward to the next pedestal and, swinging around, struck the column with his bats. The pedestal tottered, crashed. Broke. The copper pot clanged to the concrete, bounced, rolled to a noisy stop against the railing.

Liam saw the indecision on O'Dea's face. Danaher already had made a mental leap over the balcony. Liam did a racing metronome with his index finger, turned the finger downward, telling them to hold their ground. They waited five minutes. By Liam's reckoning, it was more than enough time for someone inside to react.

To be certain, he waited two more minutes, then entered

the dining room, using the pen light to mark a stop point for Danaher, who gave a victory sign.

Liam next slid the beam a few inches to the left for O'Dea, who stepped back from the circle of light to the French window and eased it shut.

The hinges made loud, rusty squeaks. O'Dea and Danaher froze. Liam sucked his breath and counted off two minutes to himself. He pointed the light beam at the door to the hallway, whispered for O'Dea to share the bats.

The noises outside her window yanked Cookie from a fitful state, not quite sleep; a restless mind full of concern for Daddy. The pictures of him she'd invented were horrible and worse for having had to hold them in until Mommy closed her eyes and drifted off to her own fears. Only then did Cookie go back to her own room and cry until her tears had turned to dust and her arms hurt too much from slinging Baby Throw Doll, trying to work the anger from her system.

From the sound, one of the pedestals outside the dining room had been knocked over, taking the flower pot along. She had toppled the pot often enough to know the racket it made, and to know the base was too sturdy for the wind to be responsible.

Peter coming home? He forgot his keys, and—

If he forgot his keys, he couldn't be driving, either.

Cookie considered a stray animal prowling the grounds. Possible. It happened once before, but the wandering pooch gave his hairy, hunky self away by yowling and howling.

She reached for the flashlight in her nightstand drawer. Aimed it at the ground. Learned the batteries were dead. She didn't want to risk the reading lamp. She slipped out of bed, padded across the room to the window, navigating the darkness by memory.

She opened the French window wide enough to poke her head outside and listen for other sounds. The dining room was clear around on the other side of the house, so there was no way to verify what she'd heard already. She stepped back inside and was about to shut the window when she heard a squeak. Next, another sound she knew, like chalk scraping a blackboard.

One of the French windows being opened.

Cookie aimed for the telephone on her computer hutch and stumbled over Baby Throw Doll. She pitched ahead, dancing for balance, and managed to stay on her feet. Her heart was racing. She lifted the receiver. The line light flashed. She punched down the disconnect button. The house was a zoo of phones, four lines and at least one extension everywhere. Any intruders could spot the light and know someone was awake. Better to let them take whatever they wanted and go. One of Daddy's rules.

A creak. Loud. Outside her door.

The loose floorboard nobody could fix.

A streak of light underneath her door, leaking inside.

Somebody at the door handle.

Cookie got Baby Throw Doll and vaulted back into bed, landed her head on the pillows, dragged the covers over her. She could hear her breathing, labored and out of control, and prayed her heart wouldn't explode and give her away; she pulled Baby Throw Doll against her, the way she sometimes dreamed of Andy.

She sensed being studied, felt a narrow ray of light tickling her shuttered eyes.

Heard a man's whispered voice deciding, "Wrong room." Felt the drift of a strong cologne bite her nostrils.

Felt the light evaporate.

Heard the door close.

Cookie waited until she was reasonably certain they had not decided to check again. She rolled out of bed and crawled to the door, turned the lock. Slipped out of her pajama bottoms and used them to cover the space between the door and the floor so no light would escape. Turned on the reading lamp.

She crossed swiftly to the hand-carved oak dresser Mommy and Daddy found for her the time they toured Germany and Austria and got a two-handed grip on one side, between the back and the wall.

The dresser wouldn't budge. It was too heavy for her to move by herself. Last time she'd had Andy to help.

Cookie stepped back, saw the solution and berated herself for being so stupid.

Starting from the top, she removed the drawers one at a time and stacked them carefully. There were twelve in all, lined up two across. The bottom ones were the heaviest, crammed with assorted and forgotten keepsake junk. After eight drawers were out, the dresser gave way to her pull, moving far enough away from the wall so she could reach the bulky towel she hid there the same morning that phony John Ford came for breakfast.

Andy was nervous about sneaking into KC's room, almost had a shit fit when he touched the Walther PPK and the .32 caliber Colt. He tried talking her out of stealing them, but Cookie was adamant. She'd heard and seen enough. Until she had more answers, if anybody was going to hide guns, it was going to be her.

He urged her to say something to Daddy or Peter, but she was trapped by her promise to KC. Finally, she shut Andy up by promising him that, once the guns were hidden in her room, he could squeeze her boobs *inside* her bra.

Cookie weighed the two weapons in her hands before deciding on the Walther PPK. She left the .32 on the dresser and moved to the bed stool. Aimed the Walther PPK at the door and wondered what to do next. Thought how never in a million years, all the times Peter took her to the Police Academy firing range in Elysian Park, did she ever think she would have to shoot one for real.

"Wrong room," the man had whispered.

What if it was the right room, and she had the gun in her hands and aimed and—

Could she use it anywhere but in her imagination?

"Of course you can use it," Peter told her when she asked him. "You don't even think about it. Your life is in danger, that's what you think. Somebody comes after you, you must protect yourself. You must. You squeeze gently on the trigger, just like I taught you. Here, I'll show you, again. You squeeze easy. That's all you think about. You protect yourself, Cookie, you and all the things you love and cherish the most."

Mommy. Cookie was scared for Mommy.

Hers was the *wrong* room, the man had whispered.

What if Mommy's room was the *right* room?

She would die before she let anyone harm Mommy.

Cookie rushed forward and pressed an ear against the door. Ordinary sounds of silence. She pushed aside the pajama bottom, twisted the lock, worked the door open.

Heard something. Reached around for the light panel and snapped on the row of ball-shaped fixtures running the length of the hall.

Gasped at the sight outside KC's door.

Three men.

Strangers. Burglars. Killers.

Worse.

Unhesitatingly, Cookie aimed the Walther at them.

CHAPTER 50

Peter was half a block away when his headlights caught the town car parked outside in the street. He braked on the roll, cut the headlights and veered to the curb. Kept the motor running while he tried to psych out what KC had in mind by coming back . . . if it was KC.

No signs of life.

He got into the glove compartment using his left hand and pulled out the ankle holster. The .22 was inside where it belonged. On reflection, insufficient firepower if he was up against anything like the .45 she had ripped off him.

Peter pushed the .22 into his belt and snaked out of the Trans Am on the passenger side, keeping one eye on the town car, heading for something better in the trunk, a new 9-mm Beretta he'd been breaking in on the Academy range. Did a fast but thorough check of the silver-colored armory box. Boxes of ammo, but not the 92-F. He pictured the 92-F in the spare shoulder holster that was dangling from an eye hook in his locker.

He brought the .22 to his lips, kissed the short barrel. "Baby, looks like you're elected," he quietly confided, and moved on the town car using a wide-legged sidestep, the .22 aimed at arm's length.

The rear and front passenger side windows were open. He jammed the gun into the back window. The car was empty, except for a tobacco smell thick enough to feel. His eyes began shedding tears as his sinuses shut down. He settled on the front bumper and worked past a sneezing attack, concerned about Mother and Cookie and the possibility they were in danger.

Not from KC.

Because of KC.

That was something else.

CHAPTER 51

Liam made four more wrong guesses after checking the kid's room. The bedroom across the hall from her was empty, except for evidence that it was where the shit detective parked, like the kid's room large enough to house the entire clan McClory, including uncles on a visit. Two rooms had an unused smell.

He tried the double doors at the head of the corridor. They led into a bedroom suitable for everyone on the block.

The old lady was there.

He studied her tossing in her sleep and calling out to her husband in seizures of panic, showing off the kind of handsome that could trap him for hours if not for pressing business and the interfering presence of Danaher and O'Dea.

Except, there was something about her this way that made him think of the wee Ma.

It was the love she was expressing for her man, even in her restless sleep, needing his presence and his love, the way his own had done for so many months after the Brits cut the Da cold before his time.

Ma would call for the Da and sometimes speak with him, telling him about the day's happenings, asking the Da for an opinion. What to do about Liam? What to make of Francis? Decisions she never had to make alone, and not anxious to do so now. God, but Ma loved her man the way he loved her, this saint of a woman, who never got what she truly deserved, but always made him to be the best for whatever he was, encouraged him never to disappear under his brother Francis' shadow.

Liam retreated from the room and led Danaher and O'Dea back to the head of the stairs. He saw two more doors to choose from. He flipped an imaginary coin and pointed. Danaher led the way. He opened the door and bowed them to proceed him, followed by a hand gesture.

This time, no question of it being Katie's room. The curtains were drawn. He located the wall switch with the pen light. He felt comfortable about turning on an overhead. Found himself staring at more luxury than anyone Belfast would know in two lifetimes. All said, America was truly good for letting the poor know what they were missing.

The closet door was ajar.

Danaher and O'Dea found the matched set of travel cases exactly where Katie had told Liam they were. O'Dea stacked the three pieces and then moved them to the middle of the room without raising a sweat. They congratulated themselves all around before retreating behind their ski masks.

Danaher went out into the hallway first, gripping a case in one hand, a bat in the other. O'Dea followed him out, arms encircling the small trunk, supporting its weight from the bottom.

Liam turned off the room light, then brought up the rear. He set down the travel case he was carrying. Turning to draw the door closed, he accidentally tapped his bat against the wall. The fragmentary noise froze Danaher, so fast that O'Dea crashed into him and sent him sprawling onto the floor as the lights splashed on.

They seemed to see her at once, the little girl at the far end of the hallway, in red pajama tops and pink bikini briefs, aiming at them what looked like a Walther PPK.

"I know what to do," she yelled at them. "Stay where you are or I swear I'm going to blow you away."

Liam saw that her grip was steadier than her voice.

★ ★ ★ ★ ★

Don't be afraid, Cookie told herself. You do know what to do. The bro says if any one of them moves, you fire. You squeeze the trigger. You don't even think about it. You squeeze the trigger. Shoot. All of them. Mow them down. Only—

What if they don't move? Then what?

"I really mean it. I'll blow you away."

Can't reach a phone.

Call out to Mommy. Wake her up.

Tell her to call 9-1-1.

She didn't have to think about it any more.

Mommy was there, suddenly.

Getting in the way.

The stupid girl didn't appreciate the trouble she had made for herself. Liam's mind was working rapidly, like a calculator, figuring out how to wrest control of the situation, when the old lady hurried into the hall in her white flannel nightgown and slippers and ground to a halt. Her wild-eyed glance sucked in the three of them and her gun-toting child. "What is going on here?" she demanded, her voice faltering, like she couldn't decide if this was a dream.

"Mother, go back in and call the police."

"Cookie, put that gun down."

"Please, mother. I know how."

"No police!" Danaher barked the command over their voices.

Danaher climbed to his feet and, with a look at Liam, started toward the old lady and her kid, wielding the baseball bat like he expected the next pitch to be low and on the outside.

The foolish little man was showing off for him, Liam realized. He's been in America so long, he's forgotten the power of the children, Liam thought. The stupid girl is ready to shoot, as sure as birds croon.

"No police here," Danaher repeated himself. "And you'll be well off obeying your Ma, child."

Cookie told Danaher, "Stop or you're dead meat, mister." She was having a hard time convincing herself. Damn it, girl. You're thinking about it. Stop thinking about it.

"No way to talk to them what's older'n you," the man answered back.

Her mother was shouting at the same time, "Cookie, stop this immediately!"

"Mommy, get out of the way! Know what I'm doing!" Mommy moved between her and the man, stretched out her hand for the Walther. "Mommy, please! Move your ass!"

Cookie wasn't sure what startled Mommy more, the way she was shouting back or telling her to move her ass.

In the time she thought about it, the man acted on the moment. He lunged forward and batted Mommy aside. More a shove than a hit, and Mommy twirled around like a ballerina and plowed backwards into the wall. Cookie made a moaning sound and turned her head to see if Mommy was all right. Before she knew it, the man was on top of her. He snatched the Walther, pushed her into Mommy, and gloated to his friends, "Ninny had on the safety, so don't think I was any hero or a crazy man." He demonstrated by removing the safety and held up the weapon for them to see.

Cookie's eyes consumed her face. She was certain he was about to kill Mommy and her. What else could she do to stop them?

"No place for that now," Liam called at Danaher. "Too

much noise already, and we got what we come for. Can't risk making a mess and be here to greet the cops." He was worrying over the old lady, looking at the old lady and seeing his Ma. It had come on him suddenly. Like that. He shook his head and still saw her.

O'Dea raved, "Do 'em the both and still time to get the hell away from here, Snuffy."

"Christ's sake! Using me name leaves no choice."

"And my name is O'Dea, so what the bloody fuck, Danaher. You want to save on bullets, I'll do it by meself with this here baseball club and not waste a whack succeeding."

Danaher brought the Walther down to his side and took a step away. He seemed to be deciding who should go first, the mother or the daughter.

"I said we got what we come for," Liam said, but saw it was no use. Danaher and O'Dea were candidates for Bedlam now, same as when they joined in the fun on the shit cop's partner. Annie Waterman was already stripped of the truth, but Liam wasn't ready to have it end, and he would never forget the look in her eyes that made him out to be the sin of her salvation.

"Freeze first or melt in Hell, Danaher."

"Bro!" the little girl shouted.

Liam looked past O'Dea's left shoulder to the stairs and saw Peter Osborne.

CHAPTER 52

Peter was on the landing, using the banister rail to steady his grip on the .22 he had aimed at Danaher. He warned, "You, too, O'Dea, you prick, unless you think you're fucking Superman!" Not giving O'Dea more leeway than a shift of his eyes. Keeping Danaher in sight. He sensed Danaher was weighing the instant in his grin, but he couldn't decide where to shoot first, at his mother or Cookie.

Peter didn't have the problem. His shot hit Danaher in the chest, below the heart.

Danaher, an amazed look across his face, released the Walther and followed it to the floor with a wheeze and a whimper.

Without faltering, Peter used the rail as a track to get the .22 aimed at O'Dea's midsection. He squeezed the trigger. The bullet whunked into the trunk just as O'Dea lobbed the trunk at him. The trunk caught his shoulder. Pitched him off balance.

He hit the stair wall, did a forward somersault all the way down and landed with a bone-crunching thud.

O'Dea raced forward, after the Walther.

Cookie already was bending to pry the Walther from under Danaher. Her fright was giving her a strength beyond anything she ever knew she had, while at the same time her fear had made her wet her pants.

She squealed as O'Dea lifted her like a sack of silk and threw her aside. She boomed into her bedroom door louder than her yelling, and the momentum of his pitch carried her all the way into her room.

★ ★ ★ ★ ★

Liam watched the old lady leap onto O'Dea, shouting condemnation and beating on his chest. Laughing, O'Dea picked her up off the ground, dodged her blows at his head and tossed her away. She bounced off the wall, landed on her knees, somehow propelled herself at him again. O'Dea put a foot to her chest and kicked free, got the Walther, double-checked the safety and fired recklessly at the old lady, who made a contact noise.

O'Dea turned and headed for the stairwell, inquiring of Liam with a wink, "We don't want to forget about the cop, do we?" He stooped over and looked down, putting a hand on his knee to brace himself. "Looks to be knocked out cold, napping like a baby and not good enough, huh? I can do him better'n that." Another wink and he disappeared by inches down the stairs, proceeded by the Walther.

The old lady had managed to rise to her feet and up the hallway to where the .22 had been dropped by the shit cop. She scooped it up and waved it menacingly at Liam, backed around the banister post, looked down after O'Dea. Her left arm leaked blood like a broken faucet, staining the white nightgown a rich crimson.

A shot from below passed through her left thigh, but the old lady didn't appear to feel the fresh geyser of blood.

She wobbled trying to take aim.

She was open and vulnerable for O'Dea's next shot.

In her bravery, Liam saw his Ma.

Shook his head.

And still saw her.

He released the travel case and the bat. Moving like a hounded fox, he got to the old lady in time to stop her from tumbling into a head-first dive, pushed her out of the line of fire and took charge of the .22. She used the wall to hold herself upright, swallowing air. Stared in dismay at the blood. Touched it like it belonged in a dream.

Liam wanted to say something decent to her, but didn't know what.

Below, he saw O'Dea and the shit cop wrestling for control of the gun.

The cop wasn't as sleepy as O'Dea had thought.

Liam found it hard getting a bead as the advantage shifted back and forth, now O'Dea, now the cop, who was clubbing O'Dea with the plaster cast on his right hand.

Peter knew he had to do something and fast, or the son-of-a-bitch was going to kill him. He was hurting like hell and didn't know how much strength he had left. A shot cracked into the ceiling above them as he ripped off the ski mask and confirmed it was O'Dea underneath. He brought his cast down hard on O'Dea's nose, harder a second time.

O'Dea howled under the impact, the bridge of his nose smashed to pulp like raw, cheap grade hamburger, drinking his own blood.

Peter somehow held onto the Walther. Not for long.

O'Dea rammed up a fist that caught him on the forearm and sent off another wild shot.

Peter's arm was radiating surrender and sending the message to every other part of his body as O'Dea grabbed hold of the gun by the barrel. If it was hot, it didn't matter to him. He wrenched the gun free and tried to get a grip, but his hands were smeared with his own blood. The gun slipped away.

Peter thought he heard Mother saying something, but her voice was too feeble to be understood. He was afraid for her, afraid for what he'd do to the other one if he did anything to harm Mother or Cookie. Assuming he managed to handle O'Dea, who was all over him again, screaming names.

They wrestled for control of the Walther.

It went off.

Liam saw his target clearly and fired, on top of the Walther exploding. He heard a third shot and felt the heat of a bullet eating through the mask, scraping across the side of his neck, spoiling his aim.

He spun around. Saw the little girl was advancing from her bedroom, saucer eyes ablaze with determined fury behind the revolver she was pointing squarely at him, two-handed steady. She stopped less than ten feet from him, planted her feet apart and growled, "I know what to do."

"No, Cookie."

Liam understood what the old lady was saying this time. Maybe her daughter did, too, but the little girl, not bothering to think it through, closed her eyes and squeezed the trigger anyway.

CHAPTER 53

The diluted orange mist of morning drifted through the window blinds and across KC's face, rousing her to the few sounds of a city not quite ready for the weekend. She checked the time, almost six o'clock, and replaced her watch on the night stand. An unreal peace, so enjoy it while you can, she thought.

She and Frankie had been at each other through most of the night, but she wasn't tired. She felt refreshed. Fucking did that for her. She'd learned years ago not to confuse fucking with love, and it had become all too easy after Peter. She had learned not to feel guilty about it. Men didn't, so why should she?

Frankie was sleeping soundly on his side. He'd been a victim of his sexual imagination until his body refused to respond. A childish enthusiasm still nipped at the corners of his mouth. His head poked under her armpit, massaging her erect nipple with his steady breathing. A hand cupped her other breast the way it always did after they quit exhausted and sank into a peaceful sleep. His *Security Tit,* he called it.

She disengaged herself, stole into the bathroom, stretching out the body kinks en route. Lingered in the shower. (Pondering Frankie's lies.) Finger-scrubbed her teeth. (Thinking them through.) Dressed. (Fearing what she'd heard from Burkes.)

Her panties were useless. Frankie had ripped them off in the heat of lust. She dropped them in the waste basket, pulled up her jeans. Negotiated the tunic one arm at a time. Returned to the bathroom with her creel bag. Studied her complexion in the mirror while brushing and style-combing her hair. The tired lines were there, but so was the sex glow. She added eye liner and a dab of bright red lip rouge. An overlay of Obsession.

Satisfied after a last inspection, she tossed everything back inside the bag, draped it over her shoulder and started for the kitchen and her first caffeine jolt of the day. The aroma of fresh-made coffee attacked her at once, confusing her until she turned from the hallway and saw Liam staring back from the living room couch, his coffee cup raised in greeting.

"Made a full pot, Katie, with some-a that fine Colombian me brother covets . . . Speaking of whom, what you done with Himself, what's usual the early riser?"

Frankie said, "Up most of the night."

Frankie must have followed her out of the bedroom.

She turned around in time to take his hug and a playful lick on the cheek. He reeked of their odors, her scent even on his breath.

He said, "And a lot earlier the morning than this, your curious mind got to know, Liam."

Frankie finished pulling a multi-colored rugby shirt over his chest and tucked it inside a pair of loose-fitting white cotton pants. He was barefoot and his hair was glued down by sweat.

He cinched the belt and said, "Lookie here, Face, our reunion so far has cost me a whole notch." Playing to Liam, he formed a diabolic smile to fit his raised eyebrows.

Liam nodded approvingly.

"By the time we're on our merry, I fear I'll be mistaken for a toothpick," he said.

"Especially if your brother lets me have my way," she agreed, for Liam's benefit.

Liam nodded, but kept his expression vacant, the mechanical smile a silent keyboard. Frankie's smile had turned into a convenience.

KC was certain thoughts were passing between them in the silent cross-talk that families develop like a sixth sense and master for their exclusive use. She never had it with the Osbornes or the McClorys, but always could tell when it was being used. Were Frankie and Liam holding back now because of her?

Liam shook a smoke from his pack on the couch table, pulled it with his teeth and held up the pack to Frankie, who stepped over and bent from the waist to pull his own.

Frankie got the jet flame lighter from the table to light both, sucked a belly full and aimed a flume of smoke at the ceiling. He motioned KC to the couch and pulled a wicker wall chair for himself. KC squeezed into the corner opposite Liam and placed her handbag by her feet. Frankie positioned the chair on the other side of the couch table. He turned the curved back to them and straddled the seat, using the back as a hand rest, one wrist crossed over the other.

"So, Liam, how's your day so far?"

"Better'n me night, Francis."

Frankie gave the impression he understood; nodded.

The calico cat arrived from somewhere. Frankie scooped him up and held him to his chest like he was getting ready to burp a baby, stroking the back of the cat's head.

"Danaher and O'Dea? How about their night, Liam?"

"They can't complain," Liam said, and ran a finger across his throat.

Frankie crossed himself.

Liam rubbed his nose with the arch of his palm, took a drag, and let his eyes drift to her. "The goods stashed in her closet where Katie said, I grant her that," Liam said, reassuringly. He tapped a finger off his eyebrow. "All three bags outside in her car, and I can't describe the grief lugging 'em by m'self, big one especially."

"You went to the Osbornes'?" The question spilled out of KC, her worst fears with it.

"I went to the moon and back. You'll be needing petrol you plan driving any farther'n down the hill."

She brought her hand to her breast to quell the spasm rocking her body, sensed her soul sinking into her stomach. Before she agreed to anything, Burkes had sworn to her the family would be safe. Only yesterday, Burkes had said he wouldn't remove the security if she did as she was told.

We are all liars . . . There's no rule that says we can only lie to strangers.

He said that, too. Son of a bitch!

What have Liam and his bastard friends done to the Osbornes?

The question took her breath. She appealed it to Frankie with her eyes.

Frankie understood, almost like family. "So, tell me, Liam, all the news . . ."

Liam picked at his mustache and held the cigarette like an hors d'oeuvre. His eyes receded into his ruined face, barged out like glassy beacons that had located the right nightmare.

KC shuddered.

Frankie gestured patience. "Bright Eyes is with me and for me, and for the cause, Liam." He looked at her reassuringly. "What else you got to tell me, you say in front of her."

CHAPTER 54

Liam thought, Francis giving orders again, but not for much longer. And her, twisting him on the spit like suckling pig. He had enjoyed watching her fright grow thick as weeds while he explained the visit to the Osbornes, as if the punishment had been inflicted directly on her, instead of the old lady and the girl.

Finally, she couldn't look square at him and didn't try hiding the whimpering sounds that accompanied his description of the blows, the shots, except where it came to Danaher and O'Dea, like their deaths were an overdue prize. And, something different come upon her when he talked about the shit cop. Big fucking surprise there.

Liam said, "I was enraged, Francis. Danaher was dead where he fell, in the line of duty, and now the shit cop set to do the same to O'Dea. I fixed the cop in me sights and, blam, it was over for him the same instant the cop pushed the Walther to O'Dea's head and painted the walls with his brains." He averted his gaze to Katie. Clearly, she wanted to do him the same death. And Francis sending signals to go easy on her.

"The stupid girl wearing ugly hair where her common sense should be, making me a target two times, once coming close as a drunken barber." He indicated the raw gash on the side of his neck. "She was next, and last to go was the sappy old Mum, already stained blood red, but only after I showed her what for."

Katie was coiled tight as a mainspring, and he wouldn't have been surprised to find her lunging at his throat. Tears

405

ran down her face, streaked with the black of the mascara puddled on the crest of her cheekbones, like the Indian war paint he knew from Francis' old cowboy movies.

She brought her handbag to her lap.

He supposed she was after a hanky.

Instead, the leather exploded like one of the movement's own special deliveries. He felt his guts scrambling inside and saw her composed face daring him to stay alive.

"For Jesus Christ's sake, woman, a joke! Was only pulling your wings off!"

Francis threw the cat aside getting to him. The cat landed on his feet, letting him know what he thought before he charged from the room. He pushed his way past Katie and dropped onto the middle of the couch, so any second shot would have to pass through him. He grabbed the bottom of Liam's turtleneck sweater and lifted it for a better look. He made a face worth a million words. He reached for one of the embroidered throw pillows, propping it hard against Liam's wound to repress the spill.

"Damn, Liam. Always knew your big bloody mouth would one day bring you to grief."

"You're the one asked me the question, Francis."

Francis closed his eyes to the truth, then, "Got one more, you're up for it."

"If it's do I need a doc, answer is yes. Wouldn't mind ambulance either."

Francis' head barely moved. "You put Donahue up to going after Katie on the train?"

"Yes. His greed helped me do the hiring."

"Why for? We had her back working for the movement whether Katie wanted or not. Whether Katie knew or not."

Liam closed his eyes. "You'd gone soft because of her. No telling what could happen to our plans with her running around down here. I was on the bleeding train, so what we need her for anyway?"

"For me, Liam. For me."

"I'm aching something awful, Francis." The kind of chill he felt was new to him.

"Katie was under control after our charade at Milly O'Malley's, and everyone's oath no harm would befall her. I would not be here otherwise."

"Katie almost took you over once. She could take you over a next time, Francis, and we couldn't stand the risk to see our best Plowman become a traitor." The word hurt to say and to hear. His voice no longer sounded like his own. He touched his face to verify the blood spill and coughed up a handful.

"A traitor, me? Only losing can do that to me, Liam." Spontaneously, he also said the words in the finger language of their Da.

"Took less on me, Francis." He saw his brother's mind tripping on the news. "Not like I said earlier. I give it up finding no place better to turn."

"You give it up?"

"Yes," he said. He pointed to his ear and motioned Francis to the pack of cigarettes on the table.

Francis hefted the pack and looked to the ceiling for solace. He tore the pack apart to get to the bug planted inside, pushed out a sigh too big to measure. It was the same gun metal gray micro-mini they had used on Katie at the diner.

"Fucking bug me, Liam? Fucking bug me?"

"Outside now, waiting to hear enough. Government men . . . Not enough for a carnival, but nobody laughing either. The boss has the plug stuffed in his ear or up his ass, one and the same, I expect . . ."

"For God's sake, why?"

"For you and me. They said I cooperate getting them to

you before you get to the nigger and I help earn both of us a free trip home. *Both of us . . .*"

A painful look scarred Frankie's face, ugly as he had ever seen it. "So that's the smell I been smelling, Liam, bad as me suspicions. And how much more informing before we get this free trip home?" His fingers echoed the question.

"The nigger's not worth dying over, Francis."

"Do we also give up our mates? Help bring down the shuttle? Both, maybe?"

"Just looking out for us, boy. Call the government men inside and hear for yourself I'm saying the truth. For us, Francis. Like always, before she come along."

Francis shook his head.

He rose and took a step back, moved around behind Katie, sitting still as petrified wood, clearly unable to burrow out of trauma, her gun hand still sheltered inside the handbag, the snub nose of a revolver poking from a hole the size of a quarter.

Francis dipped into the handbag. He raised it up, using his other hand as a shelf. "Liam, you give them government men the wrong answer."

"You don't want your brother's blood on your eternal soul, Francis . . . Me, what's dying anyways?"

"Me brother's dying. I'm executing a traitor."

Liam looked at Francis for the lie, saw the same glint he never forgot from the day they lost the Da, after Francis pulled the trigger to become a man, as brave as any come before him.

He heard the bullet. It made a fwacking sound cutting through the throw pillow, pushed him into the crevice, then forward, and Liam welcomed death like an old friend.

CHAPTER 55

KC remained motionless as Frankie brushed his lips sensuously against her ear and whispered instructions. "Darlin', you ease your grip on the gun after I lift my trigger finger from yours . . ." He nibbled at the lobe, momentarily hid his tongue inside.

She did as she was told, frightened of Frankie for the first time in her life.

" 'At's me girl." He removed the .45 from her handbag and addressed the bug he was weighing in his other palm. "Outside, you government boy-os? You listening? I just done in a traitor, me own brother, so doing in me wife is no idle threat, you fellas decide to charge on in here. Tell what I say is true, Face."

He buffed her lips with the bug, then moved it an inch or two away. "Let 'em hear your voice, Face . . . I said let 'em hear . . ." He pressed the muzzle of the revolver against her neck, just below the ear. It was still warm. From somewhere, she found the strength to speak.

"Yes."

"A little louder, in case Doubting Thomas is out there, too."

"Yes."

"You hear, boy-os? Just keep your place and mind your manners and I'll be talking to you soon. You make one false move, we got this house wired up for Kingdom Come and I won't fear pressing the plunger."

He leaned around her and flipped the listening device. It landed with a splash inside Liam's coffee cup. "Sorry, Face, but had to let 'em know for sure. Would do m'self before I let anyone harm you, m'self included."

He squeezed her shoulder, stuffed the .45 inside his belt and walked around the back of the couch to lean over and kiss Liam on top of the head. KC saw melancholy on his face and tears not quite realized.

Angling his head at her, Frankie said, "I did so love him."

She found her voice. "And me?"

Frankie exaggerated a grimace. "Thank God you were only a spy, Face. Liam, he was a *traitor*. Difference in that, big, big difference. Why you're still alive. That and because I love you more precious than life itself."

He rummaged Liam's pockets, careful to avoid getting bloodied, and found what he was searching for, a sterling silver pocket watch. He flipped open the cover to check the time, put the face to his ear for a moment and approved.

"I was meant by our Da to have it," he said, "if ever came the day me older bro' had no further need." He shut the case and pocketed the watch. "There're people who would call me a traitor for what I've been doing, Liam." He stepped away, shoved his hands inside his pockets and considered her at an angle.

She asked ruefully, "Were you ever on our side?"

"In my wildest dreams, Face. The only side I'm on is the side that matters. Freedom. And who ever really decides which side of the fence that grows on?"

"You say you love me, but you deceived me."

He held out a stop hand. "And who deceived who first? You come into marriage with another purpose, treachery, so I aimed to give back as good as I got after Liam figured out the real truth."

She looked at her shoes. "That's not fair."

"Always meant to ask . . . How many orgasms did you fake?"

"Only the first one."

A remorseful noise. "Puts you one up on me, Mrs. Frankie McClory." He returned to her and pushed the dimple in her chin. "I'll tell you what I did do. I kept a secret from you."

"No reason for you to be any different."

"I didn't let on I was the Plowman. One last job for the money it brings. One last payday. Enough for the two of us to leave our old ways behind, burrow under the earth to start a whole new life together. All along I wanted it for the two of us, not just for me, Face. Confident I could show you to my point of view."

"You can't, Frankie."

"Your final word?"

"My only word."

CHAPTER 56

Peter studied the house in silence from the passenger seat of Burkes' Sundance Duster. Burkes was in front of him, behind the wheel, doing the same.

It had been an hour since the bug died, and Burkes had taken to rolling the earpiece inside his palm like a latter-day Captain Queeg.

The road was empty except for the unmarked in front of them and another pair across the way, one with its motor running, positioned to block the driveway fast if Frankie managed to get as far as the town car, an unlikely possibility considering the fire power he'd have to outrun.

The immediate area had been cordoned off before Burkes let Liam pull up and enter the house. Burkes' crew was augmented by SWAT teams requisitioned by Chief Spence and a crew of desk mechanics, who had set up a crisis communications center behind them in the Craftsman house about ten yards back of the manicured bristle-bush fence.

The SWATs were armed with tear gas guns, AR-180 and AR-15 semiautomatic rifles, twelve-gauge shotguns, .283-caliber long rifles and as many .45s as there were team members. Nobody was moving five feet away from Frankie's house, in any direction, without permission or a passion to die on the spot.

All the usual precautions had been taken. The neighbors most immediately at risk, two dwellings flanking the target dwelling and the four directly across from it, had been visited and given safety instructions. The usual percentage of card-carrying complainers were vocalizing how their complaints to the City Council would read, but the operation was going smoothly, otherwise.

Peter watched as a SWAT clambered over the front porch railing and duck-ran past the smaller of the two curtained windows facing the street. He set up shop to the left of the screen door. If Frankie peeked out, he would have both barrels of a shotgun ready to blow his nose for him.

Semis and longs aimed down from the ridge above them, a sheet of vine-tangled hillside still showing the scars of a canyon fire two years ago.

Six other SWATs had checked in from locations behind the house, at the rear edge of the property line. To get there, they had scaled a terraced slope from the street below.

They reported two possible exits, through the service porch door off the kitchen or through a glass slider onto a brick patio furnished in basic redwood and a sauna under a green- and yellow-paneled fiberglass roof.

The garage, blocked by the town car, had access from the yard through a side door that was padlocked. There was a free-standing tool shed; a badly-weathered greenhouse, the size of a bathroom, its door hanging by one hinge; lemon-bearing trees; a vegetable garden with neat rows of corn, tomatoes, cucumbers, potatoes; a lost patch between the greenhouse and the rusted, ivy-entangled mesh fence at the property line, full of weed meant to be harvested and smoked.

Burkes said, "You see the curtain move?" He indicated the larger window, which they figured to be the living room. "A flutter in the corner, like somebody playing peekaboo with us."

When Peter answered "No," Burkes repeated the question into the two-way and got the same answer. "The waiting starts to work on you after a while," he said.

"I don't think he'd kill her, Burkes."

"Meaning what? You suggesting we give Frankie to the count of ten and then rush inside through a cloud of gas? Just how powerful an overdose of painkiller did the kindly medics shoot up you?"

"Of course not. I'm just talking out loud." And hurting more than he wanted Burkes or anyone to know. What wasn't busted hurt, but it was nothing to talk about. He'd suffered worse on the football field and once, on the job, when a psycho armed with a metal club confused his body for a bass drum. Besides, it just as easily could have been him stretched out for the photo I.D. boys, alongside O'Dea and Danaher.

"And maybe talking through your hat, you were wearing one." Burkes softened his tone. "Hell, Peter, you're not alone with the wishful thinking, but we got a caged animal in there. He'll use KC any way he can if it gets him off the hook."

"What did Liam tell us? Frankie's love for KC was at the bottom of all the problems—"

"You mean the turncoat who also said, 'Don't worry, gents, my going in there to bring Francis out . . . Francis would never in a million years raise a finger against his brother?' " Burkes did a passable Irish accent. "We can have it chiseled on Liam McClory's gravestone."

"You're certain he's dead?"

"Heard the shots, the all-points from Frankie's lips. If he's not dead, the ambulance Liam wants is a hundred yards behind us, down there around the bend. Along with the bomb squad." Burkes held the plug at his ear like a seashell, grumbled something, and went back to playing Captain Queeg. "Terrorism and death are what those bastards know best . . . We get a clear shot, Frankie is going out, no questions asked. Failing that, we wait. Hope Frankie answers our phone call and negotiates."

"Once he realizes he's not going anywhere and he has to play the only piece left on his board."

"KC." Barely nodding. "Unless, of course, it winds up I'm wrong, Peter, and Liam was right and Frankie decides to pull a Romeo and Juliet . . . Makes good his threat to blow the place sky-high."

Peter closed his eyes to the suggestion.

An old thought strolled by, something that had been nagging at him off and on since he brought down Liam and Liam bought the deal Burkes offered. It hadn't seemed important at the time, so he let it drift away, but the thought was as tenacious as Liam's need to save Frankie and prove something to himself. Both of them.

Peter played time forward from the moment on the stairway landing:

Three shots.

He takes out Dermot with one of them. Cookie's shot narrowly misses Liam's jugular. Liam's bullet suckers into the hardwood, so close Peter can read the caliber.

A fourth shot.

Another near-hit by Cookie.

Functioning on fantasy time, he double-times the stairs and jams the Walther into Liam's back, at the base of the spine, shouting for Cookie to hang it up.

Shot Number Five.

Another near-hit by Cookie before she recognizes her brother's voice, understands his words. Charges to apply to Mother the first aid she learned in the Girl Scouts.

Mother, assuring the world she'll be fine. Waiting until Cookie had both makeshift tourniquets in place, strips of bed sheet on her left arm and above the left thigh, before she shut her eyes for what she promises will be a moment and still hasn't roused in the ten minutes it takes a fire department emergency unit and Pasadena police to get there.

Liam in the parlor when Burkes rolls up, shackled hand and foot beyond threat.

Refusing to shut up.

Wounding Peter repeatedly with descriptions of KC and his brother in bed, like some porno flick narrator who's paid by the four-letter word. Like he's warming up for the horror tales he invents later for KC, after Burkes gave him terms he can live with. (And die with.)

Burkes insists on some proof of good faith.

Liam tells them about the luggage, three wrapped boxes of explosives underneath the false bottom of the small trunk. "Not to worry," Liam says. "A wee pinch might inspire a few loud snaps in the fireplace, but they call for a timer device activated before any real damage done."

"To blow up Mr. Mustamba."

"And whatever acre of earth he's occupying at the time."

"Where?"

Gargled laughter, palms turned out. "That's the kind of information you need from Francis himself. He come with the information, where the bitch come with the goods. Suppose you know that from her already."

Burkes says, "You're saying she knew about Frankie all along?"

"Is the Pope Catholic?"

"I don't believe him, Burkes."

"Why should you, you shit cop? Nobody likes to give up on a good fuck. Ain't that so, Mr. Burkes?"

Before Peter can reach Liam, Burkes steps between them, using his arms like a horizontal log fortifying a fortress gate, pushing him back, shouting over Peter's shouts, reminding him he's a police officer and Liam is in custody.

Peter quits grudgingly, marches to the other side of the room, dumps onto a chair, drapes a leg over the armrest. Catches his breath and his temper while Burkes continues to work Liam.

The bomb squad arrives.

Checks the luggage.

Verifies Liam's story.

Liam winks at them. "Francis will inquire about the bags first off, mark me words. I'll have a story made up by then, so he'll have to come on outside the yard after them."

"The luggage stays here."

Liam's eyebrows raise. He tilts his head and squeezes out a dubious look. "Surprised at you, Mr. Burkes. Suppose Francis won't have it, trudging outside, and decides to send me for the bags? I got to show him something before I claim too much for one man to lug. You never heard how seeing is believing?" Peter takes his glance and tosses it aside. "Or, Francis just might say to the bitch, 'You go on out and help me brother.' That would please the cop over there. I might think about encouraging it, to show no hard feelings."

"Okay, Liam, I'm sold, but they stay in the car. In the trunk. I want you to understand, if the girl comes outside we move on the house. It's up to you to convince Frankie to surrender."

"He won't try no OK Corral."

"Meaning what?"

"Just cowboy talk, Mr. Burkes. Meaning my Francis has never been one to abuse the odds, especially when they ain't in his favor."

A rapping on the passenger window snapped Peter back to the car. The magnified eyes of Burkes' man, Simmons, who had been babysitting the communications center, were a showcase of uncertainty.

Burkes leaned over and rolled down the window. "You remember these, Simmons?" He held up the two-way and frowned.

Simmons angled forward, his head halfway through the opening, and replied courteously, "Just connected inside the house, Mr. Burkes." He displayed his own two-way. There was a fix to his mouth that inferred the news he'd brought was too critical to broadcast.

Burkes grunted. "It's always a matter of time," he called to Peter over his shoulder. "What demands is McClory making?" He pointed at the car interior several times and began twirling the finger, predicting a chopper.

Simmons glanced from Peter back to Burkes. "Says we have ten minutes to clear the area before he blows the house, sir. I surmise McClory intends to be inside when that happens. Mrs. McClory, too. He's asked to see Mr. Osborne—"

Peter jumped from the Duster and charged for the house without waiting to hear the rest of what Simmons was saying, ignoring the commands Burkes began shouting at his back.

"Peter, wait, God damn it! Hold up! You don't know what McClory has in mind for you! Get your ass back—"

CHAPTER 57

Peter flicked off the SWAT's warning glance with a quiet sign and pushed the shotgun aside.

The SWAT gave him a Fred Mertz look and made his brush mustache dance with his nose, uncertain how to deal with somebody who wanted to enter the house. He whispered the question into his lapel mike, by which time Peter was slamming the door closed.

At once he spotted KC. She was in the middle of the living room, trussed with hangman's rope to a sturdy, straight-backed chair. Her arms were strapped tightly to her body, vertical to the threadbare rug, and the thick yellow hemp locked her thighs and feet to the contour of the chair. If she moved, she'd tip over. The white adhesive bandage wrapped around her mouth made even a whimper impossible. The sparkle of her blue eyes was flat as day-old champagne. A swelling under her eyes and the violet fog on her cheeks were both reminders of his rage out of control.

KC flashed him a warning glance. He tracked it past her to the couch, where Frankie sat alongside his dead brother. Frankie's beefy grip obscured the label on the dark brown bottle he was nipping at. He had the .45 in his other hand aimed casually. A calico cat was bundled by his bare feet, asleep.

"Thanks for dropping by, Mr. Peter Osborne."

"An invitation I couldn't resist, Frankie."

"I supposed as much. You packing?"

"Inside my belt. Walther."

Frankie told him to put it on the couch table. "The other

419

Guinness there is for you." He followed Peter's moves with the revolver as Peter traded the Walther for the brown bottle.

The bottle was cold to Peter's touch, but not enough to discharge the heat he felt building inside his stomach. He recognized the smell in the air as his own fear. It was not a new smell to him. He smelled it every time he let his job overcome his good judgment. This time, though, it was more than the job. It was KC. Otherwise, he might have stayed outside and let the bastard check out like the Fourth of July.

No matter what the evidence seemed against KC, it was still circumstantial.

Peter couldn't sit back and let her die on the mood of a killer's kiss, never knowing her last words on the subject. Maybe he wasn't so much different from the judge after all, not in that regard. The judge meted out harsh justice, but only on certain evidence or a jury verdict positive beyond redemption.

"I'm vigilant, you're a vigilante," the judge had once accused him.

"I'm the law."

"I'm justice."

"One and the same."

"Hardly, son. Without the law, you wind up with injustice. It's like a game without rules, or a book without binding; nothing to hold the fabric of society together."

"You are preaching to me again, Judge. Maybe that's where both of us went wrong. We should have gone into the church."

"Would you have followed me there?" Flashing the fox's smile that meant he'd scored again on cross. One of the basic lessons of the courtroom lawyer. Don't ask the question if you don't already know the answer. They both knew the answer to that one.

The judge was too tough to let that heart attack shut him down for good. Maybe, when he came home from the hospital, it was time for them to sit down again, man to man, work on the questions neither had answers for, the ones that had stalked his childhood and never got any real attention from a judge who was always too busy to be a father.

Assuming, of course, he walked out of here whole.

Peter settled beside KC, leaning his weight on one leg and clamping onto the top of the chair for support. He moved the Guinness bottle against his body, to help steady his arm. He wondered how obvious his shakes were to Frankie, who examined his cast without a word.

"You really mean to blow up the place, Frankie?"

"No idle threat, mate. First thing we do we settle into a safe house is wire it good and proper for sound, the sound a-course being, *K'boom!* We have to go sudden-like, we don't have to worry 'bout what's left behind."

"People get hurt that way."

"People get hurt crossing the street or being in the wrong place the wrong time, don't have to tell you that." Smiling crooked and using Peter like they were pub-crawling buddies having one more before one more for the road.

"See that gadget?" Frankie inquired. He set down the bottle on the table, picked up a plum-colored object shaped like a fountain pen. "State-of-the-art. Them Japs, fine craftsman, wizards, whatever they touch. I give the pen a proper push and sent a message to the timer not more'n two minutes ago."

He replaced the pen and pulled out an old, silver pocket watch. "Under eight minutes and counting." He placed the watch on the table, next to the pen.

Peter checked his watch. The sweep-second hand was dragging compared to his pulse. "Do you invite me in to go

K'boom with you? What this is all about?"

Frankie's smile turned ornery. "Fuck, no. This is about her, mate. About Katie. And, it's about you and me, ever since I seen the results of your handiwork, how you come to hurt my Katie and paint dark clouds on the sunshine of her face."

"I won't deny it—"

"Can't. One look to her brands you the liar."

"I'm not proud of myself. I lost my temper."

"But you won my enmity, mate. So, I'm obliged to hurt you for how you hurt Katie, you understand? I made m'self and Katie a solemn promise."

"It's what she wants, too?"

"This is man talk, mate. Katie is me wife. She'll want what I want, and the better for it."

"Death. I can see how much she wants it."

"Do us part. You know the words as well as I know the words. Until death do us part."

"Until death do us . . . *K'boom*."

Frankie used the .45 to write a line parallel to the floor, telling him to shut up.

"Except, I aim to shoot you for the mangy cur you are, paint these walls with your blood and my retribution," Frankie said. "Know I made good my word to Katie, and so I thank you for dropping in to make the oath come true."

He addressed him in the slow, determined cadence of vengeance he had heard before, from hard cases and soft-core criminals alike, system abusers with nothing to lose but a life they couldn't shake on a trade-in.

Peter wasn't surprised KC could be attracted to Frankie. It was more than good looks, although he had the kind of simple features that appealed to many women. The magnetism to make them work. A natural, unaffected manner that probably imbued his loving with equal parts pride and possession. Frankie was a man who would kill for the woman he loved. Or, because of her.

"Fuck you and fuck your oath, Frankie. I came for KC." The words got out too fast for him to consider the consequences. He braced himself for the shot taking him down, but Frankie only grinned knowingly and glanced at Liam, for approbation.

"Well, as you can see, mate, she's all tied up at the moment." The laugh was familiar, and Peter placed it after a few seconds. Liam had laughed that way, not as warmly, but with the same unsettling undertone of tragedies recognized. "A-course you come for her. What I thought when I invited you." Frankie made a face. "I can't not a single minute fathom a person in his right mind rushing in where sweet angels fear to tread, unless a-course this person harbors a secret desire to make an angel of himself."

"You, maybe."

"Never a secret with me, mate. Only a matter-a time. However, I'm not holding out any hope for a pair of wings and a shiny halo. Sharing a coal shovel with Liam, rest his rotten soul; far and away the absolute best I see for m'self."

"Shall I untie KC or carry her out like that?"

Frankie looked at him dubiously. "You listening to him, Liam? Mr. Peter Osborne must think he is back on the playing field I heard tell from Katie. That it, mate?" A silly cackle. "This some championship football game to you? You pick up me wife, with your busted wing and all, swoop down the field and across the goal line to win, with—How much time left on the clock?"

"Five seconds."

"Appears more like six minutes," Frankie said, checking the pocket watch.

Peter verified the call on his wristwatch.

Frankie searched around for inspiration, and his voice became deceptively ingratiating. "Or, maybe, not football . . . Is KC take-away pizza to go, mate? I become very fond of take-away pizza to go. With mushrooms and anchovies. Extra cheese. Tell me, you still as fond of me wife I come to be of take-away pizza to go?"

Peter felt KC's shoulder blade pressure against his fingers. He took his hand off the back of the chair and moved around to see her face. There were two deep ridges between her brows, and her eyes flashed urgent signals. One more inch of tension in her body and the ropes might burst.

Peter moved to the table and deposited the beer bottle. Frankie tightened his aim, so he framed his face with his palms open and fingers spread, to prove his good faith. He stepped away and said, "It depends on whether you're talking to me about the whole pizza or pizza by the slice, Frankie."

"You tell me that," Frankie urged, and patted his brother's lifeless thigh. "Liam give me the impression that you took it any way you could get it." Frankie's eyes studied Peter like a lie detector.

"Not from me, Frankie. High cholesterol runs in my family." He lied, "I haven't had so much as a sniff of pizza for six or seven years."

Frankie's generous mouth moved a tic. He seemed to be sending a signal of acceptance, like he would have bought any answer that brought him the only truth he wanted to know about KC, but it disappeared at once, replaced by an ardent meanness.

He leaped to his feet, skirted the table, cracked the gun barrel across Peter's cheeks, the way Peter had hit KC.

The calico cat lifted off the rug and danced out of the room.

Peter threw up his arms to protect himself. The jarring

movement brought panic to his cast hand. The pain killers had worn as thin as Frankie's patience. He wheeled and stumbled across the floor. Dodged around the piano. Used his hands to brake against the wall. Crashed hard anyway. Screamed on the slow slide down the wall to the floor, the elastic howl like a tenor's sour note. Worked his way back to his feet, stepped over to the piano for support and turned to confront Frankie.

Frankie was settled back on the couch, massaging the back of his neck. He pushed out a long breath and said, "Mrs. McClory begged I spare you, over my own deeply-felt reservations, so that does it for us then. Wipes the slate."

There was something in the gentle way he looked over at KC that informed Peter the notion he had shared with Burkes, that Frankie would not kill KC, was on the money. Absolute. Frankie had no intention of letting KC die. Frankie had wanted him here for something besides revenge.

He shut out his pain by focusing on the problem.

The phone rang. Frankie grabbed it off the hook and used his chest to muffle the receiver while he leaned forward for another look at the pocket watch. "Tell your mates they got four minutes on the countdown," he said, holding out the receiver to him. "Or it won't be my fault what happens." He modeled a mushroom cloud with his hands and mouthed the word *K'boom*.

Peter took the phone.

He checked his watch and repeated Frankie's message, pronouncing the *K'boom*.

He listened to Burkes and put a hand over the mouthpiece. "Communications is down to two men and they clear out after this call," he said. "There'll be a car parked in front, a Duster, motor running and ready to move."

"Tell it don't go nowhere. You be right along."

"Mrs. McClory?" Peter tested the answer he already knew into the phone. "I'm bringing Mrs. McClory out with me. Right, Frankie?"

Frankie worked his lips in and out. He played with his nose and wiped his mouth with his fingers, ran them over his chin, down his neck. Smiling at KC, he said, "Love is a madness most discreet."

"What?"

"Mrs. McClory, too," Frankie agreed, and turned quiet as dust.

Peter listened intently for another moment and hung up the phone.

"Mr. Burkes says he would like you to join us, Frankie. He says the deal he made with Liam still stands."

Frankie shook his head and smiled dimly, his gaze fixed on his own goal line. "Tell the man thanks for me, mate, but me work here ain't finished yet." Picked up the watch by its chain and held it out. "Take this, you don't mind, for Katie. It's the one McClory family heirloom. Only had it for a short time m'self, and she the one gets it now."

"Three minutes," Peter said. He closed the cover and dropped it into a pocket, tapped his thigh for good measure. "Help me untie her."

"The way she is, mate. Otherwise, Katie won't go."

"Why you needed me here. To get her the hell out."

"Jesus Fucking Christ, man! No time left to give you the whole story. Take me word for it. It ends with a bang." Frankie smiled impishly, an overgrown leprechaun making a joke of the world.

Peter moved directly behind the chair. He bent over and encircled it with his arms at KC's waist. Took a deep breath and started a slow, cautious lift. Hurt. Managed it a foot off the floor. Pain. Forgot the pain.

He started duck waddling to the door, a distance of ten or twelve feet.

The rough hemp ate at his wrist and he lost his grip.

He set down the chair. Swiped the sweat from his brow. Tried again. This time, he had a better hold. If KC were ten pounds heavier, no way.

From the corner of his eyes, he saw Frankie hurry over to the window and check past the curtains. "Was a sharpshooter hanging there earlier," Frankie said.

Peter had no more energy to waste on words.

Do it, Frankie, he thought, knowing what was on the other side of the door. *God damn go and open the door.*

"I'll get the door, mate." Peter hid his reaction. "You angle off. Come charging by with your shoulder and that takes care the screen door. I seen the Duster out there, where it's supposed to be."

Frankie stepped backward, using the thick oak door as a shield while getting it open wide enough for Peter and KC to sail through.

"Mind you not to trip, mate. Throw Katie into the fucking car and floor it." His laughter was sudden and priceless. "And, you, Face, you listening, Bright Eyes? This bloody bastard ever hits you again, you kill him for me. Any bloody bastard who ever dares touch you."

Peter adjusted his walk to lead with his left shoulder and double-timed his pace just before he hit the threshold. The screen door was secured by a cheap, aluminum latch lock and didn't budge.

He lowered the chair to the floor, refusing to play a guessing game with himself on how much time remained, certain his arms would fall off momentarily.

He stretched around, pressed down on the door handle, kicked with his foot.

The door screeched open.

The calico cat dodged into the emerging day.

A pair of gloved hands seized hold of the chair and jerked it clear of the doorway.

A SWAT wheeled into position, a no-nonsense AR-15 ready to air-condition Peter's chest.

Another SWAT grabbed him by the shirt and heaved him into the waiting arms of a fourth SWAT, who prodded him down the noisy steps, poking him in the back and encouraging him in a harsh voice loud enough to launch a missile to hit the ground running, aim for the street at top speed.

Two other SWATS were racing ten or fifteen feet ahead of them, carrying KC and the chair.

All of them wore baseball caps and fluorescent orange flak vests, the backs labeled S.W.A.T., to show each other who to miss or the bad guys who to aim for.

Behind him, the AR-15 was telling a noisy story.

He had an image of Frankie behind the door, cut down before he could get off a shot, trading in patriotism for martyrdom among his people. Giving everyone else a dead terrorist, occasion for rejoicing and relief.

Ahead loomed a U-shaped hill of sandbags about five feet high and ten feet long, built at an angle across the road and invisible from the house. Burkes and Simmons waved them on from an inside corner, like Dodger coaches signaling in the winning runs.

When they were almost there, Burkes threw a go-finger at Simmons, who pulled the two-way to his mouth and shouted, "All present and accounted for! Thirty seconds to clear!"

Suddenly, a loud, penetrating siren, the guerrilla warning noise of a rescue operation.

Peter heard shouts and scrambles coming at him from all directions.

Boots chomping into grass and shuffling gravel, hitting the asphalt hard.

Nettled birds, adding a musical unreality to the roar of the retreat to safety.

The house exploded with a thunder that eclipsed all the other sounds.

The roar tore the structure loose from the foundation and it stretched for the sky, hung briefly in midair before it floundered and fell to the ground. Windows shattered and spit. The walls cracked and splintered, spilling like playing cards toward the center, collapsing on each other under the shredded shingle roof.

An orange and blue pilot light, but no fire. Self-contained destruction. The house had been prepared by demolition experts who knew what they were doing, like the companies hired to kill office buildings, to make room for progress or for a scene in *Lethal Weapon 86.*

A sudden calm.

Like noise had been vacuumed out of existence.

The first bird making inquiry.

A coyote's howl echoing in the canyon.

Other animal sounds.

The smell of wounded pine.

Fire sirens. An ambulance.

Simmons into the two-way, "Mop up. Mop up, who reads me . . ."

The breeze of activity.

Peter looked in the direction of the hand gripping his shoulder.

"You okay?" Burkes asked, chin elevated, sighting him over his half-moon glasses to examine the answer. He nodded. Burkes grunted. "You did a damn fool thing trooping in there," he said. Took his hand away and promptly obscured any evidence of genuine concern. He called over Peter's shoulder, "One of you take care of the lady, please," and trailed after his request.

Turning, Peter saw KC was still a prisoner of the chair. The SWATs had settled her onto the street facing the translucent morning sky.

She appeared unharmed. Distraught.

Drawing closer, Peter saw a sorrow in her eyes that had not been there before. He stood alongside Burkes and they watched the SWATs turn the chair upright and cut through her ropes, like fishermen gutting a fish. One of them thought to peel away the adhesive from her mouth. He did it slowly at first, then with a yank that made her wince.

"You okay?" Burkes asked.

KC ignored the question.

Burkes didn't press. He dug his hands into his pockets and barked some inconsequential directions.

KC's arms were free. She exercised them while the SWATs removed the last of the fat hemp from her body, cut loose her legs. She stretched them alternately, refused a hand, worked herself up by slowly pushing both palms against the seat of the chair. Her knees gave, and she sank back down. This time, two SWATs supported her at the elbows without asking and helped her to a steady rise. She pulled away from them and circle-walked the kinks out, stopping a few times to bend and stretch.

She walked over to them and said to Peter, "You have something that belongs to me." Her eyes drifted everywhere but into his.

He started to ask what she meant, and remembered.

Frankie's pocket watch.

He fished it out.

KC took it and studied it for certainty, clutched it in her

tight fist, navigated past them and started around the barri-
cade.

Burkes called after her, "Keys are still in the car, Mrs.
McClory."

She stopped and half-turned to confront him. Her face
was a mask of flesh wounds. "You miserable son-of-a-bitch,"
she said. "You miserable son-of-a-bitch!"

The second time loud enough to catch the canyon drifts. A
dog barked, and other animals picked up the theme.

Burkes extended his arms. "It's what I do for a living, Mrs.
McClory."

KC started down the street. Stiff. Erect. A proud walk.
She stopped. Made a precision turn and, without looking at
them, headed for the town car. Gunned the motor. Backed
cautiously out of the driveway.

Peter asked Burkes, incredulously, "What about the explosives in the trunk?"

"No explosives in the trunk."

"But, you told Liam—"

"Lied. Like Jimmy Durante used to say, *I got a million
a-them*. Your bomb guys stashed them in an evidence locker
after they substituted talc."

"She called you a son-of-a-bitch."

Burkes rubbed his cheek with the heel of his hand and
grinned. "That offer of a free trip home if he came on over to
our side. She probably thinks I encouraged the SWATs to
make a liar out of me all over again . . ."

"Did you?"

"Would have, but couldn't afford to. I needed to know
where the try on Mr. Mustamba was going down. If Frankie
was the one. But after that—" His grin grew.

"You are a son-of-a-bitch, aren't you?"

"Yeah, but a damned fine one."

Together, they watched KC navigate down the hill until she took the bend. Burkes lassoed the air with a finger. Simmons cupped a hand over his mouth, whispered into the two-way.

Burkes said, "We'll have a shadow on her before she hits the traffic light at Franklin."

"Whose side is she on, Burkes?"

"My best guess? Both sides . . ." He asked Simmons for the time and wondered, "You hungry yet? There's a deli down the hill serves a mean breakfast."

Two days later, Burkes phoned him at the office.

"We've been going through the rubble with a fine tooth comb and no sign of a second corpus, Peter. Seems Frankie McClory got his Irish ass out of there before the explosives went off."

"How?"

"C'mon down. I'll show you."

CHAPTER 58

Burkes had Peter follow him to the back of the ruins and pointed out a hardwood door in the concrete floor that the fire inspectors had found, just about where the service porch would have been. The cleared area measured about ten feet by ten feet, the door about three by six.

Peter refused an offer of help as he hunkered down to get a grip on the inlaid metal handle. His right arm was dressed in a fresh cast, and God knows where else he still hurt. A glassy-eyed ceramic glaze, the natural by-product of pain killers, suggested to Burkes that he hurt all over.

Burkes couldn't oomph up the door. Quit when he sensed his balls getting ready to search for his Adam's apple and hollered for help from Simmons. Simmons interrupted his conversation with a pair of fire marshals, picked up two yellow LAFD hard hats from the kitchen counter, like the one he was wearing, and navigated the piles of rubble.

"Beam us down, Simmons. Concrete stairway, you see it, Peter? Stairs just wide enough for one at a time." He went down first, then used his flash to guide Peter and Simmons. "Keep a tight hold on the rail, the angle is a bitch," he called up to them, and swept the darkness with his flash until he found the wall switch.

The room was about half the size the kitchen overhead had been. Four interior walls of reinforced concrete brick, utilizing two of the basic foundation walls. An unpainted steel door built into the east property wall.

The cold began eating Burkes' bones. He pocketed the flash and drew the molting fur collar of his raincoat up around his neck, buttoned it. "You understand why I told you to dress for winter?" he asked Peter, rhetorically. "Colder than the original mummy's tomb."

Burkes drew a pair of fur-lined leather gloves from a pocket, studied their cracks and peels as he pulled them on. Stroked out the raincoat wrinkles. Peter fixed his pea jacket collar, adjusted the hard hat. Wrapped himself in his arms. Cocked his head while making the library shelves lining an entire wall. The shelves were empty. The white enamel paint was chipped and peeling everywhere he looked.

Burkes watched him study the cobwebs and the dust, looking for a reason, the same way he had when he'd come down here the first time.

"The original builders might have had it in mind as a storage cellar: freshly-canned fruits, that kind of stuff," Burkes said, helping him out. The walls absorbed the echo and gave his voice a faintly hollow sound. "Or, it might've been rigged as a bomb shelter in the late fifties. Was an Atom Bomb scare that triggered a craze bigger than the Hoola Hoop or Pet Rock, and it sent a lot of people digging underground. Our immediate frame of reference falls somewhere in-between." He saw Peter was waiting to hear the rest. "Prohibition. The place was rigged as a drop point and warehouse by bootleggers when the roaring twenties started roaring. These hills up here were as remote as Tibet and safe for anybody but a dallying llama."

Peter flashed him a condescending smile. Simmons laughed out loud, as usual, maybe even got the joke. Burkes sent him a signal.

Simmons moved to the steel door and opened it with a flourish.

Inside, the light of a naked bulb dangling overhead revealed dirt side walls veined with rocks and roots and reinforced with horizontal wooden crate slats someone had pounded into the earth.

"Somebody carved a small tunnel beneath the backyard that angles to the street below, maybe a hundred, a hundred and fifty yards. Big enough for single-file traffic, humped over. A six-foot ladder is at the far end, leading topside to a door that opens trap-door style into a fenced, overgrown quarter-acre. You would not ever find the door in a million years without knowing what you were looking for."

"Your bootleggers used the tunnel to transport cases of booze back and forth," Peter said, nodding acknowledgment to his guess.

"Gets better. Had my people check the records. The deed to this house is still in the name of the wife of an Irishman with mob ties, who did a few hard years at Alcatraz for hijacking and illegal transport. Ties going all the way back to the old sod. Lawless. Fiona Lawless. The name ring any bells?"

"The mother of May Lawless?"

"The grandmother," Simmons said. "The deed to the lot below is also in her name."

"Explaining why the house would be available for Frankie," Peter said.

Burkes noticed Peter's mind working overtime, eyes rolling around the room after—what? "Or anybody else who needed a safe place to stay. Frankie took a couple chances after learning we were outside. One was to get you inside, to take Mrs. McClory safely out before the big bang. The other, greater risk was timing it so he could come down here and hide out before the SWATs got to him. Crud like Frankie McClory are miles too smart to think the enemy closes up shop and goes home because they demand it."

Peter found a comfortable position against a wall, his

hands inside his pockets, and said, "It doesn't add up, does it, Burkes?"

"What?"

Burkes saw Peter definitely thought he knew something. He showed it by the way he narrowed his eyes and ran his tongue around his lips and rubbed them together, like he was trying to decide on the best starting point.

"A thought started eating at me after Frankie said the house was wired and ready to blow," Peter said. "Remember how Liam insisted the explosives had to be in my folks' car, because Frankie would want to know about them before anything else?"

Burkes encouraged him to keep going, but Peter didn't notice.

He was talking to a spider web in a corner across the room, a finely-spun curtain hanging across much of an empty bookcase shelf.

"Liam said Frankie knew where they planned to blow up Mr. Mustamba, not him. KC had the explosives, but Frankie had the *information*." Peter pointed a finger through the ceiling, several times. "Next, we learned Frankie had explosives, too. Had explosives all along. So tell me, Burkes, how necessary could the explosives in KC's luggage really have been when Frankie already had a shit full of the stuff here?"

"It's your quarter, Peter."

"They didn't need to use KC as a mule, did they? They could have brought the plastique or whatever it was inside the luggage into the country at any time. Last month. Last year. They could have stored it down here like they used to store all that bootlegged booze. They could have stored it anywhere in the house. It's not as if you had an all-points on the address."

"Anything else?"

"Yes." Burkes caught his eyes and ushered out the words

with a hand gesture, like he was guiding a jet-liner to port. "I think you got suckered, Burkes."

Burkes nodded. "It wouldn't be the first time." Repeated the hand gesture.

"I don't have it all yet but, if I'm right, the bad guys never bought into your business on Pasadena. Instead, they decided to work your bullshit against you. They blazed a trail for you to follow while they got ready to assassinate Mr. Mustamba somewhere else."

Burkes shrugged and began pacing off the room. It wasn't nerves. The cold had worked through his hard soles and hit his joints, making them feel the way they always did when it was about to rain. He thought about a vacation in Hawaii or the Bahamas, wondered what the doctors had told Vonnie about her spurts of pain this time. He made a mental note to call her, first thing back at the office. Check up on Fritz, too.

"I'm not as big a sucker as you imagine," Burkes said, shooting a look at Simmons, who responded with palsied head shakes. "Donahue got caught by the Brits and we turned him the way we thought Mrs. McClory had turned Frankie. Donahue was the one who told us about the Mustamba contract. About the set-up on Frankie, to throw us off the scent. About Frankie being shuttled to the States to lay the ground-work. Donahue thought he had the job, thought he would be the Plowman, and that's why Donahue was on the train. Only he got frisky, and he got killed for trying to be a naughty priest. Or, because Liam McClory paid him to take out Mrs. McClory and she was too fast for him. Or, because they got wise to Donahue and Frankie convinced Mrs. McClory to punch his exit visa."

"Which?"

"Doesn't matter, Peter. Except, it helped to show us we had bigger problems than we had imagined when we set up the Pasadena showcase to move Mrs. McClory back into the apparat and take our chances she was still on our team. Suddenly, we had Liam in town. We had Frankie resurfacing. Snuffy Danaher and Dermot O'Dea breaking into your folks' place with Liam . . ."

"Why, if the explosives were a ruse?"

"To keep up the show, keep us dangling on one foot in the wrong direction while Frankie ran KC to check her loyalties and how close we were getting to the truth. Don't ask again which side she's on. I don't know which side she's on. She's with her husband now. If we hear from her, we're doing fine. If we don't . . ." Another shrug.

"What do you mean she's with her husband now? How the hell can you—"

"Simmons."

Simmons moved a few steps forward, between Peter and Burkes, like he was stepping up to a podium. He rotated his neck, cleared his throat. Gave his tie a tug.

"I've been carrying on an acquaintanceship with Miss Lawless," he said, blushing at the implication. He searched Burkes' eyes for approval. "I was keeping her company the night of the explosion, when she received a phone call. Suffice it to say, I was sufficiently close to make the caller's voice. It was Mrs. McClory. She identified herself and said she was putting her husband on the line."

Burkes said, "No question about that?"

"No question, sir," he replied, full of Southern fried indignation. " '*This is Kate McClory,*' she said. She said, '*I'm putting my husband on the line.*' "

The color drained from Peter's face. He settled onto the floor and crossed his legs.

Burkes cursed the cold privately and eased down alongside him with the warmth of companionship.

"Miss Lawless suddenly remembered she was not alone. She started to get out of bed. I had been pretending sleep and reached over to take her in my arms, but she pushed me aside, rolled out of the bed and moved into the bathroom with the telephone. I could not hear anything through the door but a mumble, then the shower running. Ten minutes later she was dressed and running out the door, reminding me where to find the instant coffee and the day-old doughnuts. I got right on the blower, but it didn't make a difference. We've had the Lawless apartment and The Quiet Man staked out ever since. No sign of her. May Lawless's lost, the same as Mrs. McClory."

Peter said, "Simmons, you're certain it was KC?"

"Yes."

"Frankie. You're sure she said Frankie?"

"Mrs. McClory said her husband, Mr. Osborne."

"And since we know he isn't here, it's pretty likely that's who she meant, Peter." Burkes rose, brushed off his raincoat, and crossed the room. He pointed at the floor. "I didn't see you paying much attention to the footprints in the dust, but the lab boys did. Those belong to Liam. The ones here match a couple of pairs of men's walking shoes left behind in the closet, so it's a pretty good bet that they're Frankie's. These babies—smaller, feminine. Mrs. McClory's. KC was down here with him, so we have to figure she was in on the escape plan."

Peter's complexion had turned to ash.

He shook his head disbelievingly.

"Why would Frankie tie her up, go through the business of—?"

"To fake us out. To keep his wife in the action, because he needed her for other things. To make the call to May Lawless. To get the Plowman to where he really wants to be. And that

439

could be anywhere. Anywhere at all. Let's hope Mrs. McClory's still on our side, that she finds out where from Frankie and gets the information to us while there's time to do something about it."

Peter looked at Burkes hard. There was something Burkes was holding back. He put the question to him. Burkes held up his hands in surrender and said, "I've been debating with myself whether to tell you now or wait."

"Wait for what?" He turned to Simmons, who found somewhere else to look.

Burkes said, "Until we had a better fix on how this one ends."

"I'm a big boy. More about KC?"

Burkes shook his head. "About Annie Waterman."

Peter swallowed hard. He was almost sorry he'd raised the question. He fixed his jaw in anticipation.

"I asked Washington to come in and do a survey for me, using some of the sophisticated shit you don't find in local police departments. I figured that I owed you that much, Peter. They picked some partials off her body and matched them against prints we lifted from your house, the records. Follicles. You know the drill."

Peter's chin inched up and his eyes closed against the news, but before Burkes could tell him, he guessed, "Liam McClory?"

"Yeah. Also the barflies, O'Dea and Danaher."

Peter nodded and kept nodding, unsure of his voice. He looked away from Burkes and Simmons, not willing to share the next few moments. Finally, he said, "When I went nuts and went after KC, I asked her about Liam. She said she didn't know—"

Burkes shrugged. "Maybe, she didn't. Meanwhile, if it's

any consolation, you know three of the four sons-of-bitches are maggot food."

Peter started to respond in kind, when he realized what Burkes had said. "Three of the—four?"

Burkes and Simmons exchanged glances, and in that fraction Peter knew what he was going to hear.

"On a lark, I had Washington add Frankie McClory to the mix. Him, too, Peter. He was there, too." Peter looked for something to lean against. "Let me say this much with some degree of certainty. If KC knew Frankie was in on it before she helped him get the hell out and away, then we know where she stands, don't we?"

"If it's true, I'll kill her, Burkes."

"I find out what I need to know first, and I won't stand in your way."

"Can't guarantee a thing, Burkes. Not a damn thing."

CHAPTER 59

Two days earlier, leaving the ruins of Frankie's safe house, KC had caught the tail immediately.

There never had been anything particularly subtle about Burkes or his methods, so she started looking for a car the moment she reared out of the driveway, filled with dread at the thought Frankie's plan might not have worked.

She pictured Frankie dead, a faceless, mangled, blood-endowed heap behind the door, unable to escape to the hatch and pull it closed behind him before the SWAT team withdrew.

She had heard the Uzis before the explosion.

The SWAT team shooting wild, or—

"That bastard Burkes," she thought, again. "That son-of-a-bitch Burkes and his free trip home."

She wanted to burst into tears, but knew she had to hold herself together until tonight, when she kept her end of her bargain with Frankie and learned once and for all where he stood.

Her hand found the sterling silver cross around her neck. She clutched it tightly during a silent prayer for his safety.

She drove like a tourist through Hollywood and, when she got to Beverly Hills, played the one-way streets until she could plunge through a signal on yellow and leave the tail behind on the red. Two fast turns later and she was by herself.

She spent the rest of the day lost among Saturday shoppers at the Beverly Center, taking in movies at the multiplex that made no sense. She kept seeing Frankie, hearing his voice as they worked out the rest of their lives, Liam silent witness to the agreement.

"So, where does that put us, Face?"

"I love you, Frankie, and I want to be with you, but not if you're a Plowman. Not if you're here to kill Mr. Mustamba. Not if you ever kill anybody ever again. I came this far with you truly believing you wanted to put an end to killing."

"I do, I do. It's the money makes it possible."

"I want to leave, Frankie. I want to leave now."

She started to get up from the couch. He stopped her with his hands on her shoulders, eased her down.

"I can't allow that, Face." He kissed the top of her head, worked loose strands behind her ears. "Without you a hostage, I'm bound to leave here like Liam, feet first."

"You heard Burkes. You come in peacefully, tell him what he wants to know about Mr. Mustamba, it's a free trip home. We start a new life somewhere—"

"I have one word for your Mr. Walter Burkes, and the word begins with bull and it ends with shit. Mr. Walter Burkes would soon as see me dead, Face. I tell him the plan, he'll up and leave me to the mercy of others, like your Mr. Peter Osborne. That's the only free trip home Mr. Walter Burkes has in mind." He pointed at Liam. "I'm damned if I do and dead if I don't, Face, so what you want? You want your Frankie-boy dead over some nigger what don't mean a wart to us in our lifetime, except for the comforts come our way with the bounty money?"

"Kill me or let me go, Frankie," she said, and shivered at the declaration.

Frankie didn't move and his hands hung lightly on her shoulders. He made a despairing sound deep inside his throat and walked around to make a show of the .45.

He flipped out the cylinder, checked the load.

Grunted approval.

Sighted the chamber.

Grunted again.

Flipped the cylinder back and offered the .45 to her.

"All but the two," he said. "Since I would never harm you and have no thoughts for offering m'self up, do me the courtesy of putting the barrel to me head and sending me on me way."

"Frankie!"

He bowed appreciatively to her alarm. "You'll be a hero in their eyes and, once the news gets back, there'll be some other Plowman come along shortly to do the nasty deed." He brought the .45 closer.

KC pushed back. The arm of the couch jammed into her. She motioned erratically, not quite sure where to put her hands, only certain she wanted them away from the .45. Frankie understood. He laid the .45 on the table carefully and turned his voice to cream suggesting, "Let me make another proposal, Face? One keeps you safe from harm and me alive?"

He led her downstairs, to the room beneath the kitchen and explained what he had in mind.

She asked about Peter.

"No harm come to him, I swear it."

"And, afterward?"

"Out of it, Face. Swear. Out of it forever. You, too. Gone where they'll never find us or even think to look. I'll do the auto repairs and you can make us fine babies and happy ever after, the lot of us."

Shortly before nine o'clock, she approached Beachwood from Franklin on the east and took the steeper Canyon Drive back route in second gear, up the winding roads to Willows. Willows was the street below the back of the Lawless house.

The street lights made circles on the asphalt and not much else. The quarter moon dipped in and out of darkening clouds. It was going to be raining tomorrow, exactly as promised by the man with the sun-drenched voice on All-News Radio.

All-News Radio was full of reports about the explosion, but all the official quotes were vague, something about a gas leak. No mention of Liam or the siege or what went down at the Osbornes'.

KC knew it had to be Burkes at his usual game, keeping a lid on the truth.

She drove past the empty lot, barely slowing down for a casual scan, turned right at the first cross street. It led to a street that took her back down to Franklin.

So far, so good.

Nothing to suggest they'd found the cellar or the escape tunnel.

Probably tomorrow, after they'd dug through the damage and couldn't find him.

Or, would they?

She couldn't halt the tears this time and turned up the radio to bury her sobbing. It didn't work. She switched to a music station and tried matching lyrics with Barry Manilow. That didn't do it, either.

She cut a U-turn through the supermarket parking lot, repeated the route. Same results. No signs of anyone laying in wait for the town car. The only police who showed up with flashing red monkey caps and sirens blaring were in her imagination.

Real was the biker who pulled up alongside her in the through lane, before she turned left up Willows for a third pass at the lot. A red bandana held his mangy, shoulder-length hair off his watermelon face. Mirrored glasses. A black vest guarding his overgrown chest and beer belly. The poster boy for *Cliché Biker* Magazine. He went from nicotine-stained teeth to a phallic tongue the length of a ruler and roared off.

She drifted to a stop across the street from the empty lot, almost parallel. Cut the lights, but kept the motor running. Checked the time on the dash clock. Nine exactly. Frankie should be along any minute.

She rolled down the window and studied the chain link fence for any sign of him. A sound from somewhere inside the high grass. A shadowed figure moved toward a corner of the fence and worked a section away from the pole until it was large enough to pass through.

A tramp stepping out for an evening stroll.

He looked around, barely giving the town car a glance, and headed up the street, away from her.

"Boo!" A scant murmur at her ear.

Only the safety belt stopped her from crashing through the windshield.

Frankie had crept up on her from behind. He leaned in, kissed her cheek. Hurried around to the passenger side and got in. Leaned over and kissed her other cheek.

They embraced hard.

Swallowed each other's kisses.

Groped through the thrill of reunion and, at the last minute, they pushed away from one another with mutual reluctance.

Once he'd regained his voice, Frankie said, "Need to make proper love to you."

"Me, too," KC said.

They pulled into an all-night station. Frankie waited in the car until KC signaled she'd reached May Lawless. He took the phone from her and, not bothering with any pleasantries, said, "May, Katie here tells me you put her off when she called before about having us a car."

"I knew to be on my guard, Frankie, all it was. I told her I had to hear it from you, first, before I did anything. The way you wanted it set up yourself."

Frankie thought about it a few seconds. "Yes, you're right on that, May, and I apologize."

"Apology accepted."

He looked around to see who else besides KC might be listening. The station was empty, except for the tanker loading the pump wells. The driver, who needed to lose forty pounds, kept adjusting his black Stetson while making small talk on the corner with an anemic hooker in a flamingo pink fright wig and hot pants.

"How fast can we have one then? As clean as a whistle and good enough to get us over to Atlanta, Georgia, with no breakdowns along the route."

"It'll take me five minutes to wash my fun zone and an hour or hour and a half after on arrangements. If you need to have the car loaded, give me another hour."

"A full load."

"A full load," she repeated, and they made the meeting for one o'clock on the roof of the Tom Bradley International Terminal parking structure at LAX.

Frankie hung up the phone and pulled Katie closer, took her in his arms. The kiss was lingering, and she felt her legs go rag doll soft.

"Atlanta?"

"Gateway to the South, Bright Eyes, ain't that what they call it? We got people there we can trust, who been away from the battle long enough to care for me more'n the cause. They'll know where best to park us for the duration."

KC put her fingers over his mouth. There already were enough lies between them.

Frankie peeled them away and smiled. He said, "Not what you're thinking, Face. It's not the nigger, or would I want you beside me eavesdropping?"

He took her by the hand and guided her back to the town car.

"Can't be rid of this car fast enough," he said. "A wonder we ain't been stopped already, especially if it's like you say, Mr. Walter Burkes trying to hitch a tail to your kite."

They arrived at LAX about twenty minutes early, and KC pulled into one of the empty spaces in the row along the wall farthest from the elevator, facing out.

A light drizzle was falling.

They settled back to wait for May.

Watched black rain clouds glide in from the ocean.

Made the kind of small talk that suspends reality in favor of fond memories and allowed them to regard the future in terms of the past.

Good enough for now, KC thought.

A jet whooshed overhead, rising at a forty-five-degree angle, and curved left toward the Pacific.

He relaxed an arm around her back, stole a hand under her tunic. He squeezed her breast so hard she knew it would be black and blue by morning, a love souvenir. What they'd come to call those reminders, love souvenirs. He barely had his hands groping inside her pants when the horn interrupted them.

A light beep. A break. Two more beeps.

The dashboard clock said one o'clock.

An arriving 747 whooshed closer than the last one, like syrup on pancakes.

There would not be many more. The sky was closing down fast.

The car was stopped with its motor running in the third traffic lane across from them. The driver waved through the distorting glass, eased forward and parked in the last empty at the end of the row. A white Oldsmobile sedan. A salesman's car.

A light gray mist made it hard to define details, but KC saw it was road dirty and wore Las Vegas rental plates. A big American flag decal on the rear window. A Just Say No bumper sticker. A vehicle easily lost under the posted speed limit anywhere in the country.

Frankie got the Walther from the glove compartment and slid it between his spine and his trousers. Passed her the .45, which he had hidden under his seat. "You hear a sour noise, you go like a bat out of hell."

"I'm sure it was May."

"The same, but always better safe than sorry."

Frankie looked at KC like she was some masterpiece hanging on a museum wall.

He reached across to stab the cleft in her chin before he opened the door.

Got out.

Traveled casually down the aisle, like he wasn't sure where he had parked his car.

KC dropped the .45 into her handbag.

She got out to wait.

Frankie turned to wave and sent her a smile that stood out briefly against the veil of fog.

KC threw back a kiss, but couldn't be certain Frankie had caught it.

Less than five minutes later, May Lawless ambled toward

KC in that disjointed puppet walk of hers, her sandals slapping noisily on the damp concrete. She had on a turquoise-colored mesh top and matching Capri pants a size and a half too small that made her rail-thin legs look like stilts and her knees bigger than her boobs. An attached hood covered her hair and framed her flaking face. Her slash of lipstick matched the orange sunbursts on her cheeks.

She stopped, stared back impatiently, took a deep drag on her cigarette and sailed it, waiting for KC to join her.

Pressed two fingers against her throat.

Looked around, anxiously.

"Keys are in the ignition," KC said, handing over the yellow parking ticket. "You'll be sure to leave it where it can be found?"

"Your man already told me, so don't worry your pretty head. We'll clean it real good and see it gets back to your people in better condition than when you borrowed it," May said, almost abrasively. "When you settle in Nashville, you call, and we'll have somebody disappear the Olds on you."

"You mean when we settle in Atlanta."

May couldn't make up her mind whether to nod or shake her head. "Nashville, he says now. So, good thing I put in the full load like he asked. Good for anyplace between here and the East Coast, Nashville or Atlanta. I wouldn't ever want to do nothing to offend Frankie, you know what I mean?" She emphasized the word "ever" like it was the end of the world.

KC just stared back. She didn't trust her voice.

May made a face that meant she wasn't surprised, and stepped closer.

"Everything he touches turns to death," May said, her voice falling to a whisper. "My friend Dermot told me that, on word came back to him from Belfast, but neither of us figured Dermot would become the proof in his own pudding.

Like Snuffy Danaher. Like even his own brother, Liam. The girl before them three."

KC gasped and averted her eyes.

She asked, "What girl, May?"

Certain of the answer.

Her throat closing around the truth.

"The cop. The detective. She come around snooping, but didn't know much of anything and was learning even less. Frankie wasn't hearing any of it. He was afraid of her mucking up his plan, so he had her taken where he could finish her off after making certain for sure that she had nothing to tell."

"You mean Liam."

May shook her head. "Frankie. He did most of the cutting and the butchering himself, a lot worse than the television let on. Made some of it a game with his brother. And had to have Dermot and Snuffy part of it. Said to prove they was one for all. Dermot came to me after it was over. He was shaking like a leaf something fierce and puking out his soul and he had to get drunk as a skunk, drunker than I'd ever seen him, before he could tell me any of it . . . Aw, Jesus!"

May began to tremble. Her eyes ripened. She backed off and half-turned to look behind her, then moved to within an inch of KC's face. "Aw, Sweet Jesus Fuck, you won't tell Frankie I said so, will you?" she said, her beating eyelids shedding crust. "He knew the way I'm talking, I'd be as likely to wind up the same as the detective."

"Just go. Leave. Get out of here. Get the car back and don't worry," KC said, numbly.

May bit down on her lower lip and squinted to be certain of what she saw. She hugged KC. "You take care of yourself, girl." She hurried into the car, and ten seconds later was tearing after an exit.

"I will," KC said to herself.

She willed herself over to Frankie. On the way, she tried to comprehend why Liam hadn't told her. It would have been his best revenge, telling her what his brother had led them into doing to Annie Waterman. A story, finally, to rip her out from between them and win back his beloved Francis.

No, of course, not.

That would have been too obvious and kind.

Liam was crueler than that.

He saw the beauty in not telling her immediately, in letting her lower herself back into Frankie's love, become a prisoner of her own emotions until she was too trapped to defy the truth, then tell her. After it was too late for her, and—

For Mr. Mustamba.

When Liam's victory could be all-consuming.

Frankie gave her the thumbs-up sign.

He eased down the trunk lid and exerted extra pressure to make the lock catch. Double-checked it. Held out a hand to test the rain.

"Just in time," he said, smiling. "Another five minutes and it should be pouring. We're not escaping from this sad case of a city one minute too soon."

He must have read the concern in her eyes. He cocked his head and put his arms akimbo, waiting for her to say something.

"May says you told her we're going to Nashville, not Atlanta."

He seemed relieved.

"That's the truth. She has a mouth on her that one, so I up and changed the story, just in case the wrong people nose around later. She come across angry at me for the deaths of Dermot and Snuffy and no way of telling what she'd be likely to say to someone."

"We're going to Atlanta."

"Atlanta, promise." Frankie tried to drown her with his grin. "I don't know anybody in Nashville, Face, not a solitary soul. So, tell me, did May say anything else I have to answer for?"

KC thought about it.

Shook her head.

Removed the .45 from her handbag and fired.

"Not to me," she said.

EPILOGUE

The new dream, no better than the old one.

One of those cardboard communities off the Interstate, hanging onto the phone in a hotel where the bath towels come with the receipt and the TV set operates on quarters.

"Where the hell are you?" Burkes demands to know.

"Between a rock and a hard place."

"Come on in, or tell me where you're calling from, and we'll come and get you." His voice trying not to lose control. How Burkes hates to lose control.

"I don't think so. Tell me about Mr. Mustamba."

"We were waiting for them. It's over, kid. We got the bastards, thanks to you. The good guys won, so, for Christ's sake, come on in."

"Burkes, did you know Atlanta is the Gateway to the South?"

"What? What the hell does that mean?"

"Nothing you'd understand. How's your dog, how's Fritz?"

"Fritz is fine. He's gonna be fine. I want you to come in, KC. I want you to come in before you get hurt. They're gonna figure it out and come after you, and—"

"It's a big country."

Burkes sighs. "You still haven't told me what to tell Peter. He's on my ass every day, asking—"

She hangs up on him.

And the new dream.

And wakens to the same old sweat and confusion of a new life without Frankie.

About the Author

Robert S. Levinson writes the best-selling novels starring Neil Gulliver and Stevie Marriner, including *Hot Paint*, *The John Lennon Affair*, *The James Dean Affair* and *The Elvis and Marilyn Affair*, optioned by 20th Century Fox for film and TV series development. His short stories appear regularly in *Ellery Queen Mystery Magazine* and *Alfred Hitchcock Mystery Magazine*, including one voted a 2003 Ellery Queen Readers Award. Bob, a former newspaperman, television writer-producer and award-winning public relations executive, is a national director at-large of Mystery Writers of America and a past board member of the Writers Guild of America. He wrote and produced the last two MWA Annual Edgar Awards shows. He and his wife, Sandra, reside in Los Angeles. More at *www.robertslevinson.com*.